ROBERT KROESE
DISTOPIA

WESTMARCH
PUBLISHING

This is a work of fiction. Any resemblance to actual persons is purely coincidental.

Published by Westmarch Publishing
westmarchpub.com

For the Raft.

....

With thanks to:

- All the Kickstarter supporters who made this book possible, with special thanks to: Dan Tabaka, Christopher Turner, Katherine Nall, Cole Kovac, Eric Sybesma, Cara Miller, Andrea Luhman, Taki Soma, Melissa Allison, Matthew J. McCormick, Neva Cheatwood, Daniel Boucher, Sean Simpson, Josh Creed, and Denise and Chad Rogers;

- my editor at Westmarch Publishing, Richard Ellis Preston, Jr.

- and the sharp-eyed and insightful beta readers who made many helpful suggestions for improving this book: Joel Bezaire, Alan MacDougal, Jessica Jobes, and Mark Fitzgerald.

Svalbraakraat

Jagged Coast

Vorspaal Mountains

T
Y

Bjill

Brobdi

Sea
of
Dis

Purivel

Dismal
Marsh

Chathain
Mountains

Truiska

Skaal River

Skuldred

Here
ʒar be
monsters

○

Skaal City

Sybesma

Skaal

The Land of Dis
And the Jagged Coast

Kovac
Mountair

0   200
Miles

Leman
Territor

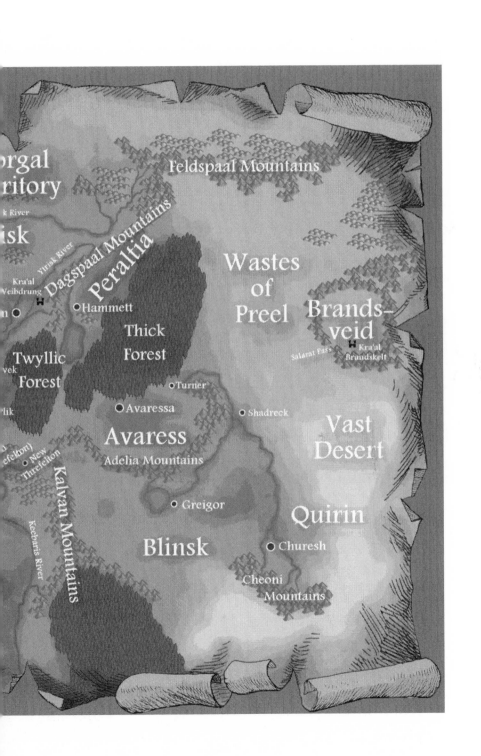

One

You have undoubtedly heard the story of Wyngalf the Bold, who is reputed to have liberated the land of Dis from the scourge of dragons. And like most who have heard the story, you likely have your doubts about its veracity. Did Wyngalf really cross the Sea of Dis on a raft buoyed by the gall bladders of seventeen mud trolls? Did he really live for a month inside the belly of a giant beaver? Did he really strangle the Beast of Borgoin with its own entrails? No. Frankly, most of the traditional story of Wyngalf is dead wrong—not to mention oddly preoccupied with the internal organs of mythical creatures.

The part about the dragons, however, is true.

History of the land of Dis prior to the Old Realm is sketchy and dominated by unverifiable and often fantastic myths, to the extent that the Dissian Heroic Age is regarded by most educated folk as little more than a stock setting for fairy tales and bedtime stories. Underlying these stories, though, are certain historical facts, and I have done my best to separate these from the fabrications. It should be noted, however, that even in a completely factual account, certain overarching themes often seem to arise unbidden; I can only say that if parts of this narrative seem to smack of moralizing or allegory, that is not my intention. I wish only to tell Wyngalf's story as accurately as possible.

At least one fact can be established with some certainty: Wyngalf of Svalbraak was a traveling evangelist for a now-defunct religious sect known as the Noninitarians, which espoused a faith so arbitrary and counterintuitive that those simple-minded enough to see its appeal were generally unable to grasp its doctrinal nuances firmly enough to convert. Wyngalf himself was surprisingly erudite, if somewhat naïve—a combination that placed him solidly in the Noninitarians' targeted demographic. He was also, truth be told, an astonishingly poor advocate for his chosen faith, and this fact was only partially explained by the intrinsic unpalatability of Noninitarianism. Wyngalf's sales pitch was so off-putting that he could have been selling skins of water in the middle of the Vast Desert and caravans would have gone miles out of their way to avoid him. The surprising thing about Wyngalf, then, was not that he failed in his effort to establish Noninitarianism in Dis, but rather that he very briefly became an extremely influential religious leader in that land. But I'm getting ahead of myself.

Wyngalf was abandoned as an infant on the doorstep of the Noninitarian Stronghold in Svalbraakrat, and he spent the next twenty-three years being indoctrinated in the stultifying nuances of that obscure faith. On his twenty-third birthday he passed the last of the Eleven Tests of Noninitarian Apostleship and was allowed to leave the Stronghold for the first time. For the next five months, he traveled down the western coast of the Sea of Dis, preaching the gospel of Noninitarianism and gradually becoming aware of the near-complete lack of interest in metaphysics that characterized the denizens of the Jagged Coast.

Wyngalf's story begins in earnest in the town of Skuldred, the southernmost town in Svalbraak, and the last in a series of settlements that had been unlucky enough to be subjected to his droning harangues on the Twenty-One Theses of Noninitarianism. The reception to Wyngalf's message in these towns ranged from complete disinterest to outright hostility (he'd actually had to flee from villagers with torches and pitchforks at one point), and Skuldred was his last chance to make a convert before having to return, an unmitigated failure, to the Noninitarian Stronghold in Svalbraakrat. The bishop would then undoubtedly strip him of his vestments and sentence him to spend the rest of his life pulling weeds in the vast radish farm that spread out for dozens of acres behind the Stronghold.

It was with these worries on his mind that Wyngalf set down his pack and hat in the town square of Skuldred, cleared his throat, and began a well-practiced sermon titled "Fourteen Points by Which the Pagan Might Be Convinced of His Errors in Thought, Word and Deed and Thereby Made Ready for Accepting the Irrefutable Truth Revealed by the Fourth Person of the Noninitarian Faith." This particular sermon was considered something of a classic among the Noninitarian clergy; it possessed such a sublime mixture of arcane dogma and abject rudeness that listeners were never sure whether to be bored or offended. It was rumored that no preacher reciting it had ever held an audience past Point Four, but despite his recent failures Wyngalf was feeling inspired, and he convinced himself that he would not only get through the entire sermon but convert the entire town of Skuldred to his faith.

"Attention, benighted pagans of insert town name here!" he recited, realizing his mistake before he'd even finished the sentence. A few confused townspeople had stopped what they were doing to stare in his direction. He smiled weakly and attempted to tip his hat toward them, but then remembered that his hat was lying brim-up in the dirt in front of him. Occasionally when he was delivering a sermon, a passerby, prompted by guilt or pity, would drop a copper or two into the hat. It was the only income Wyngalf had, and so far it had been just enough to keep him from starving. Not finding his hat on his head, he gave the villagers a sort of awkward salute and pressed on.

"I present for your elucidation these Fourteen Points by which you miserable pagans might be convinced of your errors in thought, word, and deed, and thereby approach a state of readiness to receive the truth of the Noninitarian faith, as revealed by Ganillion, the Fourth Person of the Blessed Noninity. I begin with Point One, by which you are Brought Low by recognition of your Essential Wretchedness."

"Boo!" cried a man skirting the edge of the square with a sack of potatoes slung across his back. "Sod off!" shrieked a woman clutching an infant to her chest. The rest of the villagers shook their heads and muttered to each other or ignored him completely.

Wyngalf's confidence began to falter. The Bringing Low of the Pagans was his favorite of the Fourteen Points, and ordinarily the sheer offensiveness of it tended to keep the audience's attention, but the insults being hurled at him thus far were few and seemed half-hearted. He took a breath and continued:

"Being that you are pagans and therefore ignorant of the joys of a life Enriched by the Fifth and Seventh Persons of the Noninity, you are likely to greet my words with hostility. Know, however, that I do not take offense at your brute ignorance, but rather greet your outbursts as the First Proof of the Wretchedness of Pagans. For as Ontenogon himself once said, 'The fool sees his own foolishness reflected in the wisdom of the teacher.'"

This passage prompted no epithets, only shrugs and mutters. Wyngalf had expected the people of such a remote town to be desperate for entertainment, but they seemed too busy or jaded to pay much attention. This did not bode well for the other Thirteen Points.

"What's this all about then?" said a small voice behind him.

Wyngalf spun, finding himself face to face with a teenaged girl. She wore a hooded cloak against the wind, but Wyngalf could see that underneath, her clothes were of high quality. She had a pretty face framed by auburn curls that spilled out of the hood. He guessed she was around seventeen.

"Run along, girl," said Wyngalf. "A child's mind is too immature to grasp the subtleties of the Twenty-One Theses of Noninitarianism."

"You don't look like much more than a child yourself," said the girl. "And I thought you said there were fourteen," said the girl.

Wyngalf sighed heavily and rolled his eyes. "There are Fourteen *Points* that must be drummed into the pagan mind to make it ready to receive the Revelation of the Fourth Person of the Noninity. Once the mind has been prepared, he must then master the Twenty-One Theses of Noninitarianism."

"He or she," corrected the girl, and Wyngalf rolled his eyes again. "What's Noninitarianism?"

"Why, the belief in the Blessed Noninity, of course!"

"You believe in a nonentity?"

Wyngalf sighed again. "*Noninity*," he said. "A single God in Nine Persons."

"Oh!" exclaimed the girl. "It seemed from your sermon that you believed in only one god. You're saying there are *nine*?"

"No!" snapped Wyngalf, irritated that even the most basic teachings of Noninitarianism seemed to go right over these people's heads. "There is but one God, who reveals Himself as nine distinct persons. These are the Nine Co-Equal Persons of the Noninity."

"I don't understand," said the girl. "How can a single God be— "

"Of course you don't! You're a polytheistic pagan, and a silly little girl at that. And you've heard only one small fragment of the first of the Fourteen Points! Now, please run along and allow me to get back to my sermon." The girl shrugged and walked away. Wyngalf turned to see that what little audience he'd had was dispersing. "Vile, depraved souls!" he shouted, trying to remember where he'd left off. "Fools and harlots!" But it was no use. His diatribe had devolved from insulting to incoherent. He took a deep breath and started from the beginning: "I present for your elucidation these Fourteen Points...." But he no longer had anything like an audience. A large swath of the square roughly coterminous with the reach of Wyngalf's voice was now empty. Villagers were hugging the edge of the square to avoid him, as if word had gotten out that he was a carrier of some particularly virulent strain of plague. "It doesn't seem to be catching!" he shouted at three men skulking single-file along the wall of an inn at the far side of the square.

He sighed, composed himself, and started for a third time. This time he powered through, oblivious to his lack of audience. He told himself that if nothing else, it was good practice. He managed to recite the first three Points without once consulting the book of the *Six and a Half Revelations of Saint Roscow*, but the Fourth Point was by far the longest and most tedious, and he wasn't sure he had it in him to slog all the way through it. It was late afternoon, he was tired and hungry, and he was beginning to lose his voice. Wyngalf had spent the morning walking from the village of Truiska to the north, arriving in Skuldred just after noon, and all he'd had to eat was a handful of dried radishes he'd found at the bottom of his otherwise empty pack. There'd be no supper tonight, and he'd be lucky to find a doorway to sleep in. There was little glamor to the life of a Noninitarian missionary.

As he faltered at the Prelude to the Fourth Point, he noticed one figure standing still in the middle of the square, apparently listening to him. For a moment, he thought perhaps he had gotten through to someone, but his hopes of making a new disciple faded when he realized it was the same girl he'd dismissed earlier. Noninitarians had a strict policy against proselytizing to anyone under the age of eighteen, ostensibly because children lacked the intellectual sophistication to grasp the finer points of the Noninitarian faith, but Wyngalf had also noticed that children tended to ask innumerable impertinent questions that made it virtually impossible to get through the Fourteen Points. It just wasn't worth the trouble.

"Are you finished?" the girl asked.

"No!" Wyngalf croaked, his raspy voice undercutting his air of authority.

"Okay," said the girl, and stood silently, watching him.

Wyngalf tried to remember where he'd left off in the Prelude to the Fourth Point, but he was unnerved by the way the girl was looking at him. "Why do you ask?" he said.

"My father told me to invite you for supper when you're finished."

Wyngalf's stomach began to growl so loudly that he was certain that even the villagers skulking along the outskirts of the square could hear it. "Supper?" he asked, and he had to catch himself before saliva ran down his chin.

The girl nodded. "My father is the town fishmonger. When traveling preachers come to town, he always has them over for supper. It should be ready soon, but I can tell him you're too busy saving souls if you want."

Wyngalf looked out at the empty square. The sun was sinking low in the west, and a chill breeze had picked up.

"I can pick up tomorrow where I left off," he said.

"Good," said the girl. "Come with me."

Two

The fishmonger's residence, a large, two-story affair set against the hills that bordered Skuldred to the west, appeared to be the most luxurious house in town. The girl, who had introduced herself as Evena, invited Wyngalf inside and escorted him to the dining room, where her father and mother seemed to be waiting for them. The entire house was filled with the odor of cooked fish. Evena ran through the introductions in such a polished manner that Wyngalf got the sense he was playing a part in a drama that had been performed many times before. He hoped it didn't end with an itinerant preacher dismembered and preserved in a barrel of brine.

"Father Wyngalf," said Evena, "this is my father, Bulgar the fishmonger, and my mother, Erdis. Father, mother, this is Father Wyngalf, a missionary representing the Noninitarian Church."

Wyngalf bowed slightly, and Bulgar and Erdris stood and did the same. Evena directed Wyngalf to an empty chair at the table, and the four of them sat. On the table in front of them was a platter of some kind of fish, along with bread and a plate of assorted vegetables. Wyngalf's mouth began to water anew.

"Welcome, Father Wyngalf," said Evena's parents in unison, cordially but without great warmth.

"I thank you for inviting me into your home," Wyngalf said. "It isn't necessary to refer to me as 'Father Wyngalf,' however. Simply Wyngalf will suffice."

"Fine," said Bulgar the fishmonger. "Wyngalf it is." He was a compactly built man with a bald head and a heavily waxed moustache that stuck out on either side of his head with the points turned slightly forward, like the horns of a bull. His wife was a pear-shaped, doughy woman with braided blond hair and a blotchy red complexion.

"Simply Wyngalf," said Wyngalf.

"Yes," replied Bulgar. "That's what I said. Wyngalf."

"Beg your pardon," said Wyngalf. "It's a common mistake. Ministers of my faith are customarily addressed 'Simply,' to remind us of our humble status as servants of the Noninity."

Bulgar stared at Wyngalf, expressionless. "I fail to see how I could address you any more simply, Mister Wyngalf."

"Simply Wyngalf," said Wyngalf.

"Wyngalf," said Bulgar.

"Simply Wyngalf is fine," said Wyngalf.

"Wyngalf," said Bulgar again.

"Simply Wyngalf, if you please."

"You would like me to call you simply Wyngalf?"

"If you don't mind."

"Wyngalf," said Bulgar once more.

"Close enough," said Wyngalf, who was growing faint from lack of food. Everyone at the table breathed a collective sigh of relief.

"Father Wyngalf, would you mind saying the blessing?" asked the fishmonger's wife.

Wyngalf couldn't muster the will to object. "Of course," he said, with a weak smile. He clasped his hands on top of his head as was customary for the Noninitarian pre-meal blessing, and waited for the others to do the same. When they had complied, he closed his eyes and launched into the Eight Part Expression of Gratitude for Wholly Undeserved Nourishment. He was so hungry, though, that he decided to skip Parts Four through Seven and made a mental note to utter the Prayer of Supplication for Failing to Fully Execute a Sacrament before bed.

"Goodness, that was quite a blessing!" said Erdis, when he had finished Part Eight. The abbreviated blessing had taken about ten minutes.

You don't know the half of it, thought Wyngalf, but he just smiled.

"You must be famished, Wyngalf," Erdis said. "Please, eat."

Wyngalf ate. The fish—haddock? herring? halibut?—was dry and bland, and the vegetables were boiled beyond recognition, but it was the best meal he'd had in weeks. Whatever Bulgar the fishmonger and his wife had in store for him, he was convinced at the present moment that it was worth it. They exchanged pleasantries and commentary on the weather as they ate, and Wyngalf was goaded into speaking a little about his travels in between bites, but if the couple had any motive other than charity in inviting Wyngalf to their table, it was not evident. Evena in particular was very interested in his travels, and seemed disappointed that Wyngalf had spent most of the past five months preaching and begging for food rather than engaging in "adventures." It was clear that the girl had never left the environs of Skuldred, and possessed an exaggerated notion of exotic lands full of adventure just beyond the horizon.

When they'd finished eating, Evena cleared the table. As the warmth of the wine spread through Wyngalf's body, he found himself struggling not to stare at the girl. She was a bit young, yes, but undeniably attractive, and it wasn't uncommon for girls of her age to marry. Noninitarian devout were not technically sworn to celibacy, but were forbidden to engage in relations with anyone who had not accepted the Twenty-One Theses of Noninitarianism, so the practical result was generally the same. In any case, Wyngalf got the impression her father wouldn't approve of any advances he might make toward her. He wasn't sure what role he played in Bulgar's mind, but he was fairly certain that it was not potential suitor for his daughter.

After clearing the table, Evena returned carrying a large leather book along with a quill and inkwell, which she set on the table in front of her father. Anxiety clutched Wyngalf's overfull stomach as it occurred to him that the fishmonger was going to present him with a bill.

"So, Noninitarianism," said Bulgar, flipping through pages of the ledger as if to find his place. "That's a lot of gods to keep track of."

"Only one," said Wyngalf, lifting his glass to take a swallow of wine. Evena had produced a bottle of reasonably good white, and Wyngalf was enjoying his third glass.

Bulgar frowned and glanced at his wife, who shrugged. "I understood that you worship a pantheon of nine deities."

Ordinarily Wyngalf would have sighed heavily and launched into a diatribe on the Essential Unity of the Blessed Noninity, but between the warmth of the house, his full stomach, and the effects of the wine, he couldn't muster the effort. "Nine persons, one God," he said, holding up his index finger.

"Hmm," said Bulgar, studying a page in the book.

"What's that?" asked Wyngalf.

"Investment ledger," said Bulgar.

"My father keeps track of all of his investments," said Evena, a hint of pride in her voice. "He's invested in all the major religions."

Wyngalf swallowed hard and then coughed several times. "He *what?*"

"Shandorism, the Cult of Varnoth, Followers of Grovlik, the Eupardian Pantheon…" said Bulgar, running his fingers down the page. "I had to limit my investment to the thirty major Eupardian deities. You have to draw the line somewhere."

"Whenever a preacher comes to town," Erdis explained, "we have him over for supper so he can tell us about his gods. We're not religious people, but Bulgar is a very practical man."

"I don't like to take unnecessary risks," said the fishmonger, still studying the page in front of him.

"My husband invests in each of the gods, depending on their influence and…" she trailed off, as if trying to remember the wording.

"Reputed authority over one's fate in afterlife," said Bulgar, dipping the quill in the ink. "We all want to go to heaven, after all. Your religion does teach of a glorious afterlife, does it not?"

"Of course!" exclaimed Wyngalf. "After death, those who have been filled with the Spirit of Royahim the Imbuer, the Seventh Person of the—"

"Fine, fine," said Bulgar, jotting something in the book. "And how many followers does Nonitarianism have?"

"Um," said Wyngalf. "A few hundred in and around Svalbraakrat."

Bulgar paused with the quill hovering above the page, eyeing Wyngalf disapprovingly. He looked like he was about to slam the book shut and throw Wyngalf back out into the street.

"But of course we have a strong missionary presence in the north," said Wyngalf. "And I left several months ago, so I don't have the latest numbers...."

"An estimate is fine," said Bulgar. "Ten thousand? A hundred thousand?"

Wyngalf nearly spit out his wine. "Closer to the first, I would guess," he said after he'd swallowed, assuring himself that it wasn't technically a lie. As far as he knew, there were fewer than twenty Noninitarian missionaries in total, and most of them weren't much more charismatic or competent than Wyngalf.

"Excellent," said Bulgar, making a note.

"My husband says that the popularity of a religion is an indication of the relative power of its deity."

"How's that?" asked Wyngalf, raising an eyebrow.

"A powerful god would inspire more followers than a weak one, wouldn't he?" said Bulgar, as if he were talking to a child.

Wyngalf, as a representative of perhaps the least popular religion along the Jagged Coast, would ordinarily have taken issue with this assertion, but he wasn't sure this was the best tactical move for him. "To be clear," he said to Bulgar, "you're planning on making a donation to the Noninitarian Church commensurate with the relative clout of our God?"

"An investment," corrected Bulgar.

"So you're going to give me money."

"If I judge your god to be a wise investment, yes."

"And you expect to make a return on this 'investment?'"

"I'm not going to ask for the money back, if that's what you're wondering," said Bulgar. "I expect you to use the money as your god wishes. Buy a goat to sacrifice, build a temple, whatever it is you do. My goal is to maximize the odds of me and my family prospering in the afterlife."

Erdis and Evena smiled beatifically at him.

"But that's not how—" Wyngalf started.

"I'm not interested in the mechanics of it," said Bulgar. "I have no head for theology. I'm good at one thing: selling fish. I do very well at it. So I'm delegating. I give you money, you work it out with your god, goddesses or combinations thereof to get me and my family into Heaven or whatever it's called. Got it?"

"Yes, but I can't just—"

Bulgar held up his hand. "Understand that I'm paying you to be a steward of this money. To make decisions. The more of those decisions you involve me in, the less you are worth to me as a manager. Some preachers fail to grasp this point, and insist on explaining the fine points of their religion to me. The more religious claptrap I get stuck in my head, the less room I have for business. If I forget the going rate for dried cod because my brain is full of angels dancing on the head of a pin, I make less money. Less money means no money for you. Are you with me, Father Wyngalf?"

Wyngalf nodded. This was the first time in his recollection that getting a donation depended on him *not* proselytizing, and it put him in a bit of an ethical quandary. What would Bishop Frotheckle say about accepting money from a man who insisted on remaining ignorant of the sublime truths of Noninitarianism? On one hand, any donation would help the church fulfill its mission—but on the other, wouldn't he be taking advantage of the spiritual poverty of Bulgar and his family? Wouldn't it make a more powerful statement if Wyngalf were to refuse to take Bulgar's money on principle? Perhaps this was a test, sent by Grimilard, the Second Person of the Noninity, to discern Wyngalf's worthiness as a missionary. He imagined indignantly turning down Bulgar's offer and denouncing the man's attempt to reduce matters of eternal significance to a business transaction. He would then dramatically stomp out of the house, and Erdis and Evena would throw themselves at his feet, begging him not to go. Bulgar would repent of his wickedness, tear up his ledger, and give his entire fortune to Wyngalf. Wyngalf would use the money to build a grand cathedral in Skuldred, which would stand forever as a monument to Wyngalf's humility and asceticism. This scenario seemed like a long shot, though.

"How much money are we talking about?" asked Wyngalf.

"Well," said Bulgar, "as I'm sure you're aware, at ten thousand adherents, you're one of the smaller sects along the Jagged Coast." Wyngalf nodded, telling himself it would be rude to correct Bulgar's understanding of the reach of the Noninitarian faith. "And you're monotheistic, which means that I don't have to spread my investment among multiple deities."

"You give polytheistic religions more money simply because they have more gods?" asked Wyngalf, puzzled.

"Of course," said Bulgar, as if the point were self-evident. "You can't expect a whole pantheon of gods to be satisfied with the amount I'd give to a single deity."

"But that's a fundamental misunderstanding of the relationship—" Wyngalf started, but he was met with a cold stare from Bulgar. He paused a moment, trying to think of how to put the point in more acceptable terms. "What I mean to say is, there are questions of the division of labor." This earned him a broad smile from the fishmonger.

"Excellent point," Bulgar said. "As you say, in a monotheistic scheme, the single deity is responsible for more work, and should be compensated with this in mind. But that's not my responsibility."

"What do you mean?"

"What I mean is that I'm sure that creating the cosmos was a great deal of work, but it happened before I got here. I didn't ask for it to be created, I wasn't consulted on the specifics, and I don't intend to pay for it. The same goes for most of the nonsense that these gods and goddesses get up to. Screwing ducks and planting oak trees in each other and whatnot. My interest is in getting my family into heaven, so I spread my money around to all the deities I know of. I'm simply playing the odds."

"It still seems to me," said Wyngalf, "that you're unfairly penalizing monotheistic religions. After all, what's to stop me from making up five hundred deities and asking for money for each of them?"

Evena furrowed her brow, and Bulgar and Erdis stared at him in apparent horror. "Why would you *do* something like that?" Erdis asked, and Bulgar nodded. It was as if the idea of a religious charlatan exploiting them had never occurred to them.

"Well, *I* wouldn't," said Wyngalf. "But less scrupulous individuals…" He trailed off as the three continued to regard him with confusion. Wyngalf had encountered less extreme instances of this phenomenon in the past: certain hard-nosed businessmen (and their families, evidently) tended to develop an overly idealistic notion of the clergy as men untouched by material concerns—a romantic notion that it wasn't in Wyngalf's interest to correct. In any case, the only way he knew to disabuse them of this idea was to explain the Noninitarian doctrine of Essential Wretchedness, and Bulgar had explicitly forbade him to preach religious doctrine. "Never mind," he said. "It's an obscure point of doctrine that I'm sure you would have no interest in."

Bulgar nodded, and his wife and daughter breathed audible sighs of relief. "Now," said Bulgar. "I'm a little uncertain how to enter a... what did you call it? A nonity?"

"The Blessed Noninity," said Wyngalf. "Nine Persons making up a single... you know what? Just put it down as nine gods." If Bulgar was going to be making a donation based on a complete misunderstanding of Noninitarianism, it might as well be a misunderstanding that was beneficial to Wyngalf. And the church, of course.

"Very good," said Bulgar. "And is one particular god in charge of eternal judgment and/or the afterlife?"

"Well," said Wyngalf, cringing slightly at the heretical nature of the question, "Shotarr the Purifier, the Ninth Person of the Noninity, is ultimately responsible for the punishment of unbelievers, but of course his task is dependent on the functions of Xandiss the Auditor, who—"

"Team effort," Bulgar declared, scratching a note in the ledger. "And what do you plan to do with the money I invest in your gods?"

Wyngalf frowned. "I understood that you didn't want to be apprised of the details."

"I'm not interested in the mechanics of how you procure eternal salvation for me and my family," said Bulgar. "But of course I need to have some idea what you'll do with the money, if for no other reason than I need to know how much to give you. Some gods can get by with very little, while others have very expensive tastes."

Wyngalf nodded, once again amazed at Buglar's naïve credulity. The man was fortunate that Wyngalf was not greedy or unscrupulous. Now that Wyngalf's belly was full, all he really cared about was having a warm place to sleep tonight, and he had no doubt Bulgar's hospitality would extend that far. But Bulgar clearly wanted to make a significant donation—no, *investment*, and Wyngalf felt something of an obligation toward the church to make the strongest case he could for that money. Wyngalf had no doubt the bishop would find a use for the money, however much it ended up being, but he didn't think Bulgar would want to hear about the much-needed repairs to the rectory. No, Wyngalf needed to come up with something far more dramatic to loosen the fishmonger's purse strings.

Nor was Bulgar's fortune the only factor contributing to his desire to concoct a particularly inspiring proposal. Pretty Evena stared eagerly into Wyngalf's eyes, obviously still hoping that he would turn out to be the far-traveling man of adventure she had made him out to be. And at this moment, Wyngalf wanted nothing more than to be that man. Not some impoverished preacher traveling from town to town, barely surviving on the pity of strangers, but a fearless adventurer, who sought out danger, vanquished monsters, and told grand tales of his heroic exploits.

If only he had met Bulgar and his family at the outset of his journey, when he was still filled with enthusiasm and big dreams. He'd have had no trouble back then spinning bold tales of what the church could accomplish with a little more money. But five months had passed since then, and he was feeling considerably less optimistic. Skuldred was the end of the line for him, and his hopes and dreams had diminished to the point that he thought no farther ahead than his next meal. He'd suggest that he needed money for a grand missionary expedition, but there was nowhere left to go. To the west was uninhabitable swamp, to the east was the Sea of Dis, and to the south was wilderness populated only by goblins, ogres and other miscreants. One might as well proselytize to the fish as to the soulless humanoids in the southern lands. As he imagined himself preaching from the bow of a ship to a rapt audience of tuna and manta rays, an idea occurred to him. Lubricated by the wine, the words left his lips before he realized what he was saying.

"An expedition," he announced, holding up his wine glass. "To the land of Dis."

Stunned silence followed. A silence so dense and oppressive that Wyngalf knew with absolute certainty that he had made a terrible mistake. He knew almost nothing of the land of Dis, save that it was far away across the sea. People in the towns he'd traveled through had a tendency to speak of taking on some unpleasant chore "after I return from Dis," meaning never. As far as Wyngalf knew, no one ever actually traveled there, although he was unclear on the reasons for this. He had been entertaining a vague notion that he could use the idea of an expedition to the land of Dis as a sort of placeholder for some indeterminate future expenditure. Bulgar would give him a pouch of gold coins and he would return to the Stronghold at Svalbraakrat (after staying at a string of fancy inns on his return journey) with something to show for his year of travel. But it was clear from the reaction of Bulgar and his family that they took his pronouncement very seriously.

Bulgar leaned forward, staring at Wyngalf in amazement. "Your gods have told you to go to the land of Dis?"

Wyngalf swallowed hard. He couldn't very well admit at this point that the notion of traveling to Dis was a mere whim. Still, there had to be some way of wriggling out of any sort of specific commitment. "Yes, well," he said. "They expressed some general interest in the area. As for the exact details of the—"

"When did you arrive in town?" asked Bulgar.

"Just a few hours ago," said Wyngalf, puzzled.

"Did you speak to anyone? Any fishermen or their families?"

"He was preaching in the square all day," said Evena. "I saw him."

Bulgar nodded thoughtfully, taking in her words.

"There are only a few who know," said Erdis. "And most of them are at sea. There's no way he could have talked to any of them."

"It was meant to be!" cried Evena, leaping out of her chair to embrace her mother, who was nodding in happy bewilderment.

"How's that?" asked Wyngalf, more confused than ever.

Bulgar solemnly closed his ledger and set it on the table. "Among my business interests are three fishing vessels," he explained. "Occasionally I go along on fishing expeditions to oversee the operations firsthand. I happened to be on one of the ships when a sudden storm rolled in. There was no time to get to port, and we were swept out to sea by the wind and crashing waves. Those of us on board were certain the ship was going to capsize and we were all going to drown. The crew prayed to all their gods to no avail, and finally the captain announced in desperation that if any god would save them, he would take the ship on a journey across the sea to the land of Dis to proclaim the god's power and mercy. The sea calmed within moments, and the ship was able to return to port. But of course no one knew which god had saved them, so nothing more was said of the proposed journey."

Another agonizing silence.

"But now we know!" Evena exclaimed at last. "Your gods saved my father's ship!"

Wyngalf smiled weakly. "Well, let's not jump to any conclusions," he said. "My gods... that is, my *God*, has a wide variety of competing interests, and while it's certainly possible—"

Bulgar shook his head. "No, it's settled. Never in my thirty years of investing in religions have I seen anything like this. I'm betting everything on your nine gods, Father Wyngalf. Whatever it takes to make your expedition to Dis happen."

"*My* expedition?" asked Wyngalf, barely able to speak.

"Of course!" said Bulgar. "Your own humility blinds you to the truth. Your gods have selected you to lead a missionary expedition to the land of Dis."

Wyngalf felt the color drain from his cheeks.

"How exciting!" cried Evena. "An adventure!"

Three

Three days later Wyngalf, still clutching to a remnant of hope that that he could find some kind of loophole in his commitment, found himself losing his breakfast over the port side of a herring buss called the *Erdis Evena*. He'd never imagined when he suggested a voyage across the Sea of Dis that there might be a ship in Skuldred capable of making the journey. And as he wiped his chin and surveyed the half-rotted railing surrounding the deck of the *Erdis Evena*, he wasn't entirely convinced he was wrong.

The *Erdis Evena* was the largest of Bulgar's three ships, a round-bilged keel ship with three masts. It was about sixty feet long and fifteen feet wide, and had a crew of nineteen plus Wyngalf. Wyngalf gathered that there were supposed to be twenty men, but the first mate, a man named Fendrelli, had apparently come into some money unexpectedly the day before, gotten extremely drunk, and was in no shape to join the expedition. Another man was promoted in Fendrelli's place, and the ship embarked as scheduled.

Bulgar the fishmonger, having organized and paid for the voyage, had evidently come to the conclusion that his own destiny lay elsewhere. He and his wife saw Wyngalf off. Evena, despite her excitement about Wyngalf's "adventure," was nowhere to be found. It saddened Wyngalf a bit not to see the girl waving from the docks with her parents, but he assumed she had been overwhelmed by emotion at the thought of his departure.

Wyngalf learned that the *Erdis Evena* was the same ship that had nearly capsized in the storm a week earlier. He knew little about the mechanics of fishing, but to the extent he thought about it, he had assumed that fishing ships stayed relatively close to shore, filling their nets and returning at the end of the day. This was mostly true, but enterprising businessmen like Bulgar had evidently learned that they could acquire larger volumes of fish more efficiently by sending larger ships out farther, and leaving them at sea for days or weeks at a time. These ships used long nets that hang like curtains across the travel paths of the herring schools. The nets would be taken aboard at night and the crew would process and salt the fish for barreling.

There was no reason in theory, Wyngalf supposed, that such a ship couldn't successfully navigate the Sea of Dis, although he'd never heard of it being done. The crew seemed confident enough in their chances, but Wyngalf wasn't sure how much of that was due to their misplaced faith in him as the prophet of the gods who had saved them from drowning a week earlier. Or *was* it misplaced? He supposed that the One True God (in Nine Persons) must have saved them, in some sense. And that same God (or one of His Manifestations) had brought Wyngalf to Skuldred at just the right time to convince Bulgar of that fact. But was this voyage part of some divine plan to bring the gospel of Nonitarianism to Dis, or was it simply Wyngalf's punishment for failing to repudiate the fishmonger?

By the third day at sea, his nausea had diminished to a tolerable level, but he found in its place a growing sense of unease about his role in this expedition. The initial enthusiasm of the crew about undertaking a divinely ordained mission had begun to fade, and increasingly they were looking to him for reassurance. At first Wyngalf ascribed their uncertainty to the expected length of the voyage, but it became clear from conversation with crew members that several of them originally hailed from fishing villages to the north, where voyages of two or three weeks were not at all uncommon. As far as he could tell, the voyage to Dis was expected to take just over a week, depending on the weather. Clearly the crew possessed some deep shared foreboding about the journey that arose from some factor of which Wyngalf was unaware. Wyngalf knew almost nothing of seafaring and figured that whatever was spooking the crew was beyond his control, so he avoided pursuing the matter as long as possible. He was having enough trouble as it was mustering the enthusiasm to deliver the occasional pep talk about the crew's divinely ordained destiny.

The captain of the *Erdis Evena* was a man named Savikkar. Savikkar seemed competent and reasonably well-respected by the crew, although he had an air for the dramatic; the men tended to roll their eyes and mutter under their breath when he started in on one of his stories of seafaring derring-do in decades past. He was the man who had proclaimed that he would undertake a voyage across the Sea of Dis if the crew were spared. That meant he was largely responsible for Wyngalf's current circumstances, so Wyngalf, not certain whether to regard him as the agent of his glorious destiny or an instrument of divine vengeance, found himself with conflicting feelings toward the man.

The quarters below deck were adequate, if not particularly comfortable or spacious; the crew slept in hammocks that hung three high in a large room that took up about half the space below deck. The other half was taken up by a hold that was ordinarily filled with the crew's rations, bags of salt, and barrels for storing the salted fish for transport back to the mainland. Currently, though, the proportion was tilted heavily toward rations and other supplies, as fishing was not the primary purpose of this voyage. Wyngalf was a little unclear what the purpose actually was, other than traveling across the sea to the land of Dis. He knew very little about this semi-legendary land across the sea, and no one had said anything about what they expected Wyngalf to do when they got there. He supposed they expected him to disembark at whatever port they found and immediately begin making converts to his religion. The fact that he'd been aboard a ship with twenty men for three days without making a single convert didn't seem to trouble them; like Bulgar the fish merchant, the men evidently believed they could somehow further the divine plan of Wyngalf's god without troubling themselves with the details of his faith. No one had yet asked him a single question about Noninitarianism; the prevailing view among the crew seemed to be that risking their lives on a journey across the Sea of Dis was devotion enough, and maybe they were right.

Like all sailors, the crew were a superstitious lot; they were constantly uttering strange oaths and engaging in bizarre and arbitrary rituals like sprinkling salt on their shoes or rapping on their foreheads with their knuckles. Probably they simply didn't have room in their crowded pantheon of gods, spirits and sea sprites for another deity—even if that deity was the one who was ostensibly in control of their destiny. They were also, like most sailors, an uncouth and smelly group, and Wyngalf was grateful the weather had so far been mild, allowing him to spend nearly all of his time above decks. He'd been issued raingear constructed of oil-impregnated canvass, but thus far hadn't needed to use it. His nausea hadn't receded to the point where reading was possible, so his copy of the *Six and a Half Revelations of Saint Roscow* and the *Noninitarian Prayer Book* remained wrapped in wax paper in a satchel in his hammock, and he occupied his time by praying to Illias the Interceder and contemplating the meaning of the twists of fate that had brought him to this point. He tried very hard not to think about the challenges that faced him in the Land of Dis and the growing sense of dread that seemed to grip the crew, but finally broached the subject during a rare pause in one of Captain Savikkar's unlikely and obscene anecdotes involving mermaids and death rays.[1] Other crew members tended to flee from Savikkar when he told these stories, so it was just Wyngalf and the captain leaning against the railing during this pause in which Wyngalf's curiosity finally got the better of his fears.

"I've noticed," Wyngalf said, "that the men seem to be developing some trepidation regarding our voyage."

Savikaar shrugged and puffed a few times on his pipe, looking out over the open sea. "Just nerves," he said. Wyngalf saw that he was staring at dark clouds on the horizon. The wind had begun to pick up, and it seemed to be coming from the direction of the clouds.

"But what are they nervous *about?*" asked Wyngalf. "Dis is a strange land, to be sure, but what horrors could it possibly hold that

---

[1] A breed of ray once thought to subsist on sailors who fell overboard, death rays in fact feed on mollusks, crustaceans and, occasionally, naughty children who stray too far from shore.

cause such unease while we are still at least a week from landfall? They seemed quite optimistic at first, but the closer we get to Dis, the more troubled they become."

Savikkar shook his head. "Oh, it's not *Dis* they're worried about," he said. "It's what they fear we'll encounter before we get there."

"What?" Wyngalf asked, watching the sky darken to the east. "Another storm?"

"The men have been through many storms," said Savikkar.

"What then? Why does no one ever cross the Sea of Dis?"

"Men have crossed it."

"Far to the north," said Wyngalf. "I have passed through many seaports on my way down the coast, and I have never heard of a ship departing for—or returning from—the land of Dis. Why? Is there some hazard in the middle of the sea? Rocks? Whirlpools? Sea monsters?"

Savikkar said nothing, taking a long draw on his pipe.

"Sea monsters?" Wyngalf asked again. "They can't seriously believe—"

"No good to talk about it," said Savikkar curtly.

"But surely it's your responsibility as captain to allay the crew's unfounded fears about mythical creatures!" cried Wyngalf.

Savikkar again said nothing.

"They *are* mythical, right?"

"We don't speak of such things," said Savikkar. "Bad luck."

Wyngalf stared in disbelief. "What's bad luck is having your crew paralyzed with fear of something that doesn't exist. If you simply tell them there are no sea monst—"

"Hafgufa," interjected Savikkar.

"Excuse me?"

"We call it the 'Hafgufa.' It means 'the thing in the sea which should not be spoken of.'"

"Okay," said Wyngalf. "Simply tell the crew that there is no such thing as a Hafgu—"

"Shh!" hissed the captain. "Don't say it aloud. Bad luck."

Wyngalf threw up his hands. "Well, what do I call it then?"

"You don't!" snapped Savikkar. "That's the whole point. It's bad luck. Drop it."

"This is ridiculous. How did you even find out about the… about the thing we can't talk about, if nobody can talk about it? Have you seen one?"

Savikkar said nothing.

"Of course not," said Wyngalf. "I'd wager no one in the crew has seen one of these things. But they whisper about them secretly, and so the rumor grows. And your unwillingness to talk about the matter openly makes it impossible to dispel the myth. In fact, by creating a mystique around the thing, you give the myth more power. So this is why no one ever goes to Dis. Because of some unfounded, superstitious fear of a monster that doesn't exist!" Wyngalf found himself nodding excitedly. He finally saw the truth: the barrier to trade between the Jagged Coast and Dis was an illusion—a blind, stupid fear of a mythical creature. "Yes, yes!" he exclaimed. "This is why we were chosen to go on this voyage. Don't you see? The true purpose of this mission is to show that faith can overcome fear! We're going to demonstrate to the world that there is nothing to fear in the Sea of Dis, and thereby reestablish communications between the Jagged Coast and Dis!" And I shall be renowned in both lands, he thought, as Saint Wyngalf the Fearless! Or perhaps Saint Wyngalf the Navigator. The Reconciler? He'd let the powers-that-be at the Stronghold work out the details, but there could be no doubt that his canonization was assured.

Savikkar chomped on his pipe, shaking his head, but Wyngalf couldn't concern himself with what this superstitious old salt thought of him. He turned toward the crew members on the deck, who were engaged in various tasks with ropes and chains that he didn't understand. "Men of the *Erdis Evena!*" he exclaimed. The men stopped what they were doing and stared expectantly at him. "I have been granted a vision of our purpose!"

Men muttered to each other and shrugged.

"It's come to my attention," Wyngalf went on, "that some of you are concerned that we may encounter a certain sea monster known as the Hafgufa."

Several of the men gasped in horror at the sound of the name.

"You may rest easy," announced Wyngalf, holding up his hands as if giving a benediction. "There is no reason to fear such a creature."

The men murmured to each other. One of them spoke up: "Are you saying there is no... I mean, that the *you-know-what* doesn't exist?" His voice was hopeful, as if he had long suspected this himself, but hadn't dared express his doubts openly. Wyngalf saw expressions mirroring his on the faces of several other men. All they needed to be delivered from their irrational fear was some confident reassurance.

"Not exactly!" cried Wyngalf, and he saw disappointment come over the men's faces like a shadow. He went on hurriedly, "That is, there *could* be a Hafgufa, but I've seen no convincing evidence for it. Now, given that lack of evidence, coupled with the principle of Horkuden's Knife, which is a rhetorical device for eliminating propositions that are..."

The men's eyes were glazing over. "Is there a Hafgufa or not?" one of them yelled.

"What I'm saying," Wyngalf explained, "is that I believe that if there is a Hafgufa, it's largely metaphorical. And therefore our struggle against it is metaphorical as well. What we are fighting against is not a sea monster that is somehow 'out there,' but rather a sea monster that exists in our own souls. There is, perhaps, a little Hafgufa in each of us."

Pandemonium is the only word for what happened next on the *Erdis Evena*. One man, who had been suffering sea sickness all morning, tore off his clothes and threw himself onto the deck, his body jerking in spasms, screaming that a metaphorical Hafgufa had taken up residence in his belly. Wyngalf was relieved to see several other men subdue him, until one of them produced a knife, clearly intending to cut the monster out of him. The men pinning the victim cheered on the attacker, one of them proclaiming that he wielded Horkuden's Knife, the only blade capable of destroying the vile parasite. Other men joined the fray, some of them trying to get in on the action, others apparently trying to stay the knife. The motives of even this latter contingent were not entirely reasonable or altruistic, though: several of them were screaming something to the effect that it was too dangerous to try to cut the monster out, and that the man should be thrown overboard. Two other men had also stripped and thrown themselves to the deck, apparently convinced that they too were inflicted with metaphorical Hafgufas. Others stood by in stunned silence or screamed in terror.

"Stop!" cried Wyngalf. "There is no reason to fear! The Hafgufa can't get you unless you let it!"

But it was no use. He didn't know how to speak to these men in a way that they could understand. They didn't understand nuance, logic or figures of speech. It was like trying to preach to children. Very large, violent, sweaty children. With knives.

"Let that man go, you worthless dogs!" roared Captain Savikkar, shoving Wyngalf out of the way. He brought his right fist down on the nape of the neck of the man with the knife, stunning him, and gripped the collar of another, jerking him backwards so that he stumbled and fell flat on his back. Another man got a knee in his ribs, and a fourth received a slug across the jaw. "You!" Savikkar growled, wagging his finger at the naked man in the center of the fracas, "get your clothes on! The rest of you, douse the sails and batten the hatches!"

The spell of terror was broken almost instantly as the men stopped and stared at the darkening eastern sky. The storm was nearly upon them.

"Move, you scurvy bastards!" howled Savikkar. Wyngalf noticed that miraculously the captain's pipe was still clutched in his teeth. "And there'll be no more talk of the *you-know-what*!"

The men set to their respective tasks without another word. "Remarkable!" exclaimed Wyngalf, observing the unfolding scene in awe. "You must teach me the secret of addressing groups of uneducated, superstitious and fearful men such as these. Why, if I could—"

"Not another word, preacher," Savikkar growled, "unless you want to swim the rest of the way to Dis. Now get below decks where you can't cause any more trouble."

Wyngalf started to object, but thought better of it. Chagrined, he retreated to his hammock, where he spent the next half hour listening to the wind howl and the ship creak and moan. In between waves crashing against the hull, he heard the frantic yells of the men doing whatever it was they did in a storm. Wyngalf was the only one below decks, and he felt worse than useless. He'd not only managed to feed the superstitions of the men, causing them to panic, but he'd distracted them from the onslaught of the storm. If they still harbored any illusions that Wyngalf's presence granted them some kind of divine protection, this storm was going to disabuse them. If they survived.

The pounding of the rain and howling of the wind continued to get louder and Wyngalf's hammock swung crazily as the ship pitched and rolled at angles he'd have wagered were impossible. The ship groaned as if it were about to be torn apart at the seams. He could no longer hear the shouts of the men, whether because the storm was drowning them out or because they'd all been tossed overboard he didn't know. The only thing that broke through the constant roar of wind and waves was the occasional deafening clap of thunder. No light could get to him below decks, though. He clamped his eyes shut in the darkness and did his best to pray to Illias the Interceder for deliverance.

The roar of the wind suddenly got even louder, and Wyngalf opened his eyes to see that someone had opened the hatch. A figure stood at the doorway, lit from behind by dim light filtering down from above.

"Preacher!" hollered a voice. "You're needed above deck!" Barely controlled terror gripped the man's voice.

Wyngalf opened his mouth to request an explanation, but the hatch slammed shut. The man was gone. "What in the name of Abasmos...?" Wyngalf murmured to himself. He couldn't imagine what they might want him above deck for, unless they intended to throw him overboard to placate the angry sea. He considered hiding, but if they really wanted him above decks, that would be a temporary solution at best. If they had to drag him out, it would only make them angrier—although it was hard to imagine what they might do to him that would be worse than throwing him overboard. He sighed. Better to face his fate with a modicum of courage.

He managed to get out of his hammock and crawled to the hatch, fighting the movement of the ship. Then he clambered up the ladder to the deck. As he peeked his head out, the rain slapped him in the face and he realized he'd forgotten to don his severe weather poncho. But before he could return below decks, a rough hand grabbed him by the collar and practically dragged him onto the deck. Unable to keep his feet on the pitching ship, he fell to his hands and knees. Wind pelted him with rain, drenching his clothing. He turned to see who had "helped" him onto the deck. It was Captain Savikkar.

"You're up," shouted Savikkar.

Wyngalf stared at him dumbly, not knowing what to make of this statement. Did Savikkar expect him to perform some sort of miracle to calm the storm? He shook his head. "I can't do anything about a storm!" he yelled.

Savikkar laughed wildly. "It's not the storm I'm worried about," he cried. "I need you to do something about *that!*"

He pointed over the bow of the ship, and Wyngalf turned to see what he was indicating. At first, between the billowing waves, the intense rain and the dark sky, he didn't see it. But then a flash of lightning perfectly framed the thing in silhouette. It was like a mountain rising out of the sea. A small island, he thought? Why would the captain ask for his help with—

No, not an island. The thing was getting bigger as he watched. Or rather, more of it was emerging from the sea. And he saw, as the lightning flashed again, that the peak of the "mountain" had developed a number of vertical cracks, like a praying man slowly spreading his fingers. Tentacles, thought Wyngalf. My God, the thing is *alive*. It had to be three hundred feet tall—and that was just the part visible above the water. Its tentacles writhed menacingly, spreading as if to make a cage for the ship. It was so huge that Wyngalf would have expected the displaced water to push the *Erdis Evena* away from it, but if anything the opposite was happening. Wyngalf saw that the creature had parted its tentacles in such a way as to form an opening to admit the ship, and it was sucking vast quantities of water into its gullet. The ship was being slowly but inexorably drawn into the whirlpool.

"The Hafgufa," Wyngalf murmured weakly.

"Metaphorical Hafgufa," yelled Savikkar, with a grin, slapping Wyngalf on the back. "Go take care of it!"

Wyngalf stared at him in horror. Was Savikkar joking with him, or did he really expect Wyngalf to somehow mollify the Hafgufa? Either way, Wyngalf realized, the man was completely insane. He'd cracked under pressure—and this wasn't the first time. Wyngalf should have known there was something wrong with the man when Bulgar had told him how Savikkar had promised an unknown god that he would journey across the Sea of Dis if his crew were spared. It was funny how often madness was confused with faith.

At this point, though, Wyngalf had little choice but to embrace the man's madness and hope that his own faith was still worth something. The crew was paralyzed with fear, and he doubted there was anything they could do anyway. They had taken down the sails, and oars wouldn't be of much use against the maelstrom. Only divine intervention could save them now. The Nine Persons of the Noninity worked in mysterious ways, and maybe the Hafgufa had been sent as another test. The only thing for it was to rise to the challenge and hope his faith was strong enough to save them. It was the only chance any of them had.

Wyngalf got to his feet and made his way slowly to the bow of the ship, struggling against the pitching of the deck and the rough winds. By the time he reached the railing, the ship had been drawn into a torrent of water that was now pulling it rapidly toward the creature's maw. On either side of the channel were massive tentacles, larger than the great stonewood trees of the northern provinces of Vostolook, huge slimy arms writhing in the air like fingers beckoning the ship to its doom.

Wyngalf gripped the railing with both hands and stared into the vortex, wondering what it was that his God demanded of him. He refused to believe this was the end. There had to be some reason he had been brought to this point. Whether this voyage was the result of sheer coincidence or evidence of a divine joke, he still believed that ultimately the Noninity had some kind of purpose in mind for him. That meant it couldn't end here—at least, not as long as Wyngalf's faith held firm.

"Behold, foul monster of the deep!" cried Wyngalf. He doubted the creature could hear him through the wind, and doubted even more that it would be able to understand him if it could. But expressions of faith needn't be constrained by practicality or logic. He was convinced that somehow he could bend the monster to his will if only his faith were strong enough. "We are on a divine mission to bring the Blessed Truth of...."

He quavered as he noticed something huge and black encroaching on his field of vision to the right. He turned just in time to see the tip of a tentacle whip toward him. But it slowed as it curled around behind him, as if the monster was being repelled by some invisible force. Hope swelled in Wyngalf's breast. He'd done it! His faith had—quite literally—bent the sea beast to his will. The tentacle writhed around him, but remained just over an arm's length way. Try as it might, it couldn't touch him. Feeling encouraged by this clear display of divine power, Wyngalf was emboldened to command the creature to spare the *Erdis Evena*. He began again, with renewed confidence, "We are on a divine mission to bring the Blessed Truth of Noninitarianism to the distant land of Dis. Return to the depths from which you came, that we might continue unmolested!"

The tentacle—only about the thickness of his waist at its nearest point—hung in the air, motionless except for a faint quivering along its length. Wyngalf resisted the urge to reach out and strike the creature, as it seemed like that might be tempting fate. There was no need to lord it over the beast. It was simply an unthinking agent of the divine plan, sent to test Wyngalf's faith. He could no more be angry at it than he could feel animosity for the storm that still raged around him. Both would be forced to subside in the face of the unimaginable power working on Wyngalf's behalf.

As if in response to this thought, the tentacle began to straighten and withdraw, slipping closer to Wyngalf as it did so. Wyngalf shuddered with relief. He'd passed the test, beaten the mighty Hafgufa, unspeakable terror of the Sea of Dis. Men would write songs of this day—about what the all-powerful Noninity had done through its humble but unquestionably courageous servant Wyngalf. He couldn't help admiring the thing; the grace with which it moved held an undeniable beauty. Still, it was getting awfully close. Finally he was overcome by the urge to put a little distance between himself and the tentacle, and found himself leaning ever-so-slightly away from it to give the thing a wider berth. He'd already passed the test; there was no point in pressing the issue.

Anyway, that was what he was thinking when the tentacle whipped toward him and swept him off the bow into the sea.

Four

Wyngalf couldn't say how many hours he treaded water. In the chaos that followed his being thrown overboard, it was all he could do to keep from drowning amidst the swells and crashing waves. For a little while he caught an occasional glimpse of the ship or a tentacle writhing in the distance, but both gradually receded in the churning murk, and he was left alone in the storm. Eventually the gales died down, and only he remained, bobbing helplessly on the ocean swells. What happened to the *Erdis Evena* was a mystery. Maybe Wyngalf really had driven the creature away, or maybe the ship had been pulled beneath the sea by the maelstrom. There was no way to be sure.

It would have been nice to know that the ship survived, given that Wyngalf was almost certainly going to drown, but even that consolation was denied him. In all likelihood the *Erdis Evena* and its crew had been sucked into the maw of the Hafgufa. He supposed he would find out in the next life, if his faith in the afterlife was not also misplaced. Even if they had by some miracle survived, the mission had lost its preacher and therefore its raison d'être. He wondered if they would go on to Dis without him, pulling into some distant port as emissaries of a faith of which they were almost entirely ignorant. Perhaps they would tell tales of Wyngalf the Martyr, who had thrown himself into the sea to save the crew. "To Wyngalf!" they would cry, raising their glasses to him in a tavern across the sea. "We don't know what he believed in, but there can be no doubt that he believed it!"

The water was chilly but tolerable; even as the sun fell in the west and the air grew colder, Wyngalf remained fairly certain that he'd die of thirst or exhaustion before hypothermia set in. He doubted very much, in fact, whether he'd make it through the night. Some part of him wanted to dive deep underwater, let the salt water into his lungs and have it over with. But a larger part of him still believed he'd have to meet his maker[2] and be judged for his actions[3], and suicide was never acceptable, even under these dire circumstances.

As the orange disc of the sun touched the sea, Wyngalf became aware of a dark object floating in the water some distance away. It was hard to tell how large it was or how far away, because of the fading light and the swells that blocked it from view most of the time, but it appeared that it might be large enough for Wyngalf to climb on top of it. It would probably only delay his inevitable fate, but all he could think about at present was having a moment to rest his arms.

Not yet, though. If he was going to reach the floating thing before darkness fell, he was going to have to move fast. He forced himself to ignore the tiredness in his limbs and pushed himself toward the object. The sun continued to drop behind the horizon, and at first it seemed as if he was making no progress at all. But gradually the floating thing became larger, and he pressed on.

---

[2] Abasmos the Creator, the first person of the Noninity. The name of Abasmos is considered too sacred to speak aloud, so Noninitarians usually refer to him simply as "The First Person."

[3] By Xandiss the Auditor, who evaluates the sum total of each person's actions upon their death using a system that only Xandiss himself fully understands. Orthodox Noninitarianism teaches that Xandiss simply compares a person's good deeds with his or her wicked deeds and, if a negative balance is found, passes the person's soul on to Shotarr the Purifier. More recently, some liberal theologians have posited the idea that Xandiss also gives the individual credit for various sorts of obstacles in life that may have made it more difficult for the individual to live a virtuous life. This school of thought, known as Standard Deductionism, is considered heretical by mainstream Noninitarians.

Wyngalf was a reasonably good swimmer, thanks to the lap pool the bishop had installed on the grounds of the Stronghold three years prior. It was one of the few diversions available to the acolytes, and if Wyngalf survived this he promised himself that he would express his undying gratitude to the bishop. But as the sun dropped below the sea and the floating thing remained a few swells away, the chances of that happening seemed slim indeed. Still he pressed on, paddling languidly in the direction he thought the object lay. In the last remaining gray light, he spotted it again as a swell passed under him, and he pushed himself toward it with renewed effort. He finally found it with his fingers rather than his eyes, a curved wooden surface bobbing in the waves. It was a fish barrel that had apparently been thrown from the *Erdis Evena*.

He climbed on top of it and formed his body to the barrel's curve, spreading his weight as evenly as he could. The thing had just enough buoyancy that he could with minimal effort keep his head and trunk out of the water, with his hands and his legs below the knees submerged. He shivered as the night air hit his damp skin, but his aching limbs thanked him for the respite. If he could just make it through the night, his clothes would eventually dry in the sun, and then—well, he'd die of thirst. But first things first.

At some point, he fell asleep. He was only aware of this because he was awoken by a strange sensation. An impossible sensation, in fact. It seemed to him that someone had been knocking on the barrel, trying to get his attention. After a moment, it stopped and he went back to sleep. Some indeterminate amount of time later, it happened again. He still refused to believe it had happened, though, attributing the sensation to a manifestation of his discomfort due to cold, hunger and thirst. Once again, he slipped back into sleep. The third time, the rapping continued sometime after he regained consciousness, and was followed by the sound of a small voice.

"Say again?" Wyngalf murmured, not entirely convinced he hadn't dreamed it.

The voice spoke again. "I said, is somebody out there?"

Wyngalf was so startled, he nearly lost his balance. It was all he could do to keep from falling backwards into the water. "Who... who is that?"

"Father Wyngalf?" said the voice, small and muffled. It clearly came from inside the barrel.

"Evena?" cried Wyngalf hoarsely. "What in heaven's name are you doing in there?"

"Floating, I think," said Evena. "Can you get me out?"

Wyngalf stared dumbly at the barrel. A crescent Moon had come out, and he could just make out the steel band wrapped around the boards in front of him. He moved his fingers to the top of the barrel, feeling the lid, which had been secured with pitch.

"I don't think so," said Wyngalf. "Why are you in the barrel?"

"I wanted to go with you on your adventure," said Evena. "So I stowed away. I paid one of the mates, a man named Fendrelli, to seal me in this barrel and load me on the ship. He was supposed to get me out after we'd been at sea for a day."

"He missed the ship," Wyngalf said. "You've been stuck in this barrel for *three days?*"

"It hasn't been so bad," Evena said. "I've got water. I ran out of food, but I haven't been hungry anyway."

Wyngalf nodded. He had barely eaten since the ship had left Skuldred. "Can you breathe okay?"

"I have an air hole," she said. "Here, in the top."

Wyngalf reached around the top of the barrel and felt around until his fingers felt a round hole, about the diameter of a large coin. Three of Evena's delicate fingers were sticking through it. He took hold of them and squeezed. They were surprisingly warm.

"What happened to the ship?" she asked. "I heard the storm. There was a lot of commotion, and then a terrible sound like the hull being ripped apart. Next thing I knew, I was bobbing in the waves. I called for help for hours, but no one came. I thought I was going to die out here."

"You still might," murmured Wyngalf.

"What?"

"We just have to survive the night," Wyngalf said.

"And then what?"

"I don't know," Wyngalf admitted. "Maybe once I can see something, I can get you out." Although you'll probably be no better off, he thought. "Just try to get some sleep." He gave her fingers another squeeze and then let her hand go.

"Okay."

Evena grew quiet again, and when she didn't stir for a while, Wyngalf supposed she must have fallen asleep. He drifted off too eventually, lulled to sleep by the rhythm of the swells. He had just sunk into a deep sleep when he was thrown violently from the barrel into the water.

Disoriented, he had no idea which was way up, and began to thrash around in a semi-conscious panic. He was trying to locate the surface, but his hand struck something rough and hard. The sensation was so unexpected that he didn't know what to make of it. Eventually he got it into his addled brain that the rough thing was some kind of floor, and he oriented his feet toward it and pushed off. His head broke through the surface and gasped for air. He felt the swell sinking and suddenly he was standing on the rocky ground, the water barely reaching his armpits. A few seconds later, the water rose again, lifting him off the rocks.

He couldn't see a thing. The Moon had either gone down or was hidden behind clouds; the sky was a uniform charcoal below which was the near-total blackness of the sea. He paddled furiously, spinning himself around in an attempt to locate either the barrel or the rock it had struck, but the swells played tricks on his eyes. "Evena!" he called, but there was no response.

A moment later he was once again standing on rocks, this time in even shallower water. He wanted to run, to get away from the capricious ocean that would in another moment lift him high above the rocky floor—and drop him just as quickly—but he had no idea which direction to go. So he simply stood there until another swell caught him, shoving him up, up, up…

And then fell down, down, down, bracing himself for contact with the rocks, which could be five or fifty feet down. If he landed wrong, lost his balance and struck his head, he was done for.

But he once again landed with his feet on more-or-less level rock, in water that reached barely to his chest. Not only that, but he could just make out a larger rock formation towering over him a few yards away. At the peak of the swells, the top of it was probably only a few feet underwater. It appeared to be shaped like a pillar, about ten feet in diameter, with sharply sloping, irregular sides and a plateau at the top. If he could get to it, he'd have a firm place to stand. Even if it didn't connect to any larger land formation, at least he'd have a momentary respite from the swells that threatened to crack his skull open like an egg.

He dove into the water in the direction of the rock, willing himself toward it even as he felt the water once again shoving him skyward. By the time the swell reached its zenith, he figured he must be on top of the rock. At least, he hoped he was—if he'd miscalculated, the swell would drop him on one of the sloped sides leading up to the plateau, and he'd tumble down the side, bashing and bruising himself until he either hit water or another rock big enough to break his fall.

But as the water receded, he found himself gently deposited on his hands and knees on the almost perfectly flat surface of the rock. He got to his feet and peered into the darkness, seeing now that the column was actually part of a small promontory that jutted out from what appeared to be a larger mass of rock. Land.

There was no telling how big the island was, or whether it was all as harsh and inhospitable as this unforgiving rock, but it was solid ground, and that struck Wyngalf as near-miraculous occurrence. Once again, he had cheated death—at least for a little longer. But what of Evena? Had she been spared death in the shipwreck only to die in a barrelwreck?

"Evena!" he called again, but still there was no answer. The water rose, but only to his waist, and when it receded again, he made his way quickly across a lower patch of ground to get to the larger rock formation. He scrabbled up the sharp slope just ahead of the rising swell, finding himself standing on dry ground. He called for Evena once more, and this time he thought he heard a response. Making his way carefully over the rocky ground toward the sound, he called again, and this time he was certain he'd heard her. Evena was alive.

He found her sitting on a flat section of rock, hugging her knees and shivering.

"M-m-m-my b-b-b-b-barrel b-b-b-b-broke," she said, as he sat down next to her. She was soaking wet. The barrel must have smashed open on the rocks, and she had managed to climb up here. Wyngalf put his arms around her and squeezed her tightly. They sat there shivering together until morning.

Five

Dawn revealed that the island was not much larger than Wyngalf had imagined—perhaps three stone throws across. Most of it was comprised of rough, porous rock, although there was a small stretch of sand in a recessed area near the center. As this offered a bit more comfort and shelter from the wind than the expanse of flat rock on which he and Evena had spent the night, they made their way over the rocks and lay down on the sand, soaking up the warmth of the sun. They dozed there until almost noon, when Wyngalf was awoken by thirst. He left Evena to sleep while he climbed back onto the rocks. He managed to find several small puddles of rainwater that had collected in depressions in the rock and lowered himself to slurp water with his mouth until the thirst abated. An intense feeling of relief lasted for about ten seconds, after which his awareness was seized by a ravenous hunger. He pushed this away and continued exploring the island.

There was nothing to do about the hunger; other than a few small trees, scraggly shrubs and weeds, there was no vegetation on the island. Wyngalf spent half an hour traversing the perimeter of the island to make sure of this. He knew that various small crustaceans, mollusks and fish made their homes in tide pools, but the ocean swells here were apparently too irregular to be amenable to such denizens. Except for a few barnacles and moss clinging to the rocks, he saw no life in the water at all. He had the feeling that their stay on this island was going to be short and unpleasant.

When Wyngalf returned to the sandy area, Evena was awake and looking around for him in near-panic. He had to suppress a laugh at this; where did she think he had gone? But, adopting his best reassuring preacher manner, he explained that everything was going to be alright and told her about the water he'd found. The mention of water snapped her out of her panic; he had no sooner pointed to the area where he'd found the puddles than Evena had set to scrambling over the rocks toward it.

Wyngalf found it difficult not to stare at Evena as she clambered away from him. She had chosen a much more practical outfit for her "adventure" than the frilly dresses Wyngalf had previously seen her in—a pair of rugged trousers, a plain green blouse, and boots that might have been borrowed from her father—but the way the damp fabric clung to her body, it only accentuated her femininity.

When she had disappeared over the rocks, Wyngalf allowed himself a moment of despair. He sank to his knees and pounded the sand with his fists. Once again, he had been spared death, but why? His pack along with his provisions and the rest of his meager belongings had gone down with the ship, and whatever Evena had brought along had been lost when her barrel splintered apart. They had no food, no real shelter, and minimal fresh water. What was the point of not drowning only to die of starvation a few days later?

No, he thought, forcing himself to get to his feet. This was another test. His faith had sustained him thus far, and he wasn't about to abandon it now. He'd thought that his God had abandoned him when the Hafgufa swept him off the deck of the *Erdis Evena*, but he realized now with sudden clarity that it was his own betrayal that had led to him being thrown overboard. If he had remained firm in his faith, the monster would have withdrawn innocuously, but he had flinched—and his momentary weakness had cost the crew their lives. It was only through the infinite mercy of Illias the Interceder that Evena had not perished as well.

He and Evena had been spared for a reason. He didn't yet know how, but somehow they would get off this island and continue their mission. He just needed to have faith.

He was still pondering this when Evena reappeared, climbing over the rocks with something cradled in her arms. He realized after a moment that it was several planks from the barrel that had been crushed against the rocks.

"I found these floating in a pool over there," Evena said, indicating somewhere over her shoulder. "I thought we might be able to build—"

"A signal fire!" cried Wyngalf, suddenly encouraged. He had seen the planks as well, but had been too focused on the idea of locating food to give them any heed. As far as he knew, they were hundreds of miles from civilization and shipping lanes, so it was very unlikely that anyone would see a fire—or respond to it, if they did—but seeing Evena with the planks cradled in her arms, he was suddenly convinced it was a sign from Ganillion the Messenger. The fragments of the barrel should have been swept out to sea, but somehow these planks had been caught in one of the shallow pools on the periphery of the island. Once again, his faith had been rewarded!

They laid the planks out on the sand to dry, and then set about gathering branches from trees and shrubs that grew sporadically about the island. It was hard work, since they had no knife or tools of any sort, but after a few hours they managed to assemble several small piles of brush. The idea was to get the fire started with the planks and then, once it was burning strongly, to feed it with progressively greener vegetation to create smoke that could be seen from a long distance. During his preparations for his missionary journey, Wyngalf had learned—in theory—how to start a fire simply by rubbing two pieces of wood together. He'd never managed to actually perform this feat, even with perfectly dry wood that had been specifically cut for the purpose, but he was certain he could do it, given sufficient motivation.

After collecting as much brush as they could, they rested under one of the small trees while they waited for the planks to dry. Evena argued that they should start the fire when it got dark, as it would be more visible from a distance, but Wyngalf suspected she was more concerned about keeping warm than alerting anyone to their plight. The sandy area's recessed position made it very unlikely that the fire could be seen even by a ship that had drifted so far off course that it came within a few miles of this island. They might have tried to get a fire started on one of the rocky outcroppings, but Wyngalf hadn't been able to find a flat area big enough, so they were stuck trying to get the fire going on the sandy plateau. He was convinced that a plume of thick smoke was their best bet, and it would do them no good to stay warm for one night if it doomed their one chance to get off the island. Even with all the fuel they'd collected, the fire wouldn't last much longer than a few hours. In any case, it was going to take at least a full day for the planks to completely dry. So they would have to spend another night shivering together in the dark.

Wyngalf was not entirely inexperienced in matters of the opposite sex; the Noninitarians couldn't afford to turn away any prospective devout, so the Stronghold admitted both men and women. The sexes were largely sequestered in separate sections of the Stronghold, but occasionally met for communal meetings and worship services, which were notorious occasions for fraternization. Such activity was officially frowned upon by the Noninitarian hierarchy, but little effort was put into stopping it. Cynics grumbled that turning a blind eye to this illicit hanky-panky ensured a steady supply of "orphans" to be turned into future devout, and the seemingly arbitrary enforcement of anti-fraternization regulations tended to bolster this claim: it was rumored that Bishop Frotheckle kept a secret record of the familial connections between the various orphans and worked assiduously to prevent devout from unknowingly engaging in incestuous relations with one another. Wyngalf had on a few occasions given in to the temptation of sneaking away with one of the devout from the opposite side of the Stronghold, but his own uncertain lineage—as well as his lack of confidence in the record-keeping of the bishop—kept him from letting things go too far.

Ordinarily, then, spending the night with an attractive young woman who was almost certainly not a blood relation might have been a serious temptation for Wyngalf, but the first night they had been so cold, wet and tired that the idea of doing anything more strenuous than shivering had seemed singularly unappealing. They had since dried off and gotten some rest, but now a feeling of protectiveness had come over Wyngalf. It was, after all, his fault that Evena had stowed away on the *Erdis Evena*, and it could hardly have been a coincidence that the two of them had been marooned here together. Wyngalf had a responsibility to watch out for her. In any case, despite her confidence and physical maturity, she was not much more than a child. Perhaps some time in the future, if they somehow survived this, and Wyngalf had successfully indoctrinated Evena regarding the Fourteen Theses of Noninitarianism… but he still had his doubts whether Evena possessed the intellectual development to appreciate the sublime truth of his faith, and in any case she seemed in no mood for theological discussion at present. Her thoughts were on more immediate matters.

"You didn't want to go," said Evena as they sat on the rocks watching the sun set over the ocean. "On the voyage to Dis, I mean. I could see it in your eyes when my father proposed the expedition. I thought you were crazy. Who wouldn't want to go on an exciting adventure to a faraway land? But now I understand. You were right. This was a bad idea. And I was stupid to come along."

Wyngalf shrugged. "You lived a sheltered life," he said. "So did I, up until five months ago. So I understand the desire for adventure. The problem with adventures, I've found is that they are by definition unpredictable, and usually when something unpredictable happens, it's something bad."

"So you've been in predicaments like this before?" asked Evena hopefully, as if Wyngalf might be in possession of some universally applicable wisdom that could save them.

"Oh, no," Wyngalf admitted. "Nothing quite as desperate as this. I've been robbed, chased by wolfbats, nearly burned at the stake a few times. But being stranded on a deserted island in the middle of the Sea of Dis is a new one."

Evena nodded glumly. "We're going to die here, aren't we?"

"No," said Wyngalf, trying to exude confidence. "We could easily have gone down with the ship. I believe the Noninity saved us for a reason. We just have to keep faith."

"Your faith didn't save my father's men. They were all killed by the Hafgufa."

"You don't know that," said Wyngalf. "In any case, perhaps those men served their purpose already."

"They served their purpose and now your god is done with them?" Evena asked, a hint of pique in her voice. "Like an old pair of shoes whose soles have worn through?"

"It is not for us to question the ways of the Noninity," snapped Wyngalf, a little too harshly. He was taken aback by Evena's brash impertinence. If he was honest with himself, he was also feeling a bit defensive. If he hadn't flinched during his test with the Hafgufa, the men on the ship might still be alive. But there was no point in dwelling on the matter; if they were going to get off this island, he needed to keep his faith pure—and that meant pushing away any doubts about his own foibles. "Look," he said. "What I mean is that we can't help those men now. All we can do is hope for the best. I have to believe there is a reason we made it this far."

The sun had dropped below the horizon, and Evena got to her feet without a word and climbed back down to the sheltered sand. Wyngalf followed. They spent another night huddled together for warmth, Wyngalf once again acting the very model of propriety.

Some time after noon the next day, Wyngalf judged the planks to be dry enough to attempt a fire. He broke one of them into several pieces by smashing it with rocks, and then spent the next six hours experimenting with various methods of rubbing the pieces of wood together in an effort to create a spark, occasionally taking breaks to get water or pound the sand with his fists and curse in frustration. He was so hungry that he took to chewing on splinters of wood that broke off during his efforts. It didn't help. The sun began to set, and he was forced to admit he'd failed. They spent a third night huddled against the cold. Wyngalf had never before felt so defeated.

He awoke early the next morning to the smell of smoke. At first he thought he was imagining it, but he opened his eyes and turned to see Evena beaming at him, a small fire burgeoning among a stack of splinters in front of her. He jumped to his feet and ran to it.

"Don't let it die!" he cried. She nodded, and gently placed a few more fragments of wood on the stack. "Don't smother it!" he yelled.

"Wyngalf!" she snapped. "Calm down." Her fierce tone struck him like a slap across the face. He nodded dumbly, embarrassed to have faltered in his faith in front of Evena.

Evena shrugged. "I learned how to do it from watching you," she said.

"You're too kind," replied Wyngalf.

"Well, I learned how *not* to do it, anyway."

Wyngalf wanted to chide the girl for her impertinence, but found himself repressing laughter. "Glad I could help," he said, falling back onto his elbows. He smiled as the fire grew and he gave thanks to Pamphloss the Provider for granting him the means of procuring their survival. The smile soon faded, though. The smell of the smoke had put him in the mind of breakfast, and his mouth was salivating in anticipation of food. But the odds of anyone seeing the smoke and coming to rescue them were, he had to admit, vanishingly slim. In all likelihood, he'd already eaten his last meal. And he'd vomited it over the side of the *Erdis Evena*. Once again, his faith was proving weak.

Tending the fire at least gave them something to do. They built it gradually larger and larger, and then, when they had a roaring fire going, they started to throw green, leafy branches on it. Plumes of gray smoke went up a few feet and then, when it had reached the open air above the sheltered area of the island, dissipated almost completely in the wind. Wyngalf fell to his knees, defeated.

"There's no way anybody is going to see that!" he wailed.

"You give up too easy," Evena chided. She threw another branch on the fire.

The girl's childish mood swings were beginning to grate on Wyngalf. It was all well and good to have a positive attitude, but Evena's hope, like her preceding glumness, was just an arbitrary sentiment that didn't connect to anything, like a house without a foundation. If his own emotions were sometimes volatile, it was because he was grappling with profound issues of faith and destiny. Evena's mood swings were just sound and fury, signifying nothing.

"It's pointless!" he protested. "There's no land for hundreds of miles, and no ships come within twenty leagues of here. And even if one strayed near us, and someone in the crew happened to look in this direction, why would they go even farther out of their way to rescue a couple of strangers? We're doomed."

"Boy, are you moody," said Evena.

"I'm not moody!" Wyngalf snapped. "I'm grappling with profound issues of faith and destiny!"

Evena shrugged but didn't reply. She continued to watch the fire, adding more branches to increase the output of smoke. But no matter how many she put on, the smoke never made it more than thirty feet into the sky before dissipating into an almost invisible haze. It didn't take even as long as Wyngalf had estimated to go through all their fuel. The piles of branches were both gone, and the fire still continued to emit only an embarrassingly small column of inoffensive gray smoke. Soon even that shrank to almost nothing. So their signal fire had come to nothing, and now they were doomed to spend another evening freezing and hungry in the cold.

As the fire died down and Evena too began to succumb to despair, a breeze picked up, fanning the flames but further dissipating the smoke. It was a strange sort of wind, as it somehow penetrated the shelter of the rocks and seemed to have no clear direction. In fact, as Wyngalf watch the remaining flames whip around erratically, it seemed to him as if the wind were originating from directly *above* them. A moment later, he and Evena were suddenly shrouded in shadow, and they looked upward in unison to see what was above them. What Wyngalf saw struck fear into his heart.

It was a gigantic, scaly green reptile, with vast, bat-like wings. And it was getting bigger.

Wyngalf and Evena sat there with their necks craned back and their mouths agape as the dragon lowered itself toward them. Wyngalf wanted to run, but there was no place on the island to go. If the dragon was determined to eat them, there wasn't a thing they could do about it. As the creature drew closer, its great leathery wings sent blasts of wind toward them, extinguishing the fire and showering them with sand. Wyngalf clamped his eyes shut and held Evena close to him. All he could do was hope that it would be over with quickly.

Then, suddenly, the rushing of the wind stopped, and Wyngalf cautiously opened his eyes. Evena must have done the same thing, because they screamed in perfect unison. Not five feet away from them was the emerald dragon's head, craned downward on its long scaly neck to peer at them. The dragon's head was the size of an oxcart. Its eyes were like great yellow marble bowls, and its teeth were like carving knives. They felt its hot breath emitting in long bursts from its nostrils.

Wyngalf and Evena wrapped their arms around each other and cowered together, waiting to die.

Six

"Wow!" the dragon exclaimed, its voice like a baritone choir, "*that was a long flight.*" He paused, apparently trying to get his breath. "It must be 300 miles from the shore of Dis to this island. But sometimes you have to leave the beaten path to find a gem in the rough, and this place is definitely..." He trailed off, craning his long neck to survey the island. "...rough. Good grief, I've had bowel movements larger than this island. Easy beach access, I'll give you that, but the amenities are positively primitive. This place is going to need a lot of work." He spun around and climbed up the rocks behind him, spreading his wings to keep his balance. Wyngalf had to duck to avoid being smacked in the head by the dragon's tail. When the dragon reached the top of the rocks, he made a long, slow survey of the island. Wyngalf noticed he tended to hold his head cocked slightly to the left, as if favoring his right eye. After some time, the dragon spread his wings, leapt into the air, and glided back to the sandy patch where Wyngalf and Evena stood. "It's got potential," the dragon said. "But I'd definitely put it in the fixer-upper category. How are the schools?"

"*Schools?*" asked Evena.

"You're surrounded by fish," said the dragon, with a touch of condescension. "Surely you've looked into the schools? Of course it doesn't particularly matter if you're planning on focusing mainly on tourism. What's the zoning?"

"Zoning?" said Wyngalf. "I'm afraid I don't—"

"And have you thought about public transportation? You're quite a ways from the main shipping lines, you know. I only noticed you because of the smoke, and it took me most of the morning to get here. Not exactly commuter friendly. If you plan to develop this property, these are things you need to think about."

"Mr. Dragon, sir," said Evena, "We don't mean any offense, but—"

"Ah, my apologies!" cried the dragon. "Sometimes I get so wrapped up in my work that I forgot to introduce myself. My name is Verne." He reached down with his right claw and carefully pulled something small from behind one of the scales on his chest. As he held it toward them, Wyngalf realized it was a small card made of paper. Wyngalf took it from Verne. It read:

Verne the Dragon
President and CEO,
Green Hills Real Estate

Offering development, sales
and commercial management
services to the Southwestern
Dis region

Call Verne and
"Dis land can be your land!"

"Nice to meet you, Verne," said Evena, who seemed to have overcome her initial terror. "This is Wyngalf. I'm Evena."

"Enchanted," said Verne, with a slight bow.

"Verne is a strange name for a dragon, isn't it?" asked Evena.

"That's what people used to tell my parents," Verne said. "Why 'Verne'? they'd ask. And my parents would say, 'No, he's just small for his age.'"

"I don't understand what this means," said Wyngalf, staring at the card.

Verne frowned. "It's a pun," he said. "Dis land is your land. Dis land is yours, dat land is mine. You don't get it?"

"I get it," said Evena, with a cautious smile. "Very clever."

Verne grinned at her.

"No, I get the pun," said Wyngalf. "I mean, I don't understand the rest of it. You sell land?"

Verne nodded excitedly. "Buy, sell, develop, manage," he announced. "I'm always on the lookout for hot new properties, and this one is *smoking!*" He spread his wings in apparent excitement, looking at them expectantly.

Wyngalf and Evena stared blankly at him. Verne frowned, turning to look at the pile of wood from which a barely visible wisp of smoke was rising. He opened his mouth, spitting a stream of fire. The wood burst into flame. He turned back to face them.

"*Smoking!*" Verne exclaimed again, and turned to look at them. They continued to stare, unsure how to respond.

Verne scowled, letting his wings settle to his sides. "It's smoking," he said. "Get it? Because of the—"

"Yeah, I get it," said Wyngalf. "I think you've misunderstood our situation, though. We're not *selling* this island. We don't even—"

Verne nodded. "I see how it is. Hardball, eh?" He began to pace back and forth in front of him, his huge tail swishing ominously over their heads. "Look, I'm not going to lie to you. Islands are hot these days, and not just the volcanic ones. Get it? Not just the.... Everybody loves islands. They're great for families. Why, just the other day I was showing a volcanic island to a nice family with three young kids. I love kids. 'Don't touch the floor, it's lava!' I told them. Poor, disfigured little bastards." He stopped and turned to face them again. "The highest I can go on something like this is four hundred gold pieces."

"Four hundred gold pieces!" cried Evena in disbelief.

"Alright, four fifty," said Verne, "but that's my final offer."

"Verne," said Wyngalf. "You're not listening. We're *marooned* on this island. We lit that signal fire because we were—"

"Holding out for a better offer, huh?" said Verne, scratching his chin nervously with his claws. "How many dragons do you think are buying real estate in this area anyway? That's a serious question. Four? Six?"

"To be honest, I didn't know there were *any* dragons around here, much less dragons with an interest in real estate."

"Right," said Verne. "Right! Of course. There are no other real estate dragons out here. It's not like another dragon is going to see your signal and make you a better offer any minute now." He straightened up, folding his arms in front of his chest. "So you're stuck with mine. Four hundred and fifty gold pieces. Take it or leave it."

"Verne," said Wyngalf. "We can't take your offer because we don't o—"

"We'll let you have it," Evena interrupted.

Wyngalf and Verne both turned to face her. "You mean for *free?*" asked Verne.

"Yes," said Evena. "On one condition. You have to give us a ride to the mainland. You have to take us to Dis."

Wyngalf bit his lip. He was not at all sure that asking a dragon for a ride was a good idea. Dragons, he knew, were irredeemably evil creatures, and accepting assistance from one would seem to indicate a weakness in his faith. But what if this was their only chance to get off the island? Would the Noninity forgive him for temporarily allying himself with a dragon if he did it so that his holy mission might continue?

Verne cocked his head at her suspiciously. "Wait a minute," he said. "Do you even *own* this island?"

"Finders keepers," said Evena. "We claimed it when we got here two days ago."

"Claimed it, did you?" said Verne skeptically. "Then what's the island's name?"

"Its *name?*" asked Evena.

"You can't claim a piece of land without giving it a name. If you didn't name it, it's still up for grabs, legally speaking. Personally, I would call it Verne's Island."

"Oh, the name!" Evena exclaimed. "Yes, we gave the island a name. Of course we did. Didn't we, Wyngalf? When we first got here, I said, let's call it, um..."

Wyngalf's brain went blank as he tried to come up with a suitable name for the island. He found himself saying, "Ta..."

Evena added, "...ba..."

"...ka," Wyngalf finished.

"Tabaka," Evena announced. "Yep, that's what we called it."

"Tabaka?" asked Verne. "What kind of name is Tabaka?"

"In our native language, it means..." Evena started.

"Green dragon," offered Wyngalf.

Verne cocked his head to the side for a moment, considering this. He nodded. "I like it. Tabaka it is. Okay, you have a deal. I'll give you a ride to Dis in exchange for a one hundred percent interest in Tabaka."

"Evena," Wyngalf said nervously, turning to face the girl. "Perhaps we should discuss this before we sell, um…."

"Tabaka," said Evena.

"Right. Before we sell Tabaka."

Verne nodded. "I understand this is a big decision for you folks. I shall give you a moment to conference." The dragon stood, pivoted on his huge, scaly feet, and settled down again facing the opposite direction. His tail whooshed back and forth over their heads.

"I'm not sure I trust this Verne," Wyngalf whispered. "Dragons are notoriously devious."

"This is our only chance!" Evena whispered. "You said it yourself. There's no hope of a ship rescuing us."

"You just need to have faith," Wyngalf said. "Illias the Interceder will send someone."

"He did!" cried Evena. "He sent Verne!"

"Dragons are vile, wicked creatures," Wyngalf snapped. "The Noninity wouldn't send a dragon. A hippogriff, perhaps, or a wyndbahr." This was the problem with Evena's sort of faith: with no real grasp on the scope of the spiritual struggle in which they were engaged, she seized upon the first possibility of rescue that came along.

"Well, you can stay here and wait for the next hippogriff," said Evena. "I'm going with the dragon."

"You can't do that!" cried Wyngalf. "He'll drop you in the middle of the sea!"

"Wyngalf, if Verne had wanted to kill us, he'd have done it already."

"Dragons are sadistic," Wyngalf insisted. "He's probably just toying with us."

Evena sighed in frustration. "Isn't your God omnivorous?"

"Omnivorous?" asked Wyngalf, confused.

"All powerful," said Evena.

"You mean omnipotent?"

"Yes! Omnipotent. He controls everything, right?"

"Technically, yes. Each of the Nine Persons of the Noninity is responsible for different aspects of—"

"Good. So if he controls everything, then everybody ultimately works for Him. Including dragons."

"That's a vast oversimplification of how the Noninity works," said Wyngalf. "The Noninity permits a certain level of evil in the world to refine us and allow us to reach our true potential. Dragons are part of that evil. They are not to be trusted. Don't you see? We're being tested. The Noninity has sent this dragon as a temptation, to determine if we will continue to trust the Noninity or if we'll succumb to the temptation to take the easy way out."

"Being carried across the ocean by a dragon is the 'easy way out'?" asked Evena. "Your god sounds like kind of a jerk."

Wyngalf stared at her, stunned by the unthinking blasphemy of her comment. This is why one didn't discuss theology with children. He needed to change tacks before she said something truly unforgivable.

"Look," he said. "You were never supposed to come along in the first place. This is *my* divine mission, not yours. "How about if we ask our friendly dragon to fly to Skuldred and tell your father where we are. He can send a ship to rescue us. You can return home where you belong, and I'll go back to Svalbraakrat, where the bishop can organize a proper expedition to Dis."

Evena regarded him for a moment, and then began to nod.

"So you see the wisdom of my plan?" he asked.

"I see that you're a coward who is going to die alone on an island," replied Evena. "I'm going to Dis with the dragon. You may do what you like."

"Evena!" cried Wyngalf. But it was no use. She had stood up and caught the end of Verne's tail in her hand to get his attention. The dragon gingerly turned around to face them.

"Have we made a decision?" Verne asked genially.

"I have," said Evena. "I'd be much obliged if you could take me across the sea to Dis."

"My pleasure, Miss," said the dragon. "I take it your friend has decided to remain here?"

"I'm afraid my religious beliefs prevent me from making a deal with a dragon," said Wyngalf. "I mean no offense."

"Sure, sure," said Verne. "I'm not going to pressure you to do anything against your principles. Just make sure you've cleared out by the time I get back."

"Cleared out?" asked Wyngalf, puzzled.

"If I give Evena a ride, the island is mine," said Verne. "That means you're trespassing. Anyway, clear out by the time I get back and we won't have a problem." He turned to Evena. "Ready, dear?"

"Ready," she said.

"Excellent," said Verne. "Climb aboard." He rested his head on the sand in front of them, and she moved to climb onto his neck.

Wyngalf regarded Verne uncertainly. "What if I can't get off the island by the time you get back?"

"Well, you'll be incinerated, of course," said dragon.

"Incinerated!" Wyngalf yelped.

Verne frowned. "Wait, what's the word for when somebody gets kicked off an island?"

"Evicted?" Wyngalf asked.

"Right!" Verne said. "Sorry, you'll be evicted."

"What does that mean exactly?"

"It means you'll…" Verne frowned again. "What's the word for when somebody gets burned to ash?"

Wyngalf swallowed hard. "You're going to burn me alive?"

"Not if you don't want me to. I had assumed you would prefer a quick incineration to being dropped in the middle of the sea, where you will eventually drown. I apologize if I was being presumptuous. Right between the wings is your best bet." This last was directed at Evena, who had gotten onto Verne's back and was crawling to the flat section of his body between the wings. "That's it," said Verne. "I'll try to be careful, but you can hold onto the base of my wings to keep from slipping off, in case there's turbulence."

Evena spread herself flat on the dragon's back, gripping the base of his right wing with her right hand. Verne sank into a crouch, spreading his wings as if to leap into the air.

"Wait!" cried Wyngalf.

"Yes?" said Verne, with a touch of impatience. "You've made your position on negotiating with dragons quite clear, Mr. Wyngalf.

Frankly, I admire your willingness to be incinerated rather than sacrifice your principles. You don't see a lot of that kind of pig-headed idealism these days. Hold on, dear." Verne made to leap into the air again.

"Just wait a second!" cried Wyngalf again. "If I accept a ride from you, you agree that we're trading the island for transport to Dis. Once we get to Dis, we're even. We don't owe you anything else. We both go our separate ways."

"That was the arrangement," said Verne, sounding bored. "But I'm not going to wait around all day for you to decide. If you're going, get on board now."

Wyngalf bit his lip. "What if I refuse to sell? The island is half mine, you know."

"Then neither of you gets a ride to Dis," said Verne. "This is an all-or-nothing deal."

"Don't you dare," said Evena, glaring at him from on top of the dragon. "Come on, Wyngalf. This is our only chance to get off the island. Don't let your faith blind you to what's right in front of you."

Wyngalf regarded Evena and then the dragon. This test—if it was a test—was getting more complicated all the time. On one hand, all of his schooling warned him that dragons were not to be trusted. On the other hand, if Evena was going with the dragon, was he not obligated to go with her to see that no harm came to her? Perhaps the test was not simply to resist the dragon, but to resist his fear of the dragon—to have faith that the Noninity would protect him from harm even while he was in the clutches of a dragon. If he could discuss the matter with Bishop Frotheckle, he had no doubt they'd be able to come to some theologically satisfactory conclusion to the conundrum, but he didn't have that luxury. He needed to make a decision, and fast. In the end, he concluded that the Noninity could overcome any obstacle, including Wyngalf's own lack of discernment. He strongly suspected that the bishop would call that sort of thinking rationalization, but the bishop wasn't here to play his part in the dialogue.

"Fine," he said. "Let's go to Dis."

"Ask nicely," said Verne.

Wyngalf gritted his teeth. "I would be much obliged, Verne," he said, "if you would carry us both to Dis."

"Certainly," said Verne. "Climb aboard." He once again rested his head on the sand in front of them, and Wyngalf climbed onto his neck. Wyngalf crawled up the long neck and settled in next to Evena, gripping the base of Verne's left wing.

"Ready?" asked Verne.

"Ready!" cried Evena. Wyngalf shut his eyes tight and molded himself to Verne's back as best he could. Evena, to his right, reached out to clutch his left hand. They were pressed hard against Verne's back as he launched himself into the sky, and Wyngalf felt powerful muscles shifting beneath the scales, working hard to keep them aloft. He had to admit the dragon was an amazing creature, even if he was an irredeemably wicked beast. They continued to gain altitude for some time before leveling out. Evena shrieked in exhilaration, and Wyngalf forced himself to open his eyes.

They were soaring several hundred feet above the ocean, which was an endless plane of blackness broken only by barely discernible white crests. Wyngalf's eyes watered from the wind, and he blinked away tears. Looking up, he saw a layer of puffy clouds sliding slowly past overhead. Occasionally they would break through a low-hanging cloud and Wyngalf would feel a sheen of water vapor condensing on his cheeks.

"Ordinarily I'd fly above the clouds," Verne called back to them, "but the air is a bit thin and cold up there."

Wyngalf nodded silently. He was already shivering as the wind pulled the heat from his body. Dragons were built for this sort of thing; humans were not. It struck him that for an irredeemably evil beast Verne was extraordinarily attuned to the needs of his passengers. Perhaps dragons weren't so bad after all—or this particular one wasn't, anyway. If he intended to kill them, he was certainly taking his time about it.

Wyngalf had no idea how fast they were traveling. Faster than any horse could run, for certain, and probably ten times as fast as the *Erdis Evena* traveled. Still, the journey took several hours, and it was late afternoon by the time the dragon finally set down on land.

"Here we are," said the dragon, as they slid off his back. "You didn't specify where you wanted to go, so I just landed on the nearest promontory. The town of Sybesma is just over that ridge. If you start walking now, you should be able to reach it by nightfall. I'd get you closer, but I tend to make a bit of a scene when I land near towns, as you can imagine. If the locals hear how I rescued you from that island, they'll make a big deal out of it, probably insist on throwing a party in my honor, keep me up all night with toasts to my health and proclamations of gratitude, that sort of thing. We dragons tend to be a reclusive lot, and frankly I'm exhausted from the journey. I hate to be rude, but I'd prefer to just get back to my lair and get some sleep."

"Quite understandable," said Evena. "Please don't feel obligated to do any more on our account. We're already deeply indebted to you for saving our lives."

"Yes," mumbled Wyngalf begrudgingly. "We would certainly have died on that island if you hadn't rescued us." He was grateful, but he couldn't help feeling a bit foolish about his prejudices toward the dragon.

"No trouble at all," said Verne. "I'm happy to be of assistance. It was a pleasure doing business with you both. Well, I should be going. Good luck on the rest of your journeys."

"Thank you," said Evena.

Verne lifted his wings as if to fly away, but then paused, lowering them again. "Say," the dragon said. "I have one question, if you don't mind."

"What is it?" asked Wyngalf.

"I'm curious," said the dragon, "how you ended up on that island in the first place. No ships travel that far out from Dis."

"We didn't start out from Dis," said Wyngalf. "We left five days ago from a town called Skuldred on the far side of the sea. We ran into... unforeseen difficulties." This wasn't entirely true, of course. The only one who hadn't foreseen the difficulties was Wyngalf. But dwelling on that point wouldn't bring the crew back from the bottom of the sea. "We spent the past two days on that island."

Verne cocked his head at Wyngalf. "You're saying it's only a three day journey by ship from that island to the far shore of the Sea of Dis?"

"Most of the mainland is somewhat farther," replied Wyngalf, "but Skuldred is at the tip of a peninsula that juts two hundred miles or so into the sea." Wyngalf wasn't sure what interest Verne had in far-off cities, but after what the dragon had done for them, he thought it only polite to humor his questions.

"Wyngalf," said Evena quietly. "If I could talk to you for a moment..."

"Interesting," said the dragon, cutting her off. "I am fascinated by the cultures of foreign lands. I've visited nearly all the towns in this region, and I have to say, I've grown a bit bored. I think I've taken in all they have to offer."

"Skuldred isn't exactly what you'd call exotic," said Wyngalf, "though I suppose it has its charms. I only spent a brief time there myself, but Evena's family lives there."

"Interesting," said the dragon, glancing at Evena. "And would you say this Skuldred is a rich city? Culturally speaking, I mean."

Wyngalf shrugged. "It's a typical port town," he said. "A lot of fishermen and dock workers. Although of course there is a small class of merchants who do what they can to keep the arts alive. Evena's father is actually the town fishmonger. Very agreeable chap, if a bit preoccupied with financial concerns."

"Wyngalf!" Evena hissed. "I don't think you should—"

"Oh, quite," said the dragon. "Some people are far too concerned with amassing fortunes of gold, when there are so many more important things. Sadly, it often takes a tragedy for them to realize this."

Wyngalf nodded, surprised at the wisdom espoused by the dragon. Clearly he wasn't the monster Wyngalf had taken him to be. "Speaking of tragedies," he said, "if you do visit Skuldred, I'm sure Evena would greatly appreciate it if you could stop by her father's house and let her know Evena made it safely to Dis. She stowed away on the ship without his knowledge, and he must be worried sick about her."

Evena had taken to poking Wyngalf in the ribs in an effort to get his attention, but he continued to ignore her. Obviously she had been right about Verne; it wasn't necessary for her to keep rubbing it in. This is what came of not letting children know their place.

"I'll be certain to send my regards," said Verne. "It is strange, though, that I've never heard of this port, if it's so close. Do the people who live there not trade? Why do no ships from Skuldred ever visit the shores of Dis?"

"You know," said Wyngalf, "I wondered that myself. Turns out there's a gigantic sea monster in the middle of the Sea of Dis. I assumed it was just a superstition, but I can assure you it's quite real and frankly terrifying. That sort of thing tends to cut down on trade. But of course sea monsters are of no concern to you, as you could fly right over them."

"Indeed I could," said the dragon, thoughtfully.

"Yes," Wyngalf went on, "and of course you could probably fly from here to Skuldred in less than a day. Why, the island where you found us couldn't have been more than 200 miles from Skuldred. You were probably two thirds of the way there. A few more miles and you'd have seen the lighthouse, with your sharp eyes."

"Wyngalf!" Evena snapped.

Wyngalf glared at the girl. "My dear child," he said, adopting a manner of superiority, "you are being quite rude. You've made your point. I was wrong to doubt our friend Verne—" He turned to Verne. "—if I may call you that—" Verne nodded obligingly. "—merely because he is a dragon. He has been nothing but helpful, and it seems to me that satisfying his curiosity about our homeland would be the least we could do to repay him for his assistance."

Evena slapped herself on her forehead and stomped away.

"I apologize for my companion," said Wyngalf. "I can't imagine what has gotten into her."

"No need," replied the dragon. "She's been through quite an ordeal. Obviously suffering from hunger and exhaustion. Speaking of which, I should let you go. Just one last thing: you said there was a lighthouse…?"

"Oh, yes," said Wyngalf. "You can't miss it. Just fly directly west of that island and you'll see it. It'll lead you right to Skuldred."

"Much obliged," said Verne. "Again, good luck on your own journeys. Perhaps we will meet again someday."

"I look forward to it," said Wyngalf. "Thank you once again for your help."

"Don't mention it," said the dragon. "You've been a great help to me as well." The dragon spread its great wings and leapt into the sky, leaving Wyngalf to puzzle over this last remark. At last he shrugged and went after Evena, who stood sulking just down the road.

"What was that all about?" Wyngalf demanded. "Verne saved our lives, and you can't humor him with a few moments of conversation?"

Evena turned to glare at him. "Has it occurred to you to wonder why Verne was so interested in the lands across the sea?"

"He said it himself," Wyngalf replied, puzzled at Evena's tone. "He's bored. He's seen everything there is to see in Dis, and he's interested in learning about new lands and different cultures."

Evena stared at him as if he were some peculiar specimen of beetle. "How have you survived this long?" she asked. "I didn't know it was possible for anyone to be this naïve."

"What are you talking about?" asked Wyngalf, irritated anew at Evena's impertinent tone.

"Back on the island, you were going on about how dragons are irredeemable, vile monsters, and now suddenly Verne is your best friend? It never occurred to you that he was *using* us?"

"Using us for what?" Wyngalf asked, puzzled. "We have nothing to offer him."

"Except the location of the town where *my family lives!*" Evena shouted. "He had no idea there *were* any cities across the sea. We could have told him we were from anywhere. You basically drew him a map to my parents' house!"

"I think you're overreacting," said Wyngalf. "We have no reason to suspect Verne's motives were anything but benign."

"He's a *dragon!*" cried Evena. "You don't think there's any reason to question the motives of a *dragon?*"

"I'm a bit puzzled by your sudden change of heart," said Wyngalf. "Where was this skepticism about dragons back on the island?"

"We were in danger of starving to death!" Evena exclaimed. "It's not that I trusted Verne. I just couldn't imagine how taking Verne up on his offer could make our situation worse. But I have to hand it to you, you seem to have found a way."

"Let me get this straight," said Wyngalf. "You think Verne flew 300 miles out of his way, rescued us and flew us all the way to Dis just to get us to tell him about Skuldred? So he could, what, go there and burn it down?"

"I don't know!" cried Evena. "But you have to admit it's a possibility. Ships never come here from across the ocean because of the Hafgufa. So Verne just assumed that any cities across the city were too far away for him to fly to. But as you so helpfully pointed out, there's no reason at all he couldn't fly to Skuldred in a day. All he's got to do is look for the lighthouse!"

"Alright, alright," said Wyngalf. "I understand your apprehension. But I think your concern for your family's wellbeing is clouding your judgment. Yes, Verne is a dragon, and dragons do have a certain reputation for laying waste to cities, but nothing in Verne's behavior indicates he has any interest in such base activities. Also, it's a long way across the sea, even for a dragon. He would have to be a particularly cruel and avaricious—not to mention devious and deceitful—dragon to fly all the way to the Jagged Coast in search of new cities to pillage. After all, aren't there enough cities here in Dis to satisfy a dragon?"

Evena begrudgingly admitted that Wyngalf had a point.

"In any case," Wyngalf said, "there's nothing we can do about it now, and we need to get some food and find a place to sleep. Verne himself said there was a town called Sybesma just over the hill. If that turns out to be the case, and the townspeople haven't been harassed recently by a dragon, can we agree that your concerns are misplaced?"

Evena nodded tiredly. They were both exhausted. The sun was nearing the horizon, and a chill had crept into the air. Without another word, they began walking up the hill toward in the direction Verne had indicated. After some time, Evena stopped, a curious expression on her face. "I smell smoke," she said.

Wyngalf nodded. "Supper time," he said. "If we pick up the pace, we may get there in time to beg for a bowl of stew." But as he said it, he realized something was wrong. It wasn't the aroma of cooking fires that he smelled, but rather the stale scent of smoldering charcoal. He pushed down the uneasy feeling in his gut and forced himself to smile. "Come on," he said to Evena. We don't want to miss supper."

She nodded uncertainly and followed him. Wyngalf came to the crest of the hill, and Evena stopped beside him. They looked down into the valley to see where they would be spending the night. Evena gasped.

The town of Sybesma was nothing but rubble and piles of smoking ash.

Seven

In the dying light Wyngalf could just make out a small cloaked figure moving about the rubble. Without thinking, he ran down the hill to the ruins of the town, leaving Evena to gape in horror at the scene. As he descended the hill, he lost sight of the figure for a minute, but since there were few remnants of any structures over shoulder height still standing, it was not difficult to locate him again. The man was sifting through the ruins, seemingly oblivious to Wyngalf's approach. For a moment, Wyngalf stood in the gloom studying him. There was something off about the man, but, viewing him only in silhouette, Wyngalf couldn't pinpoint it. He was short and hunched over, with a large head and weirdly overdeveloped forearms. Eventually it came to him: the creature wasn't a man at all, but a goblin—one of the race of vile humanoids that were known to plague less civilized lands like Dis. The Jagged Coast had long ago exterminated goblins, as well as ogres and many other species of misbegotten humanoids, but Wyngalf had seen many illustrations from the Dark Ages in the library of the Noninitarian Stronghold, and recognized the form—although this creature was certainly smaller than he'd been led to expect.

The goblin was sifting through a pile of what appeared to be cookware, and seemed to have no idea Wyngalf was there. It occurred to Wyngalf to simply step quietly away and leave it to its pillaging, but he and Evena would have to spend the night somewhere, and their best chance to find some kind of shelter lay in this ruined town. That meant dealing with the goblin. Wyngalf had noticed a glint of metal among the ashes between him and the goblin, and he realized now that the object was a sword.

Wyngalf took a deep breath and lunged forward, grabbing the sword by its hilt. He assumed his best swordsman's crouch (lacking other entertainment options, he had spent many hours sparring with the other Noninitarian devout, albeit with wooden dowels rather than sword), pointing the tip at the goblin.

"Explain yourself, goblin!" Wyngalf shouted, doing his best to sound intimidating. "What have you done to this town?" The obvious cause of the village's destruction hadn't eluded Wyngalf, but his mind had seized on the presence of the goblin as an alternative to admitting that Evena had been right about Verne. Again.

The goblin stood up straight, peering at Wyngalf in the gloom. After a moment, it shuffled closer to him and bowed deeply. Wyngalf saw that it held a large bag that was presumably filled with spoils it had collected from the ruins. Straightening up again, the goblin began, "I beg your indulgence, kind sir. Your suspicions regarding me are indeed well-founded, as I am a member of an accursed race of subhumanoids whose penchant for pillaging is well-known. However, in this particular instance I must regrettably inform you that the conclusion you've reached regarding my culpability in the devastation of this village is erroneous. It was, I'm afraid, quite ruined when I got here."

Somewhat taken aback by the goblin's articulate response, Wyngalf nevertheless pressed on. "Tell the truth, vermin!" he cried, waving the sword at the goblin. "You and your clan razed this town and murdered its inhabitants to sate your rapacious bloodthirst!" Wyngalf knew as well that goblins were cowardly creatures, attacking only when their numbers were sufficient to guarantee a massacre.

The goblin sighed. "Alas," it said. "Would that it were true, but my clan has but one member, and he is I. These days my clan, such as it is, occupies itself mainly with efforts to stave off hunger. Our rapacious bloodthirst goes largely unsated."

"Lies!" cried Wyngalf. "Admit that you destroyed this town!"

The goblin shook his head apologetically. "I'm afraid these lands are terrorized by a great green dragon who goes by the name

Verne," said the goblin. "I arrived here some time after catastrophe befell it, but I can only surmise that the devastation you see before you is the work of that very same saurian. He is well known for laying waste to towns that fail to comply with his demands."

The point of Wyngalf's sword wavered.

"Why are you tormenting this poor goblin?" asked Evena, coming up alongside him. "Can't you see he's hungry and frightened?"

The goblin bowed toward Evena. "I thank you for your concern, Miss," he said, "but you needn't worry. Your companion and I were merely engaging in a spirited discussion about the cause of the ruination we find around us. The insightful young gentleman had advanced an intriguing hypothesis which—and I apologize sincerely if I'm mischaracterizing your position, kind sir—posits that I single-handedly undertook the razing of this town and the mass murder of its inhabitants. I reposted with a counterpoint, relying on information to which the perceptive gentleman, whom I take to be a visitor to this land, is undoubtedly not privy: that this region has long been subjected to the scourge of a particularly avaricious and cruel dragon. Building on this premise and certain telltale signs—such as scorched stone, fused metal and the sizeable claw marks you see on the ground before you—I humbly advanced a theory, to wit, that it is that very dragon who is responsible for the devastation of this town. It should go without saying, of course, that I do not claim any sort of epistemic certainty on the matter, and welcome robust discussion of alternative possibilities."

"I knew it!" cried Evena. "Verne destroyed this town, and now he's on his way across the sea to murder my parents!"

"Ah, so you've met Verne," said the goblin.

Wyngalf swallowed hard.

"Yes," said Evena, glaring at him. "Wyngalf just told him how to find my home town."

"Ah," said the goblin, frowning. "That would seem... inadvisable."

"Okay, look," said Wyngalf, letting the sword drop to his side. "I get it. I shouldn't have told Verne where we're from. And now that you've pointed out the signs, I'll admit that it does appear that a dragon was *involved* in the destruction of this town. But I don't think there's any reason to assume the worst. Skuldred is a long distance from here, and however wicked Verne might be, he's not going to fly across the sea just to visit random violence and destruction on unsuspecting townspeople."

"Oh, there's nothing random about it," replied the goblin. "That is," he continued uncertainly, "I've been following the exploits of this dragon for some time now, and in fact even came face to face with him once. I thought my doom was assured, but Verne evidently considered me to be beneath his concern. My observations since then have led me to conclude that he is engaged in a very carefully thought-out strategy. If you wouldn't mind indulging me, I'd be only too happy to outline my thoughts on the matter."

Wyngalf wasn't particularly interested in hearing the opinions of a goblin, but Evena shut him down with a glare. "Please do," she said to the goblin.

The goblin bowed slightly to Evena again. "Like all dragons," he said, "Verne's primary aim is to amass as much gold and other treasure as possible, and he accomplishes this by demanding tribute from all the towns within several hundred miles of his lair, which lies in the mountains to the northeast. Ordinarily the townspeople comply without question, but occasionally it is necessary for him to make an example of a town whose residents have failed to meet his demands. Hence the devastation you see before you. Verne is not entirely without mercy, however: he seems to have given the denizens some warning of his intentions."

"Why do you say that?" asked Evena.

The goblin cocked his head at them curiously, as if he suspected Evena was teasing him. After a moment he explained, "Surely you noticed the complete dearth of corpses, indicating that the townspeople fled in advance of the dragon's assault."

Wyngalf surveyed the rubble in the gathering dark, noticing that the goblin was right: despite the near-total devastation of the town, he hadn't seen a single corpse. "You see?" Wyngalf said, turning to face Evena. "Verne is a reasonable dragon. Perhaps a bit overly acquisitive, but rational in his application of violence. Worst case scenario, he may shake down the citizens of Skuldred for a few gold pieces."

Evena, staring at the smoking ruins around her, seemed unconvinced. "Does Verne own this town?" she asked the goblin.

"*Own* it?" the goblin said, confused.

"He seemed quite concerned with following the appropriate formalities regarding the acquisition of our island," Wyngalf explained.

"You have an island?" the goblin asked.

"We did," said Evena. "For about five minutes. We traded it for passage to Dis."

"Ah," said the goblin, with a nod. "Yes, that's the saurian modus operandi. A dragon will set up a complex system of rules and then attempt to impress you with how well he is following them. Of course, the rules are completely arbitrary and fashioned with the sole purpose of making certain the dragon gets what he wants. If you ever happen to catch a dragon violating his own rules, he'll claim some obscure loophole, and if you back him into a corner, he'll just modify the rules to accommodate his behavior. In your case, that wasn't necessary. He simply traded an island he didn't want for a trip he was going to make anyway, in order to distract you from what he actually wanted, which was information about your homeland."

"You're not making any sense," said Wyngalf. "You're saying that this incredibly clever dragon somehow never figured out there are entire cities just across the sea, ripe for extortion?"

"It does seem paradoxical," the goblin admitted with a nod. "But that is the nature of dragons. Simultaneously very clever about certain subjects and very dimwitted on others. They are particularly gullible when it comes to gold and other forms of treasure. It may be helpful to think of them as analogous to young human males, whose reasoning is easily compromised by the presence of an attractive female of the species."

"That may well be," said Wyngalf, anxious to change the subject, "but Verne's behavior hardly excuses looting and pillaging. The residents of this town have lost enough without goblins rooting through their few extant belongings looking for baubles and trinkets." His eyes fell to the bag, which the goblin had set down next to him.

"It is fortunate, then," said the goblin, indicating the sack, "that I have collected only a variety of vegetables, dried meats, and other foodstuffs."

Saliva shot into Wyngalf's mouth at the mention of food. It had been so long since he'd eaten that he'd almost managed to put the concept of food out of his mind, but now it suddenly slammed into his consciousness with such force that it made him dizzy. It was only light-headedness that prevented him from rushing at the goblin with his sword and taking the sack. The goblin regarded him with a curious expression. If Wyngalf didn't know that goblins were vile, selfish creatures that thought only of satisfying their own base urges, he might have thought he saw pity on the monster's face.

"I hesitate to make this offer," said the goblin, "as I understand from your comments that you have a strong ethical compunction against theft, even in cases of dire need and where the ostensible victims have no use for the items being appropriated, but if you can overcome your qualms, I'd be more than happy to share a portion of what I've—"

"We'll take it!" cried Evena, clearly as frantic as Wyngalf was at the idea of eating.

"Please," Wyngalf croaked. "That is, I think we can set aside our ethical concerns for the moment, given the circumstances." Wyngalf seemed to be setting his scruples aside a lot frequently.

The goblin nodded and picked up the sack. "Follow me, if you would be so kind," it said. It turned and trudged away. Wyngalf and Evena followed unquestioningly. Soon they found themselves surrounded by the remains of a small stone cottage. The rubble seemed to have been cleared away from the center of the dirt floor, and a small campfire was burning there.

"I hope you can forgive the crude accommodations," said the goblin. "I only arrived here myself a few hours ago, and it's the best I was able to arrange under the circumstances. Please, have a seat."

The three of them sat around the fire and the goblin handed the sack to Evena while it tended to the fire. True to the goblin's word, the sack contained a variety of mostly nonperishable foods that it had apparently scrounged from the rubble of the town. A large jug of water sat nearby. Wyngalf helped himself to the water and then tore at some dried beef while Evena chomped into a bruised but juicy apple. Wyngalf had set the sword down in the dirt next to him, having come to the conclusion that the goblin was largely harmless—and that in any case, he and Evena were in more danger from hunger than attack by the diminutive creature.

"Not that you asked," said the goblin, while they ate, "but my name is Tobalt."

Wyngalf was momentarily embarrassed of his slight; it hadn't occurred to him that goblins *had* names. "I'm Simply Wyngalf," he said around a mouthful of jerky. "This is Evena."

Tobalt stood and bowed, then sat again, waiting patiently for the sack of food to be handed back to him. "If it isn't presumptuous to ask, what brings you to Dis?"

Wyngalf wavered between an overly literal response ("a dragon") and a more thorough answer. Either one was likely to prompt questions from Tobalt that Wyngalf was in no mood to answer. He could tell a harmless lie, but that would require Evena's cooperation, and he doubted she'd be amenable to playing along at this point. He figured his best bet was just to tell an abbreviated version of the truth and hope that the goblin's tiny, cretinous brain wouldn't prompt it to ask questions the answers to which it had no hope of understanding. "I'm on a divine mission to bring the one true faith of Noninitarianism to the Land of Dis," he said.

"Ah, Noninitarianism!" cried the goblin, nodding excitedly.

Wyngalf peered at Tobalt curiously. "You've heard of it?"

"Oh, no," said the goblin. "But unless I'm mistaken, the etymology indicates that it's a belief in a single God manifesting him- or herself in Nine Distinct Persons."

Evena, sitting between them and chomping away at her apple, was glancing back and forth between Wyngalf and Tobalt, an amused expression on her face.

"Yes," said Wyngalf uncertainly. "That's... correct."

"I assume you're familiar," said Tobalt, "with the Quadrinitarian beliefs of the Cult of Varnoth?"

"I'm... aware," said Wyngalf. He'd studied a wide variety of religions as part of his education at the Stronghold, although much of this education consisted of learning the ways in which the various religions of the world fell short of the sublime truth of

Noninitarianism. "I didn't realize the Cult of Varnoth had made many inroads into Dis," he said.

"It hasn't," said Tobalt, with an apologetic shrug. "The only religion with a large following in this region is Ovaltarianism. But I'm a bit of an aficionado of obscure sects. I find the syncretism between the monotheistic religions and the polytheistic schemas they've supplanted particularly interesting. For example, the idea of a single god, Varnoth, existing in four distinct persons seems to be a concession to the entrenched belief in the four pagan deities that predominated in the region."

"Well," said Wyngalf. "I don't know about that." He wasn't sure he liked where this conversation was going. This goblin, although he was clearly unable to comprehend the finer nuances of theological matters, seemed to have memorized passages from some heathen study of religions, and his careless comments were in danger of corrupting young Evena. Wyngalf had thus far made only halting attempts at explaining the Fourteen Points to her, and she simply wasn't prepared for this onslaught of nihilistic paganism. It puzzled him that a goblin would possess such an unnatural interest in religious matters. It was well-known, even to those who hadn't accepted the One True Faith, that goblins were devoid of souls and therefore incapable of appreciating matters of eternal significance. As for Ovaltarianism, which the goblin claimed was the predominant faith in the area, Wyngalf had never heard of it, and he suspected the goblin was misremembering the name of some other sect. Why was it that the only people who showed an interest in matters of faith were monsters and children, who could not possibly benefit from the sublime truths of Noninitarianism?

"Ah, I've offended you," said Tobalt, with what seemed to be genuine remorse. "'Tis my lot, I'm afraid. It was my penchant for engaging in abstruse discussions on topics of philosophical interest that precipitated my ostracization from my clan. For as you so helpfully pointed out, Simply Wyngalf, my kind tends more toward bellicose and rapacious pursuits, and has little tolerance for abstract intellectual concerns. As I am regrettably ill-suited to tasks of a belligerent nature, as well as given to embarking on ill-timed musings on abstract and recondite matters, I was largely a burden on my clan. They tolerated me as best they could, but ultimately there was no denying that I was a liability, and it was agreed that it would be best for everyone involved if I were allowed to pursue my intellectual interests free of the constraints of a primitive and violent tribal society."

"They shunned you," said Evena, a note of pity in her voice.

"It was a mutual decision," said Tobalt, staring into the fire. "One night, nearly three weeks ago, I was assigned to guard duty at the entrance to the cave several miles south of here in which my clan makes its home. I was frequently selected for this task, as it generally involves little more than staying awake and banging a drum if one witnesses anything suspicious, and it was deemed by the clan leadership—after witnessing my unremarkable but effective drum banging technique—that I was capable of such activities. As it happened, on this particular night I happened upon a particularly vexing philosophical problem, which I have somewhat immodestly taken to referring to as Tobalt's Paradox." The goblin paused. "Before continuing, might I ask your level of familiarity with naïve set theory?"

Wyngalf and Evena stared at the goblin, unsure how to respond.

"I can see I need to back up a bit," said Tobalt. "I beg your indulgence while I provide some background. You see, according to naïve set theory, any definable collection is a set. Now let's suppose that T is the set of all sets that are not members of themselves. It follows that if T is not a member of itself, then its definition dictates that it must contain itself. But it occurred to me that evening that if it contains itself, then it contradicts its own definition as the set of all sets that are not members of themselves. You see the problem."

"You were preoccupied," said Wyngalf.

"No!" cried Tobalt, shaking his head vigorously. "Well, yes. But what I meant is that the definition of T is self-contradictory. I mean, so much for the idea of a logically consistent theory of definable collections!" He looked expectantly at them.

"Perhaps," Evena ventured, "it isn't necessary for us to understand the exact nature of the conundrum to see its relevance to your situation."

Tobalt thought for a moment, nodding slowly. "Yes," he said at last, clearly disappointed in their lack of interest in the finer points of the discussion. "Of course. I suppose the key point here is that while I was preoccupied with this paradox, a party of adventurers slipped past me into the cave entrance and slaughtered sixteen members of my clan. It would have been far worse, but the party took a wrong turn and happened upon a pack of giant rats which they were unprepared to face, and were forced to flee. I was unaware that anything was amiss until I was knocked over by a hefty gentleman in heavy plate armor fleeing the cave. It was decided in the wake of the massacre that perhaps I should pursue my philosophical interests elsewhere. Since then, I have survived principally by scavenging in the wake of Verne's attacks. Needless to say, I am often hungry and cold, not to mention deeply troubled by the intrinsic incoherence of naïve set theory." The goblin continued to stare glumly into the fire.

"Well," said Evena, "we are quite grateful for your company. Were it not for your resourcefulness and generosity, we certainly would have starved." She elbowed Wyngalf in the ribs.

"Ah," said Wyngalf, who was lost in reverie as he ruminated on a very dry hunk of bread. "Yes. We're quite beholden to you." With some effort, he managed to smile at the goblin. As pleased as he was to have some food in his stomach, Wyngalf was getting a little tired of being forced to depend on the whims of random monsters for his survival. He understood that the Noninity worked through the actions of all creatures to bring about its divine will, but ever since he arrived in Skuldred, Wyngalf had felt like he was being tossed about by capricious forces he could neither influence nor comprehend. What was the point of being on a divine mission if none of the actions he undertook of his own volition ever amounted to anything? Faith was admirable of course, but at some point, he needed to seize control of his own destiny.

"We're happy to pay you," Evena said, "I lost most of what I was carrying, but I've got a pouch with some coins in it sewed inside my trousers."

"I thank you for your kind offer," said Tobalt, "but it is unnecessary. I consider your indulgence of my feeble attempts at philosophical discourse to be more than adequate compensation for these meagre foodstuffs."

Tobalt was so pathetically earnest that Wyngalf found it difficult to sustain whatever animosity he had toward the goblin by virtue of his membership in a vile and accursed race. Tobalt would never be able to rid himself of his essentially base nature, of course, and his pseudo-metaphysical jabbering amounted to nothing more than an amusing quirk, but he seemed to be harmless. Wyngalf was so certain of this that when he found himself nodding off in front of the fire, he didn't fight it. His faith had gotten him this far, and if the Noninity had fated him to be slain in his sleep by a runt of a goblin with philosophical pretensions, he wouldn't resist. His last thought, before falling asleep, was to hope that the goblin could manage to cut his throat quickly.

Eight

Wyngalf awoke stiff and groggy, but alive—and pleased to find that he had evidently been right about Tobalt's harmlessness. Sunlight streamed through the nonexistent ceiling of the cottage, alighting on Evena's fair hair as she slept, curled up next to the remnants of the fire. The sword lay on the ground where Wyngalf had left it, and Tobalt was nowhere to be found. Wyngalf suspected—correctly as it turned out, for Tobalt reappeared with his sack full not long after—that the goblin had gotten up early to get a head start on his scavenging. Tobalt had found an old coat that would fit Wyngalf and a cape that Evena could wrap around her shoulders. As the fire had died and the morning air was cold, they accepted these with almost as much enthusiasm as they had shown for the food the night before. When they were a bit more comfortable, Tobalt revealed the other contents of his sack: moldy bread, salted pork and some very dry prunes.

After breaking fast and exchanging a few morning pleasantries, the conversation turned to what they were going to do next. Having successfully made landfall in Dis and sated his hunger, Wyngalf was feeling much more optimistic about his prospects. It was clear to him now that he had failed to save any souls along the Jagged Coast not because of any deficiency in his method, but because his destiny lay in the virgin territory of the land of Dis. He had no doubt that in Dis he would find thousands of people ripe for the good news of Noninitarianism, rather than the jaded merchants and dimwitted laborers he had encountered so far. He'd begin making converts as soon as he reached a good-sized city, and within a few weeks the congregation would begin construction on the first Noninitarian church in Dis. The troubles he had encountered so far were minor obstacles on his path toward canonization as the greatest missionary Noninitarianism had ever known.

Evena, meanwhile, insisted that they make for the nearest seaport, where she could charter a ship to take her back to Skuldred so that she could make sure her town was still standing. Wyngalf pointed out that even if she could convince a ship's captain that her father would pay the cost of the voyage upon her arrival in Skuldred, it was still very unlikely that any captain would agree to undertake such an expedition. Undoubtedly the legend of the Hafgufa was widespread on this side of the Sea of Dis as well; it was only the unusual circumstances of Wyngalf's arrival, the insanity of Captain Savikkar and the intervention of Verne the dragon that made their eastward journey possible. No amount of money would convince a sane man to undertake the return voyage. Wyngalf had heard of ships crossing the sea from ports to the north of Svalbraakrat, so perhaps by traveling many miles out of her way she could avoid the Hafgufa, but she was unequipped for a long journey overland. And even if she made it to one of the northern ports, she would still have to convince a captain to take her across the sea and then south along the coast to return her to Skuldred in order for him to receive payment from her father. Another option would be traveling overland to the south, but that would take her through hundreds of miles of desolate wastelands, much of it populated by trolls and other dangerous monsters.

Tobalt eventually broke the impasse. He recommended—in his halting, ingratiating way—that they head north toward Skaal City, which was a large, bustling port, and a hub of the Dissian Shipping Guild. According to Tobalt, the Shipping Guild boasted members all along the coast of Dis, and he suggested that Evena might be able to negotiate with them to arrange for her to take a series of voyages that would ultimately bring her back home. Wyngalf wondered how it was possible for a shipping guild to exist in a place where captains were afraid to cross the sea, but evidently a healthy amount of trade was conducted up and down the coast of Dis. Members of the Shipping Guild often entered into cooperative arrangements to ship goods long distances, with the Guild acting as a sort of bank and impartial arbiter. Tobalt suggested that Evena's father would, upon her safe return, pay the captain of the ship that brought her home. The captain would keep his share and hand over the rest to a branch of the Shipping Guild at his earliest opportunity. The Shipping Guild would then make sure the other ship owners were paid for their part in transporting her.

As Tobalt explained the complex system by which the Shipping Guild ensured payment to its members, making it possible for ship owners to profit from being a link in a long chain of transactions without having to worry about where their cargo was coming from or where it was going, he began to suspect that the goblin was spinning a yarn to deceive them. At first Wyngalf thought Tobalt was saying that all the ship captains worked for the Guild, which dictated where they would go and when, but the goblin insisted that was not the case. The ship captains were free to go wherever they wanted and to accept or refuse cargo as they saw fit; all the Guild did was give them options and information. If, for example, a shipment of Peraltian wool was due at Brobdingdon on a certain date, and it needed to be transported to Skaal City by a certain date, the Guild clerk in Brobdingdon would issue a bulletin which got handed out to any captains passing through the port. A small bounty was offered to the captain who first delivered this bulletin to any participating Guild port, so information about pending shipments tended to spread quickly along the coast. Captains who were Guild members (which was essentially all of them, as far as Wyngalf could tell) would review the bulletins posted at the Guild office whenever they came into port, and if a certain captain was going to be unloading cargo at Brobdingdon around the time that the Peraltian wool was due to arrive, he might inform the local Guild clerk of his willingness to pick up the wool at Brobdingdon and deliver it to Skaal City. That information would then be passed along to the clerk in Brobdingdon, who would accept the offer and issue an updated bulletin indicating that the wool shipment was no longer available. The whole thing was such a chaotic mess that Wyngalf was certain the goblin had misunderstood it.

"And how do you happen to know so much about how goods are shipped along the coast of Dis?" he asked.

"It's one of my interests," said Tobalt sheepishly, slightly embarrassed of his lengthy discourse on the matter. This was a habit of Tobalt's that Wyngalf hadn't yet decided was endearing or irritating: he would expound at length on the most obscure details of some issue and then apologize, as if ashamed of his encyclopedic knowledge. As with his discourses on religion, of course, it was unclear whether Tobalt was evincing actual knowledge or simply parroting notions he'd come across at some point without any real understanding. Wyngalf tended to think it was the latter. And yet, it wasn't in his interest to argue with the goblin: if Skaal City really was the bustling port that Tobalt made it out to be, then it was most likely his best prospect in the area for making converts and founding a church. If he could get Evena to agree to accompany him there, it would allow him to look after her for a bit longer and perhaps talk her out of trying to return to Skuldred until they had a better understanding of their options. After all, what could she hope to accomplish by returning home now? Even if she got on a ship tomorrow, it would be weeks before she got to Skuldred—and if Verne really wanted to destroy the town, she wouldn't be able to stop him. Her parents would be worried sick about her, of course, but she had known that when she decided to stow away on this adventure.

Evena reluctantly agreed that traveling to Skaal City sounded like their best bet, and Tobalt offered his own services as a guide and scavenger for the journey. "Perhaps too," he added, "I might offer some measure of protection against others of my kind. Goblins, as you no doubt are aware, have a penchant for waylaying innocent travelers, and my presence among your party might give them pause regarding the pursuit of such endeavors in your case."

Wyngalf didn't particularly like the idea of traveling with a goblin, as he suspected it would reflect poorly on his cause to potential converts, but he couldn't deny the sense of Tobalt's words. According to Tobalt, Skaal city was two day's journey if they took the meandering road along the coast, but he claimed to know a shortcut through the hills to the northeast. Assuming Tobalt was telling the truth, it would save them another night sleeping in the cold, and that alone was worth enduring his company. In any case, Tobalt was unlikely to be permitted to travel inside the confines of a human city, so it would be easy enough to ditch him once they got to their destination.

They spent the morning trudging north along the poorly maintained road that ran along the rocky coast. They met no other travelers; Tobalt explained that there were several towns along the road further to the south, but a few of these had suffered the same fate as Sybesma, and the most of the residents of the remaining towns had fled to Skaal City, which was deemed to be safe from the dragon's attacks. Whether this was because the city militia was somehow capable of repelling Verne's aggression or because the city's rulers met the dragon's demands was unclear. Fortunately, they were spared the sight of any more ruined towns; just after noon, they stopped for lunch, finishing off the contents of Tobalt's sack, and then turned east toward a low ridge, beyond which Tobalt promised there lay a long valley that snaked through the hills for several miles. Eventually, he said, they would come out onto a flat plain just south of Skaal City.

As Tobalt promised, after they scaled the ridge, they found themselves looking down on a valley that snaked through the hills. It wended vaguely northeast, the direction in which Tobalt claimed Skaal City lay. They made their way down to the valley floor and followed it through the hills. As the valley took a turn to the east, a suspicion crept into Wyngalf's mind that this was all some sort of elaborate plan to lure them to a goblin lair. It was hard to imagine how waylaying two destitute travelers could be worth all this trouble, though, and ultimately they had little choice but to trust Tobalt; without him they'd likely starve or be killed by bandits or goblins anyway.

Wyngalf was still reflecting on this when the afternoon sun, which had been beating down hard on their backs, was suddenly blotted out. Evena and Tobalt instinctively turned to see what could have plunged them into shadow so quickly, but Wyngalf simply stopped in his tracks and sighed. He had a feeling he knew precisely what that shadow portended. For a moment he was able to maintain the belief that it had simply been a fast-moving and very dark cloud, but that illusion was spoiled almost immediately by a familiar gusting wind.

"Run!" cried Tobalt, and Wyngalf was vaguely aware of Evena and the goblin rushing past him to take shelter among some nearby boulders. The idea of trying to hide from a dragon in this sparse landscape struck him as so absurd it was almost humorous. If Verne wanted to kill them, hiding behind rocks wasn't going to help. For that matter, if he had wanted to kill them, they'd never have made it off the island. Reluctantly Wyngalf turned to face the dragon.

"Hello again!" Verne exclaimed, alighting on the ground just in front of Wyngalf. In his clutches was a great wooden chest. "I thought that was you, Simply Wyngalf."

"Hello, Verne," said Wyngalf, without emotion.

"Is that any way to greet an old friend?" said the dragon, a tone of exaggerated offense in his voice. "What happened to your gratitude for saving you from that island? And why are your friends hiding in the rocks over there? A little rude, don't you think?"

"I believe we've repaid you for that bit of kindness," said Wyngalf, eyeing the chest. Despite his hopes to the contrary, he was afraid he knew where the chest had come from.

The dragon grinned at him, revealing rows of knife-like teeth. "Fair enough," he said. "Admittedly, it is due to your thoughtful assistance that I was able to locate the town of Skuldred and apply the appropriate pressure to extract a considerable amount of gold from its citizenry—more than enough to make the trip across the sea worthwhile. Ordinarily it's such a bother to convince the townspeople to ante up. You'd think it would be a simple matter: show up, raze a few buildings, demand ten thousand gold pieces, and wait for people to shower you with gold. But the logistics are surprisingly challenging. Most of the time the townspeople just run around in a panic, and it's difficult to get them to calm down to the point where I can even explain to them what I'm after."

"Perhaps," said Wyngalf through gritted teeth, "if you didn't start off by razing buildings."

"I've tried that approach as well," said Verne with a thoughtful nod. "But then they don't take you seriously. Sometimes I get shot at with arrows, which is irritating. So these days I usually start off by torching a few barns on the periphery of the town. That lets them know I mean business. Of course, occasionally the fire gets out of control and burns down the rest of the town, which is counterproductive. If people get the idea that I'm just arbitrarily razing towns, they're less likely to meet my demands. It's a delicate balance."

"I can imagine," said Wyngalf humorlessly.

"Fortunately, everything seems to be working out with Skuldred. I arrived yesterday evening and incinerated a few storehouses on the edge of town. Perfect timing; the whole town could see the fire. Then I landed in the town square and asked to speak to Bulgar the fish merchant. I may have implied that I'd abducted Bulgar's daughter, Evena; it seemed a harmless lie under the circumstances. The fire was still burning when Bulgar appeared, begging for me to return his daughter. An hour later, I was on my way back here with a chest full of gold. Easy-peasy."

Out of the corner of his eye, Wyngalf caught Evena peeking around the boulder.

Wyngalf's hand fell to the sword at his side. He'd found a matching scabbard in the ruins and had attached it to his belt. "And now you've come to collect her?"

Verne laughed. "Oh, goodness no. This is just the down payment." He patted the chest with his right claw. "I don't plan on returning her for some time. Frankly, I might never bring her back, depending on how things go. But I did want to stop by and make sure she's still alive, just in case. And to thank you for your help, of course." He craned his head to peer at Evena, crouched beside the boulder. "Hello, dear," he said with a smile. "I see you've made a new friend." His gaze fell to Tobalt the goblin was cowering behind Evena. "Take good care of her, goblin," he said. "I may need her back one of these days."

Tobalt nodded dumbly, shaking with fear.

Evena stood, her fists clenched at her sides, staring at the dragon. "What have you done to my home?" she demanded.

"As I was telling my friend Simply Wyngalf," Verne said, "I've harmed no one in your fair town. So far, anyway. I'll return once a month, and as long as they provide me with the gold I ask for, the town will remain unharmed."

"I demand that you take me back there," said Evena, standing to face the dragon. "Immediately!"

Verne laughed, a deep, rumbling laugh like furnace bellows stoking a coal fire. "Oh, you *demand* it?" he said. "I'm afraid, my dear, you're in no position to *demand* anything. You know, you were much politer when you thought you were going to die on that island."

Evena bit her lip. "Please, Verne," she said. "Take me back to Skuldred."

The dragon paused, seeming to give the matter some thought. "No," he said at last. "I don't think I'll be doing that just yet. It's better to let your parents worry for a while. If it becomes necessary to make a show of goodwill, I'll be back for you."

"How will you find me?" asked Evena.

Verne chuckled. "Don't worry about that," he said. "You couldn't hide from me if you tried." He pulled his long neck back and faced Wyngalf once again. "Anyway, I should get this gold back to the lair. Just wanted to stop by and make sure you're all okay. Wouldn't do to rescue you and then have you fall victim to the local monsters. But you're almost to Skaal City now, so I'm sure you'll be fine."

"Assuming you've left Skaal City in better shape than Sybesma," said Wyngalf.

"Ah yes," said Verne, with a sheepish smile. "Sorry about that. I'd actually forgotten I'd razed that town. They got behind on payments, and I had to make an example of them. Understand that's a relatively rare occurrence; generally the townspeople in this region are pretty good about meeting their commitments. I've never had a problem with Skaal City, for example. The mayor is a fine man, very responsible. Collects taxes from his citizens and passes on the bulk of what he collects to me. He skims off the top, of course, but I look the other way as long as my demands are met. And I help him out on occasion as well. It's what you might call a mutually beneficial arrangement. Well, I won't keep you from your important mission any longer." He spread his wings, wrapped his claws around the chest, and launched himself into the sky. "Goodbye for now!" he cried.

Wyngalf watched Verne recede in the eastern sky. The dragon was just disappearing behind the hills when suddenly Wyngalf was thrown to the ground. The back of his head struck the ground, and for a moment he was dazed. Eventually he became aware of a dull thudding against his chest. Evena had tackled him and was now straddling his midsection and pummeling him with her tiny fists. She didn't have the strength to do any real damage, and Wyngalf almost burst out laughing at the feebleness of her attack—and then he saw that tears were streaming down her cheeks.

"It's your fault!" she cried. "Verne is going to kill my parents, and it's your fault!"

Wyngalf resisted the urge to seize her wrists, figuring it was better to allow her to take out her anger on him. The cumulative effect of her bony fists striking his rib cage was only a mild discomfort, and already her blows were becoming softer and less frequent. "I'm sorry," he tried to say, but it came out as a series of syllables broken by the percussion of her fists: "I-I-I-I'm So-o-orr-ee-ee-ee-ee."

"Sorry isn't good enough!" Evena screamed. "Don't you realize what you've done? It's not just Skuldred. A dragon's greed knows no limits. He'll move on to Truiska, then Purivel and all the other towns along the coast. Eventually he'll probably even reach your beloved Svalbraakrat!"

Wyngalf winced, thinking of the precious relics the bishop kept in the catacombs beneath the Noninitarian Stronghold, among them the silver Chalice of Illias, the jewel-encrusted tibia of Saint Roscow, and the miraculous bronze Statue of Ontenogon, the ears of which provided the Holy Wax used by the bishop for the seal on official church documents. Verne would no doubt have no compunction about razing the Stronghold itself for such treasures.

"I-I-I-I'm S-s-s-o-o-o-orr-ee-ee-ee-ee," he said again. "I-I-I-I d-di-i-i-i-d-nt kn-n-n-o-o-o-o-w-w-w w-w-w-wha-a-a-a-t I-I-I-I w-w-wa-a-a-as-s-s d-do-o-o-o-o-i-i-i-ing."

"What?" Evena asked, pausing with her fists clenched in the air.

"I didn't know what I was doing," said Wyngalf. "I wasn't thinking. I was hungry and exhausted and not thinking clearly. I'm sorry I told Verne where your parents lived. I'll do whatever I can to make it up to you. I'll help you get back home."

Renewed anger swept over Evena's face for a moment, and Wyngalf braced himself as she raised her right fist over her head.

But then she collapsed with a defeated sigh, rolling onto the dirt next to him. Tobalt watched this scene unfold with mute interest.

"It's no use," Evena groaned, lying flat on the ground, her fists clenched against her eyes. "There's no stopping him now. He'll take every piece of gold my father ever earned. And when that's gone, he'll burn the town down."

Wyngalf sat up, putting his hand on Evena's shoulder in an attempt to reassure her, but she pulled away. At a loss, he looked to Tobalt, imagining that the goblin might have a suggestion. But for once, the garrulous goblin was silent. He simply stared back at Wyngalf and shrugged. There was nothing any of them could do about a dragon.

Nine

Wyngalf, Evena and Tobalt arrived at Skaal City just after dark. The guard was dubious at first regarding Wyngalf's claim to be a traveling missionary, but when Wyngalf launched into a recitation of the first of the Fourteen Points, he threw open the gate and hurried them inside, presumably so he wouldn't have to listen to any more of Wyngalf's stultifying spiel. The guard cast a puzzled glance at Tobalt, who had thrown his hood over his head to conceal his features, but didn't try to stop him. Wyngalf had actually expected Tobalt to be refused entry to the city, which would forestall the need to ditch him later on, but either the guard didn't realize Tobalt was a goblin or figured that he was such a miserable specimen of the race that he was no real threat.

"You'll need to surrender your sword," the guard said to Wyngalf. "No swords over thirty-two and a quarter inches allowed in Skaal City without a permit."

"We have good reason to believe our lives are in danger," said Evena.

"In that case," the guard said, "we should be able to expedite the permit process."

"How long will that take?"

"Thirty days."

"Thirty days!" cried Wyngalf. "We could be dead by then!"

"I don't make the laws," said the guard. "You should have anticipated being in grave danger thirty days ago."

"I didn't even know I was going to be on this continent thirty days ago!"

"Sounds like a lack of planning all around," said the guard. "Look, you didn't hear it from me, but you might be able to pick up a black market sword somewhere, if you're really desperate."

Wyngalf sighed. He unbuckled the sword and handed it to the guard. "Do you know where we could find lodging tonight?"

"Sure," said the guard, taking the sword. "There's an inn just down the street on the right."

"Thanks," Wyngalf muttered. They turned to leave.

"Hey, buddy," said the guard. Wyngalf stopped and turned to face him.

The guard grinned at him. "Want to buy a black market sword?"

It was probably just as well that Wyngalf was unarmed at that point, or he might have done something he later regretted. While he silently fumed, Evena handed the guard ten gold pieces and he gave her the sword. "Let's go," Evena said, taking Wyngalf's arm.

They made their way down the street in the direction the guard had indicated, Wyngalf muttering the whole way about the injustice of the having to pay for a sword he already owned. Neither the fact that it was Evena's money they'd spent nor Tobalt's reminder that he had essentially stolen the sword in the first place soothed his resentment.

Following the guard's directions, they found themselves standing in front of an establishment called The Battered Goblin. Assuming this was the inn the guard had spoken of, they went inside. If Tobalt had reservations about the name of the establishment, he was wise enough not to voice them.

They walked through the dimly lit common room, where an odd assortment of a dozen or so people ate and drank, casting curious glances at the three strangers as they entered. It was dark enough that it would be unlikely for anyone to identify Tobalt as a goblin from more than a few feet away. Unfortunately, the innkeeper, a sullen, slovenly man, evinced a bit more suspicion about the strange little hooded figure lurking behind Wyngalf and Evena than the guard at the city gate had, and Wyngalf was about to take Tobalt aside and suggest that he spend the night in the alley when Evena spoke up.

"We'd prefer a private room if you have one," she said. "Our son tends to snore." She produced three gold coins from her purse and placed them on the counter in front of her.

"Your... son," said the innkeeper dubiously, his eyes darting from Tobalt to the coins and back to Tobalt again. The light in the inn was dim, but not *that* dim. Behind them, a dozen or so men sat at tables drinking beer and talking boisterously. A few of them had begun to take notice of the strange trio, and Wyngalf was anxious to retreat someplace where there were fewer drunken and undoubtedly xenophobic locals.

"He has a... condition," said Evena, putting another coin on the counter. Wyngalf inhaled sharply. He didn't know how much gold she had in that purse, but she was going to be broke pretty fast if she had to pay four gold pieces just for a place to sleep every night. Whatever they owed Tobalt for his assistance, having a goblin as a companion was going to be expensive—not to mention dangerous—in Skaal City. It just wasn't going to be practical to keep him around long-term. It was unfortunate for Tobalt that he'd been spurned by his own kind, but he wasn't going to fit in any better among humans. In the morning, Wyngalf would explain the situation, and they would go their separate ways. In the meantime, though, they needed to get him out of sight before there was trouble.

The innkeeper looked at the coins on the counter and bit his lip. His eyes went to Tobalt, and then to the men behind them, drinking their beer and muttering quietly. The men stared back, as if daring him to take the money. Wyngalf doubted they had figured out that Tobalt was a goblin, but they clearly sensed something was off. If the innkeeper had just taken the money and shuffled them off to a room, there wouldn't have been a problem, but his hesitation had provoked suspicion. Wyngalf saw Evena pulling another gold coin from her purse in an effort to seal the deal, but putting more money on the counter was only going to escalate things. The more she offered, the more suspicious their situation became. Already one of the men—a lanky old fellow with long, grayish-white hair—had gotten out of his chair and was limping slowly toward them. He was a mean-looking man, all sinew and gristle. A large burn scar covered the right side of his face and continued down his neck.

Wyngalf's hand went to his sword: he didn't want to start a fracas, but if the man's intention was to unmask Tobalt, all pretense would evaporate and they'd be tossed into the street—if they were lucky. It was best to prepare for the worst.

But the man stepped past Tobalt and, before Wyngalf understood what was happening, snatched the coin out of Evena's hand. "A round for the house?" he said loudly, as if responding to something Evena had said. "A splendid idea!"

Evena started to protest, but Wyngalf nudged her. He didn't know what the old man's game was, but if a round of drinks would distract the crowd for a moment, he was all for it. Cheers went up and everyone in the room raised their mugs to Evena. The old man handed the coin to the innkeeper, who took it and slid it into his pocket. He moved to refill the men's mugs, but the old man caught him by the shoulder. "First, a room, Merton," he said sternly. "For the handsome couple and their..." – he glanced at Tobalt and shuddered slightly – "*son*."

The innkeeper nodded, sliding the coins off the counter into his pocket. "Through that doorway," he said. "First door on the left. Orbrecht, if you wouldn't mind...."

"Glad to be of service," said the old man, whose name was evidently Orbrecht. He turned to Wyngalf and Evena. "This way." He limped through the doorway the innkeeper had indicated, and the three followed, anxious to get out of the common room. He took a lamp from where it hung on a hook in the wall and walked to a door at the end of the hall. He opened the door and walked inside. The three followed. Orbrecht hung the lamp on another hook, and Wyngalf looked around to see that they were in a windowless room lined with several small cots. Orbrecht smiled and said, "Only the best for a wealthy young couple and their extraordinarily good-looking son."

Tobalt bowed slightly at the compliment. He hadn't said a word since they'd entered the inn, so as to better preserve what little illusion remained that he was a human being. Even in the lamp light and partially obscured by his hood, Tobalt's goblinesque features were evident. Orbrecht was either nearly blind or being deliberately disingenuous.

"Yes," said Wyngalf uncertainly. Orbrecht continued to stand there smiling at them, and Wyngalf began to wonder if the man expected some sort of tip. Five gold pieces seemed like more than enough for these accommodations, and while he appreciated Orbrecht's help, he was suspicious of the man's motives. If he was planning on shaking them down by threatening to reveal Tobalt's race, Wyngalf wished he would be a little more explicit about it. He was too tired to play games. "Yes, well," Wyngalf said, stretching his arms and yawning, "it's been a very long day." He was actually more hungry than tired, and expected Evena and Tobalt were as well, but they might have to get by with no dinner tonight. He didn't dare go back to the common room to face questions about his strange companion from the men gathered there.

Orbrecht nodded in understanding, but gave no indication that he planned on leaving.

"Is there... something we can do for you?" asked Evena at last.

"There is, actually," said Orbrecht, with a nod. "I take it from your accents that you fine folks are not from around these parts, and in any case you're too young to remember the Frontier Wars."

A moment of awkward silence followed. Tobalt shifted nervously.

"*I* remember, though," said Orbrecht. "Oh, yes. Lost my leg in the Second Frontier War." He pulled up his trouser leg to reveal a wooden peg below the knee. "Goblin bite," he said. "I killed so many of 'em, I lost count. By Grovlik, do I hate goblins! Orbrecht the Goblin-Killer they called me. At the Battle of Vornulpa, I must've killed forty of 'em. Only thing keepin' me from killing more goblins was the ones I already killed. Piled up to my knees, they were. I had to climb over them just to get to the ones what were still alive. 'Cept one of 'em wasn't dead. Not quite. Had just enough life in him to get his foul yellow teeth into my leg. I ran him through, but by then it was too late. Goblin bites are nasty things, they are. My leg turned colors I'd never seen before. Finally had to saw it clean off at the knee. Did it myself, with a leather belt cinched around my thigh. Took me six tries, as I kept blacking out. I hated goblins even more after that, if you can believe it."

Wyngalf cleared his throat, his hand having surreptitiously moved to his sword hilt. "Yes, well," he said. "My wife and I thank you for your service. Without sacrifices such as yours, this city wouldn't be safe for families like ours."

Orbrecht grinned at him. "Let's get a couple things straight," he said. "For starters, I didn't lose my leg so that you could bring a filthy runt of a goblin into this town." He pulled his cloak aside and swiftly drew a dagger from a sheath at his belt. "Second, I can slice your neck wide open before you can even get that pig-sticker out of its scabbard."

Wyngalf swallowed hard, slowly raising his hands. He suspected Orbrecht was bluffing, but Wyngalf wasn't about to trust Evena's life to his own decidedly amateur combat proficiency. "Alright," he said. "We don't want any trouble. What do you want? Money? If you're going to kill us, I'd appreciate it if you'd just get it over with. It's been a very long day."

"Ha!" Orbrecht yelped. "I'm not going to kill you. Not unless you try something stupid with that sword, anyway. You're the most interesting thing that's happened in this sorry excuse for a city for weeks. All I wants is to know your story." He placed the dagger back in its sheath and sat down on one of the cots, looking at Wyngalf expectantly.

"Our *story*?" asked Wyngalf.

"Aye," said Orbrecht. "How you came to be traveling with a goblin, for starters."

Tobalt had retreated into the corner, and in the dim light he looked almost human.

"I'm afraid you're mistaken," said Wyngalf. "It's true that our son is not *conventionally* handsome..."

Orbrecht's smile faded, and the lamplight glinted off the dagger blade as he slid it several inches out of its sheath.

"Okay, okay!" cried Wyngalf, holding up his hands again. "We'll tell you."

"The truth," snarled Orbrecht. "No sugar-coating. I'll know if you're lying."

Wyngalf nodded.

"Good!" exclaimed Orbrecht, letting the dagger slide back into its sheath again. "Please, have a seat."

Wyngalf, Evena and Tobalt each sat down on one of the cots.

"Well," Wyngalf began. "I'm a missionary representing the—"

"Hold on!" cried Orbrecht, getting to his feet. The three of them jumped at the sudden movement, but Orbrecht simply hobbled to the door and left, slamming the door behind him. Wyngalf and Evena stared at each other, confused.

"Do you suppose he's gone to find a larger knife?" asked Tobalt.

"I don't think he intends to hurt us," said Evena.

"We should be ready, just in case," said Wyngalf. "If he tries anything, I'll go for his throat. Tobalt, try biting his leg. The good one."

Tobalt nodded and exercised his jaw as if readying himself for this task.

But when the door opened a moment later, Orbrecht reappeared with a large platter full of food. Behind him was the innkeeper, bearing a jug of wine and a small wooden table. The innkeeper shuffled past Orbrecht and set the table in the middle of the room, where it could easily be reached by all the cots. They set the food and wine on the table.

"Anything else, Orbrecht?" asked the innkeeper.

"That'll do for now, Merten," Orbrecht replied. The innkeeper nodded and left, closing the door behind them. Famished, Wyngalf and Evena tore into the food—bread, vegetables and some sort of stew of indeterminate constituency. Tobalt crept nervously forward, as if not certain whether he was welcome.

"Come, then, goblin!" Orbrecht barked. "I haven't killed a goblin in twenty years, and if I was going to start up again, I'd find a more robust specimen than yourself. I could beat you to death with my wooden leg."

"I thought you hated goblins," said Tobalt uncertainly, in which was perhaps the shortest sentence Wyngalf had ever heard him utter.

"Oh, I do," said Orbrecht. "Hate them with a passion. Vile, revolting creatures. But I hate them as a *group*, not as individuals. And while it is doubtful you will ever overcome the base instincts of your accursed race, nor, I think, make suitable penance for the crimes you have undoubtedly committed, to say nothing of the sins of your forebears going back to the slime pit from which the first pair of proto-goblins emerged, hateful and stinking, I have nothing against you *personally*."

The goblin accepted this explanation with aplomb. "I am indebted to you, kind sir, for your forgiveness and pragmatism," he replied. "For while I did not choose to be a vile subhumanoid, I must confess that at times I forget to be suitably abashed at my goblinhood. To my shame, in fact, I sometimes delight in the thought of such activities as skulking and pillaging, which, as you undoubtedly know, are hallmarks of the goblin race. It is, I suspect, only my own congenital unsuitability for such pursuits, and not my stunted sense of morality, that prevents me from attaining the depths of depravity that is characteristic of my fellows."

"Don't get me wrong," said Orbrecht. "I'd run you through as soon as look at you if I met you on the field of battle. But then I suppose that's true of your friends here as well." He grinned at Wyngalf and Evena.

"But we're not on a battlefield," Evena reminded him.

"Aye," said Orbrecht. "It is curious, though, a young couple smuggling a goblin into an inn. The way I figure it, you're either an exceptionally kindly and sophisticated goblin, or these two are a couple of exceptionally crude and vile human beings. When I figure out which, I'll know whether you need killing or not. Anyway, on with the story!"

Wyngalf narrowly avoided choking on a mouthful of stew, and once again launched into his story. He doubted Orbrecht would believe the part about being rescued by Verne, but he couldn't think of a likelier explanation for their surviving the shipwreck, and he guessed that it was better to tell a story that Orbrecht might find fantastical than risk being caught in a lie. In any case, Orbrecht seemed at least as interested in entertainment as he was in truth, and you couldn't beat a dragon for sheer entertainment value. But when Wyngalf got to the part where Verne landed on the island, Orbrecht scowled, and Wyngalf wondered whether he'd miscalculated.

"You accepted a ride from a dragon?" Orbrecht asked. He sounded more disapproving than dubious.

"We had no choice," said Evena. "We'd have starved."

Orbrecht nodded thoughtfully. "Red or green?"

"The dragon?" said Wyngalf. "He was green."

Orbrecht scowled again. "Ah, that would be Verne."

"That's what he said," Evena said, nodding.

"And what did he want in return?"

"He didn't ask for anything," Evena said. "But after he brought us to Dis, we... that is, I suspect..."

"He wanted to know where we were from," said Wyngalf. "And I told him. It never occurred to me that he might not know there were lands across the sea. It was a stupid mistake, and it was all my fault. Evena tried to warn me, and we hadn't even met Tobalt yet. So if you want to kill someone, you should just kill me. Let them go."

"Relax, lad," said Orbrecht, holding up his hands. "Dragons are tricksy, and Verne's a particularly tricksy one. I'd not run you through merely for being taken in by the likes of him. Now, if you please, continue with your story."

Wyngalf told him about finding Tobalt scrounging in the ruins of Sybesma, and meeting Verne again on their way to Skaal City. "Tomorrow we're going to the Shipping Guild to see if we can negotiate for passage for Evena back home to Skuldred. So here we are."

Orbrecht nodded. "A word of advice," he said. "When you tell the Shipping Guild clerk about how you got here, leave out the dragon."

"You don't think he'll believe us?" Evena asked.

"Oh, to the contrary," said Orbrecht. "I think he *will* believe you. If the Shipping Guild finds out Verne is keeping you on this side of the sea as ransom against your hometown, they might not be willing to help you. Very little happens around here without Verne's approval."

"Yes," said Wyngalf. "We've heard all about his extortion scheme. If the city doesn't pay, he threatens to burn the place down."

Orbrecht snorted. "He doesn't *have* to threaten. People in this city are tripping over themselves trying to make Verne happy. Bunch of cowards, if you ask me. You know how I got this?" He turned his face so they could get a good look at the burns. "Not from the incisors of a goblin, I'll tell you that!" He gave Tobalt a jab in the ribs, and the goblin chuckled good-naturedly.

"You *fought* Verne?" asked Evena, in awe.

"That I did, lass. I and several score of brave men, years ago, when such could still be found in this city. I led an expedition to the dragon's lair in the Kovac Mountains to the south. We sneaked into his lair to attack him while he slept. Unfortunately, he woke up. We fought well and bravely, but the odds were against us."

"But how do you fight a dragon?" Wyngalf said. "Those scales must be almost impenetrable."

"The eyes, lad," said Wyngalf. "The eyes are the weak points. I myself shot an arrow into his left eye. It's the only reason I'm alive today. He couldn't see straight to aim his fire. The rest of my men weren't so lucky."

"Verne killed them all?"

"Every last one, save me," said Orbrecht gloomily. "As I lay there on the cave floor, my face half burned off, I begged him to finish me, but he refused. Told me to warn the people of Skaal City what would happen to anybody who trespassed in his lair. But I left him with a reminder as well. He's still blind in the eye I shot the arrow into. Tries to hide it, but if you look close, you can see that eye never moves. I'd return to finish him off, but I'm an old man now, and I can't do it alone. Sadly, there are few brave men left in this city. The bravest of them all was the father of Morten, the innkeeper. He was my best friend. The dragon took his head off with one swipe of his claws. Ever since then, Morten has given me room and board, and I do what I can to look out for him. "

They sat for a moment in silence. The food was gone, and Wyngalf was growing sleepy.

"But that's none of your concern!" declared Orbrecht, getting to his feet. "Tomorrow you'll be on your way home across the Sea of Dis. I thank you for your company and your story. In my estimation, not one of you needs killing at present. Not even you, goblin, runt of an accursed brood though you may be. I bid you all goodnight!" With that, he hobbled out of the room, closing the door behind him.

"Strange man," said Evena.

Wyngalf nodded.

"I like him," said Tobalt.

Ten

They awoke early the next morning and managed to smuggle Tobalt out of the inn while it was still dark. They streets were mostly deserted, but they tried to avoid the major arteries through the city to be on the safe side, taking narrow streets that wound through a seemingly random configuration of slums and tradesmen's shops. They relied on Tobalt, who could see better in the dim light, to guide them. Unfortunately his sense of direction did not seem to be on par with his vision.

"Knowledge of our precise whereabouts seems to have eluded me," said Tobalt, coming to a halt in the middle of the street.

"You mean we're lost," said Evena.

"There's someone up ahead on that corner," said Wyngalf. "I'll ask him how to get to the harbor. Wait here." Tobalt and Evena remained behind as Wyngalf went to speak to the man, who was standing so still that Wyngalf wasn't entirely certain it wasn't some kind of dummy dressed up in a cloak. But as Wyngalf approached, the man threw back his hood and turned to face him, his completely bald head shining in the moonlight. The man was thin and gaunt, but his age was impossible to determine. A smile seemed to be playing at the corners of his mouth.

"Uh, hello," said Wyngalf uncertainly. Stopping a few feet from the man, he noticed the man had a prominent marking on his forehead: a vertically oriented oval. "I was hoping you could tell me the way to the harbor."

"Fleeing the city, are you?" said the man. "My name is Arbliss. Your accent is strange, sir. Are you perhaps from across the sea?"

Wyngalf wasn't keen on revealing the details of their situation to a stranger, but if satisfying the man's curiosity was the price of getting to the harbor, then so be it. "My friend and I are from the Jagged Coast, yes," he said. "We need to get her on a ship home."

"Your friend, eh?" said the man, peering down the street behind Wyngalf. "A young woman, yes? And a goblin!"

"Look," said Wyngalf, growing impatient, "can you tell me the way to the harbor or not?"

"Oh, yes," said the man with a wink. "I can give you directions to the *harbor.*" The man was now speaking with unnecessary volume, and enunciating in a way that made Wyngalf think of a dramatic performer on a stage.

"Okay, then," said Wyngalf, when the man didn't elaborate. "Any time now would be fine."

The man took a step toward Wyngalf, and Wyngalf's hand went to the hilt of his sword. But the man simply leaned forward and said into Wyngalf's ear, "We've been waiting for you. My name is Arbliss. I am keeping it safe." He pulled back a few inches and winked at Wyngalf.

"Simply Wyngalf," said Wyngalf, mimicking the man's whisper despite himself. He shook the man's outstretched hand. "You're keeping what safe?"

Arbliss chuckled softly. "That's it," he whispered, then pantomimed locking his lips with a key. He slid the imaginary key into a pocket inside his cloak.

"So," said Wyngalf impatiently, "the harbor?"

The man slapped himself on the O on his forehead, then held up his index finger. With his other hand, he reached inside his cloak, pulled out the imaginary key, and pantomimed unlocking his lips. "The harbor," he announced, reverting to his loud, theatrical manner, "is *that* way."

"Thank you," said Wyngalf, turning to leave. But the man's hand shot out, gripping him by the shoulder. He pulled Wyngalf close and whispered into his ear, "I will tell the others. We will be ready when you return." He gave Wyngalf's shoulder a squeeze, relocked his lips, and then turned and walked away without another word.

Wyngalf shook his head and walked back down the street to where Tobalt and Evena waited.

"What was all that about?" asked Evena.

"No idea," said Wyngalf. "But he says the harbor is over there." He indicated the direction the man had pointed.

"It's as good a direction as any," said Evena. Wyngalf and Tobalt agreed. They set out down the road, and it soon became evident that the strange bald man had been telling the truth: the streets began to slope gradually downward, approaching sea level. After a few minutes, they could smell the sea air and hear gulls crying in the distance.

The sun was just coming up when they arrived at the harbor, but already the docks were aflutter with activity: large men were grunting and sweating as they carried crates and barrels up a ramp to a ship about twice the size of the *Erdis Evena*. There seemed to be a great deal of bickering and confusion on and around the ramp, and Wyngalf realized after a moment that some men were loading the ship while others were simultaneously unloading it. Occasionally a collision would occur and work would cease while the two parties swore and shook their fists at each other. It seemed only a matter of time before a full-on brawl broke out.

Tobalt pointed out a weathered sign reading "Shipping Guild Office," with an arrow underneath the text that seemed to point directly out to sea. After a moment, Wyngalf realized the sign was directing them to a tiny shack near the end of the dock, just past the ship that was the center of all the commotion. "You'd better wait here," Wyngalf said to Tobalt. Tobalt nodded and slinked away some distance down the road, where he wouldn't draw attention. Not that anyone was looking their way; everyone in the vicinity seemed to be involved in the drama unfolding around the ship. Wyngalf and Evena continued down the dock toward the office.

The office was a tiny, square building resting atop a wooden framework that raised its floor a couple feet above the surrounding dock, presumably to give its occupant a good view of the goings-on around it. There was a window facing each side of the dock, and through a small window in the door they could see right out to the bay through the window in the far side of building. Entering the office, Wyngalf and Evena found a little balding clerk furiously shuffling through papers on a small desk. They waited for some time for him to finish what he was doing and acknowledge their presence, but after a few minutes they began to think he was either deliberately ignoring them or simply shuffling papers recreationally. Wyngalf amused himself by watching the chaos unfolding around the ship just outside the north-facing window, but he could tell Evena was rapidly losing her patience, and he feared she was going to make a scene and spoil her chances of getting on a ship. Wyngalf cleared his throat loudly, but this also had no effect. "Good sir," Wyngalf said at last. "My friend seeks passage to Skuldred."

The little man stared for a moment at the papers as if trying to determine where the sound had come from, then eventually looked up at Wyngalf and Evena, who tried to smile inoffensively.

"Skuldred?" the man asked, as if mildly offended. "Where's that?"

"It's on the Jagged Coast," said Evena, but the man continued to stare obliviously.

"Across the Sea of Dis," Wyngalf offered.

"Across the Sea?" said the man absently. "Nobody goes across the Sea."

"I wasn't figuring on going directly," said Evena. "I thought if I could get to one of the ports in the North, I could travel across the sea from there."

"Not going to be cheap," said the man.

"My father has money," Evena replied. "He's the richest man in Skuldred."

The man cocked an eyebrow at her. "Where?"

"Skuldred. That's where I want to go."

"Well, why didn't you say so?" the man asked irritably. "You can't get there directly. You'll have to take a ship to one of the ports up north first."

"What a splendid idea," Evena said. "I wish I had thought of that."

"Yes, well, I've been doing this for quite a while, Miss," said the man. "Where did you want to go again?"

"*Skul*-dred," Evena said, through gritted teeth. Wyngalf put his hand gently on her shoulder in an attempt to calm her.

"Skuldred," the man said uncertainly, and his eyes fell to the papers on his desk again. He lifted one stack to peer at one of the sheets, ran his finger down a column of text, and then tapped his finger on a line about halfway down. "Here we go!" he exclaimed.

Wyngalf smiled at Evena. For all the appearance of chaos, it appeared that the clerk had a very precise system after all.

But then a scowl came over the clerk's face. He clutched the paper in his hand and suddenly ran past them out the door, slamming it behind him. Sheaves of papers fluttered across the room in his wake.

"I wish people would stop leaving in the middle of conversations like that," Wyngalf said. They watched out the window as the little man ran down to a ship farther down the docks, waving the paper in the air.

Evena sighed. "I'm thinking about trying the barrel trick again. There was a lot less paperwork involved."

Wyngalf nodded, not entirely certain whether Evena was joking. "It might come to that," he said. Even if they could get the clerk to acknowledge them and agree to let them on a ship, there was no telling where they might end up.

While they waited for the clerk to return, Evena began picking up the papers that had fallen to the floor. As she did, she sorted them into separate stacks according to some criteria that were unknown to Wyngalf.

"Do you think that's a good idea?" Wyngalf asked. "The clerk might not take kindly to you disturbing his system."

"System!" Evena snorted. "He has no system. That man is an idiot. My guess is that his only qualifications for this job were the ability to read and perform simple arithmetic." She picked up a page from the floor, glanced at a column of figures and sighed. "Scratch the arithmetic part. My father wouldn't have hired this guy to dispose of fish heads."

Wyngalf looked on nervously as Evena went through the papers on the desk, arranging them in well-ordered stacks. "I know you think you're helping," he said, "but that clerk, idiot though he may be, is our only chance to get you on a ship back home. Upsetting him probably isn't the best... oh boy." Through the window he saw the clerk jogging back toward the office, muttering to himself.

Wyngalf turned to face the door and braced himself for the clerk's entry. The door swung up, and the little man walked in, still muttering to himself. He stopped short, apparently surprised to find someone inside his office. "What are you doing here?" he demanded, glaring at Wyngalf. "You can't be in here."

"We were here when you left," said Wyngalf. "Remember? We were asking about passage to—"

"What in Dis do you think you're doing?" the clerk exclaimed, peering around Wyngalf to see Evena straightening the stacks of paper on his desk. "You've upset my whole configuration!"

"Configuration?" Evena scoffed. "More like catastrophe. You had your outgoing mixed with your incoming, your accounts payable shuffled with your accounts receivable, your bills of lading filed with your customs declarations.... It's a miracle any ships ever get out of this port with their proper cargo." As if to punctuate her point, there was a loud crash outside as a rope snapped and a crate slammed into the dock, smashing to pieces. The contents—some kind of large green melons—hit the deck and began to roll in every direction. Several men tripped over the melons, dropping their own cargo, and soon the entire dock was an impassable bottleneck of crates, sacks and angry men yelling at each other.

"Look what you've done!" cried the clerk. "That ship is due in Brobdingdon in three days, and now it will never get there in time!"

"What *I* did?" said Evena. "If I'd been running this place, you wouldn't have been in this mess in the first place!"

"Okay, let's all take a deep breath," said Wyngalf, trying to sound reasonable. "Sir, my friend meant no harm. She was only trying to help, and in her youthful enthusiasm she made the mistake of thinking—"

"I didn't make any mistake!" Evena cried. "*He's* the one making the mistakes!"

"Evena," Wyngalf chided. "It isn't your place to—"

"Just get out," moaned the clerk, staring hopelessly at the neatly arranged papers on his desk.

"Please, sir," said Wyngalf. "We can make it up to you. We're young and strong. We can help you get the ship loaded." He glanced out the window at the commotion on the dock. Several fistfights had broken out, and anyone who wasn't involved in the fracas was either egging on the combatants or standing around in slack-jawed befuddlement. The ship's cargo seemed to have been forgotten completely. "Or unloaded, whichever."

"It will take me the rest of the day just to clean up this mess!" cried the clerk, indicating the impeccable stacks of paper. "I don't know what's coming and what's going!"

"Don't be silly," said Evena. "It's perfectly clear. This stack is—"

"Grovlik have mercy," the clerk moaned. "The guildmaster is coming!"

Wyngalf and Evena followed the man's gaze out the window in door, which faced the shore. A very well-dressed, aristocratic-looking gentleman was walking pertly up the dock toward the office.

"I'm sacked for sure," the clerk lamented, then ducked under the desk. For a moment, they thought he was attempting to hide, but he appeared a few seconds later with a metal strongbox in his arms. He thunked it down on the desk, pulled a key from his pocket, and opened the lid. Inside were several hundred gold and silver coins. The clerk shoveled these into his coat pockets and, before Wyngalf and Evena realized what he was doing, threw open the window opposite the door. "Good luck!" he yelled as he climbed out the window, and ran away down the dock. He seemed to be headed for a small rowboat at the end of the dock.

"Our helpful clerk seems to have planned his escape," Wyngalf noted.

"If he'd applied that level of attention to his job," said Evena, "he might not *need* to escape."

They watched as the man unwound a rope from a post, tossed it in the boat, and then leaped into the boat. The weight of the coins in his coat pockets put him off balance, though, and after rocking precariously several times, the boat capsized and he disappeared with a splash into the dark water. They continued to watch for several seconds. He didn't come up again.

"Or not," said Evena.

"What are we going to do?" asked Wyngalf. Having given up on the clerk resurfacing, he had turned to watch the guildmaster approaching through the opposite window. He was almost to the office.

"Follow my lead," said Evena. "And hide that box."

"I'm not sure I like the sound of that," said Wyngalf, but he grabbed the box and put it back under the desk. As he stood up, the door opened and the guildmaster stepped inside. Wyngalf hadn't noticed before that the man wore a rapier at his belt. Furrowing his brow, the guildmaster looked from Wyngalf to Evena and then back again.

"Who the devil are you?" he asked Wyngalf. Wyngalf opened his mouth but couldn't think of anything to say.

"New clerk," said Evena. "You're the local guildmaster, I take it?"

"Of course," said the man, turning to face Evena. "Lord Otten Popper. I oversee this branch. What's become of Halbert?"

"Had to let him go," said Evena. "You just missed him, in fact. He was released with a small severance package. This is the new clerk, Fedric." Popper turned back to Wyngalf, who smiled weakly and nodded at him.

"Nice to meet you, sir," said Wyngalf, holding out his hand. But Popper simply stood there, regarding Wyngalf coldly. Wyngalf let his hand fall to his side, and as the man continued to stare, Wyngalf began to feel some pressure to effect a more convincing impression of a clerk. He picked up one of the stacks of paper and begun to thumb through it, as if his work was too pressing to be halted for more than a moment. He pretended to lose himself in the minutiae of one of the documents, and finally he felt the guildmaster's glare switch back to Evena.

"And who might you be, lass?" he asked.

"Lady Evena Herringbone. I came down from Central this morning to oversee the installation of the new clerk. You may know my father, the notoriously reclusive Count Herringbone."

"Doesn't ring a bell," said Popper. His right hand moved toward the hilt of his rapier.

"Understandable," said Evena. "He is, after all, notoriously reclusive."

"I know nothing of any new clerk," said Popper.

"That doesn't surprise me," said Evena. "Halbert has been losing bulletins left and right. Fortunately, Fedric has already made significant progress in addressing the organizational failings of this office."

Popper again regarded Wyngalf, who was running his fingers along an indecipherable line of text and muttering to himself. The guildmaster's eyes fell to the neat stacks of papers on the desk. "It does look more organized," he mused quietly. "Halbert always insisted that he had a system, though."

"That he did," said Evena. "Unfortunately, his system was designed to make it impossible for anyone but Halbert to understand what was going on in this branch, and at that it was quite effective. Central is instituting a system based on the Tabaka protocols, to standardize the flow of information between branches."

"The Tabaka…" Popper began.

"You'd know all about it if Halbert had been doing his job," Evena said. "I don't mean to accuse him of anything, you understand. Other than incompetence, of course, which he possessed in spades."

Shouts could be heard outside, and the guildmaster turned to look out the window. Another crate crashed to the dock, splintering to pieces and spilling its cargo. "What is going on out there?" he asked.

"More of Halbert's doing," said Evena. "We're still hoping to get the *Numinda Fae* to Brobdington on schedule, but Halbert really made a hash of the logistics, I'm afraid. Fedric has been working on it all morning."

The guildmaster scowled at the chaos outside and then turned back to Evena. Doubt came over his face. "How old are you, anyway?"

"Old enough to resent the question," said Evena, with a touch of patrician annoyance. Wyngalf had to hand it to her, she made a pretty convincing aristocrat. But Popper seemed dubious.

"This is all highly irregular," he said, shaking his head. "Central doesn't have the authority to send a new clerk without my approval. No, something is off here." His hand clutched the hilt of his rapier. "Who are you, really?"

"I'm afraid I don't have time to go over this all with you again, Lord Popper," said Evena. "Fedric and I have work to do. I'm going to have to ask you to leave."

"You're asking *me* to leave?" exclaimed Popper. "I'm the guildmaster! You can't ask *me* to leave. No, I'm sorry, Miss. You're quite charming, but I don't believe for a moment you're from the Guild Central Headquarters. You're far too young, and your accent is decidedly not of Dissian origin." He drew his rapier and held the tip of the blade a few inches from Evena's throat. "You have five seconds to tell me who you really are, and what you've done with Halbert. If I believe you, I *might* let you live."

While pretending to be engrossed in the papers on the desk, Wyngalf moved his hand surreptitiously to the hilt of his own sword. He didn't think Popper had noticed he was wearing one, as his coat covered the hilt and the scabbard was hidden by the desk. He doubted he was a match for an aristocrat who had undoubtedly received combat training as part of his primary education, but if he could surprise Popper while he was preoccupied with Evena, they might have a chance.

But Evena evidently had something else in mind. "These matters don't concern you, Fedric!" she snapped. "You can be replaced as easily as Halbert, you know. Now focus on your work. That ship *will* leave on time."

Stunned, Wyngalf dropped his hand to his side. "Yes, Ma'am," he found himself saying. "Er, Lady Herringbone." Nothing to do now but hope that Evena knew what she was doing. Wyngalf went back to shuffling papers.

"You can drop the supercilious act," said Popper, to Evena. "This man is no more clerk than I am. Let me guess: you're a couple of traveling con artists, and you somehow managed to convince Halbert to leave his post so that you could clear out the strongbox. But I came along just in time to foil your plan."

"Yes," said Evena. "That's exactly right. And before we robbed you, we decided to really stick it to you by updating your antiquated filing system. Now if you're through making spurious allegations, we've got a lot of work to do."

Popper stood open-mouthed for a minute, the point of his rapier wavering near Evena's chest. Wyngalf, still pretending to be engrossed in the papers, watched him out of the corner of his eye. He wasn't sure if Popper was actually beginning to doubt himself or if he was simply stunned at Evena's gall. After some time, the guildmaster spoke.

"Who is the governor general of the shipmaster's guild in Vardis?" he asked, narrowing his eyes at Evena.

Evena sighed. "Please, Lord Popper," she said. "I understand your desire to fulfill your due diligence regarding this office, but we really don't have time for these sorts of games. Perhaps once the *Numinda Fae* is on its way to—"

"Answer the question!" snapped Popper. "If you're from Central, it should be no trouble for you at all." When Evena hesitated, he grinned. "Just one simple little question. Then you can go back to work."

Evena shook her head. "I don't know why I subject myself to this," she said. "I really don't. I could have taken a cushy job at Central, but instead I spend my time traveling on creaky old ships to backwater ports like this one to try to make sure all the guilds are within three iterations of the current Tabaka protocols. And what thanks do I get? A rapier pointed at my throat." She glared at Popper, but the point of his blade didn't move. She sighed again. "If you must know, the current governor general at Vardis is Iliana Pravis."

"Ha!" cried Popper. "Nice try, but I'm afraid you're wrong. The current governor general is my brother-in-law, Bander Willshott of Breem. Alright, outside, both of you. I'd rather not get blood all over the floor of the guild office."

Wyngalf sighed and set down the papers. The jig was up. They'd come all this way only to be murdered by a petty aristocrat with a chip on his shoulder.

Eleven

Wyngalf began to shuffle toward the door, but Evena didn't move. She shook her head again and chuckled.

"Your imminent death amuses you?" said the guildmaster.

"No," said Evena. "I'm amused by your lack of familiarity with guild politics, not to mention developments of note within your own family."

Popper scowled at her. "What in Dis are you talking about?"

"Again," said Evena. "I'm not surprised the news never reached you, given Halbert's 'system.' Wyngalf, could you please hand me the interoffice bulletin from a fortnight ago."

Wyngalf nodded, and his eyes fell to the stacks of paper with their indecipherable markings. For a moment, he stood there, frozen.

"Third stack from your left," said Evena. "It'll be the eighth document down."

Wyngalf riffled though the stack until he reached the eighth sheet of paper.

"Hand it to Lord Popper, if you please," said Evena.

Wyngalf did so. The guildmaster took the sheet with his left hand, still scowling at Evena. "What is this?" he sniffed. "Some sort of...." He trailed off, studying the document. "By Varnoth's eyes, my brother-in-law has been replaced!"

"Suspected embezzlement," she said. "He was relieved of his position three weeks ago. Iliana Pravis was elected to replace him in a special meeting of the guild council. I'm a bit surprised you didn't hear about it from Willshott himself, but his silence on the matter may be a result of his cooperation with the guild's ongoing investigation."

"Investigation?" said Popper, looking up from the paper with a somewhat dazed expression on his face. "What are you talking about?"

"I can't speak to the details," said Evena, "but you can see why the council would want to limit Willshott's communications with others who may have been involved in the conspiracy."

"Conspiracy!" the guildmaster cried, letting his rapier fall to his side. "What are you saying? The guild suspects me of being involved in my brother-in-law's crimes?"

"As I said, I can't speak to the details," Evena replied. "Suffice it to say that threatening a guild representative with a rapier is unlikely to reflect well on you in the eyes of the council."

"What?" cried Popper. "No! I wasn't threatening you!" He hurriedly sheathed his sword. "That is, I was acting in what I assumed were the best interests of the guild. I thought you were con artists out to rob us!"

"Or perhaps you knew exactly who we are, but you were worried about what we found in Halbert's files," said Evena.

"No, no, no!" Popper exclaimed. "I mean, if there's anything improper in that paperwork, it's all on Halbert. The man was woefully incompetent. Why, I was going to fire him myself. That's why I'm here, actually. I don't know about anything in those files. That is, obviously I'm familiar with the business. What I mean is that I'm unaware of any improprieties. Of which I'm sure there are none. You didn't, ah, find any, did you? Improprieties, that is?"

"Scads of them," said Evena, and Popper cringed. She let him worry for a moment before continuing: "But so far they seem to be explainable by Halbert's incompetence. The only thing causing me to suspect you of complicity in Willshott's crimes is your continued interference in our work."

"Interference?" said Popper. "Am I interfering? No, far from it! I was merely attempting to ensure that everything was running smoothly. But you clearly have everything under control."

"That we do," said Evena coldly. "Now if you don't mind, we have a ship to load."

"Very good!" Popper exclaimed. "Then if there's nothing else, I'll be on my way."

"Nothing else at this time, Lord Popper. I'd appreciate it if you could swing by in the morning to make sure Fedric has everything he needs. I'll be leaving for Brobdingdon on the *Numinda Fae*."

"So soon?" asked Popper, whose demeanor toward Evena had changed completely. "You just got here. I'd be much obliged if you could stay a bit longer. I've been trying to get this office in shape for years, but Halbert, you know... he was quite hopeless. But together, you and I could turn this office into the jewel of the Guild's operations on the coast. With my vision and your administrative prowess, we'd be quite the team. Perhaps over dinner...."

"That sounds lovely," said Evena. "But I'm afraid I have pressing business awaiting in Bjill. We're looking at a pumice miner strike up there."

"Good heavens," said Popper. "That sounds dreadful. Those pumice miners are rough people. If you need an armed escort, I'd be quite willing to accompany you." He patted the rapier hilt at his belt.

"That's very kind," said Evena, "but unnecessary. Besides, I need you to keep an eye on Fedric here. He has quite a knack for details, but he lacks your capacity of visionary thinking. I'll be returning in six weeks to make sure things are running smoothly, and—assuming you and Fedric have things well in hand by that time—I'd be more than happy to meet with you to discuss your ideas for improving this office."

"Wonderful!" exclaimed Popper. "Well, I'll leave you to it, then. Good day to you, m'lady." He bowed slightly and then turned to Wyngalf, who was still absently thumbing through papers. "Shape up, Fedric!" Popper snapped. "Lady Herringbone and I will broach no lollygagging!" He grinned ingratiatingly at Evena, and she managed to affect a reasonably convincing facsimile of a smile back at him. He turned and exited the office, closing the door behind him.

"Tell me, Wyngalf," said Evena, watching though the window as Popper trotted self-importantly back down the dock, "does your religion teach that every being in creation serves some purpose?"

"Of course," said Wyngalf. "Everything must work together to further the purposes of the Divine Noninity."

"And what purpose does someone like Lord Otten Popper serve?"

Wyngalf thought for a moment. "Well," he said at last, "the purpose isn't always immediately evident."

"You know what I think?" said Evena. "I think some people don't have any purpose. I think God made a mistake, and then tried to cover it up by calling those people aristocrats. Someday people are going to realize that the nobility aren't actually good for anything, and a lot of noblemen are going to lose their heads."

Wyngalf frowned at the blasphemy, but he couldn't help sympathizing with the sentiment. "'Never underestimate the resilience of useless men,'" he said.

"What's that?" Evena asked.

"One of the pagan thinkers I read in the stronghold library," said Wyngalf. "Poltec the Cynic. He taught that every civilization requires a class of useless people to remind itself that humanity's ultimate struggle is not against evil, but against utter pointlessness. So you see, Popper does serve a purpose. He exists so that you and I will wonder why he exists."

"That's stupid," said Evena.

"Yes," Wyngalf agreed. "Poltec wrote his Treatise on the Useless Class while working in middle management at a brand image consulting firm. It was only upon finishing it that he realized he had done no actual work for six years. He hung himself shortly after the treatise was published."

"What's 'middle management'?" asked Evena, furrowing her brow. "And what's a 'brand image consulting firm'?"

"Alas," said Wyngalf. "The answers to those questions are lost to history. So what was all that business about a conspiracy involving Popper's brother-in-law? How did you know all that?"

"Oh," said Evena with a sheepish smile. "I saw something about Bander Willshott being replaced as governor general of the shipping guild by Iliana Pravis. The rest of it was improvisation."

"But... that's *amazing*," said Wyngalf. "You happened to read that one bulletin out of all this stuff, and you remembered the details with such precision. And then you were able to fabricate a story to fool Popper!"

Evena shrugged. "I could recite the contents of every document on that desk," she said, "and tell you exactly where each of them is. It's a gift. The first time I recited a six-page shipping manifest from memory, my father summoned a priest to perform an exorcism. Fortunately his business sense kicked in when the priest demanded fifty gold pieces for the operation. He decided it was more cost-effective to put my demonic talents to work for him in his office. I was basically running the place by the time I was twelve. Of course, grownups don't like taking orders from twelve-year-olds, so the ship captains and warehouse foremen were always trying to trip me up. I had to always look like I knew what I was doing, even if I didn't. I found that even if I didn't know something, I could usually fake it until I figured it out. I got pretty good at bluffing. After a while, they gave up trying to stump me. Which was too bad, in a way, because it was the only real challenge that job offered. I could run my father's business in my sleep."

Wyngalf stared at her, trying to determine if she was putting him on. He decided she couldn't be; there was no other way to explain her performance with Lord Popper. "That's why you stowed away," he said. "I thought you were just a spoiled kid. No wonder you were bored."

"Boredom doesn't even begin to describe it," said Evena. "I'm good at keeping track of details. That doesn't mean I enjoy it. I craved novelty and excitement, but every day it was more shipping logs, inventory lists, and price matrices. Meanwhile, I met almost every day with ship captains who had traveled many leagues up and down the coast and experienced all manner of adventures. Probably many of their stories were embellished, if not completely fabricated, but that didn't lessen their appeal. I'd been planning to stow away eventually for months, and when you showed up with your divine mission, I decided it was time. And so here we are."

"Trying to get you back home," added Wyngalf.

"Circumstances have changed," said Evena.

Wyngalf nodded. "Indeed they have. So what do we do now?"

"We get that ship loaded," said Evena. "And then I get on it and head north to Brobdingdon."

They spent the rest of the day coordinating the unloading and loading of the ship. That is, Evena coordinated it; Wyngalf was reduced to barking orders at the puzzled dock workers. The foreman at first resisted their efforts to take control of the situation, but it very quickly became painfully evident that Evena was miles ahead of him in her understanding of logistics, and the workers were so desperate for firm leadership and frustrated with their lack of progress (the cargo that had been loaded onto the ship so far turned out to be almost entirely the same cargo that had been unloaded an hour earlier), that it took very little prompting to coax them into tossing the foreman into the bay. Fortunately, as his pockets were not filled with gold coins, he was able to swim away with nothing injured but his pride. Halbert the clerk, sadly, still had not resurfaced.

For all the incompetence of the management, though, Wyngalf was amazed at the volume and variety of goods that moved through the port of Skaal. This one ship contained textiles made from Peraltian wool in the mills of Brobdingdon, crates of pumice from Bjill, animal hides originating from the Vorgal territories far to the north, salt from the Trynsvaan, knickknacks produced by the gnomes of Swarnholme, and a dozen other sorts of cargo. These would be unloaded and replaced with fruits and nuts from the vast orchards to the east of Skaal, spices from as far away as Churesh, ceramics and jewelry from Avaress, and cured meats butchered in Skaal City from the herds of cattle that roamed the plains to the southeast.

Once the ship was emptied and the loading process seemed to be going more-or-less smoothly, Wyngalf took a step back to marvel at the assortment of goods being delivered to Brobdingdon, from whence it would be distributed throughout Ytrisk.

"Impressive, isn't it?" asked Evena, coming up next to him. "The machine runs pretty well when you replace the stuck gears. It's a tribute to the guild's organization, really. Even having complete idiot in charge of the operation for Grovlik-knows-how-long didn't do any serious damage. Remove the idiot, apply a little common sense, and goods begin to flow freely again. It makes me wish we had something like the shipping guild back home. On the Jagged Coast, every city manages its own trade, and there's very little communication between the ports. We could greatly benefit from more coordination among the ports, but the local authorities in each town are more concerned with holding onto what power they have than increasing trade."

"Hmm," said Wyngalf, nodding. There was something bothering him, though. "I can't help thinking that Skaal City would be better off if it didn't send all these riches away to Brobdingdon. Can't the people here use meats and spices?"

"Of course," said Evena. "But the idea is that Skaal benefits more from sending these goods to Brobdingdon than Brobdingdon benefits by sending its goods here. If the Skaal authorities play their cards right, they'll still get the better of Brobdingdon."

"Ah," said a voice from behind them. "Mercantilism." They turned to see Tobalt, who had sneaked up behind them.

"Excuse me?" said Evena.

"You're evincing the central tenet of mercantilism, which views international trade as a zero-sum game," said Tobalt. "Although it clearly is not."

"I'm sorry," said Evena, raising her eyebrow at Tobalt. "Are you claiming to know more about the shipping business than I do?"

"My apologies," said Tobalt, with a slight bow. "I make no such claim, and apologize for giving you that impression. Your expertise in the finer points of the business clearly outstrips my amateur understanding by a fair margin. I meant only to correct one minor point, which is that speaking in macroeconomic terms, mercantilism is a misguided ideology, as it assumes that in any voluntary transaction between two powers, there is, to put the matter bluntly, a winner and a loser. Trade in such a scheme becomes, therefore, a zero-sum game, the goal of which becomes to get the better of one's adversary. It is, sadly, this sort of misguided thinking that leads inevitably to the situation that you described as being endemic to the Jagged Coast: an unwillingness to expand trade out of fear of one's fellows getting the upper hand. My theory is that this dynamic in human affairs is a holdover from prehistoric times, when cooperative arrangements were limited in scope to one's one tribe or clan. As evidence of this, I present my own race: unable to cooperate on a large scale, goblins subsist by waylaying travelers and raiding the settlements of more developed races. Yet it is this same inability to cooperate in groups larger than a single clan that will be our undoing. Humans, able to take advantage of a much greater pool of talents and resources, gradually displace us with their superior technology and long-term strategic thinking. The process is slow, but I'm afraid that ultimately my race is doomed unless we can learn to adapt. And with few exceptions, goblins aren't much for learning."

Wyngalf and Evena stared at Tobalt dumbly.

"Macro what?" asked Wyngalf after a moment.

"I beg your forgiveness," said Tobalt. "As I say, it's a minor point, of interest mainly to members of a race whose congenital short-sightedness threatens its own extinction. Being human, you obviously have the luxury of remaining oblivious to such existential concerns."

Evena and Wyngalf traded glances. It was becoming increasingly unclear whether Tobalt was apologizing to them, lecturing them, or making fun of them. While Wyngalf was still mulling his response, Evena spoke up.

"Perhaps we should leave this discussion for another time," she said, nodding toward the *Numinda Fae*. The last few crates were being hauled up the ship's ramp.

"So this is it?" asked Wyngalf. "You're leaving?"

"I have to," replied Evena. "I wish I could accompany you on the rest of your adventure, but I need to get home. My mother and father must be worried sick about me, thanks to Verne."

"I understand," said Wyngalf, with a nod. "Are you certain you'll be safe on that ship? Perhaps I should come with you, at least to Brobdingdon."

"I'll be fine," Evena said. "Word has spread among the seamen that I'm a high-ranking official with the shipping guild. Nobody is going to mess with me. And you need to think about starting your church. There's no need for you to accompany me."

Wyngalf nodded, still uncertain about letting her go.

"It's okay, Wyngalf," she said. "I know you didn't mean to tell Verne about my hometown. And in any case, you were true to your word. You got me on a ship. Once I get to Brobdingdon, I'll catch another across the sea, and then travel down the coast back to Skuldred. It will take some time, but I will make it home."

"But what will you do when you get there? You can't stop Verne from destroying Skuldred."

"No," she admitted. "But at least my parents will know I'm safe. My father has plenty of money. We can flee town and resettle somewhere out of Verne's reach. Perhaps I'll suggest Svalbraakrat. When you return after your divine mission is complete, you can find me."

Wyngalf smiled, feeling a flutter in his chest. "I would like that," he said.

"Goodbye, Wyngalf," said Evena, with a smile. "And goodbye, Tobalt. You're certainly the most... *interesting* goblin I've met."

"And the *only* goblin you've met, I would wager," said Tobalt with a bow. "It is to my utter regret you were inflicted with such a poor representative of my species."

Evena turned and walked up the ramp. She gave them a final wave, and then set about to snapping orders at crew members, who scurried in response to her commands.

"I think she'll manage," said Tobalt.

"It would appear so," said Wyngalf. "Let's see if we can sneak you into a tavern and get something to eat."

Twelve

Wyngalf and Tobalt located a tavern overlooking the harbor. It was now late afternoon, so the place was nearly empty, and the proprietor, who seemed to be half-blind, made no indication that he noticed anything amiss about Tobalt. He might simply have been desperate for business, but Wyngalf slipped him a couple of extra silvers just in case. Evena had given them enough money to get by for the next few days, and they were famished. The two companions sated their hunger with fish and bread while they waited for the *Numinda Fae* to cast off. For the moment Wyngalf had stopped thinking about ditching Tobalt. With Evena gone, Tobalt was the closest thing he had to a friend on this continent. And, truth be told, the goblin's idiosyncrasies were starting to grow on him. When they were full, they sat drinking beer and staring out at the harbor.

"I'm sorry to see Evena go," said Tobalt, setting down his mug. "She seems a fine specimen of humanity."

"That she is," replied Wyngalf wistfully. "I mean, does. She seems fine, that is." Wyngalf was not ordinarily a big drinker, as alcohol impeded communication between his brain and his mouth. Sometimes this resulted in him saying things that he later regretted, as had happened at Bulgar the fishmonger's house. With that incident fresh in his mind, he was now overcompensating, considering each word as it came out of his mouth, like a man tripping on cobblestones because he's preoccupied with his own shoes. "I'm not sure I trust this chaotic transport system you seem so enameled of," he said. "Enameled of? I'm not sure I trust this transport system you like so much. I'd have preferred to hire a single ship to transport Evena home."

"But doing so would be prohibitively expensive, would it not? Assuming you could get a captain to agree to make the voyage."

"Yes," said Wyngalf. "So we have no choice but to rely on a series of sea captains, each acting in their own self-interest. His own self-interest? A series of self-interested sea captains. How do we know that one of them won't take advantage of her?"

"I get the impression Evena can take care of herself," said Tobalt, "but in any case, I suspect there is little reason to worry. From what I can gather, the shipping guild's system, when it isn't bottlenecked by idiocy and incompetence, seems to work fairly well for transporting goods all up and down the coast of Dis and even across the sea from the ports in the north. There seems little reason to think that it will not serve equally well to transport Evena home."

"Still," said Wyngalf, "I don't like it. Too many things can go wrong between here and Skuldred. I should have gone with her."

"Forgive me if I'm being presumptuous, Simply Wyngalf," said Tobalt, "but I was under the impression that your purpose here in Dis was to spread the Noninitarian faith."

"Of course," said Wyngalf. "But I also have an obligation to make sure Evena gets home safely."

"Unless I am mistaken," Tobalt said, "Evena herself released you of that obligation. And in any case, although my assessment of the situation is undoubtedly flawed, I fail to see how accompanying Evena on her voyage would increase the likelihood of her returning home safely. Unless you possess information to which I am not privy, I would, begging your forgiveness, venture that perhaps your true motivations are otherwise."

Wyngalf took a moment to parse the goblin's statement and decided he wasn't entirely sure he liked what he seemed to be implying. "Are you calling me a liar?" he demanded.

"Certainly not," said Tobalt. "What I am trying to say, in my own imprecise and evidently provocative manner, is that I suspect you might have feelings regarding Evena beyond those of mere obligation and protectiveness, of which perhaps you are not entirely aware."

"Pah," muttered Wyngalf dismissively. He wasn't entirely certain that this qualified as a rebuttal, but consoled himself with the thought that adhering to the proper forms of discourse was probably pointless in a discussion with a dimwitted subhumanoid anyway. He finished his beer and signaled for another.

"I cannot say I blame you," said Tobalt, undeterred. "She is, as I've indicated, a prime specimen of the human female, well into her fertile years. I might add that her allure transcends even the boundaries that separate your kind from subhumanoids such as myself, although of course I have no delusions regarding potential reciprocation." Wyngalf furrowed his brow at Tobalt and the goblin went on, hurriedly, "But more germane to your case, I suspect you harbor some uncertainty about your mission, and perhaps on some level seek to delay it out of fear of your own inadequacy for the task."

"I trust the Noninity," announced Wyngalf. "It brought me here to start a Noninitarian church in Dis, and that's what I'm going to do. My own furballs are no barrier to the will of the nonimpotent monimity."

"I'm sorry," said Tobalt. "Your furballs?"

"Furballs!" exclaimed Wyngalf, then scowled and tried again, enunciating more carefully. "Foy. Bulls."

"Ah, foibles!" said Tobalt. "In other words," said Tobalt, "you have your doubts, but you are one hundred percent certain that those doubts are unfounded."

"Yes," said Wyngalf, and then shook his head. "Wait, no. Look, what I'm saying is that ultimately the Noninity is in control of everything, so there's no point in worrying about it."

"Ah," said Tobalt. "Interesting."

"What?" Wyngalf demanded. "Spit it out, gobble-bin!"

"Oh," said Tobalt with an apologetic shrug, "I just find it fascinating that although a moment ago you were fretting about Evena's treacherous journey home, you are now assuring me that everything is under the control of a supernatural entity of which, if I'm not mistaken, you have no direct experience."

"You think I'm contracting myself," said Wyngalf, wagging his finger at Tobalt. "Contra*dict*ing myself. But I'm not. My concern about the chaotic nature of the shipping guild's transport system arises from my faith. Goblins do not have a monopoly on vile, depraved conduct, Tobalt." Having hit his stride, Wyngalf pressed on, relying on his rote memorization of Noninitarian theology to overcome the effects of the alcohol. "Humans too are base, self-interested creatures when left to their own devices. When the Creator first brought order out of chaos, human society was perfect. But Ravast the Corruptor infiltrated the First City, undermining the divine order with his message of self-interest. People began to believe that each man was the best judge of his own interests, and as this cancer spread, the hierarchy established by Abasmos crumbled. The Noninitarian faith is a devotion to the belief that for men to live in harmony, this divinely ordained order must be reestablished. The haphazard nature of the shipping guild's so-called 'system' is evidence of Ravast's corruption of human society, and is therefore not to be trusted. While the Noninity is now and always in control of all creation, men will not be truly happy and free until they are given the opportunity to live in accordance with the divine will."

Tobalt nodded thoughtfully. "If I may be so bold to ask," said Tobalt, "in this new order which you envision, would the Noninitarian leadership happen to play a pivotal role?"

"If you're suggesting that Noniminitarianism is motivated by a desire for temporal power," replied Wyngalf, "you could not be more mistaken. My brethren are interested only in the advancement of the divine will and the restoration of human society to its proper relation to the Monimitiminy. Monimity. Its proper relation to the one true God."

"But when this divine order is established, it will look very much like a pyramid with the Noninitarian bishop at the top, will it not?"

Wyngalf scowled again. With the beer muddling his thought processes, it was difficult to formulate a coherent counterargument. "Listen, gobblebin," he started, but before he could complete the thought, the room was suddenly cast into shadow for a split second as something very large passed in front of the window, blocking out the sun.

"Tell me that's a big cloud," Wyngalf said. "A really big, dark, fast cloud."

"As much as I would like to allow you to persist in that delusion," said Tobalt, looking out the window, "I'm afraid I would be doing you a disservice, unless you intend to redefine the word 'cloud' to mean 'a large, winged reptile that breathes fire.' That shadow was, if I am not mistaken, Verne, the very same dragon you have encountered twice on your journey already."

Wyngalf groaned and turned to look out at the harbor, where the *Numinda Fae* had just left the dock. Squinting against the evening sun, he could just make out a winged creature that seemed to be heading directly for the ship. "Evena!" he cried.

"It would indeed appear that Verne somehow managed to ascertain the whereabouts of—"

But Wyngalf had already gotten up from the table, and was stumbling toward the door. Tobalt went to him and helped him outside. As the cool breeze off the bay struck his face, Wyngalf's head cleared somewhat. He steadied himself and then ran toward the ship, which was now a stone's throw from the dock. The great bat-like form of Verne the dragon hung suspended above the ship, flapping its wings.

"Simply Wyngalf!" Tobalt called after him. "Forgive me for failing to see the wisdom in your actions, but I admit to being a bit curious as to what exactly you...." But the rest of his words were lost in the breeze and the clomping of Wyngalf's boots on the dock. He skidded to a halt at the end of the deck and watched helplessly as Verne lowered himself to within a few yards of the *Numinda Fae*. The crew stood on the deck, paralyzed with fear. Evena had to be among them, but Wyngalf didn't see her.

"It has come to my attention," Verne's voice boomed across the bay—and anyone in the vicinity who wasn't already agape at the scene now turned to face him—"that amongst this ship's passengers is a young woman who has not been cleared for travel from this port. This is the third serious breach in customs regulations this week, and I'm afraid I can't allow such abuses to continue. I'm going to have to incarcerate you."

Wyngalf heard snippets of confused discussion from the ship.

"I don't have all day," said Verne after a moment, still hovering just off the ship's bow, "Get off the ship or you'll be incarcerated."

More confused babbling on the ship. Wyngalf saw a few of the men move toward the railing, but none of them seemed very eager to jump into the bay. A few of them put their hands up.

"Your choice," said Verne, and he craned his head back as if taking a deep breath.

"Jump!" cried Wyngalf from the dock. "Get off the ship!"

Around half of the thirty or so men on the deck seemed to have a sense of what was coming. Maybe a dozen of them managed to get over the railing before the fire came. The cone of flame swept over the deck, engulfing the men and tearing through the sails. The blast lasted only a few seconds, but it was enough to set the whole ship aflame. Those that could get to the bay did, while the others died, flailing and screaming. It was a ghastly sight. But Wyngalf forced himself to keep watching, looking for some sign of Evena.

"Dreadful," said a voice next to him, which he was dimly aware belonged to Tobalt. "My knowledge of such matters is, of course, largely academic, but I would be hard-pressed to name a method of execution more agonizing than dragonfire. Although perhaps the survivors are more to be pitied, as they—"

"Shut up, Tobalt!" Wyngalf growled. "Look for Evena!"

"I beg your forgiveness, Simply Wyngalf," said Tobalt, squinting in the bright sunlight. "I'm afraid my instinctual reaction to traumatic circumstances is to retreat to the realm of the theoretical in an attempt to blunt the effect of the—"

"Tobalt! Shut your face and help me find Evena!"

"Many apologies," said Tobalt. "She's over there." Tobalt was pointing to a dot bobbing in the water about fifty feet past the flaming wrecking of the *Numinda Fae*. Only her head was visible—and that only intermittently—but it was clearly Evena. She seemed to be struggling to remain afloat.

Wyngalf slipped off his boots and unbuckled his scabbard. He handed it to Tobalt. "Hold this," he said.

"Forgive me for my presumptuousness," said Tobalt, taking the scabbard, "but perhaps in your present condition—"

Wyngalf dove into the water.

Thirteen

Wyngalf's memories of what happened next were fuzzy. A shock of cold, and then a blur of flailing about and gulping salt water. Somehow he must have eventually made it to Evena, because there was a lot of kicking and scratching at one point. The next thing he knew, he was doubled over on a sandy beach, retching up an unpleasant mélange of fish, beer and seawater. Once his stomach was empty and he could breathe freely, he rolled onto his back, exhausted. His head was killing him, and he closed his eyes against the glare of the evening sun.

A shadow passed over him, and for a moment he thought Verne was going to finish him off. But as he opened his eyes, he was relieved to see that it was just Tobalt, still holding the scabbard and sword. Standing next to him, looking bedraggled but otherwise unharmed, was Evena. He smiled. "I... rescued you," he murmured.

"I rescued *you*, you idiot," said Evena. "I was trying to help one of the ship's mates to shore, but when you started pawing at me I had to let him go just to keep my head above water. We only survived because you eventually passed out. I dragged you all the way here."

Wyngalf frowned. "So the man you were helping...?"

"Drowned," said Evena. "But don't feel too bad. I don't think he was going to make it anyway. Only twenty or so made it to shore, and many of them are badly burned."

Wyngalf sat up and looked around. They were on a small beach just north of the docks. Around them were members of the crew who had made it ashore. Several of them lay on their backs, moaning, while others tended to them. In the distance, Wyngalf could hear the occasional scream. In the bay, the wreckage of the *Numinda Fae* continued to burn. He was about to ask where Verne had gone when he felt a familiar breeze kicking up sand around them. A moment later, the dragon alighted on the beach in front of them. Nearby, men screamed and shouted, and those that were able ran. But Wyngalf just sighed. He managed to pull himself to his feet, with Evena and Tobalt helping him.

"Curse you, dragon!" Wyngalf growled, ignoring the pounding in his head and the churning in his gut. "What gives you the right to say who leaves this port? What gives you the right to kill men whose only crime was trying to earn an honest living?"

"Hey," said Verne, holding up his claws in a mock-defensive gesture, "Don't blame me. I *told* them I was going to incarcerate them."

"*Incinerate* them," snapped Wyngalf. "You breathe fire, for Shotarr's sake. Learn the blasted word. *Incarcerate* means you're going to put them in prison."

Verne smacked his forehead with the back of his claw. "No wonder they didn't jump earlier," he said. "Incinerate, incinerate, incinerate. Got it. So, what are you guys up to?"

"I *was* trying to get home," Evena snarled. "But you knew that."

"I may have heard something to the effect," said Verne. "If it makes you feel better, you almost got away with it, thanks to that dimwitted clerk. He was under strict instructions to alert me of any young women seeking passage across the Sea of Dis, but the man has the memory of a brain-damaged squirrel. Fortunately, my good friend Lord Popper thought he might get in my good graces by telling me about a change in the management of the local shipping guild office earlier this morning."

"If you wanted to stop me," Evena snapped, "why didn't you just tell the ship to turn around? Or pluck me right off the ship? Why did you have to kill all those people?"

Verne shrugged. "I need to make a dramatic demonstration once in a while to remind the locals who's in charge. And as an added bonus, no captain in Skaal City is going to let you within a hundred yards of his ship in the near future. I'm afraid you'll be sticking around for a while, my dear. Try not to take it personally. It's just business."

"It's not business!" Evena cried. "It's extortion!"

"I suppose," said Verne absently. "Seems like a semantic distinction to me. Anyhoo, I should get going. Got some villages in the east to terrorize tonight. Busy, busy, busy!" He raised his wings as if to fly away.

"I'm going to kill you," said Wyngalf quietly.

Verne dropped his wings and cocked his head toward Wyngalf. "I'm sorry," he said. "Could you repeat that? I didn't quite hear you."

"Come closer then," said Wyngalf, his lips curling in a slightly deranged smile. Evena and Tobalt stared at him. He felt a pinch on his right arm just below the shoulder which he vaguely realized was Evena's fingernails digging into his flesh.

Verne smiled and craned his neck to bring his head closer to Wyngalf, as if amused at Wyngalf's seething anger. Wyngalf could feel the dragon's hot breath on his face, and he saw now that the crazy old warrior Orbrecht had been telling the truth: Verne favored his right eye. The left eyeball never moved, and it had a slightly hazy appearance to it. One jab to his good eye and Verne would be completely blind.

Wyngalf laughed maniacally. "What, you aren't frightened of me, are you? Come closer, so we can talk man to man. Or man to dragon, as the case may be."

Verne hesitated a moment, but then obliged, moving his head even closer. Whatever suspicion he had about Wyngalf's behavior was outweighed by his curiosity. His teeth were now just inches from Wyngalf's nose, and his eye was within reach of sword point—if Wyngalf could only get the sword from Tobalt, who stood quaking in terror on his left. He was clutching the scabbard in his left hand, its tip resting in the sand.

"Now," said Verne, his breath like a furnace on Wyngalf's face, "were you making some sort of *threat*, Simply Wyngalf?"

"Not a threat," said Wyngalf, grinning. "More of a promise."

The dragon chuckled, and his good eye glittered at Wyngalf. Wyngalf glanced at Tobalt, who remained oblivious both to Verne's weakness and Wyngalf's plan. If only Tobalt were holding the sword on his right side! It was going to be a mean feat to get to the sword and lunge at Verne's eye before the dragon could react. He'd have a better chance if he could get Tobalt to turn around. He couldn't very well ask Tobalt to hand him the sword and still expect to take Verne by surprise.

"A promise!" exclaimed Verne. "Oh, this is exciting. And when will this momentous event occur? I want to make sure my affairs are all in order before I'm, you know, slain."

"Soon," said Wyngalf. "Be assured of that."

Verne's good eye remained fixed on him, and the dragon's mouth fell open. Wyngalf wasn't sure if the dragon was about to laugh in his face or engulf them in fire—or do both, simultaneously. Wyngalf could only hope that his need to keep Evena alive and unharmed was greater than his desire to eliminate Wyngalf as a threat. She stood silently at his right, her fingers clutching Wyngalf's bicep ever tighter. Tobalt stood to Wyngalf's left, quaking so violently that Wyngalf could hear the goblin's bones vibrating. Wyngalf was just thinking that this was the longest Tobalt had ever been silent in his presence when the goblin spoke, his voice quavering and faint.

"I'll be the first to admit that my experience in such matters is limited," Tobalt ventured, his voice quavering, "but perhaps antagonizing the fire-breathing dragon is not the most advisable course of action."

"You should listen to your goblin friend," said Verne. "He's got a good head on his shoulders. For now." Verne turned to face Tobalt and snapped his teeth together menacingly. Tobalt looked like he was about to bolt.

"Don't worry, Tobalt," said Wyngalf. "Verne's not going to bite your head off."

"No?" said Verne, focusing his eye again on Wyngalf.

"No," said Wyngalf.

"And why, pray tell, not?"

"Because goblin heads taste terrible," said Wyngalf. "What you want to do is slow roast him around the middle. This part here—" He poked Tobalt in the belly with his finger. "—is good eatin'."

Tobalt's face was rapidly going pale. "I don't mean to be presumptuous..." he began, but trailed off, unable to complete the thought.

"You don't say," said Verne, regarding Tobalt's belly. "Still, it's hardly worth the trouble. I could swallow him in one bite." He snapped his jaws at Tobalt again, and that was about all the goblin could take. His eyes rolled up and he collapsed onto the sand. Wyngalf had actually been hoping Tobalt would make a run for it, but this would do. As the goblin fell, Wyngalf leaned toward him as if trying to catch him. Supporting Tobalt's weight for a moment with his left hand, he reached behind the goblin's back and grasped the hilt of the sword. As he drew it, he let Tobalt fall, and then lunged toward Verne.

His aim was perfect, but he was a split-second too slow. Verne blinked, and the tip of the sword bounced harmlessly off the dragon's armored eyelid. Only the faintest scratch on the surface of the scales was visible. Verne reared his head back, out of range of Wyngalf's blade. Undaunted, Wyngalf stood with his sword pointed firmly at the dragon's head. If he was going to die, he was going to die with the sword in his hand.

Verne he began to laugh. "Poor Wyngalf," said the dragon with mock pathos. "It seems you're an even worse swordsman than a preacher."

The point of Wyngalf's sword wavered.

"Oh, I forgot to mention it the other day, didn't I?" said Verne. "I did a little research on you. Had a nice conversation with Evena's father, the fish merchant, when I was in Skuldred. He was rather troubled that you ran off with his only daughter and then allowed her to fall into the clutches of a dragon."

"You lie," growled Wyngalf. "I had nothing to do with Evena stowing away on that ship, and Evena's father knows it."

"I may have stoked his suspicions about you a bit," Verne admitted. "He called you all sorts of names, most of which have slipped my mind. The only ones I can recall off the top of my head are 'scoundrel,' 'rascal,' and 'poor addition to my investment portfolio.'"

"That does sound like my father," Evena admitted.

"You made such an impression on him that I decided to do a little research," Verne continued. "I inquired at a few nearby towns, and after the locals had finished screaming and running in circles, a few of them acknowledged that they remembered you. Well, at first they didn't know what I was talking about. I kept asking about a traveling preacher named Wyngalf, but all I got blank stares. It wasn't until I thought to describe you as a 'wandering imbecile' that a few people thought they remembered you. It was the walk that clinched it, though."

"The walk?" asked Evena.

"Sure," said Verne. "Tell me you haven't noticed the way he walks." Verne straightened up on his rear haunches, and then craned his neck forward, dropped his wings and began a slow, shambling walk along the shore. When he'd gone a dozen paces or so, he turned around and shambled back toward them.

Wyngalf heard Evena stifling a laugh, and he turned to glare at her.

"What?" Evena said. "You have to admit, he nailed your walk."

"I do *not* walk like that!" Wyngalf fumed.

"The denizens of the towns along the western shore of the Sea of Dis beg to differ," said Verne. "The consensus is that you're a harmless wandering beggar who was most likely dropped on his head as a child. From a very tall tree. Repeatedly. Nobody seemed to have any idea that you were any sort of missionary, I'm sorry to report."

"The Jagged Coast wasn't ready for the good news of Noninitarianism!" said Wyngalf. "That's why my divine mission brought me to Dis."

"Unfortunately," said Verne, "this is where your 'divine mission' ends, Simpleton Wyngalf. As much as I'd like to keep Evena for leverage—and keep you and your goblin around for entertainment purposes—I'm beginning to think it's just not worth the trouble. I'll just have to rely on the threat of incarceration to—"

"Incineration!" shouted Wyngalf.

"Sorry, I'll have to rely on the threat of *incineration* to keep gold flowing from Skuldred. The hostage angle seemed like the logical play, but it's just too much work. Anyway, it's been nice knowing you. Now, you can run if you like, but I'll warn you that's just going to make it take longer. Your best bet is just to cower together in fear while I *incinerate* you." Wyngalf craned his neck back and opened his mouth wide. Wyngalf dropped the sword and clamped his eyes shut, squeezing Evena tightly.

"Wait!" cried Evena. "If you keep us alive, I can make it worth your while!"

Verne paused, regarding her dubiously. "And what do you have to offer me, dear, that I don't already have?"

"A treasure hidden in the town of Skuldred," Evena said. "An extremely valuable jewel that is hidden under a cobblestone on of one of the streets."

"Nonsense," said Verne. "Why would anyone hide a jewel under a street? Desperation does not become you, dear."

"There's a bit of a story behind it," said Evena.

"I do love a good story," said Verne thoughtfully. "I suppose I could delay incinerating you while you tell the story. All right, out with it."

Evena nodded and cleared her throat.

"Any time now, dear," said Verne.

Evena smiled nervously and took a deep breath. "An emissary from a kingdom in the north was traveling through Skuldred many years ago on his way to visit a prince in the south," she began. "He had on him a priceless jewel that he was instructed to give as a gift to the prince, in order to secure an alliance against a third kingdom, to the west."

"And he hid the jewel under a cobblestone?" Verne interrupted. "Ridiculous."

Evena went on, undeterred. "A plague happened to be sweeping through Skuldred at the time the emissary and his entourage arrived in town, and the entire entourage was stricken. With his bodyguards weakened, the emissary was afraid the locals would overcome him and steal the jewel, so at night he sneaked out and hid it under a cobblestone of one of the city streets. But when the emissary himself fell ill, he began to worry that the location of the jewel would die with him. So as he lay on his death bed, he told the secret to three members of his entourage, in three parts: he told the first man the name of the street; he told the second man how many paces to walk from the beginning of the street; and he told the third man how many cobblestones to traverse from the edge of the street. Now the emissary picked these particular men because he knew they hated each other and would be unlikely to cooperate to steal the jewel for themselves. He expected that if he were to die, the three servants would return to the king in the north and pass along the information that he had given them. The king would then be able to send another emissary to retrieve the jewel."

Verne still looked skeptical, but she definitely had his interest now.

"The emissary died the next day, and of his entourage, only the three servants entrusted with the location of the jewel remained alive. The three decided that two of them should remain in Skuldred to guard the jewel and one of them should return to the king. But each of the three servants was afraid to leave town, thinking the other two would work together to find the jewel—for with any two pieces of the puzzle, the jewel could be located by spending a few days overturning cobblestones. So the three servants took up residence in Skuldred, each of them taking on some sort of menial work to support himself while he waited for the others to make their move. But none of them ever left, and none dared to start looking for the jewel out of fear of tipping off the other two about what he knew. In time, they all became respected members of the community, took wives, and had families. The three servants died within a few months of each other, and it's generally thought that their secrets died with them. But I never believed it. I was convinced that the three servants would have passed down their secrets to their heirs. Due to my father's position, I have a fair amount of influence in the town, and over the past three years I managed to locate two of the men's heirs and confirm that they know two of the three secrets. The third heir took a bit more work to find, but I finally located him just a few weeks ago. I'm the only one who knows who the three heirs are."

"So you know where the jewel is?" asked Verne dubiously.

"No," Evena replied. "I only know who the heirs are. I was never able to get any of them to talk to me. As wealthy as my father is, no amount of money could persuade them to talk, and I have no other form of leverage to use on them. I can't very well threaten to incinerate them."

Verne cocked his head at her. "Which one is that again?"

"The burning one," said Evena.

"Oh, right!" said Verne. "And I can, is that it? You happen to have just enough information to allow me to get the jewel, but not enough to get it yourself?"

"Exactly," said Evena. "That's why I ran away with Wyngalf. I'd spent three years trying to solve this mystery, but when I solved it, I still couldn't get the prize. Strolling down the streets of Skuldred, knowing that I'd probably walked right over it a dozen times, was too much for me. I decided to seek my fortune elsewhere."

"It's a preposterous story," said Verne. "Honestly, I don't think I've ever heard anything so ridiculous." But something in the dragon's voice told them he wanted to believe it.

"You wouldn't be the first to doubt it," said Evena. "Very few in Skuldred today acknowledge that just beneath their feet lies a treasure of inestimable value."

Verne cocked his good eye toward her. "*How* inestimable?" he asked.

"*Extremely* inestimable," said Evena. "You know that chest of gold you carried across the sea yesterday? The Jewel of Skuldred is worth at least twenty of those."

"Twenty!" exclaimed Verne, in awe.

"And that's being conservative," said Evena. "Some experts think it might be worth as much as a million gold pieces."

"A million!" cried Verne, flapping his wings in excitement. Then he grew suddenly somber again: "You're certain the story is true?"

"I swear on my life that everything I've told you is true," said Evena. "And I'm willing to give you the names of the three heirs, *if* you let us live."

Verne studied her for a moment. "And this isn't some kind of elaborate hoax to keep me from incinerating you?"

"Absolutely not," said Evena. "Cross my heart."

"Okay," said Verne. "Because if it is, I'll come back and kill you in a much slower, more painful manner."

"No danger of that," said Evena. "Since I'm telling the absolute honest-to-the-Noninity truth."

"It had better be, for your sake."

"It is."

"Great!" exclaimed Verne. "It's a deal. What are the names?"

"Ashor, Wiggin, and Brisby," said Evena. "Can you remember that? Just go to the town square and ask to see Ashor, Wiggin and Brisby."

"Ashor, Wiggin and Brisby," said Verne. "Got it." He spread his wings and then paused. "Hey, how do you know I won't kill you now that you've told me?"

"Because you want to make sure I was telling the truth, remember? If I lied to you, you were going to kill us slowly and painfully."

"Right!" said Verne. "Good point. Okay, wait here. I'll be back tomorrow to make you regret you were ever born if you lied to me. Which you didn't."

"Nope," said Evena. "That story was one hundred percent true."

"Glad to hear it," said Verne. "Because none of us is going to enjoy the weeks of agony I plan on subjecting you to if you've lied to me. Well, see you when I get back!" He spread his wings again and shot into the sky. Wyngalf and Evena watched him disappear into the sunset. Next to them, Tobalt sat up in the sand.

"That was a fascinating story," Tobalt said quietly. "If you don't mind my asking, though, is any of it true?"

"Not a word," said Evena. "Ashor, Wiggin and Brisby were three dogs my father owned when I was a child."

Fourteen

"Are you *crazy*?" asked Wyngalf. Now that Verne was gone, he was suddenly aware of the pounding in his head and the queasiness in his stomach. "You lied to Verne about the treasure in Skuldred? Do you have any idea what he'll do to us when he finds out?"

"You're welcome!" snapped Evena. "If I hadn't made up that story, we'd be dead already."

"At least he'd have killed us quickly!" cried Wyngalf. "When he gets back, he's going to slowly roast us to death, probably over several days, if not weeks. There's no place to hide from him. We might as well swim out into the bay and drown ourselves. And have you thought about what he's going to do to your hometown when he finds out this jewel of inestimable value doesn't exist?"

"Of *course* I've thought about it!" said Evena. "I've been thinking about nothing but Verne razing my home ever since you told him where it was. But unlike you, I refuse to give in to my fears. Verne can kill everyone I love, anytime he feels like it. If I let my fear of what Verne will do control my actions, then I may as well be dead already. At least now I've bought us some time."

"Time to do *what*?" asked Wyngalf. "Sit here and wait for our inevitable doom?"

"So much for your faith in the all-powerful Nonentity," Evena sneered.

"Even Saint Roscow despaired in the face of abject stupidity!" Wyngalf snapped. Evena stared daggers at him.

"If I may be so bold," Tobalt said, "while I certainly sympathize with Wyngalf's concerns, and while I enjoy a hearty philosophical debate, particularly one that highlights the differences between a consequentialist view of ethics and a deontological perspective, the exigent manner of our current circumstances would seem to demand that proportionately more attention be given to determinations yet to be made."

"He's saying we should stop arguing and focus on what to do next," said Evena.

"I know what he's saying!" Wyngalf snapped.

"Excuse me," said a fourth voice, and they turned as one to face a small, gray-haired woman who had come up behind them. "I couldn't help but overhear your exchange with Verne. That was extremely brave of you."

"Thank you," said Wyngalf and Evena in unison, then turned to glare at each other.

"Both of you," said the woman. "It's been a long time since I've seen anyone stand up to Verne like that. Makes me nostalgic for the days of my youth. I was part of the resistance to the dragon's takeover of Skaal City. My name is Glindeen."

"Nice to meet you, Glindeen," said Evena. "I'm Evena. These are my friends, Tobalt and Wyngalf. Wyngalf is the ugly one."

Tobalt smiled sheepishly at her remark, while Wyngalf did his best to ignore it.

Glindeen nodded at Wyngalf and then turned to face Tobalt, her eyes wide with interest. "A goblin!" she cried. "How wonderful!" Addressing Tobalt in a loud and excessively enunciated manner, she said, "Hello, dear! How are you!"

"I'm quite well, given the circumstances, Madam," said Tobalt, "and might I add that I'm gratified by your—"

"Oh my, he's adorable!" said Glindeen. "I love subhumanoid races. They have so much to offer, don't you think?" She was now back to addressing Wyngalf and Evena. Forgotten, Tobalt folded his arms glumly in front of him.

"You were one of those who fought with Orbrecht against Verne?" Wyngalf asked.

"That old nut?" said the woman with a scowl. "No, Orbrecht's methods were a bit extreme for me. My friends and I hoped to find a peaceful resolution to the dragon problem."

"A peaceful resolution?" asked Wyngalf. "What do you mean?"

"We focused mostly on demonstrations and marches. One of our burn-ins had over three hundred participants."

"*Burn-ins?*"

"We rubbed red dye on our skin to make it look like we had been burned by dragon fire," Glindeen explained. "Then we lay down in the street and pretended to be dead for three hours."

"And this… helped somehow?" asked Wyngalf, puzzled.

"It was a generational thing," said Glindeen. "You kind of had to be there."

Wyngalf smiled politely and nodded.

"Anyway, these days we're a bit more practical in our means of resistance."

"We?" asked Evena. "Who is 'we'?"

"That's actually why I approached you," Glindeen said. "I'm one of the leaders of a group that is opposed to Verne's needless violence and provocation. We're about to have an emergency meeting in the wake of today's events, and I wanted to invite you."

Wyngalf glanced around at the survivors on the beach. Many were still lying on the sand, moaning in pain.

"A meeting?" Wyngalf asked. "Right now? It seems like your efforts might be better spent helping the survivors of the attack."

"We all have our jobs to do," said Glindeen curtly.

"And whose job is it to help these men?" asked Evena. She glanced at Wyngalf—a glance that said *I'm still mad at you, but you're right about this one thing.*

Glindeen shrugged. "The meeting will start shortly, in the back room of the Alewives Tavern. It would be good to have you there." She turned and walked away. The breeze picked up, carrying with it moans and screams of the injured.

"It seems kind of horrible to leave these men here like this," said Evena.

"Yes," said Wyngalf. "We should try to help them, as best we can."

"If I may interject," said Tobalt, "there is very little we can do for a single burn victim, let alone a score of them, given our lack of resources and medical supplies. Furthermore, we have perhaps one full day at our disposal before Verne returns, intent on ending our lives in the most agonizing way possible. Perhaps, given these facts, our time might be best spent attempting to resolve this quandary. If there truly is some sort of underground resistance movement afoot, attending this meeting might be our best chance for assuring our long-term survival."

Wyngalf and Evena took another look around and reluctantly agreed. There wasn't much they could do for these men, and if they were going to live for more than another day, they needed to find some leverage to use against Verne—or at least find a way to get out of town without him finding out about it.

Wyngalf turned to see Glindeen making her way up the seaside road toward a dilapidated building they took to be the Alewives Tavern. "All right," he said, "let's see what this meeting is all about."

By the time they got to the tavern, Glindeen was already inside. On the door to the back room of the tavern a sign had been tacked up that read:

Emergency meeting of the Society Against Unnecessary Reptilian Invasions And Negligence

"SAURIAN," said Wyngalf, sounding out the acronym. "That seems like an ill-advised choice."

"It's just a name, Wyngalf," said Evena. "Not everybody is obsessed with finding hidden meanings in texts."

"I confess to being a bit puzzled at the inclusion of 'Negligence,'" Tobalt added.

"They probably just needed another word to make the acronym work," said Evena.

"So they deliberately made it spell *SAURIAN*?" said Wyngalf.

"Stop overthinking it, you guys," said Evena. "We're late." She opened the door.

The meeting was just coming to order. It consisted of roughly two dozen men and women seated in chairs in a rough circle. Glindeen smiled as they stepped inside, and then she introduced a gaunt young man with short hair and a long, scraggly beard named Dwalen. Dwalen stood up in the center of the room and launched into a lengthy tirade about the unnecessary death and suffering Verne had caused. Wyngalf had to admire the man's skill at oration, but the speech seemed a little too polished to have been written in the wake of the afternoon's tragedy. Wyngalf got the sense he had delivered the speech many times before, and simply updated certain sections with references to recent events to keep it sounding somewhat fresh. Those in attendance seemed to be faking enthusiasm with varying degrees of success. While he talked, Wyngalf and his companions helped themselves to hors d'oeuvres from a table at the back of the room.

When Dwalen finally sat down, Glindeen thanked him and then directed the group's attention to the newcomers. "Everyone, this is Wyngalf and Evena," she said. "They come from across the sea!" Impressed and—Wyngalf thought—possibly dubious murmurs arose from the crowd. "And look," Glindeen added, "they've brought a goblin with them!"

Several of the attendees made approving sounds. Those near Wyngalf and Evena greeted them cordially, doing their best to pretend not to notice their seawater-drenched clothes. Several of them smiled uncertainly at Tobalt, as if he were some sort of exotic but harmless animal. "Hello there," said one man, reaching out to pat Tobalt on the head.

"I'd be much obliged," said Tobalt, "if you would refrain from doing that."

The man chuckled. "Feisty little guy, aren't you?"

Tobalt glared at him.

"I think the subhumanoid races have so much to offer," Glindeen gushed to a group of onlookers to her left. "Don't you?"

Murmurs of enthusiastic agreement were heard. "*So* much to offer," echoed another woman.

"Yes, well," said Tobalt. "I suppose each race has its respective fortes, and without resorting to stereotypes, I can confirm that goblins, generally speaking, are—"

"Wyngalf, dear," said Glindeen, with a smile, "Could you please instruct your goblin to be quiet during the proceedings? We have to maintain a certain level of decorum, after all."

"You can tell him yourself," said Wyngalf. "He's standing right in front of you."

"Of course!" exclaimed Glindeen. She turned somewhat uncertainly toward Tobalt. "Be *quiet*, goblin," she instructed. "The humans are talking."

Tobalt opened his mouth as if to say something, but then closed it again. He fumed silently, his fists clutched at his sides.

"You'll have to forgive their somewhat disheveled appearance," said Glindeen to the group. "Wyngalf and Evena were present during the tragic events that occurred this evening." Tobalt, forgotten, slinked away to a corner.

"Goodness," said the man who had patted Tobalt. "That must have been terrifying. Were you on the *Numinda Fae*?"

"I was," said Evena. "Wyngalf swam out to rescue me." She glanced at Wyngalf, and he acknowledged the ambiguity in her words with an appreciative nod.

"How terrible," said the head-patter.

"So you know first-hand how bad it's gotten," said Dwalen, the scruffy-bearded man who had spoken earlier.

"Yes, we do," said Wyngalf. "And that wasn't our first encounter with Verne. We saw what he did to the town of Sybesma."

Sympathetic murmurs arose. "We've heard about what he did to Sybesma," said Glindeen. "A clear case of negligence, if ever there was one."

"*Negligence?*" asked Evena. "It seemed like a lot more than negligence. He razed the entire town."

"Well, yes," said Glindeen. "But I doubt that was Verne's intention. Sometimes he gets a little over-exuberant. And that brings us to our next matter of business. Hendrick, could you make sure the door is locked?"

The head-patter nodded and went to the door, securing a small deadbolt lock.

"Dwalen," said Glindeen, "do you have it?"

Dwalen regarded her uncertainly. "Are you sure we can trust them, Glindeen?" He turned to face Wyngalf. "No offense, but we just met you, and we know that Verne has spies throughout this town."

"I saw them stand up to Verne," Glindeen said. "I'll vouch for them. Wyngalf, why don't you tell us what happened?"

Wyngalf did his best to explain what had occurred at the harbor, without going into too much detail about their history with Verne.

"It's all true," Glindeen said. "I saw it myself."

"They could have staged that whole scene," said Dwalen. "We can't risk letting *it* fall into his hands at this point."

"We have no choice," said Glindeen. "The time for caution has passed. We can't allow another incident like this. We must act!"

Dwalen nodded. "All right," he said. "But let's make it official. Glindeen, do you nominate Evena and Wyngalf for full membership in the Society Against Unnecessary Reptilian Invasions And Negligence?

"I do," said Glindeen.

"I'll second the nomination," said Hendrick.

"Hold on," said Evena. "What does that mean exactly? What are the obligations of membership?"

"It's just a formality, dear," said Glindeen. "It extends to you the protection of the Society and allows us to share with you—" She glanced at Dwalen. "—certain sensitive documents that are crucial to our resistance against Verne's aggressions."

"Can we have a moment to talk it over?" Wyngalf asked.

"Of course," said Glindeen. "But please be quick about it. Time is of the essence."

Wyngalf and Evena retreated to the corner, where Tobalt had been glumly observing the proceedings.

"Allow me to apologize in advance for my admittedly goblin-centric appraisal of what is clearly a uniquely human sort of gathering," said Tobalt as they approached, "but I think these people are assholes."

"I don't like them either," said Evena. "There's something off about them."

"I agree," said Wyngalf. "But I don't see that we have much choice. Without some help from the Society, we'll all be at Verne's mercy by tomorrow night. They seem to be plotting something pretty big. Maybe they can actually stop Verne, or at least help us get out of town before he returns."

"So we accept their offer?" asked Evena.

"On one condition," said Wyngalf. "They accept *all* of us."

Tobalt nodded appreciatively. "While I have my misgivings about this group, I am in agreement that joining them offers our best chance for survival past the morrow. Further, it seems to me that our chances are augmented by acting in concert, and I'm gratified that my subhumanoid status has not blinded you to that fact."

"You're welcome," said Wyngalf. "Okay, let's tell them."

The three of them walked back to Glindeen, who was conferring quietly with several of the other members. "Have you made a decision?" she asked as they approached.

"Yes," said Wyngalf. "We'd like to be part of your group. But you have to accept Tobalt as well."

"Tobalt?" asked Glindeen, puzzled.

"Our goblin," said Wyngalf.

"Oh, it has a name!" cried Glindeen. "How delightful. Of course your goblin can join. The subhumanoid races have—"

"So much to offer, yes," said Evena. Glindeen beamed at her.

"Okay," said Dwalen. "Let's vote. All in favor of inducting Wyngalf, Evena and their goblin into the Society Against Unnecessary Reptilian Invasions And Negligence?"

Over a dozen hands went up, including Glindeen's and Dwalen's.

"All opposed?"

A few hands went up in the back.

"Congratulations!" Glindeen exclaimed. "Welcome to the Society!"

Several of the members went forward to congratulate Evena and Wyngalf, and to pat Tobalt on the head.

"I'm afraid we'll have to save the rest of the introductions and congratulations for later," said Glindeen. "We've got pressing business to attend to. Dwalen?"

Dwalen nodded solemnly and pulled a leather binder from inside his coat. He handed it to Glindeen, who opened it to reveal a sheet of paper with several lines of writing at the top. Below the writing was a list of signatures. She held it out for Wyngalf and Evena to see.

"What's this?" asked Evena, studying the text.

"It's a petition of grievances," said Glindeen proudly.

Wyngalf squinted at the text at the top of the page. It was written in a flowery script that was difficult to read, but he could make out several phrases, including "extremely disappointed," "a thorough review of these events," and "appropriate safeguards be adopted." Below this were two columns of horizontal lines, numbered from one to 100. Someone had signed his or her name next to every line through 87.

"I don't understand," said Wyngalf. "What is the point of this?"

"You have to sign it," said Glindeen, motioning toward another woman, who was approaching with a quill and a jar of ink. "You and Evena, I mean. Your goblin can dip one of his fingers in the ink and make a smudge on the line if he wants." She smiled at Tobalt, and he glared back at her. "When we get to 100 signatures," she continued, "we're going to present it to Verne."

"And then what?" asked Evena.

"What do you mean?" asked Glindeen, furrowing her brow. She pulled the petition away and folded the binder under her arm.

"I mean, what happens after you present it to Verne?"

"That's up to Verne," said Glindeen. Dwalen and several of the others nodded in assent.

"Right," said Wyngalf, "but what happens if he doesn't meet your demands? What are the consequences for failing to comply?"

Nervous chuckles arose from the group.

Glindeen smiled. "I think you have a somewhat naïve idea of how things work here," she said. "When Verne set up this system—"

"*Verne* set up the system?" exclaimed Evena.

"Of course," said Glindeen. "As I was saying, when Verne set up this system, he wisely provided a means for the citizens of Skaal to express any concerns they have about his rule. He promised that if a petition reaches 100 signatures he would read it, consider it very seriously, and respond publicly."

Wyngalf and Evena simply stared at her, dumbstruck. Eventually, Tobalt spoke up.

"Pardon the intrusion," he said, "but if I might make an inquiry: if Verne is cognizant of this process, what is the rationale for the clandestine nature of these proceedings?"

Glindeen regarded Tobalt as if he had just vomited a hairball onto the carpet. She turned to Wyngalf. "I'm sorry," she said. "Could you tell me what your goblin is babbling on about?"

Wyngalf answered, "He's asking why you bother with the secrecy if Verne knows all about the petition process."

"Oh!" said Glindeen. "We thought it would be nice if it were a surprise."

"It will have more punch if he doesn't see it coming," Dwalen explained. "He'll be all like, 'Wow, where did *that* come from?'"

"When he sees how serious we are," Hendrick added, "we're confident he'll adopt some changes in his methods."

Evena was still speechless. Tobalt simply shook his head. "And if he doesn't?" asked Wyngalf.

"Well," said Glindeen, trading glances with Hendrick and Dwalen. "We were hoping it wouldn't come to this, but some of us have been talking about organizing another burn-in. Dwalen is part of a musical theater troupe, and he can get us some makeup."

"We're dead," murmured Evena. "Verne is going to torture us to death."

"Don't be silly, dear," said Glindeen. "Verne doesn't torture people. The absolute worst he'll do to you is slowly burn you to death, one layer of flesh at a time."

"That's a fairly subtle distinction," said Tobalt. Glindeen ignored him.

"This is insane," said Wyngalf. "You understand that Verne is a murdering psychopath, right? He's not going to stop his reign of terror because you hand him a sheet of paper! When you invited us here, we assumed you had some plan for stopping Verne. A way to kill him, or—"

Gasps of shock arose from the group.

"Kill Verne!" Glindeen exclaimed. "My goodness, now you sound like that lunatic Orbrecht. I'm sorry if you've misunderstood our purpose here, but that isn't the sort of group we're running. We believe in working for change within the system."

"The system that Verne set up," said Evena.

"Listen to me, dear," said Glindeen, the amicable tone in her voice having turned harsh. "We've been in Skaal City a lot longer than you three. We've seen the terrible things Verne has done. But we've also seen the good that he does. Sure, he incinerates a ship once in a while, but ninety-nine times out of a hundred, ships depart from that port without incident. And frankly, If you hadn't gone aboard without proper documentation—"

"You've got to be kidding me," said Evena. "I was fleeing for my life."

"Because you antagonized Verne," said Glindeen. "Don't get me wrong; I admire the way you stood up to him. But that resistance has to be directed through the proper channels. It's pointless to try to confront Verne directly. And have you thought of what would happen if you succeeded? Let's suppose we all go home, get our hands on whatever weapons we can find, and all confront Verne at once. Let's further suppose that by some miracle Verne is actually cowed by our demonstration of solidarity, and he flees to his lair in the Kovac Mountains, never to be seen again. Then what?"

"I don't understand the question," said Evena.

"Well, have you thought about what Skaal City would look like after Verne is no longer in control? He's been the ultimate authority in this region for as long as anybody can remember. Can you imagine the chaos that would ensue if he were just to disappear?"

"I suppose there might be some disorder in the short term," said Evena, "but eventually the people would sort things out."

"You have a much higher opinion of ordinary townsfolk than I do," said Glindeen. "People need order in their lives."

"Of course," Wyngalf interjected. "But there's no rule that says that order has to be enforced by a fire-breathing dragon!"

"Actually," said Dwalen, "there is." He took the binder from Glindeen, opened it, and pulled another document from under the petition. He held it out for Wyngalf and Evena to see. A heading at the top read:

RULES FOR SKAAL CITY

Below this was an enumerated list of twenty-six rules. Dwalen tapped his finger on number eight, which read:

Order is to be enforced by a fire-breathing dragon.

"Well," said Wyngalf, "he's got you there."

"I suppose Verne wrote this as well," said Evena.

"Of course," replied Glindeen. "Look at number twelve, regarding the petitioning of grievances. It's actually a very well-thought-out system."

"I'm sure," said Evena. "Devised by Verne, with a mind to maximize Verne's wealth and power."

"Not at all," said Glindeen. "Many of the rules were actually written to provide for the welfare of Skaal City's residents. For example, number twenty-three: once a year, Verne is required to fly over the city's slums and drop gold pieces in the streets for the poor. For a lot of those people, that's the majority of their income for the year. Would you really sentence those people to die just so that you can get rid of Verne?"

"Okay," said Wyngalf, "but the amount of gold he gives to the poor of Skaal City has to be a tiny fraction of his total horde—not to mention that the gold he's distributing was extorted from other citizens in the first place."

Hendrick frowned at this. "Can we agree not to use emotionally charged words like 'extorted?'" he asked.

Glindeen and Dwalen nodded, and several others murmured their agreement. "Yes," said Glindeen. "I don't see the point of such incendiary language."

"Incendiary language!" shouted Evena. "We're talking about an actual fire-breathing dragon who is threatening to burn us alive, and you're worried about incendiary *language*?"

"I'm not sure I like your tone," said Glindeen.

"Let's all try to remain calm," said Wyngalf. "There has to be a better way to address these problems. What if we went to the mayor and demanded that he stand up to Verne?"

"Feel free," said Glindeen, glancing at Dwalen, who smiled sheepishly.

"*You're* the mayor?" asked Wyngalf.

"That I am," said Dwalen, "and I have to say, you're quite right about Verne. I've see his uncouth behavior firsthand, and I'm as disappointed as anyone in the current government's response."

"You *are* the current government!" Evena cried.

"Yes," replied Dwalen, "which is why I'm spearheading this petition drive. Well, Glindeen is spearheading it, but I support her spearheading it one hundred percent. I'm sort of an honorary silent co-spearheader."

"A coward, in other words," said Evena.

"Would a coward personally deliver the petition to Verne?" Dwalen demanded.

"You're going to hand the petition to Verne?"

"Not exactly," said Dwalen. "I was going to just leave it somewhere he could find it."

"But you're signing it."

"It was decided that it would be better if no sitting government officials were directly connected to the petition," Dwalen explained. "But I support the goals of the petition unreservedly, albeit in an unofficial and behind-the-scenes manner. Please don't quote me on that."

"I think we're done here," said Evena.

She turned and headed toward the door. Wyngalf went after her, followed by Tobalt.

"So you're not going to sign the petition?" asked Glindeen.

Evena and Wyngalf kept walking, but Tobalt stopped and turned to face her. "I'll sign it," he said. "If you don't mind the primitive scribblings of a subhumanoid defacing your petition."

"Of course," said Glindeen. "The petition is open to all our members, regardless of race or other handicap."

Tobalt smiled and took the quill from the young woman who was still standing next to Glindeen. Glindeen opened the binder and held it up nervously for Tobalt. He dipped the quill in the ink, and wrote, in a graceful and confident hand:

Tobalt the Goblin

"Why, Tobalt," gasped Glindeen. "That's beautiful! You should be so proud of yourself."

"Very kind of you to say so," said Tobalt. "Mastering the skill of calligraphy required me to exert a great deal of effort to overcome the brutish simple-mindedness that is endemic to my race." Then, after handing the quill back to the woman, he stuck his thumb into the jar of ink and made a giant smudge on the paper next to his name. "Perhaps," he said, "it is not yet too late for you to do the same." He turned to follow his friends out the door.

Fifteen

"What a joke," said Evena, as they walked down the street away from the tavern. "Those people have no intention of doing anything about Verne's reign of terror."

"It would appear not," said Tobalt from behind her. It was unlikely that any of the residents hurrying home in the gathering gloom would notice or care that a goblin was wandering the streets, but Tobalt kept close behind his human companions just in case. Exhausted from the day's misadventures, the three had decided to return to the Battered Goblin and then get up before sunrise in an attempt to sneak out of the city without alerting any of Verne's spies. How they were going to manage this was unclear; Wyngalf could only hope that an idea would occur to him in the morning when he had his full wits about him. Leaving by the gate they had arrived through was probably a bad idea, as the city guards were undoubtedly agents of Verne. In fact, Wyngalf realized that was probably the only reason Tobalt had been allowed in the city in the first place: Verne had warned the guards they were coming. It would be much easier to keep track of them if they were inside the walls of Skaal City, where Verne had plenty of spies, rather than wandering around in the wilderness of Dis. Hopefully they could find a place where they could slip over the wall unseen, and then make their way as far north as they could before Verne returned from across the sea.

They had only made it a few dozen paces from the Alewives Tavern, though, when a man's voice called to them from behind. They spun around, shuffling Tobalt behind them as quickly as they could. The last thing they needed now was some goblin-hating hooligan to pick a fight with them. But they needn't have been concerned: the source of the voice was Hendrick, the man who had patted Tobalt's head at the meeting.

"I say, hold up!" the man cried, hurrying toward them. The three of them stood and watched as the man approached.

"If you don't mind," said Evena tiredly, "We have a long day of fleeing ahead of us, and we're not in a mood to listen to any more rubbish from the Society of Saurian Bootlickers."

"Seconded," said Wyngalf. "Peddle your petitions elsewhere, Hendrick."

Hendrick halted a few feet from them. "I don't blame you one bit for your disappointment with SAURIAN," he said, trying to catch his breath. "In fact, that's why I came after you."

"Explain yourself," Evena said. "Make it quick."

"I'm a spy," said Hendrick, and Wyngalf's hand went to his sword. Evena took a step back, and Tobalt bared his pointy teeth. "You misunderstand me!" Hendrick cried. "I'm not a spy for Verne. I secretly work for the true resistance *against* Verne. An organization called Skaal Merchants Against Saurian Hegemony."

The three of them stood for a moment, working out the acronym. "SMASH?" said Wyngalf.

"Because we want to smash Verne's grip on Skaal City," said Hendrick, pounding his right fist into his left palm. "We're forming an armed resistance to repel Verne's aggressions against the citizens of this city. I'm on my way to a meeting right now, and I'd love to have you accompany me."

Wyngalf and Evena traded glances.

"I know what you're thinking," said Hendrick. "But our meetings aren't like SAURIAN's. We don't screw around with petitions and pointless demonstrations. We're serious about fighting Verne. Come with me and you'll see."

Wyngalf regarded him skeptically. "So you're not just a toothless organization, trying to fight Verne while abiding by rules that Verne himself wrote?"

"Absolutely not," said Hendrick. "We believe in a higher law. Human beings were not meant to be subjugated by dragons. We resist Verne not with petitions but with the sword."

"We're not merchants," said Evena.

"Oh, that name is a bit of a holdover from our initial membership," said Hendrick. "Lately we've been trying to broaden our appeal beyond the merchant class. Your social status is no barrier to entry, I assure you."

"Well," said Wyngalf, "SMASH certainly sounds better than the other group. But I think we've decided we're better off just getting out of the city as quickly as possible."

"SMASH has considerable resources," said Hendrick, "but if you leave the city we can't protect you. SMASH is a Skaal-based organization devoted to advancing Skaalian interests. You can't get away from Verne by fleeing the city. If he wants to find you, he will. Your best bet is to stay here with us." Seeing that they remained dubious, he added, "Listen, just come with me to this meeting. If you don't want to join us, you can still leave in the morning. We won't keep you long."

Evena sighed heavily. "I suppose we can spare a few minutes," she said.

"I assume that our goblin..." Wyngalf began. "That is, I assume that our friend Tobalt is welcome?"

Hendrick bit his lip. "I'll be honest with you. SMASH's membership includes several veterans of the Frontier Wars, and many of them aren't keen on goblins. That said, I think that if I tell them how you stood up to Verne in the harbor, they'll overlook the fact that Tobalt is of an inferior race."

"Much obliged for your candidness and consideration," said Tobalt, with a slight bow. Hendrick smiled and looked for a moment like he was going to pat Tobalt on the head again, but a glare from Tobalt made him reconsider.

"Would you give us a moment to confer privately?" asked Wyngalf.

"Of course," said Hendrick. "But don't take long. We're already late."

Wyngalf nodded and the three of them huddled together while Hendrick stepped away.

"Speaking only for myself," said Tobalt, "I find the unabashed bigotry that evidently characterizes the membership of this coterie to be somewhat refreshing, particularly in light of our distasteful encounter with its rival organization."

"I agree," said Evena. "Hendrick is being much more up front with us about SMASH than Glindeen was about SAURIAN. Maybe these people really can help us. And he's right, we don't have much of a chance on our own. Even if we get outside the city without being seen and travel all day tomorrow, Verne will probably find us by sundown."

"All right," said Wyngalf, nodding. "We'll give them a chance."

They informed Hendrick of their decision, and he guided them down the street to a chandler's shop. Taking a key from behind a loose brick, Hendrick unlocked the door and let them inside. They followed him through the dark store to another door, which opened into a back room where perhaps a score of men and women stood in a room dimly light by lanterns on the walls. This group had a decidedly different feel from the SAURIANs. The attendees were well dressed and neatly coifed, and the meeting itself seemed like a much more ordered affair. Many of the men wore medals and ribbons that identified them as military veterans; the others appeared to be mostly upper class merchants and petty noblemen. Several members of all three contingents turned to glare disapprovingly at Tobalt as the three entered.

A small, short-haired woman with cold eyes and a terse mouth had been speaking when the door opened, but she stopped and addressed Hendrick. "You're late, Hendrick," she said. "And I see you've brought some... *guests* with you." The way she said the word, it didn't sound like she ever had guests if she could help it.

"Apologies for my tardiness, Havartis," said Hendrick. "And for the surprise guests. But I think you'll be very interested to hear from them when I tell you who they are."

"All right, then," said the woman, evidently named Havartis. "Let's hear it. You have the floor, Hendrick."

Hendrick moved to the head of the room, beckoning for the three companions to follow him. "Hello," he said to the group, who watched in stern silence. Several of them continued to stare menacingly at Tobalt. "As I think you all know, I was tasked with infiltrating the meetings of our rival group, known as SAURIAN." Hendrick paused a moment as well-practiced boos and hisses went up from the crowd. "Yes, yes," he said. "A cowardly and villainous lot, to be sure. I attended their most recent meeting just before arriving here, and as expected, they're up to their usual tricks. Petitions and demonstrations and whatnot. But there was one interesting development: Glindeen introduced the three individuals you see before you, and attempted to get them to join SAURIAN." More boos and hisses. "Yes, quite right. Scoundrels, all of them. You'll be happy to learn, however, that our three friends saw right through Glindeen's sales pitch, rightly concluding that her organization does little more than grant a veneer of respectability to Verne's tyranny."

"What were they doing at a SAURIAN meeting in the first place?" shouted a man in the back.

"Order, please!" Havartis snapped.

"It's quite all right," said Hendrick. "I don't blame you for being suspicious. Evidently, Glindeen witnessed them engaging in a rather bold confrontation with Verne himself at the harbor today. She mistakenly thought they would be sympathetic to the SAURIAN cause, but clearly they have a more realistic notion of the threat we face than she does. When they rebuffed Glindeen's offer, I went after them and invited them to this meeting. I think they would be excellent allies in our struggle against Verne."

Inconclusive murmurs arose from the audience.

"But perhaps I should let them speak for themselves," Hendrick said. "Everyone, this is Wyngalf, Evena, and their, uh, servant, Tobalt." Tobalt scowled slightly at this, but remained silent. "Wyngalf, would you be willing to say a few words? Perhaps explain to us exactly what happened at the harbor today?"

"Yes, well," Wyngalf began. "Evena was actually the cause of all the trouble." Evena shot a glare at him and he continued hurriedly, "That is, Verne sank that ship because she was on it. It wasn't her fault. Er, maybe she should explain it."

Evena rolled her eyes at him and began, "We came from the land across the Sea of Dis. I've been trying to get home, but Verne is extorting money from my father by holding me hostage here."

"What do you mean, holding you hostage?" asked a woman in the audience. "You don't want to be in Skaal City?" Murmurs of disapproval arose from the attendees.

"Don't get me wrong," said Evena. "It's a perfectly fine city, but I—"

"What I think our beautiful young guest is trying to say," Hendrick interrupted, "is that she *thought* she wanted to leave, but her confrontation with Verne made her realize that this is where she belongs." He turned to Evena. "Right, dear?"

Evena opened her mouth to object, but the nods and sounds of approval from the audience gave her pause. "Er, yes," she said. "I... love it here. In Skaal City."

Polite applause and more approving murmurs.

"As she was saying," Hendrick went on, "Evena had been kidnapped by pirates and was being forced to leave Skaal City when Verne attacked the ship she was on. She dove into the bay to avoid being killed. She would have drowned if her friend Wyngalf hadn't been nearby to rescue her. No sooner had they made it safely to shore than Verne accosted them. Tell us how you got him to leave you alone, Evena."

"Well," Evena started uncertainly. "I sort of tricked him into flying across the sea," she said. At this, the attendees burst into cheers and applause.

"I told you they would be good allies to have," said Hendrick. "That's the kind of bold individual initiative we admire in this organization."

Evena shot a puzzled glance at Wyngalf, who shrugged. It wasn't exactly clear what these people were cheering about, or why Hendrick felt the need to embellish Evena's story, but they still seemed more reasonable than the SAURIANs.

"As you can imagine," Hendrick said, "When Verne returns, he's not going to be very happy with our new friends. They're going to need our help. I move that we vote on whether to extend official SMASH protection to Wyngalf and Evena."

Murmurs of approval arose from the crowd.

"What about Tobalt?" asked Wyngalf.

Hendrick frowned. Uncertain murmurs arose from the crowd. "I don't believe our bylaws will permit us to extend protection to a goblin. He's welcome to stay with you and benefit from the protection we provide you and Evena, but we can't officially provide protection for him."

"I'm not sure I see the practical difference," said Wyngalf.

"What does this protection consist of, exactly?" asked Evena.

"Ah," said Hendrick with a smile. "I thought you might ask that." He turned to a young man in the front row. "Colin, could you give our guests a demonstration?"

The man nodded and walked to the back of the room, where he knelt in front of a large wooden chest. When he stood up, he was holding a longsword in each hand. He walked back to the front of the room and made several deft sweeps through the air, first with the sword in his right hand, and then the left.

The room broke into polite applause, and Hendrick looked at Evena and Wyngalf expectantly. They traded confused glances and then looked to Tobalt, who seemed as puzzled as they were.

"I don't understand," said Wyngalf. "You're assigning Colin to protect us?"

Chuckles arose from the crowd, and Colin stepped forward with a smile, holding out the two swords: one to Wyngalf and one to Evena.

"You're giving us swords," said Evena.

"Well, they'll be paid for through your membership dues, but yes. All members of SMASH get them."

"To symbolize the protection we're getting?" asked Wyngalf hopefully.

The room burst into laughter. When it died down, Hendrick said, "Wyngalf, this *is* your protection. I mean, if another member of SMASH is nearby and you run into trouble, he'll certainly help you out, but every member is ultimately responsible for his own protection. We believe every man and woman has a right to carry a sword to protect him- or herself."

"Okay," said Wyngalf, "but you realize that we're dealing with a *dragon*, right? His hide is practically impermeable, and he can kill twenty men in a second with his breath. I mean, I had a sword with me at the harbor, and it didn't help me a bit. Please tell me you have some kind of plan other than just giving everybody swords."

"A plan for *what* exactly?" asked Hendrick.

"To kill Verne!" cried Wyngalf. "Isn't that what this is all about? I thought you people were the resistance!"

Uncertain murmurs from the audience. Hendrick regarded Wyngalf dubiously. "Listen," he said. "You have to understand that resistance to Verne's encroachment on our freedoms is a long-term effort. It isn't realistic to talk about killing him. What we're aiming to do is to give the citizens a way of resisting him when he oversteps his bounds."

"But killing is the only resistance a dragon understands!" Evena exclaimed. "You either comply with his demands or you kill him. There aren't any other options!"

The mood of the audience was turning decidedly against them.

"That's dangerous talk," said Hendrick quietly. "I suggest we drop the topic of killing Verne before things get ugly."

"Drop the topic?" cried Evena, who was near tears in frustration. "You're as bad as the SAURIANS with their talk of 'incendiary language.' Look, it's very simple. If we don't kill Verne, he's going to kill us. And eventually, he'll kill all of you as well, if you persist in the idea that you're part of some kind of resistance. If you're going to be the resistance, then resist! Help us kill Verne!"

"Listen," said Hendrick sternly. "There will be no more talk of killing Verne. You're newcomers here, so you aren't aware of Skaal City's precarious position in the land of Dis, but trust me when I tell you that we have many enemies. Goblins, for starters," he said, glancing at Tobalt. "But also barbarian tribes and... *others*." Ominous murmurs arose from the audience. "And while it may not be immediately apparent to you, Verne provides an invaluable service for us by protecting us from those enemies. Why, just the other day he razed a town that was harboring dangerous anti-Skaal extremists."

At this, Tobalt spoke up. "I beg your forgiveness for insinuating myself into your proceedings," he said nervously, "but if you are referring to the town of Sybesma, I'm afraid I must offer a correction to your assessment. Based on my own admittedly incomplete analysis of Verne's activity and my knowledge of that settlement, I've concluded that Verne razed the town as a means of intimidation, not to root out any particular undesirable element."

"Nonsense," Hendrick growled. "Verne doesn't kill indiscriminately. In fact, he made a public pronouncement the other day in which he very clearly outlined his reasons for destroying Sybesma."

"And Verne would never lie about such matters," said Wyngalf sardonically. Hendrick glared at him.

"You realize," said Evena, "that this is the very same dragon who burned a dozen men alive in a completely unprovoked attack in the harbor less than two hours ago."

"That's completely different," said Hendrick. "Verne has no business interfering in Skaal's internal affairs or our trade with other cities."

Wyngalf shook his head, dumfounded. "So," Evena said, "if I'm understanding you correctly: when Verne is acting inside the confines of Skaal City, he's a vicious tyrant, but when he is razing villages outside of Skaal City, he is to be trusted implicitly."

"Now you're getting it!" cried Hendrick. "The goal of SMASH is not to kill Verne, but simply to make sure his efforts are channeled in the appropriate direction. By arming the citizens of Skaal, we provide a disincentive for Verne to act against our citizens, which frees him up to raze towns elsewhere." Hendrick beamed at them.

"Wait," said Wyngalf, aghast. "You *want* him to destroy towns?"

"Of course not," said Hendrick. "We abhor violence and look for peaceful solutions to our disagreements with other towns whenever possible. But outside of Skaal is a very dangerous, uncivilized land whose denizens do not value peace and freedom as we do, so we rely on Verne to murder or subjugate them as he sees fit. Don't get me wrong; we're well aware that Verne sometimes gets a little overly enthusiastic in the execution of his mission, but frankly we'd rather see a town like Sybesma destroyed than risk Sybesman extremists coming here and killing Skaalians."

"Are Sybesman extremists a big threat in Skaal City?" asked Wyngalf.

"Oh, yes," said Hendrick. "Ever since the flaming oxcart incident twelve years ago, we live in constant fear of anti-Skaal extremists, and Verne assured us that Sybesma was a hotbed of anti-Skaal extremism."

"And you don't think Verne maybe is exaggerating the threat to keep you dependent on him?"

"It's possible, I suppose," said Hendrick. "But it's better to be safe than sorry."

"But you're *not* safe!" Evena protested. "I thought that was the whole point of this organization. You told us that Verne was a threat to the citizens of Skaal. You can't let Verne run rampant outside the city, razing towns and killing willy-nilly and then expect him to be well-behaved inside the city. And while I hate to burst your bubble, your swords aren't going to make a damn bit of difference to him. He's a fire-breathing dragon, for Grovlik's sake. You think a few paunchy merchants waving swords around is going to frighten him into submission?"

Hendrick frowned at this. "I hope you're not questioning our right to carry swords," he said.

"What?" said Evena. "No. Carry all the swords you want. You can each carry six for all I care. But you're not going to scare Verne by strolling around town with swords hanging off your belt. To be honest, I don't think you people are any better than the SAURIANs with their petitions and burn-ins. You obsess about swords because you don't really have any intention of doing anything about Verne."

"You'd obsess about swords too if people kept trying to take your swords!" cried a man in the back.

"If anybody tries to take my sword," yelled another man, "they're going to get it. Blade first!" Whoops and cheers went up from the crowd.

"That's not what we're talking about," said Evena. "Nobody is trying to take your swords."

"Ha!" shouted a woman near the front. "Just last week, SAURIAN sent Verne a petition signed by eighty-seven Skaalians demanding that Verne confiscate any swords longer than thirty-two and a quarter inches."

"So that's where that stupid rule started," said Wyngalf. "Is there something magical about thirty-two and a quarter inches?"

"Oh, don't get me started on *magical* swords," the woman said. Sympathetic murmurs arose from the crowd.

"OK," said Evena, "so some people are trying to take your swords. But my point is that—"

"Verne will take my sword from my charred, smoking fingers!" yelled a voice somewhere in the middle of the group. Cheers from the crowd.

"We're getting off topic," said Evena. "All I was trying to say is that while you're arguing over sword lengths, Verne is—"

Her words were cut off by a deafening crash, and all assembled turned to watch as the door to the room flew off its hinges and landed several feet inside the room. Armored men with very long swords poured into the room. One of them shouted, "City guard! We've heard reports that you're hiding a cache of several thirty-two and three eighths inch-long swords. Put down your weapons and surrender!" Several more men filed into the room, followed by a woman they recognized: Glindeen. Her eyes alighted on Wyngalf and Evena. "I should have known you two would turn out to be SMASHers. And you, Hendrick! I knew you weren't to be trusted."

"You're the one who can't be trusted," declared Hendrick. "I transferred my loyalties to SMASH when I realized that SAURIAN has no interest in defending the freedoms of ordinary Skaalians."

"He's right, Glindeen," Havartis said, taking a step back as the swordsmen moved to encircle the group. "You've betrayed your principles. Don't you see? You used to resist Verne, and now you're doing his bidding!"

"That's fine talk coming from someone who gets thousands of gold pieces from Verne every month for having his spies on your payroll," sneered Glindeen.

"I have no idea what you're talking about," said Havartis.

"Oh," replied Glindeen, "so Verne just happened to incinerate your biggest competitor's ship today?"

Gasps went up from the crowd. "Is that true, Havartis?" asked Hendrick. "Did your spies tip off Verne?"

"That's an absurd accusation!" Havartis cried. "Verne doesn't need my help to find out when ships are leaving the harbor. And if my man in the shipping guild office happened to mention that there was a fugitive on board a certain ship, I can hardly be blamed for what Verne did with that information."

"It's your fault all those people were killed!" Evena cried.

"Nonsense," Havartis snapped. "It was just politics. It's no more my fault that Verne destroyed that ship than it's Glindeen's fault that Verne razed the town of Sybesma because the Sybesmans were undercutting her on textile prices."

More gasps from the crowd. "I wondered why you were suddenly so worried about anti-Skaal extremists in Sybesma," said Hendrick.

"How dare you bring that up, Havartis," said Glindeen. "We had an agreement!"

"You two are scheming behind my back?" exclaimed Hendrick.

"Drop the hysterics, Hendrick," Havartis snarled. "I know what you've been doing with Glindeen during your overnight 'strategy sessions.'"

"You bastard!" yelled another man near the front. "Glindeen is mine!" He launched himself toward Hendrick, drawing a short sword. He was intercepted by one of the swordsmen, who stabbed him right through his midsection. As the man screamed, two of the other SMASHers came to his defense, drawing their own blades. Soon the entire room had erupted in a fracas, with Glindeen and Havartis both shrieking incomprehensibly as they tried to regain control of the situation.

Wyngalf and Evena drew back from the fray as it escalated, and after a moment Wyngalf realized that Tobalt was no longer with them. He caught sight of the goblin creeping along the wall of the room toward the doorway. Giving Evena a nudge, he followed. The three of them managed to slip outside the room without anyone stopping them. They made their way through the chandler's shop to the street and then followed Tobalt through the shadows down an alley to another street.

"I think we're safe," said Wyngalf. "They're too busy fighting each other to worry about us."

"That was some world class skulking, Tobalt," Evena said. "Nicely done."

Even in the dim moonlight, it was evident that Tobalt was blushing. "Many thanks for your kind words," he said sheepishly. "'Twas in truth a rather amateurish exhibition of stealth by the standards of my race, but it sufficed under the circumstances. I hope that someday you'll have the opportunity to witness a feat of skulking that better showcases the preternatural furtiveness that is the hallmark of my kind—or fail to witness it, rather."

"That would be very nice," said Evena, with a polite smile.

"There they are!" cried a voice from the shadows. The clanking of armor on cobblestones followed.

"Curse my inadequate skulking!" Tobalt moaned. "Run!"

They ran.

Sixteen

They'd only gone a few yards down the street when they heard clanking coming from the shadows in front of them as well.

"They've got us surrounded!" cried Wyngalf. "Tobalt, what do we do?"

"Alas," panted Tobalt, already out of breath from exertion, "my skulking abilities, paltry as they are, do not extend to extricating a group of individuals from a hot pursuit situation."

"We're caught," said Evena, slowing to a halt. "There's no way out!"

Wyngalf and Tobalt cast their eyes around desperately but could find nothing to belie her lament. All the shops on the street were closed. They could only go forward or back, and either way they would run into the city guard. Wyngalf drew his sword.

"What are you doing?" Evena said. "You can't fight off all those men!"

"I have to try," said Wyngalf. "If they catch us, we'll be stuck in Skaal City. When Verne comes back, they'll turn us over to him."

The three put their backs together, with Wyngalf facing the direction they had come, and Tobalt and Evena facing more or less the other way. Tobalt bared his fangs and did his best to look menacing. In both directions, armored men with swords emerged from the shadows.

Something moved in the shadows just to Wyngalf's left. "This way!" a man's voice barked. He saw now that a door had opened, and someone was beckoning to him. A vision of yet another gathering of impotent, dithering plotters flashed into his mind, but he pushed it away. Whoever waited in the shadows, he was their only chance.

"Follow me!" Wyngalf cried. He sheathed his sword and began running toward the voice, hoping that Tobalt and Evena were following.

"Inside, hurry!" snapped the man, and Wyngalf slipped past him into a dark room. After advancing a few steps inside, he stopped and turned—and the svelte figure of Evena crashed into him, followed by Tobalt. Behind them, he caught a glimpse of the stranger framed in the moonlight pouring through the doorway, but the door slammed shut before he could make out the man's features. Wyngalf heard a door latch and a heavy deadbolt slide into place. They were in total darkness.

"Keep going!" barked the man, and Wyngalf turned and took a few uncertain steps in the dark. "Move to your left until you feel the wall," the man's voice said. "Then take six steps forward. Reach out with your right hand." The man's voice seemed vaguely familiar to Wyngalf, but he couldn't place it.

Something crashed loudly into the door behind them. "City guard!" shouted a voice. "Open up!"

Wyngalf did as instructed. His hand brushed against something that he realized after a moment was a doorknob. He gripped it and turned, pulling the door open, revealing nothing but more blackness.

"There's a staircase right in front of you. Take it until you reach a small stone landing. Then stop."

Wyngalf once again followed the man's instructions, keeping his bearings by running his fingertips along the stone wall to his left. When he got to the landing, though, the wall disappeared. The air was cool here and the way the sound of his footsteps was swallowed by the darkness, he got the sense he was had entered a very large space. Evena came up behind him, resting her hand on his shoulder. It was impossible to know how big the landing was or what lay beyond it.

"Now what?" called Wyngalf to the man, who was still at the top of the staircase, doing something that involved heavy iron chains. Presumably he was securing the door against the invaders. Farther behind them, Wyngalf thought he heard wood splintering.

"Feel for the edge of the landing with your foot," yelled the man.

Wyngalf shuffled forward until the toes of his right foot slid his right foot forward until it reached an edge. As far as he could tell, it was a straight vertical edge that ran the length of the landing. Another staircase?

"Found it," Wyngalf called. "Now what?"

"Jump," yelled the man. "As far as you can."

"You've got to be kidding," said Wyngalf. "There's *jumping?*"

"If you want to live," snapped the voice, "you'll jump."

A crash sounded against the door, and the chains jangled loudly. Wyngalf stepped to the edge with his left foot and dangled his right foot over, feeling for a step. He didn't find one, but maybe he just wasn't reaching far enough. As he reached down a little farther, his left knee buckled and he nearly fell forward into the gaping nothingness. Overcorrecting, he threw his weight backwards, collapsing into Evena.

"Jump!" barked the voice from above.

With Evena's help, Wyngalf straightened up and stepped once again toward the edge. His rational mind told him that if the mysterious man had wanted them dead, he'd have left them to be captured by the city guard, but all his instincts told him this was wrong. This had to be another staircase. He could picture it in his mind. If he jumped, he would sail several feet into the air and then plummet to the steps below. He'd be lucky if his injuries only amounted to a few broken bones. On the other hand, breaking his neck would be preferable to being slowly incinerated by Verne.

Another crash sounded, and the chains jingled again. "Jump, you fool!" hollered the voice again. But still Wyngalf hesitated.

"Do it, Wyngalf," urged Evena. "I'm right behind you. If you jump, I jump."

Wyngalf inhaled deeply, put his toes just over the edge, and jumped.

For a sickening moment he was in freefall, then his feet struck wood and he tumbled to a halt, ending spread-eagled on his face. Beneath him was some kind of creaky wooden platform made of spongey wood that smelled of mildew and rot. A second later, Evena slammed into the platform next to him, and he managed to pull her toward himself in time to make way for Tobalt, who followed. He felt Tobalt scrambling past him, and a second later someone else—presumably the man who had rescued them—landed with a thud. The platform groaned and sagged beneath their weight, and Wyngalf wondered how far they would fall if it gave out—and what they would hit at the bottom. Wyngalf started to get to his feet, but the creaking boards under his feet made him think better of it.

"Stay on your hands and knees," said the man's voice. "Keep your weight distributed. No telling how much these old boards can still bear." He moved past Wyngalf as he spoke. "All right," he said, once he was in the lead, "Follow me."

Just then, they heard another crash followed by the sounds of splintering wood and heavy iron chains spilling down the stone steps. For a moment the silhouette of a man was visible in the dim moonlight coming in through the doorway. The silhouette disappeared and was replaced by another as the man in the lead began to clank rapidly down the stone steps. Guard after guard poured down the steps, raising a horrendous cacophony of clanking. The first man let out a yelp as he reached the edge of the landing and fell, but his cry was all but drowned out by the sound of more men following him down the steps. The men were fearless, Wyngalf had to give them that. One after another they clanked down the steps and across the landing, and then disappeared with a yelp into the yawning abyss below.

"What the Skaal City Guard lack in foresight, they more than make up for in foolhardiness," said the man ahead of Wyngalf. "This way." Wyngalf heard him scuffling away in the dark. Not seeing any alternative, Wyngalf followed. Evena and Tobalt crawled along behind them as guards continued to clank down the step and disappear with terrified yelps. After some time, Wyngalf's hands hit cold stone.

"You can stand up here," said the voice. "Originally a stone bridge went across the whole chasm, but a thousand years ago or so part of it collapsed. Smugglers rebuilt the missing section out of wood a few hundred years ago, but these caverns fell into disuse when the shipping guild loosened trade restrictions, and some of their scaffolding has rotted away." There was a sound like metal striking stone, and Wyngalf saw the flicker of sparks a few feet ahead of him. The man who had led them down here was kneeling over a pile of dry grass, trying to light it with flint and steel. He couldn't make out the man's face in the dim light.

"Where are we?" asked Wyngalf.

"Goblin tunnels," said the man. A small flame had caught the grass, and the man blew gently to stoke it. Once the fire was burning on its own, the man held something over it, and a moment later a torch burst into flame. He held it aloft, and for the first time they saw the face of their rescuer.

"Orbrecht!" cried Evena, recognizing the old man's haggard face from the night before.

"The same," said Orbrecht.

"How did you find us?"

"I've been looking for you since I heard about your encounter with Verne this afternoon. Thought you might need some help getting out of town. Should have figured you'd have fallen victim to the recruiting efforts of those SMASH idiots."

"We were approached by the SAURIANs before that," said Evena.

"Ugh," said Orbrecht. "Even worse. Did they make you sign a petition?"

"Tobalt signed it," said Evena. "Is that bad?"

"Eh," Orbrecht shrugged. "It'll probably get you on some kind of list of agitators, but I wouldn't expect much else to happen. Anyway, with a little luck you'll be long gone before Verne returns." He held the torch in front of him and began walking. "This way."

The cavern was too large for them to see the walls, and if not for the rough-hewn stone ceiling overhead, Wyngalf could easily have imagined that they were walking outside on a cloudy, moonless night. The bridge was only about three paces across, so they traversed it single-file. After some distance, though, it widened, and around the same time the walls became visible. The cavern gradually narrowed until they were in a winding tunnel not much taller than a typical goblin. Wyngalf, following closely behind Orbrecht, had to duck to avoid hitting his head on low-hanging rocks.

"What is this place?" asked Wyngalf.

"Ooktaank Havask," said Orbrecht. "The Skaal City authorities sealed off most of the tunnels nearly a century ago. Most Skaalians don't even realize their city is built on top of an abandoned goblin city."

"A goblin city?" asked Wyngalf. "I didn't realize goblins *had* cities." He lost sight of Orbrecht for a moment as the tunnel curved sharply to the right. Tobalt could probably see just fine in the semi-darkness, but Evena could only stumble after Wyngalf's shadow. Wyngalf reached behind him until he felt Evena's hand, clasped it tightly, and then hurried to close the gap between him and Orbrecht.

"They don't," said Orbrecht. "Not anymore. But at one point, several thousand of them apparently lived down here in these caverns. Some say the dwarves built it originally and the goblins invaded and took it over. Others say that the ancestors of today's goblins were smarter and more civilized than the current breed of cowardly thugs. No offense, goblin!"

"None taken, sir," said Tobalt, bringing up the rear.

"How can these caves even exist?" asked Evena. "We can't be more than half a mile from the harbor. Shouldn't this whole place be underwater?"

"It's a miracle of engineering, for sure," said Orbrecht. "That's one of the reasons people think the dwarves may have built it. They're the only ones who could have pumped the water out of the caves and sealed the rock well enough to keep out the seawater for hundreds of years."

"Pardon me for asking, kind sir," called Tobalt, "but are you certain even the dwarves possess such technology? I'm unaware of any other dwarven cities in coastal areas. I know they have employed steam-powered pumps to remove water from mineshafts, but in my admittedly cursory study of dwarven culture, I found nothing to indicate they are capable of moving water on this scale, to say nothing of keeping it out."

"The know-how to build such pumps may have been lost at some point," said Orbrecht.

"Quite true," said Tobalt. "But—and forgive me for my impertinence—is it not true that the technology could just as easily have been lost by goblins as by dwarves?"

"I don't know what you're talking about," said Orbrecht gruffly, glancing back at Tobalt. The tunnel had widened a bit, and they seemed to be on a mild slope downward.

"I apologize for my lack of clarity," said Tobalt. "If I may be permitted another opportunity to explain: you are offering the superior dwarven knowledge of engineering as evidence for the proposition that this city was constructed by dwarves. Yet you yourself admit that the dwarves do not currently possess said knowledge. The obvious answer to this quandary, as you've indicated, is to suppose that a race once possessed such knowledge but then lost it somehow. You've told us that goblins once lived here. I suspect there is no evidence that dwarves ever did, or you would have mentioned it. Horkuden's Knife suggests, therefore, that if a race once possessed the knowledge to build such a city and then lost it, that race was goblins."

"What in Grovlik's name is Horkuden's Knife?" asked Orbrecht, the torchlight revealing a scowl on his face.

"A rhetorical device," said Wyngalf. "It's essentially the principle that when one is attempting to explain a particular phenomenon, one should not unnecessarily introduce extraneous elements. In your explanation for this city, the dwarves are an extraneous element. It's simpler to assume that the goblins built it."

As much as he hated to admit it, Tobalt was right. It was one thing to parrot answers memorized from some text; it was quite another to demonstrate the appropriate use of Horkuden's Knife in an analytical discussion. Perhaps Tobalt really did possess something like a human level of intelligence. That hardly proved he possessed a soul, of course, and in the end that was what really mattered. However well Tobalt might understand matters of philosophy and theology intellectually, he would never be able to grasp the sublime nature of the Noninity.

"Well, I don't know," said Orbrecht. "Maybe the goblins used this rhetorical device of yours to pump the water out. Nobody really knows for sure, I guess." They came to an intersection of four tunnels, and Orbrecht took the one to their right. They were silent for some time as they followed him through the narrow, winding tunnel. Eventually it opened into a cavern about the size of Evena's house. A stone staircase wound around the edge of the cavern.

"Take the stairs up," said Orbrecht, grabbing another torch from a pile in the corner. He lit the torch from the one he was holding and then handed it to Wyngalf. "When the tunnel branches, go left. It will eventually come out at the river, just outside the city walls. Follow the river north until my man finds you. Ugly son-of-an-ogre named Krell. Missing his right ear and three fingers on his left hand. He'll get you safely away from the city, hopefully before Verne returns."

"You're not coming with us?" asked Evena.

"I have other matters to attend to, I'm afraid," said Orbrecht.

"Why are you helping us?" asked Wyngalf.

"Anybody who stands up to Verne is a friend of mine," Orbrecht replied. "I figured you would need some help getting out of the city."

"There's got to be more to it than that," said Wyngalf. "I don't believe you take just anyone down into your secret goblin tunnels. You sought us out, first at the inn, and again this evening. What are you up to, Orbrecht? What are these 'other matters' you have to attend to?"

"We don't have time for this," said Orbrecht. "Every second we waste is a second that could have been spent getting you farther away from Verne."

"I'm with Wyngalf," said Evena. "As much as we appreciate your help, Orbrecht, we're getting a little tired of being shuffled about by people who don't really have our interests at heart. We're not going anywhere until you tell us why you're so interested in us."

Orbrecht sighed. "The Ovaltarian Prophecy," he said.

"The what?" asked Wyngalf.

"Of course!" cried Tobalt. "How stupid of me. I should have seen it!"

"What?" said Evena. "What are you talking about, Tobalt?"

"The Ovaltarians believe that a messiah, known as Ko-Haringu, will arrive from a distant land across the sea," said Tobalt. "The prophecy states that he will be a traveling philosopher accompanied by a woman and a..." Tobalt hesitated.

"A what, Tobalt?" asked Evena.

"A brute that talks like a man," said Orbrecht.

Tobalt's head hung low, his enthusiasm about Orbrecht's revelation having given way to sullenness as he realized the part he was expected to play in the prophecy.

Orbrecht went on, "It is said that Ko-Haringu will survive three encounters with a dragon. After the third encounter, he will flee. But ultimately he will rid the land of Dis of the scourge of dragons."

Wyngalf's thoughts drifted to the man with the oval marking on his forehead who had given him directions to the harbor. No wonder he had acted so strangely. "And how does he do that, exactly?" asked Wyngalf.

"The prophecy is a little unclear on that part," Orbrecht admitted.

"So, just to be clear," said Wyngalf, "the prophecy made sure to insult Tobalt, but it couldn't be bothered with the specifics of how I'm supposed to kill Verne?"

Orbrecht shrugged. "I didn't write it," he said. "And frankly I never put much stock into it until the three of you wandered into the inn that night. Your timing was perfect."

"What do you mean?" asked Evena.

"I'd rather not go into details," said Orbrecht. "Suffice it to say that I have many allies in Skaal City, and we have been working in secret for a long time to offer a real alternative to the SAURIANs and the SMASHers. I believe the time has nearly come for us to seize control of our destiny."

"After I rid the land of the scourge of dragons," said Wyngalf.

"Right," said Orbrecht.

"And you're sure the prophecy doesn't explain how I'm supposed to do that?"

"It's a prophecy, not an instruction manual," said Orbrecht. "If you're the Ko-Haringu, I'm sure you'll figure it out."

"And if I'm not?"

"Then you probably won't figure it out."

"That's not very reassuring."

"Not my job to be reassuring," said Orbrecht. "Now get out of here. I've got work to do."

Somewhere in the distance, they heard the echoes of metal clanking on stone: some of the guards must have figured out they needed to leap across the gap in the scaffolding, and had followed them through the tunnels.

"Go!" hissed Orbrecht. "I'll lead them off in another direction."

The three companions whispered their gratitude to Orbrecht and then started up the winding staircase.

Seventeen

Wyngalf, Evena and Tobalt emerged from the tunnel at a cave opening in a hillside in the middle of a copse of trees somewhere outside Skaal City. Down below, they heard the Ytrisk River rushing past, and they started through the underbrush toward it. Unable to hold the torch while scrambling through the brush, Wyngalf eventually gave up and tossed it behind him into the cave opening. In any case, it was probably better not to attract the attention of any guards that might be patrolling outside the city.

The moon had come out, but the partial cover of the trees made it impossible to see where they were going. They had to feel their way through the scrub, earning dozens of scrapes and scratches by the time they emerged onto a narrow path at the edge of the river.

"This way," said Tobalt, turning to his left and heading upstream on the path. Wyngalf and Evena followed, trusting the goblin's superior night vision. They had no idea how far they would have to walk before Orbrecht's friend Krell found them—*if* he found them—but they had little choice but to try to put as much distance between them and Verne as possible. It was now nearly midnight, and presumably Verne had already arrived at Skuldred and determined that Evena's story was pure fabrication. He was probably on his way back across the sea now, seething with rage. Wyngalf couldn't help but hope that the dragon's fury didn't fade during the long journey back to Dis: if Verne were angry enough, he might kill them instantly rather than slowly torture them to death. Even with Tobalt leading them through the darkness, they were traveling so slowly that Wyngalf figured they'd only be a few miles from Skaal City when Verne returned—and the river path would surely be one of the first places he looked. If they didn't pick up their pace soon, they were doomed, Ovaltarian prophecy or not.

No sooner had this thought occurred to him than he heard the whinnying of horses just up ahead. "Is someone there, Tobalt?" he asked.

"I'm afraid my nocturnal vision, acute though it is, does not allow me to see through trees," answered Tobalt. But not long after, a dim light came into view. Wyngalf realized it was a hooded lantern. "Who goes there?" a gruff voice demanded.

"My name is Wyngalf," said Wyngalf, putting himself in front of Tobalt. "These are my companions Tobalt and Evena."

"What's wrong with your friend?" the man asked. It was hard to make him out behind the lantern, but he seemed to be leaning to look past Wyngalf at Tobalt.

"Orbrecht sent us," said Wyngalf, ignoring the question. "Are you Krell?"

"Your friend looks like a goblin," said the man. "Orbrecht di'n't say nuthin' 'bout no goblins."

"But he did instruct you to escort me and my friends away from Skaal City, did he not?"

"Yeah, but he di'n't say nuthin' 'bout no goblins."

"So I gathered," replied Wyngalf. "But as it happens, one of my friends is a goblin, and Orbrecht instructed you to help me and my friends."

The man, who Wyngalf took to be Krell, was silent for some time, evidently attempting to piece together the elements of Wyngalf's syllogism. "Usually I kill goblins," said the man after a moment, as if he expected Wyngalf to grant him permission to dispatch Tobalt on the spot.

"You won't be killing this one," said Wyngalf firmly. "This goblin is my friend. Got it, Krell?"

Krell grunted something halfway between agreement and disgust. "I got horses for ya," he said. "Dunno if any of 'em will let a goblin ride 'em."

They approached, and in the dim light Wyngalf confirmed that the gruff stranger was indeed missing his right ear and three fingers on his left hand. He was standing at the head of a row of four horses, whose reins were tied together. Without another word, Krell untied the horses and climbed into the saddle of the horse farthest upstream, apparently waiting for Wyngalf and his companions to do the same. Tobalt climbed onto the horse in the rear without hesitation; if there was any natural antipathy between horses and goblins, one wouldn't know it by the horse's reaction. Wyngalf helped Evena onto the horse in front of Tobalt's, and then climbed onto the horse behind Krell. Before Wyngalf was even comfortably in the saddle, Krell doused his lantern, grunted a "giddup," and the four horses began to move as one up the path. Wyngalf could only hope the horses could see better than he could—or knew this path well enough to navigate it in the dark. They continued in silence down the path for some time.

As the journey wore on, Wyngalf began to worry that Orbrecht hadn't thought their escape through: while it was pleasant enough to travel by horseback, the horses weren't making any better time on the narrow river path than they could have done on foot. But at this point they had little choice but to trust Krell. As Wyngalf relaxed with the rhythmic movement of his mount's muscles, he realized how exhausted he was. They hadn't had a moment's rest since Verne attacked the *Numinda Fae*, and it was all he could do to remain upright in the saddle. He was just dozing off when his mount suddenly broke into a gallop. Only the bedroll strapped to the horse's back behind him kept him from falling completely out of the saddle. He managed to get hold of the reins and pull himself upright.

The blackness that had hung over them was gone; they had emerged from the path through the woods and were now flying across an open field under a clear sky lit by a near-full moon. Ahead of him was the dark figure of Krell on his horse, leading the way, oblivious to the fact that he'd just very nearly lost one of his charges. Wyngalf ventured a glance behind him and confirmed that Evena and Tobalt remained on their mounts behind him. He wondered if they had been as shocked as he was at the sudden burst of speed. He couldn't see their faces, and talking over the galloping hooves was impossible. The only thing to do was hold on and hope for the best.

Wyngalf leaned forward against the horse's hot, sweaty neck, and soon acclimated to the horse's faster gait. He dozed off several more times, and couldn't say with any certainty how far they had traveled when his horse finally slowed to a walk again. Ahead of them loomed something large and dark, and Wyngalf realized after a moment that they were headed into more woods. They meandered down another path under a black canopy for some time, and then came to an abrupt stop at a small clearing. Krell slipped off his horse.

"Get some rest," Krell said. "There's a bedroll and some blankets on the horses."

"What about food?" asked Evena. "We're famished."

"Jerky and hardtack in the saddle bags. Should be some skins full of water too. Be quick about it. I gotta tend to the horses before I bed down myself."

They managed to extricate the supplies from the horses and had a small meal huddled together in the dark while Krell led the horses off somewhere, presumably to get them water. Then they bedded down, sleeping like the dead until Krell roused them with rough commands just after dawn.

"Giddup," he barked, in the same tone he had used for the horses. When they didn't immediately respond, he gave Wyngalf a kick in the ribs. "Giddup!" he barked again. Wyngalf bit his tongue and got groggily to his feet. When they had broken fast and attended to their other basic needs, they got back on their horses. Still sore from the previous day's ride and not feeling particularly well-rested, Wyngalf would have liked nothing better than to remain in the clearing and rest for a few more hours, but he knew that by now Verne would be back in Dis, and was probably at this moment inquiring of his spies in the city regarding them. Assuming Verne didn't learn anything relevant from the spies, he would then start checking the obvious escape routes: ships that had recently departed from the harbor, the main roads leading out of Skaal City to the south and east—and the path along the river. From what Wyngalf recalled of his studies, dragons were middling trackers but they had incredibly powerful vision. Even allowing for Verne's partial blindness, they had to figure that he could see for several miles. Wyngalf doubted that Verne would be able to track them from the river across the plains, but even if he simply proceeded in a spiral out from Skaal City, scouring every inch of ground, it wouldn't take him more than a few hours to find them. They needed to get much farther away—or find a very good hiding place—to be safe from Verne's wrath.

"How many miles do we have to put between us and Verne to be out of danger?" asked Wyngalf.

Krell snorted in disgust. "Ain't miles that's gonna save you from Verne," he said. Wyngalf tried to get him to elaborate, but he wouldn't say another word. Once again, they could only follow in silence and hope that Krell had their best interests at heart.

Wyngalf heard the sound of moving water ahead, realizing that they must be coming upon another river. Soon after, Krell dismounted and motioned for them to do the same. They followed Krell as they led their mounts down to the river and into the water. The river moved swiftly here, but it seemed to be less than five feet deep in most places. Krell guided them through the shallower areas, and it didn't take long to cross. They made their way up the steep bank on the far side, remounting when they found a continuation of the narrow wooded path.

After some time the woods gave way to rolling hills, and the three companions took advantage of the opportunity to ride side-by-side and converse regarding their circumstances.

"What do you suppose he meant by that?" asked Evena. "That miles aren't going to save us from Verne?"

"I haven't a clue," said Wyngalf. "Krell doesn't strike me as very bright. Or helpful."

"Where do you think he's taking us?" asked Evena.

"You're welcome to try asking," said Wyngalf. Krell remained several yards in front of them, and gave no indication of having any interest in their conversation.

"If I might be permitted a supposition," said Tobalt, "I would venture that our destination is the fair city of Brobdingdon. It would have been faster to travel on the road that runs along the river, but of course our choleric guide wished to keep off the main roads to avoid Verne's spies. Thus he led us along the river and then cut north across the plains to the west of the Chathain Mountains. To my knowledge, the only settlement of note anywhere in the vicinity is Tyvek, and traveling there would require us to head back south, closer to Verne's lair. That leaves Brobdingdon as our likely target."

"Okay," said Wyngalf. "But how does that help us? It's only a couple hours' flight from Skaal City to Brobdingdon, and I'll bet that Verne has spies there as well."

"From what I gather of Verne's activities," said Tobalt, "he rarely ventures farther north than Tyvek. I have not been able to ascertain the reason for this limitation, however."

"Maybe the Brobdingdonians have defenses against Verne," said Evena. "Towers with big crossbows or something."

"It's difficult to imagine a weapon that might frighten Verne," said Tobalt. "But there must be some reason that Verne was willing to fly many leagues across the sea to terrorize your hometown rather than simply follow the river north to Brobdingdon."

"Yes," said Evena. "And thanks, by the way. I'd almost forgotten that my parents and all my friends are probably dead because of me."

"Because of me, you mean," said Wyngalf.

"I'm terribly sorry I mentioned it," said Tobalt. "I was merely attempting to discern our reticent chaperon's intentions."

"It's fine, Tobalt," said Evena, exerting obvious effort to affect a conciliatory tone. "Anyway, we're all going to be dead soon enough. Whatever Verne's reasons are for staying away from Brobdingdon, I'm sure he'll make an exception for us. I don't know why we didn't just stay in those dwarf tunnels under Skaal City."

"*Goblin* tunnels," muttered Tobalt.

"We couldn't hide down there indefinitely," said Wyngalf. "And according to the Ovaltarian prophecy, we're supposed to flee, not hide."

"Don't tell me you're taking that prophecy business seriously," said Evena, looking askance at Wyngalf.

"The Noninity works in mysterious ways," said Wyngalf. "It isn't impossible that Ganillion the Messenger entrusted some ancient prophet of Dis with some small fragment of the Blessed Truth of Noninitarianism in order to facilitate my mission here."

"Wow, are you full of yourself," said Evena. "You're actually saying you think you're this Hairy Cuckoo Messiah?"

"Ko-Haringu," said Tobalt. "And I have to admit, the correlations between the prophecy and Wyngalf's journey are striking. If I were of a more superstitious bent, I would be tempted to believe it myself."

"But you don't believe it," said Evena.

"Horkuden's Knife," said Wyngalf. "It's the simplest solution."

Tobalt scowled. "I'm withholding judgment on the matter," he said. "At present, I cannot offer a more compelling explanation for the correlations than the one Orbrecht provided. But whether or not Wyngalf truly is the Ko-Haringu, it may be possible for us to use the prophecy to our benefit."

"How do you figure?" asked Evena.

"Quiet down back there!" Krell growled.

"What's the harm in a little conversation?" asked Wyngalf, growing irritated with their guide's sullen manner. "Particularly since there's a good chance it's the last one we'll ever have."

"If you wanna make sure o' that, keep distractin' me," Krell growled. "Otherwise, keep an eye out for Verne."

"What good will it do us to see him coming?" asked Wyngalf. "We can't fight him." The others nodded in assent: they were on an exposed plain with no cover. If Verne was anywhere in the area, they were doomed.

"See those peaks over there?" said Krell, pointing to their right. "Them's the Chathain Mountains. Lots o' caves and places to hide. If we see him coming, we might be able to get to one of 'em in time."

They peered into the distance. It seemed a long shot to Wyngalf, but he supposed it was better than nothing. He didn't ask why they didn't travel closer to the mountains; the terrain was obviously rougher in that direction. The three companions remained silent for the rest of the day, with Evena and Wyngalf watching the skies for signs of Verne. Tobalt, whose eyes were not attuned to bright light, rode with his gaze downcast.

Just before dusk, they reached a copse of trees that would have to serve as cover from Verne for the night. They ate dried meat and hard tack again and then bedded down for the night. Krell woke them rudely before dawn, and it took considerable effort for Wyngalf to convince himself that this was preferable to being awakened by dragon fire. Sore, tired, and hungry, they set out on their horses once again. The sun was in their eyes, which meant they were heading almost due east. If Verne wanted to surprise them, this would be a good time—not that he needed the element of surprise; they were once again on an open plain with no cover for miles.

But they survived the morning unscathed, and just after noon they turned slightly northward. Tobalt was right: they were going to Brobdingdon. Wyngalf wondered how this detour fit into the prophecy of the Ko-Haringu and the Noninity's plans for him. Perhaps Ganillion the Messenger was telling him that Skaal City was not ready for the Blessed Truth, and that he was destined to start his church in Brobdingdon instead. The more Wyngalf thought about it, the more sense it made. All the struggles he had faced so far were intended to guide him toward Brobdingdon and make his ultimate success all the sweeter. He would begin converting the citizens of Brobdingdon shortly after their arrival, and soon the faithful would begin construction on a grand cathedral that would someday tower over city. Wyngalf, as the Bishop of Brobdingdon, woud send missionaries into the far reaches of Dis—even Skaal City, once he determined the people there were ready for the Blessed Truth of Noninitarianism.

A few hours later, they came upon a paved road running roughly north-south, and Krell led his horse onto it and turned left.

"Is it safe to be on the road?" Evena asked.

"No choice," Krell answered. The three companions followed.

"I'm afraid our surly conductor is correct," said Tobalt. "We are on a narrow strip of land between the Rivers Ytrisk and Skaal. Without traveling far to the south, there is no place to ford either river. This is the only way to Brobdingdon. We can only hope that Verne is occupied with other possible escape routes long enough for us to get there unmolested."

Just before dusk, they left the road and made camp in another small copse of trees. Krell judged it too dangerous to start a fire, so again they ate in the dark and then bedded down for the night.

They set off early the next morning for Brobdingon, hoping they were far enough away from Skaal City to escape Verne's attention. Fortunately, they were aided in this by a persistent fog that hung over the river basin most of the day. Even with Verne's sharp eye, he would have to be within a stone's throw to see them. By the time the fog dissipated, they were but a few miles from the walls of Brobdingdon. The landscape was dotted with small farms and estates, and Wyngalf found himself wondering if these were free from Verne's tyranny. If the influence of whatever force kept Verne away from Brobdingdon extended this far, then perhaps they were safe already. But somehow Wyngalf suspected that Evena was right: for them, Verne would make an exception. Wyngalf wouldn't feel safe until they were inside the walls of Brobdingdon—and even then, "safe" was a relative term.

By luck or providence, they made it to the city gates. A guard called down to them, asking their business in the city. Wyngalf decided to leave the talking to Krell, assuming their guide had some connections inside the city. He almost immediately regretted this decision.

"We're merchants from Tyvek," said Krell. "Let us in."

"What kind of merchants?" demanded the guard. "You don't look like merchants. And you don't sound like you're from Tyvek. Is that a *goblin* with you?"

"Don't be stupid," Krell growled. "That's my cousin, Mingus. His mother used to eat a lot of woozleberries."

"We don't allow goblins in the city," said the guard. "And unless you can prove you have business here, I can't let you in either. Lots of spies from Skaal City about."

"We ain't from Skaal City!" snarled Krell. "And we ain't no spies neither! We're merchants, here on important merchant business! Now let us in, you rat-faced troll-hugger!"

The guard turned away, disappearing inside the tower.

"Wait!" cried Wyngalf. "You've got to let us in. There's a dragon after us!"

After a moment, the guard's face reappeared. "What kind of dragon?" he asked.

"A big, green one. His name is Verne."

The guard studied them for a moment.

"Where are you from?"

"Our guide, with whom you were just conversing, is from Skaal City," said Wyngalf, and even at this distance he could see the disdain on the guard's face. Krell grumbled and shook his head. "But my friend and I are from across the Sea of Dis. We've been running from Verne ever since we got here. We first fled to Skaal City, but the people there don't seem to understand how dangerous Verne is. We ran into some trouble with the authorities, and we were forced to flee here."

"Skaalians are a bunch of cowards," said the guard. Krell scowled but said nothing.

"That assessment has been largely borne out by my experience," said Wyngalf. "Please, this is our only chance."

"Why do you have a goblin with you? We don't allow goblins in Brobdingdon."

"He's our friend," said Wyngalf. "He's been one of the few people—er, beings—willing to stick his neck out to help us since we got to Dis. As you can see, he's a very small specimen of his race, and completely unarmed. I assure you he's harmless." Wyngalf glanced at Tobalt, who was slumped pathetically in the saddle, either attempting to demonstrate his harmlessness or express his dejection at Wyngalf's description of him.

"Well," said the guard, "any enemy of the Skaalians is a friend of Brobdingdon. But I'll need to check about the goblin. Wait here."

The guard disappeared and, not having much choice in the matter, the four travelers waited.

"Shoulda let me handle the talking," grunted Krell.

"Yeah, that was going really well," said Wyngalf.

Krell snarled at him but didn't reply. After some time, the gates began to open. They stopped just far enough apart for a horse to ride though single file. Without hesitation, Krell rode through. Wyngalf and his companions followed. They found themselves in a large, roughly semicircular bazaar filled with tents, booths, and bustling pedestrians. Bordering the bazaar were rows of buildings that grew larger as they receded in the distance, giving the impression of a city built on tiers. To Wyngalf's eye, it was a fair sight more impressive than the scattered shops of Skaal City.

They were met just inside the gates by the guard. "The mayor wants to see you," he explained. "Selvin will take your horses." Another guard came forward to take the reins.

"The mayor?" asked Wyngalf. "What for?"

"Don't know," said the guard. "I told my sergeant about your situation, and he went to talk to his boss. When he came back, he said the mayor asked to see you."

"What if we don't want to see him?" said Krell, dismounting. Wyngalf and his companions did the same.

"Then you're in luck," said the guard. "She doesn't want to see you either."

"You just said—" Krell started.

"*Them*," the guard said, indicating Wyngalf, Evena and Tobalt. "Not you. You can gather some provisions for the road and then be on your way."

Krell snorted. "Fine," he said. "Didn't wanna be here anyway." He turned to Wyngalf. "Good luck," he said, "Yer gonna need it." With that, Krell walked away, disappearing among the tents.

"Pleasant fellow, isn't he?" asked the guard.

"Be glad you didn't have to ride with him from Skaal City," said Evena.

"This way," the guard said, turning on his heel and walking smartly away.

The three companions shrugged at each other and followed.

They made their way down a series of streets and alleys, eventually coming out in front of a grand palace near the middle of the city. Wyngalf was forced to surrender his sword at the entrance, and they were escorted inside. The guard led them down a long marble-tiled hallway and then up a luxurious spiral staircase, eventually coming out at the top of a tower overlooking much of the city. Standing at the parapet was a small figure who turned to face them as they approached.

She looked to be in her mid-seventies, with short-cropped white hair and a kindly face. She was, Wyngalf realized as they approached, downright tiny—smaller even than Tobalt. If he were of the mind to, he suspected he could pick her up and throw her right over the edge of the tower before the guard could stop him. Either the authorities in Brobdingdon were trusting to a fault or they knew something he didn't.

"Hello," said the woman pleasantly, holding out her hand. "I'm Roweyna, mayor of Brobdingdon." She seemed amiable enough, but a bit haggard and on edge, as if she had been under a great deal of stress lately—and expected more of it.

They shook her hands in turn and introduced themselves. Roweyna gave Tobalt a disapproving glance, but didn't remark on his race. The guard stood by silently.

"I understand you ran into some trouble with Verne," said the mayor.

"That's putting it mildly," said Wyngalf. "If he ever catches us, he's going to burn us all alive. And he promised to do it as slowly as possible."

"Verne's a cruel beast," said Roweyna. "You must really have angered him."

"It was mostly my doing," said Evena. "I tricked him into thinking—"

"Pardon me," said Roweyna, sounding a bit nervous. "I'm very interested to hear the story, but might I ask if you could hold off until our other guest arrives."

"Other guest?" asked Wyngalf.

The mayor raised an eyebrow at the guard.

"Sorry, ma'am," the guard said. "I thought it best if you tell them."

Roweyna nodded. "Right you are," she said. "Forgive me for assuming. You see, because of Verne's ceaseless aggression, we have found it necessary to..." She trailed off, as if hearing something in the distance. She smiled and said, "Ah, here she comes now." As she said it, a shadow swept over her face. A shadow that was all-too-familiar to Wyngalf. A mysterious wind gusted down around them.

Wyngalf spun around, reaching for the sword that was not at his side. Silhouetted against the setting sun was a massive reptilian creature with giant, bat-like wings. It appeared to be settling in for a landing on the roof of the tower.

"No," moaned Wyngalf, falling to his knees. "No, no, no..."

"We're dead," said Evena, her voice choked with fear. "We came all this way and he still found us."

"It's not my place to decide important existential issues for either of you," said Tobalt, the flapping of the dragon's wings nearly drowning out his words, "but as for me, I am attempting to muster the courage to throw myself over the parapet to the street below."

"What?" cried Roweyna. "Don't be silly! None of you are in any danger."

As the dragon alighted on the bricks in front of them, Wyngalf noticed that its scales looked almost red in the light of the setting sun. No, he thought. This dragon *is* red.

"It's not Verne," said Wyngalf.

"No," said Roweyna. "*She* most certainly is not."

"Hi!" exclaimed the dragon excitedly. "I'm Scarlett. Who are you guys?"

Eighteen

"I—I'm Wyngalf," said Wyngalf, staring aghast at the giant red dragon. If anything, Scarlett was even larger and more terrifying than Verne. "Th-these are my friends, Evena and Tobalt."

"Charmed!" said Scarlett, her voice as deep and rich as Verne's, but more melodious. "What brings you to my city?"

"*Your* city?" said Evena. "You mean you own it?"

"Of course not," said the dragon. "The city belongs to the fine people of Brobdingdon. But you might say I've adopted it. We have a mutually beneficial arrangement."

"We've heard *that* before," mumbled Tobalt.

"I'm sorry, dear," said Scarlett, craning her neck toward the goblin. "I didn't quite catch that."

"Apologies," Tobalt said, quaking with fear. "I was merely making the undoubtedly misguided observation that your relationship with Brobdingdon might seem, on first appearance, to be analogous to that of Verne and Skaal City."

Scarlett nodded thoughtfully. "I can see how you would say that," she said. "However, I assure you that my relationship with Brobdingdon is quite amicable. Isn't it, Roweyna?"

"Absolutely, Scarlett," Roweyna gushed. "You've been nothing but helpful in protecting us from Verne, not to mention the barbarian hordes to the north. Why, I shudder to think what would have become of Brobdingdon during the last barbarian attack if it weren't for you." She turned to Wyngalf and Evena. "You see, the barbarians hate us for the freedoms that we enjoy here in Brobdingdon, so they occasionally send hordes of attackers in an attempt to breach our walls. The attacks would be even more frequent if Scarlett didn't seek out their camps in the hills and burn their men, women and children alive." She seemed to be trying to convince herself as much as she was them.

"That logic seems a little questionable," muttered Tobalt.

"I'm sorry," said Scarlett. "You really must learn to speak up."

Tobalt mumbled an apology.

"So you're saying that the people of Brobdingdon aren't being forced to accept your 'protection'?" asked Evena. "If they asked you to leave them alone, you would?"

Scarlett frowned, and Roweyna burst into laughter so frantic and high-pitched that Wyngalf at first thought she was having some sort of seizure. "Why would they do that?" she asked. "It's ridiculous! Ask Scarlett to leave!" She broke into her hysterical cackle again.

"Of course I would leave if I was no longer wanted," said Scarlett. "But as the beloved mayor of this fine city has indicated, that would never happen. The people here *love* me. Don't they, madam mayor."

"Oh, yes!" cried Roweyna. "That's the word I would use. Love!" She grinned maniacally.

"Now, if we're finished discussing my relationship with the people of this fine city," said Scarlett, "I'd like to hear about your encounters with my brother."

"Your brother?" asked Wyngalf, stunned. "Verne is your *brother?*"

"How is that possible?" asked Evena. "He's green."

"Dragon sibling can be of many different colors," said Scarlett. "We were of the same brood. And like most siblings, we get along fine as long as we each mind our own business. Lately, though, Verne has been getting overly acquisitive. He's been seen as far north as Tyvek, and I understand that now he's even taken an interest in towns across the Sea of Dis. If I judge your accents correctly, Wyngalf and Evena, that is from whence you hail."

It was clear that Scarlett knew most of their story already, probably having picked up bits and pieces of it from her own spies in Skaal City. Unsure of what she'd been told and having no opportunity to collaborate on an alternate version, they ended up telling essentially everything that had happened since Wyngalf arrived in Skuldred. Scarlett seemed particularly interested in the Jewel of Skuldred, asking Evena to clarify her story on several points. Evena stressed that the story was a fabrication, as it seemed their best bet to impress Scarlett was their willingness to stand up to her brother, but if anything her insistence that the Jewel of Skuldred was a fiction had the opposite of the desired effect. Wyngalf got the impression that Scarlett thought Evena was lying to protect the jewel, and the more Evena insisted there was no jewel, the more knowing smiles Scarlett sent in Evena's direction. But Scarlett played along, never explicitly voicing her doubts.

"Well," said Scarlett when they had finished their story, "it's no wonder Verne is upset with you. I'm quite a bit more lenient than my brother, but if you'd have plied me with a fantastical yarn like that, I'd have been tempted to tear you limb from limb." She gave them a broad smile, which did more to punctuate the thinly veiled threat of dismemberment than to reassure them. "If I know Verne, he's never going to forgive you for that. Why, he might even dare to confront *me* to get at you."

"But you're not afraid of him," prompted Evena, evidently hoping to play on Scarlett's pride.

Scarlett grinned again. "Of course not," she said. "He's my little brother. I hatched six minutes before he did. My point is simply that having you here puts the people of Brobdingdon at risk."

"We didn't intend to stay," said Wyngalf. "Our plan was to put Evena on a ship across the Sea of Dis so that she could return home. Tobalt and I will…" He realized that he had no idea what he and Tobalt were going to do. He had been entertaining the idea that once Evena had escaped, he would resume his missionary work in Brobdingdon, but he realized now that plan was unrealistic. Even if Scarlett permitted him to stay, he would be forever beholden to her for protection from Verne. Rather than living in fear of Verne, he'd be living in fear of Scarlett. And as for Tobalt—the people of Brobdingdon seemed even less tolerant of goblins than those of Skaal City. He would be forced to leave the city and survive on his own.

"Don't get me wrong," said Scarlett. "I'd be happy to have you here indefinitely as my guests, but I can't allow the people of

Brobdingdon to be endangered. I can handle Verne, but if he gets desperate, he could do a lot of damage before I can stop him. I'm afraid the only solution is to ship you all across the sea, to the Jagged Coast. And if you're smart, once you'll get there, you'll keep going. The farther you are from Verne, the safer you are."

Wyngalf thought of Krell's words: *Ain't miles that's gonna save you from Verne.* No matter how far they traveled, they would never be more than a day or two's flight away for a dragon. And anywhere they went, they would bring the scourge of dragonfire with them.

"Madam Roweyna will see to it that you get on a ship tomorrow morning," Scarlett went on. "I apologize for the lack of hospitality, but I'm afraid it's the only way. As a small measure of my appreciation for your help, though, we'll see to it that you have accommodations here in the mayoral palace tonight. Right, Madam Mayor?"

"Oh, yes!" cried Roweyna. "You'll stay here in one of the guest suites. You all look exhausted."

Wyngalf nodded dumbly, suddenly realizing how tired he really was.

"Well, I won't keep you any longer," said Scarlett, spreading her wings. "Very nice to meet you, and have a pleasant voyage tomorrow!"

The three companions mumbled their appreciation, and Scarlett shot into the darkening sky. The mayor escorted them back inside and bid them goodnight. The guard led them to a suite of adjoined bedrooms in the palace. Wyngalf closed the door to his room, sat down on the bed, and managed to get one of his boots partly unlaced before falling asleep.

Wyngalf was awakened by someone shaking him by the shoulder, and for a moment he thought it was Krell. Slapping the man's hand away angrily, he opened his eyes to see a small figure bent over his bed in the semi-darkness: Tobalt.

"...for rousing you at such an inopportune hour," Tobalt was mumbling, "but it's come to my attention that we are not safe here."

"We aren't safe *anywhere*," Wyngalf grumbled. "Go away." He rolled away from Tobalt, determined to go back to sleep.

"There is some truth to what you say," said Tobalt, "but I'm afraid that we are particularly unsafe in this city. Scarlett has no intention of letting us get on a ship."

Wyngalf groaned and slowly sat up. "What are you talking about, Tobalt?"

"Although I am, as has become painfully evident, a poor representative of my species, certain behaviors endemic to my kind tend to resurface when—"

"Please," Wyngalf groaned, "just get to the fargling point."

"I've been skulking again," said Tobalt, a bit sheepishly. "I overheard two of the palace guards talking about bringing three prisoners to a 'rendezvous point.' I suspect the three prisoners in question are us."

"A reasonable guess," admitted Wyngalf, rubbing his eyes. "But what's the rendezvous point?"

"A better question," said Tobalt, "might be 'with whom are they rendezvousing'?"

Wyngalf blinked and shook his head, trying to clear the fog of sleep from his brain. "Verne," he said after some time.

"That was my hypothesis as well," said Tobalt. "Either Verne or his Skaalian agents. The end result is the same."

"We're too valuable to be allowed to leave," said Wyngalf. "Ugh. I should have known. Scarlett is just as bad as her brother. She's going to use us as bargaining chips in her conflict with Verne. But what is she trading us *for*?"

"The details would seem unimportant," replied Tobalt. "The pertinent point is that if we remain here until morning, we're going to end up in Verne's clutches, and it is difficult for me to envision any scenario resulting from that eventuality that works in our favor."

"We're going to be burned alive. Slowly."

"Yes," said Tobalt. "Unless we escape these confines in short order."

"All right," said Wyngalf. "Let me get dressed, and I'll go wake Evena." He laced his boot. "Okay, dressed."

They roused Evena and explained the situation to her. Tobalt said that guards manned the doors to the palace, but there seemed to be no exterior patrol. That meant climbing out a window was probably their best bet to escape. They were on the third floor, so they knotted several bedsheets together, tied one end to Tobalt's bed, and let the other end of the makeshift rope down to the alley below. Tobalt climbed down first, and once he had verified that the alley was clear, Wyngalf and Evena followed. With Tobalt in the lead, the three of them made their way down side streets and alleys in the direction of the port.

Brobdingdon was located between the Ytrisk and Skaal Rivers, and while the Skaal River was too narrow for large ships, the Ytrisk River was navigable by most seafaring vessels. It emptied into the Gulf of Bardem about a day's voyage to the west. According to Tobalt, most ships turned southward from the Gulf toward Bascom or Skaal City (as there wasn't much in the way of civilization to the north), but a few continued across the Sea of Dis to the Jagged Coast. With a little luck, they could bribe the captain of one of these ships to take them on board. They hadn't yet decided what they would do once they got to the Jagged Coast; Evena still seemed intent on returning home to Skuldred, but Wyngalf hoped to convince her she was better off heading farther inland with him, where they would be more difficult for Verne to find.

The eastern sky was just beginning to lighten when they got to the docks. As luck would have it, the crew of a cargo ship was making preparations to depart for the island of Bjill, in the northern part of the Gulf of Bardem. The ship was only half full, as it was carrying a small load of food and supplies to the pumice miners there; it would return with a hold full of the porous stone, which Brobdingdon supplied to the rest of the continent of Dis for various purposes. The captain, a genial, portly man named Yanbo, happily agreed to take them to Bjill for five gold pieces each: usually, he said, people paid him to get them *off* that accursed island. Yanbo told them that ships also occasionally arrived at Bjill from across the Sea of Dis; he suggested they could probably hop another ship at Bjill destined for the Jagged Coast. Evena gave the man five extra gold pieces for the assurance that he'd keep his mouth shut—if Verne's spies found out they were on the island of Bjill before they could get on another ship, they were doomed.

It was just after dawn when the ship left the dock. The three companions were given firm orders to remain in the hold for the voyage; there was, according to the captain, "no room above decks for land lubbers." So they spent the day below decks, dozing in hammocks and playing cards by the dim light of a lantern. For some time they managed to avoid discussing the precarious nature of their situation and the strange sequence of events that had led to them being holed up in the bottom of a cargo ship on its way to a pumice-mining operation, but as the hours wore on, they found themselves trying to make sense of the bizarre political landscape of Dis.

"I wonder if it's true that the citizens of Brobdingdon turned to Scarlett for protection against Verne," Evena mused. "Maybe that's just a lie they tell themselves to rationalize their subjugation to Scarlett." The three of them sat around a crate they had been using as a makeshift card table. A lantern hanging on a hook swung lazily from side to side above it.

"You think it was the other way around?" asked Wyngalf. "That Skaal City turned to Verne for protection from Scarlett?"

"It is my understanding that dragons can live for thousands of years," said Tobalt. "Thus the answer to your query may very well be lost to history. But Scarlett claimed that she and Verne are of the same brood, and it therefore seems probable that the two reigns commenced concurrently, or nearly so. In any case, I would suggest that it makes little difference. The salient point is that at present, each city is perpetuating the arrangement, under the impression that allowing themselves to be enslaved by one dragon is preferable to being enslaved by another."

Wyngalf shook his head. "It's tragic to see people allowing themselves to be subjugated by a dragon in that way," he said. "It's a complete perversion of the way society is supposed to be run."

"Yes," said Tobalt, "I imagine the people of Skaal City and Brobdingdon would be much better off if the dragons were supplanted by Noninitarian bishops."

Wyngalf glared at Tobalt. The goblin's tone gave nothing away, but Wyngalf was virtually certain Tobalt was mocking him. "Are you implying that a society structured by Noninitarian principles would be no different than one ruled by *dragons*?"

"In my experience," said Tobalt, "societies are run by people, not principles. So, to answer your question, I would suggest that it would depend on the person—although even the best of men have been corrupted by the temptations of too much power."

"Then what is your solution, Tobalt?" asked Evena. "*Someone* has to run those cities. What options are there, other than a dragon, a mayor or a bishop?"

"I question the premise," said Tobalt. "Why does someone have to be in charge of Skaal City and Brobdingdon?"

"To see that society is structured in a just manner," said Wyngalf.

"To look after the public interest," said Evena.

"I'm not sure what a just society would look like," replied Tobalt. "I've never seen one. Nor have I ever seen this 'public interest' to which you refer, Evena. In my experience, individual humans have many interests, many of them competing with each other, and these cannot be added up to produce an aggregate sum, as if interests were potatoes. And while I do not claim to be a particularly bright goblin, empirical evidence suggests that most humans in power have not much better an understanding of these concepts than I do. Further, I doubt that most human leaders have any more intention of bringing about a 'just society' or working toward the 'public interest' than Verne or Scarlett does."

"I think you're being disingenuous, Tobalt," said Evena. "Even if it's a council or committee rather than a mayor or bishop, someone still has to make decisions for the community as a whole. In your idealized society, who would build the roads?"

"Perhaps the mayor," said Tobalt, "as she would have plenty of time, having been freed from the burden of structuring a just society and overseeing the public interest."

Wyngalf was still formulating his rebuttal when thunder rumbled in the distance.

"I think we've left the river and entered the Gulf of Bardem," said Evena. "We've begun tacking back and forth."

Wyngalf had noticed the ship's movements as well, but it hadn't occurred to him what the change meant. The sunlight that had been streaming through the cracks in boards above them faded, and as the night began the storm grew stronger. For several hours, the crew scampered around above in a manner that reminded him of his voyage across the Sea of Dis. He half-expected to be hauled above decks at any moment to face the Hafgufa once again. But the storm died down, and he and his companions remained below decks, unbidden and unneeded.

They spent the night sleeping fitfully in their hammocks. It occurred to Wyngalf that the last time he had an uninterrupted night's sleep was nearly a week ago, at Bulgar the fishmonger's house—and even then, his dreams had been troubled by vague forebodings of his divine voyage across the Sea of Dis. Those dreams, as it turned out, had failed to communicate the true horror of what he was to face in the upcoming days, and for that he was thankful.

As light began to creep through the slats in the boards overhead and the thudding of footsteps grew louder and more frequent, he realized it was day once again. Soon they would be on the island of Bjill, where they would have to find another ship and negotiate for passage across the sea. He hoped Evena had enough money left to convince a captain they were worth their weight in pumice.

But the day wore on, and by mid-afternoon they still had not made port. They were under orders not to leave the hold under any circumstances, but Wyngalf began to worry that something was wrong. Trying the hatch, he found it was barred shut. He banged on the hatch until footsteps approached and a muffled voice spoke up from the other side.

"Whaddya want?" the voice said.

"Shouldn't we be at Bjill by now?" asked Wyngalf.

There was a long pause. "Storm blew us off course," said the voice. "Gonna be a few more hours. They heard the man walking away. Wyngalf turned to his companions and shrugged helplessly. They spent the next several hours playing cards by lantern light. When night came again, they still hadn't arrived at Bjill. "If I were the cynical sort," said Tobalt at last, "I might surmise we are not, in fact, headed for Bjill."

"It's possible the storm blew us out into the Sea of Dis," said Evena. "If the winds are against us, it could take us a while to get back on course."

Wyngalf nodded silently, but he suspected that Tobalt was right. He should have known their escape would not be so easy. He retired to his hammock and spent several hours in prayer to various members of the Noninity, pleading for guidance, but he received no discernable reply. Clearly he had violated the divine will at some point, but he was at a loss to determine where he had gone wrong, or what he could have done differently. Had it been a mistake to flee Skaal City? It occurred to him, not for the first time, that the messianic Ovaltarian prophecy could as easily have been the word of Ravast the Corruptor as that of Ganillion the Messenger. As much as he wanted to believe that the Noninity had sent the Ovaltarian prophet to pave the way for his divine mission in Dis, perhaps the prophecy was a trap that had been set for him by Ravast—and Wyngalf had walked right into it. But did that mean that he was supposed to have stayed in Skaal City and faced down Verne with nothing but his own wits and courage? It was hard to see how that could have ended in anything but a painful death for him and the demise of Noninitarianism in the land of Dis. There was a fine line between martyrdom and a pointless, agonizing death.

Eventually his prayers and ruminations gave way to sleep, and when he awoke daylight was once again streaming through the cracks of the hold. The ship still hadn't made port at Bjill. Tobalt and Evena were already up, playing cards. When Wyngalf's gaze met theirs, he knew they were all thinking the same thing: they'd been double-crossed. None of them said it aloud, but there was only one place the ship could be heading.

Wyngalf spent a good hour pounding on the hatch and pleading to talk to the captain, but there was no reply. They spent another day in sullen near-silence. The ship made port just after dark, and they were hauled above decks. "Sorry," said Captain Yanbo, who stood on the deck waiting for them. "Got a better offer." He held out a pouch full of coins to Evena, evidently intending to return her money. She spat in his face. One of the mates drew his sword, but the captain held up his hand. "It's fine," he said gruffly, wiping his face with his sleeve. "Just get them off my ship."

The seamen marched them down the gangplank to the docks. The moon was hidden by clouds, but even in the near darkness, the outline of the harbor was familiar.

"Welcome back to Skaal City," said a well-dressed man standing on the docks, who seemed to be waiting for them. Flanking him on either side were several of the city guard. Two of them were holding torches. The three companions were prodded toward him, and in the flickering light Wyngalf could just make out the man's features.

"Lord Popper," Wyngalf said. "I'm surprised you're still in charge of the Shipping Guild office after our last encounter."

"Oh, I'm not," Popper said with a smile. "It's been an eventful few days," he said. "I won't trouble you with the details. All you need to know is that Dwalen has been removed from the mayoralty and the SAURIANs are no longer in power. After some negotiations between the aristocrats of the city and the SMASHers, it was decided that I was the most satisfactory choice for the position."

"You must be joking," said Evena. "*You're* the mayor?"

"I'm quite serious," replied Popper. "And there are going to be a lot of changes around here."

"You mean like Verne no longer being allowed to terrorize the city?" Evena asked hopefully.

Popper frowned. "Don't be ridiculous," he said. "But you'll be happy to know that Verne has allowed us to pass a resolution permitting all law-abiding citizens of Skaal City to carry swords over thirty-two and a quarter inches."

"Yes," said Wyngalf unenthusiastically. "That's fantastic news."

"Of course, there was a price to pay for that concession," said the mayor. "I had to promise to deliver you to him. I issued a bounty for you through the Shipping Guild on the off-chance you might try to slip away overseas. Honestly, I thought it was a longshot, but here you are." He turned to the guard on his right. "Take them to the dungeon," he said.

The three companions were escorted from the docks.

Wyngalf, Evena and Tobalt were taken to a small cell in a dungeon beneath the palace. The dungeon appeared to be quite extensive, but it seemed to be empty except for the three of them and a few other lonesome souls who murmured and clanked somewhere in the near-total darkness. Wyngalf supposed the dungeon was comprised of tunnels that had been reclaimed from the goblin city underneath Skaal City, and for a brief, hopeful moment he imagined that they might escape through that network of tunnels again. But of course the dungeon's overseers would long ago have blocked off any escape routes: the walls of their cell were solid stone. The only light came from a torch flickering down the hall.

Feeling more defeated than ever, Wyngalf walked across the cell and sank into the pile of straw that sufficed for a bed. Evena sat down next to him, while Tobalt stood forlornly with his hands on the bars of the cell door. The guard's footsteps receded in the distance, leaving only the faint sounds of other prisoners languishing in the darkness.

"I can't believe they put that idiot Lord Popper in charge," said Wyngalf after some time.

"He may be an idiot," said Tobalt, "but he seems to have outsmarted us."

"A smarter mayor would know better than to give in to Verne's demands."

"I'm not sure I agree," said Tobalt. "It seems to me that the mayor is acting in a perfectly rational manner, as his rule depends on keeping Verne happy. Our incarceration is not the result of stupidity, but rather of rational self-interest coupled with an authoritarian power structure. We are a threat to the power structure, and therefore must be eliminated."

"I don't think it's Popper's lack of intelligence that's the problem," said Evena. "The problem is that he's a coward."

"Perhaps," said Tobalt. "But I will point out that we faced essentially the same fate under the previous regime, which is why we fled, as you may recall. Horkuden's Knife suggests, therefore, that the problem is not with the individual holding the office, but the office itself."

Wyngalf scowled. "Not this again," he said. "You aren't seriously arguing that society can function with no one in charge, and everybody just looking out for himself," he said. "I shudder to think of what such a society would look like. We'd be no better than goblins, reduced to our basest survival instincts. No offense."

"None taken," said Tobalt. "You are quite correct about the primitive and brutish nature of goblin society. But I believe you are mistaken in assuming that this sort of society is the result of an excess of individual freedom. Quite the contrary, in fact. Goblin society evinces precisely the rigid top-down hierarchy that you desire for humanity, and the results are, as you've implied, less than optimal."

"But goblins are—present company excepted—stupid and belligerent creatures," said Wyngalf. "It is no surprise that these traits persist despite the best attempts to instill order in their society."

"If I may further beg your indulgence," said Tobalt, "it seems to me that you miss the point. Goblins are not any more inherently stupid and belligerent than humans. Their stupidity and belligerence arises not *despite* their strict tribal hierarchy but directly as a result of it. Based on my—admittedly imperfect—studies of both races, I've come to the conclusion that intelligent, creative, peace-loving individuals are as common among goblins as they are among humans. But because goblin society is organized in a rigid hierarchy, such genius is rarely recognized. In extreme cases, the individual may even be banished by the clan."

"You're trying to tell me that the only difference between goblins and humans is that goblins have a greater desire for order?" Wyngalf said, dubious.

"Not the *only* difference, to be sure," Tobalt replied. "But it seems that while the desire for order exists in all sentient species, it manifests itself more strongly in goblin society. A society run by a top-down hierarchy is necessarily one in which the individual's value derives primarily from the amount of power over his fellows. It is, sadly, not the just society that you seek, but rather a society driven by envy and characterized by backstabbing and short-sightedness. By insisting that every aspect of goblin life be controlled from the top down, we eliminate the possibility of improvement through spontaneous action. Our military organization is effective, to be sure, but ultimately the strength of any society derives from the vibrancy of its culture, and goblin culture stagnates while human culture advances. We are, in the end, merely parasites on human society, and will persist only as long as the host is too weak to fully eradicate us." Tobalt stared at the lantern for a moment, lost in thought. "Perhaps, though, such an outcome is not inevitable."

"What do you mean?" asked Wyngalf suspiciously.

"Until recently," said Tobalt, "I had assumed that the excessive goblin craving for order was a congenital defect of our race, and that human beings were somehow naturally more tolerant of the disorder that accompanies individual freedom. But listening to you, it seems to me that perhaps I appreciate the human desire for freedom because I have experienced so little freedom, while you crave order because you have not seen what a rationally ordered society actually looks like. Rather than being diametric opposites on a continuum, our races may simply be poised at different points on the arc of a pendulum swinging between order and chaos. What if, in other words, there really is no difference between goblins and humans?"

"No difference!" exclaimed Wyngalf. "That's absurd. Anyone looking at us could tell we're of two completely different species."

"Of course," said Tobalt. "I don't mean to say there are no *superficial* differences. But what if there is no significant difference between a human mind and a goblin mind? What if goblins are simply humans who have given into the most extreme form of the desire for order? And conversely, humans are simply goblins who have embraced, however imperfectly, the concepts of individual freedom and responsibility. Think of it, Simply Wyngalf: thousands of years ago, before recorded history began, a great goblin civilization, renowned for its arts and literature, may have spanned the continent of Dis, while marauding bands of primitive humans harassed its frontiers. At some point, however, the tables turned. Goblins became smug and complacent, relying on a professional military to keep them safe from threats real and imagined, and trusting their leaders to perfect goblin society. Goblin society stagnated. Meanwhile, humans, forced to innovate in order to survive, developed a vibrant, resilient civilization, eventually eclipsing the goblins—and in at least one case, literally building their civilization on top of what remained of goblin society. All that remains of the uncivilized prehistoric humans are the barbarian tribes far to the north and south—whose society is structured much in the same way as goblin clans."

Wyngalf scowled at this absurd and blasphemous corruption of history, but remained silent, unsure how to respond. The more he argued that human society required order, the more he seemed to be confirming Tobalt's hypothesis that humanity was giving into the authoritarian urge that had doomed the goblins. Wyngalf didn't buy in for an instant, but he had to admit it made for an oddly compelling narrative—especially in light of their discovery of the abandoned network of tunnels and caverns beneath Skaal City.

Just then, a man's voice called out somewhere in the darkness: "Simply Wyngalf, is that you?"

Wyngalf got to his feet and moved to the door, trying to place the man's voice. It seemed familiar, but it didn't sound like Orbrecht. Wyngalf looked to Tobalt and then Evena, but they shrugged, apparently not recognizing the voice either.

"Who is that?" called Wyngalf.

"It's your servant, Arbliss," said the voice.

The name hung in the air, connecting to nothing in Wyngalf's memory.

"I've kept it safe," said Arbliss.

"Arbliss!" cried Wyngalf. Tobalt and Evena stared at Wyngalf, still puzzled. "The man who gave us directions to the harbor," Wyngalf explained to his companions. "What are you doing down here, Arbliss?" he called.

"The SMASHERs have outlawed Ovaltarianism," said Arbliss. "They think we pose a threat to their rule. Most of us have gone into hiding, and a few have been killed. They're keeping me alive because they think they can get me to tell them where it is, but I'll never talk."

"Where what is, Arbliss?" asked Wyngalf. "What are you talking about?"

He heard the faint sound of Arbliss chuckling. "That's it," Arbliss said. "Play dumb for now. Our moment is coming."

"Seriously, Arbliss," Wyngalf pleaded, "I have no idea what you're talking about. What are you keeping safe?" But Arbliss's faint chuckle was the only answer. Wyngalf sighed and sat down next to

Evena again. It was pretty clear that Arbliss was going to be of no help.

Turning to Wyngalf, Evena said, "So this Arbliss is a member of the sect that believes in the... what did you call it, Tobalt?"

"Ko-Haringu," replied Tobalt. "The messiah that will deliver the Land of Dis from the scourge of dragons."

"And he's convinced you're the Ko-Haringu," Evena said to Wyngalf. "Just like Orbrecht was. I wonder how many others there are."

"I don't see that it matters," said Wyngalf. "They're not going to be able to break us out of this dungeon. We'll rot in here until they decide to turn us over to Verne."

"So much for your faith in the Noninity," said Evena.

Wyngalf shrugged, too defeated to rise to the challenge. "I'm resigned to my fate as a martyr."

"And we get to be martyred with you?" asked Evena. "For a faith we don't even believe in?"

Wyngalf, past the point of caring what anyone thought of him, lay down on the straw and closed his eyes. He just wanted it all to end.

Nineteen

They were roused by a guard banging his sword on the bars of the cell door. "You!" he snapped, pointing at Wyngalf, "Come here." Blinking the sleep from his eyes, Wyngalf got to his feet and approached the door. The guard sheathed his sword. "Turn around and hold out your hands," said the guard, producing a pair of shackles. Wyngalf did as instructed, and the guard clamped the shackles tightly over his wrists. The guard ordered him to step away, and had Tobalt and Evena step toward the door in turn. When he had shackled their wrists as well, he unlocked the door. "Follow me," the guard barked, and they filed into the tunnel. Another guard followed close behind.

The guards escorted them through a series of narrow hallways and then up a spiral staircase that brought them to a balcony overlooking the city. They seemed to be in the mayor's palace, at the southern edge of the city square. Judging by the angle of the sun, it was mid-morning. The new mayor, Lord Otten Popper, was waiting for them, along with several other guards and a few other people whose garb suggested they were functionaries of the city government. Among these were Glindeen, Hendrick and Dwalen, who stood next to each other as if they were old friends. The ex-mayor's smile was probably fairly convincing from a distance, but it was pretty clear he wasn't thrilled to be there. Politics, thought Wyngalf, is a strange business.

The scene reminded Wyngalf of their encounter with the mayor of Brobdingdon and Scarlett in Skaal City, but so far there was no sign of a dragon. Something else was different, too: a low, rumbling sound that seemed to come from somewhere down below. Wyngalf, still trying to clear the fog of sleep from his brain, took a moment to realize that it was the sound of hundreds of Skaal City residents gathered in the streets below. They had evidently been summoned to witness a demonstration, and Wyngalf had the sickening feeling he had a rough idea of what that demonstration was going to consist of. He only hoped his death—and that of his two friends—was relatively quick and painless.

As Wyngalf was prodded toward the railing, he saw that he had underestimated the size of the crowd below. There had to be thousands of people down there—men, women and children—all waiting to see Wyngalf and his friends punished for whatever crimes there were supposed to have committed. Wyngalf glanced to his right, where Evena stood a few feet away, looking dolefully down at the crowd. Tobalt stood stoically to her right.

"Good morning, citizens of Skaal City!" cried Popper, who had stepped up to the railing on Wyngalf's left to oversee the crowd. He was greeted with cheers and applause. "As you know," the mayor went on, "there have been a lot of changes in the city of late. Two days ago, we affirmed the right of all Skaal City residents to carry swords anywhere in the city!"

More cheers from the crowd.

"Yesterday, we repealed cumbersome environmental regulations that prohibit proprietors of inns and taverns from dumping raw sewage in the streets!"

Hesitant clapping from the crowd.

"And today, we are making a stand against foreign invaders who violate our laws, disrespect our customs, and make us feel uncomfortable about ourselves!"

Enthusiastic cheers from the crowd.

"These two humans, with the help of this filthy runt of a goblin, infiltrated our fine city, sabotaged the Shipping Guild office, drowned Halbert the clerk, threatened me, and caused the destruction of the *Numinda Fae*."

"Verne destroyed that ship!" Evena cried. "I was just trying to get—"

Her words were cut short as a guard jabbed her in the back of her skull with the pommel of his sword. Wyngalf turned to intervene, but in a flash the guard reversed his sword, the blade stopping less than an inch from Wyngalf's throat. Off balance, with his hands still shackled behind his back, it was all Wyngalf could do not to fall forward onto the tip of the blade, eviscerating himself in the process. Another guard gripped Wyngalf by his shoulder and shoved him back to the railing, nearly throwing him to the street below in his enthusiasm. Wyngalf reeled as he hung suspended over the edge, and for a moment he considered throwing himself forward to break free of the guard's grip: with any luck, he would die quickly, his skull crushed on the pavement below. But Noninitarianism did not look kindly on suicide; he'd have a hard time explaining himself to Xandiss the Auditor, and Shotarr the Purifier would deal harshly with him. No, as gruesome as his death was likely to be, he would face it bravely, like the martyrs of old. He risked a glance at Evena, to his left, who seemed dazed but otherwise unhurt. Tobalt stood next to her, somber and squinting in the bright light of the morning.

"As I was saying," Lord Popper went on, "by violating shipping regulations and sneaking on board the *Numinda Fae*, these three scofflaws forced Verne to incinerate a perfectly good ship and much of its crew." He turned to look at Wyngalf and Evena, as if daring them to object. When they didn't rise to the bait, he shrugged and continued. "These are serious crimes indeed. That said, Skaal City has a long tradition of respect for the rule of law, and part of that tradition is the guarantee of a fair trial for anyone suspected of a crime—a guarantee that extends even to foreigners from across the Sea of Dis."

Boos and hisses from the crowd.

"I take these traditions very seriously," Popper continued. "In fact, I was up most of the night deliberating on the fate of these prisoners. As you know, Skaal City has many enemies—chief among these being that hub of villainy to our north, Brobdingdon."

Enthusiastic boos from the crowd.

"We are fortunate in Skaal to have a protector against those who would do us harm. The dragon Verne works tirelessly to keep us safe from barbarians, goblins, and that winged terror who does the bidding of the Brobdingdonians."

Murmurs and nods of understanding from the crowd. Wyngalf wondered if Lord Popper didn't know Scarlett's name or if he didn't speak it out of some superstitious fear, like the fear of the seamen for the Hafgufa.

"With Verne shouldering this burden for us," Popper continued, "it is all too easy for us to forget the threats that we face. But make no mistake: we are at war, and during war certain liberties must be sacrificed to ensure the security of our fine city. Further, it has come to my attention that these three prisoners have had contact with agents in Brobdingdon, and in fact have conspired against us with that foul beast who haunts our skies and terrorizes our borders. I ask you, what good are legal niceties when our very existence is threatened?"

More sympathetic murmurs.

"After long deliberation, then, I have decided that these three prisoners are to be considered enemies of Skaal City, and therefore outside of the purview of our criminal justice system. They shall be handed over to Verne so that he can extract information from them regarding our enemies and then deal with them as he sees fit."

Cheers went up from the crowd, but then were almost immediately transmuted into gasps and cries of surprise as a familiar shadow momentarily blotted out the sun behind Wyngalf. Gusts of wind followed, and Wyngalf heard the clatter of claws on the stone of the tower. Jabbed in the ribs by one of the guards, Wyngalf took the hint and turned to face the dragon. Tobalt and Evena were forced to face him as well. Verne loomed over them.

"Greetings, citizens of Skaal City!" Verne's voice boomed. "And thank you, Mr. Mayor, for that fine introduction. Pardon my late arrival; I have, as the mayor indicated, been quite busy dealing with a few of our many, many enemies. In fact, I have just located some entirely new enemies in a land I didn't even realize existed a week ago." He gave Evena a wink with his good eye. "These are extremely dangerous people with no regard for the value of human life, and I won't rest until they've been eradicated."

Cheers from the crowd. Evena glowered at him.

"But as hard as I work to keep the people of this city safe," Verne boomed, "I'm afraid that even I cannot keep out all those who plot against us. The three criminals you see before you are evidence that we must never tire in our struggle against evildoers both here at home and abroad. These three have conspired with our enemies both here in Skaal City and in Brobdingdon. They violated our laws, threatened our officials and brought about the deaths of a score of innocent men on the *Numinda Fae*. And for this, they must be punished!"

As the crowd erupted into cheers once again, Verne craned his neck to get a closer look at his captives.

"You destroyed my home!" Evena cried. "You killed my family!"

The guard made to thwack Evena with his pommel again, but Verne raised a claw to stay his hand. "It's all right," he said. "Let the girl whine. Although in point of fact, I did nothing of the kind."

Evena stared at Verne. "My parents are still alive?"

"Of course," said Verne. "I needed them for leverage."

While Evena and Verne conversed, down below the crowd had begun chanting something in unison. At first Wyngalf thought they were simply chanting Verne's name, but after repetitions he realized they were shouting "Burn them!"

"I don't understand," said Evena. "Leverage against whom?"

"Against *you*, my dear," said Verne. "You see, I was unable to locate the jewel of Skuldred using the information you provided, and I suspect that you know more than you've told me. I think you know exactly where the jewel is, and you didn't reveal its location because you suspected—rightly, I must admit—that I would kill you once I no longer had any need for you. But I'm done playing games. Tell me exactly where the jewel is, or I will kill your parents, along with everyone else in your hometown. And then I will return to kill you, slowly and painfully. Tell me the location of the jewel of Skuldred right now, and your death—and that of your two friends—will be swift and relatively painless."

As the chant of "Burn them! Burn them! Burn them!" continued below, Wyngalf stared at the dragon, befuddled. How could Verne not have figured out that Evena's story was a fabrication? That Ashor, Wiggin and Brisby were the names not of men, but of dogs? The first person Verne encountered in Skuldred would have spilled the truth. Then, suddenly, it dawned on him: Verne was bluffing. Evena's parents—and presumably the rest of the townspeople—must have fled Skuldred after Verne's initial attack. There was no other explanation. Verne had returned to Skuldred to find the town deserted, and there had been no one to ask about the three heirs who supposedly held the secret of the jewel of Skuldred. Verne's avarice had so overwhelmed his reason that in his lust for the jewel, it never occurred to him that Evena might have been lying.

Evena must have figured it out too, because she burst into laughter. She tried to stop, probably realizing that her best bet was to play along with Verne, pretending to know where the jewel was, but the idea of Verne revealing his weakness and ignorance in an attempt to threaten them was too much for her to take.

"You find the imminent death of your family and friends amusing?" Verne roared, barely audible over the chanting of the crowd, which had risen to a deafening volume. Evena redoubled her efforts to stop chortling. Lord Popper and the other dignitaries had backed away, and were cautiously watching the scene unfold.

As Wyngalf looked toward Evena, he caught a glimpse of Tobalt, who was still standing in stoic silence on the other side of her. Wyngalf now realized why the goblin was being so quiet: he was gradually working his hands out of the shackles, which fit poorly on his overly large forearms. Already his right hand was halfway out of its cuff, and now that Tobalt was standing with his back toward the parapet, the guards couldn't see what he was doing. One of them stood less than two paces from Tobalt, staring open-mouthed at Verne, his sword in a scabbard hanging off his hip. Tobalt glanced at Wyngalf, then at the sword, and finally at Verne. Wyngalf gave a curt nod in reply, realizing what the goblin was planning. It was a bold gambit, and as likely to end in incineration as escape, but it seemed to be their only chance.

"I demand to know why you're laughing!" Verne roared at Evena, who still hadn't composed herself enough to reply.

Desperate to keep the dragon's attention off Tobalt, Wyngalf took a step forward. "It was a lie, you imbecile," he said softly.

Verne instinctively craned his head closer to Wyngalf. "What did you say?" he demanded.

"I said it was a lie," Wyngalf replied. "The whole story about the jewel of Skuldred? Evena made it up. And you fell for it."

Verne glared at him, then turned his gaze to Evena, who had stopped laughing. "You wouldn't dare," he growled.

Wyngalf ventured a glance at Tobalt and saw that the goblin's hand was nearly free. Wyngalf just needed to keep the dragon's attention—and keep him close enough for Tobalt to reach his good eye—for a few seconds longer. "Not only that," Wyngalf went on, anxious to keep Verne's eye on him, "but you just revealed your hand. If you had found anyone at Skuldred, they would have told you the story was a fabrication. Which means the town was deserted when you got there. You have no idea where Evena's family is. You've got nothing to threaten us with." His anger and fear made it difficult not to shout, but he forced him to speak in low, controlled tones. It worked: as he spoke, Verne continued to move his head closer in an attempt to hear Wyngalf over the shouts of the crowd. Verne's teeth were just inches away from Wyngalf's face now, and his good eye was only a few feet from Tobalt.

"Nothing to threaten you with?" Verne asked. "Oh, Simpleton Wyngalf. I'm afraid it's time for me to teach you a lesson. *All* of you."

Verne's mouth opened, Wyngalf could see glow of fire igniting somewhere deep in the dragon's belly. But before Verne could unleash the flames on them, Tobalt bounded forward, the guard's sword in his hand. Holding the sword with two hands, he thrust it toward the dragon's face. Verne yelped and jerked his head back, and Tobalt sprawled onto the stone before him. The sword was no longer in Tobalt's hand, and as Verne shook his head back and forth, Wyngalf saw that Tobalt had very nearly struck his target: the sword was sticking out of Verne's eye socket, just below the eyeball. Tobalt had failed to blind Verne, but he had succeeded in making him very, very angry.

Verne flailed wildly, trying to dislodge the sword. As he spun around, his massive tail whipped across the top of the tower, sweeping three of the four guards clear off the roof and knocking down the remaining guard, along with Lord Popper and the other functionaries. Tobalt, still on his knees, ducked below the sweep, and Wyngalf managed to leap out of the way. Evena wasn't so lucky: She backed away, trying to get out of range, but the tip of Verne's tail struck her solidly in the chest, forcing her to stumble backwards onto the railing. For a moment it seemed like she might regain her balance, but the momentum was too great to fight: she disappeared with a scream over the edge.

"No!" cried Wyngalf, dashing toward her—but he was too late. Evena had fallen to her death, and it was his fault. He turned to face Verne, who had managed to dislodge the sword, and was now blinking and rubbing his eye with the back of his claw. "You bastard!" Wyngalf cried. "You killed her!" Without thinking, he charged at Verne, his hands still shackled behind his back. If he was going to die, he was going to at least go down fighting.

But as he approached, Verne suddenly flapped his wings and shot into the air. Unable to halt his own momentum, Wyngalf stumbled and fell to the ground. When he had managed to get back on his feet and turn around, he saw that Verne hung in the air a few feet above the center of the tower, creating great gusts of wind with his wings. Tobalt, the mayor, and the others cowered at the edges of the tower.

What got Wyngalf's attention, though, was the *second* dragon hovering above the crowd, less than a stone's throw from Verne, her red scales shining brightly in the mid-morning sunlight. A small human figure was visible on its back: Evena. She was alive. Scarlett must have caught her as she fell. Evena lay flat on Scarlett's back, gripping the base of her wings, clearly terrified. Down below, the chants of the crowd gave way to confused shouts and gasps.

"You dare to interfere in the internal affairs of Skaal City?" Verne bellowed.

"We had a deal," Scarlett boomed. "I give you the three fugitives and you give me the jewel of Skuldred."

"You didn't live up to your end of the deal, *sister*," said Verne.

"I delivered them right to you!" said Scarlett. "Put them aboard a ship and sent it right to your port."

"Ha!" Verne cried. "You expect me to believe you were behind their escape? Nice try, Scarlett, but I owe you nothing. Fly back to Brobdingdon before I lose patience."

"Fine," said Scarlett. "But I'm keeping the girl."

"No," said Verne. "The girl and her friends are mine. They must be punished for their insolence—that is, their crimes against Skaal City."

"You can keep the other two," said Scarlett. "But the girl has information I need."

Verne laughed bitterly. "If you think she's going to tell you where the jewel of Skuldred is, you're mistaken. There is no jewel of Skuldred, Scarlett. We were duped."

"You always were a terrible liar," said Scarlett.

"I'm afraid it's the truth," said Verne. "I just found out myself."

"Then you won't mind if I keep the girl," said Scarlett, who clearly didn't believe him. Wishful thinking apparently ran deep in dragons when it came to invaluable jewels.

"On the contrary," said Verne. "It's all the more reason for me to keep her. She played me for a fool, and I cannot allow that to go unpunished. Put the girl down and leave right now and I'll forgive this encroachment on my territory."

"Make me, *brother*," said Scarlett with a smile. With Evena still lying prone on Scarlett's back, gripping the base of her wings, the dragon spun around and shot into the sky. Verne shot after her.

As the two dragons receded in the distance, Wyngalf forced himself to turn his attention back to his immediate surroundings. The remaining guard, still dazed from being knocked flat, struggled to his feet in front of him. Wyngalf, eyeing the key ring at the man's waist, launched himself at the guard, catching him in the throat with his shoulder and knocking him back down. With his hands still bound, Wyngalf could do little more than roll backwards onto the man, trying to use his body weight to keep him down. As the guard tried to throw him off, Wyngalf thrust his head backwards, hearing a loud crunch as the back of his skull struck the bridge of the man's nose. The man gave a gurgling scream followed by a hacking cough as he choked on his own blood. Wyngalf slid off him, feeling desperately for the keys. After a few abortive attempts that might have been taken as amorous advances under different circumstances, he managed to locate the guard's key ring. Wrapping his fingers around the ring, he jerked it away from the guard and rolled away.

Several keys dangled from the ring, and Wyngalf could only go through them one by one, hoping to find the key that unlocked the shackles. Behind him, the guard was still coughing and gurgling, but Lord Popper had noticed what Wyngalf was up to and approached him, rapier drawn. Wyngalf struggled frantically with the keys, but it was no use; he'd never be free in time. Popper grinned and ran at him, rapier drawn back to cut Wyngalf's throat. Popper was nearly on him when he suddenly collapsed on the bricks, screaming. Crouching behind Popper was Tobalt. Blood streamed down the goblin's chin, and Wyngalf realized with sudden shock of horror and gratitude that Tobalt had taken a chunk out of the mayor's calf.

While Lord Popper howled in pain, the guard continued to cough and gurgle, and the other city dignitaries cringed uncertainly at the perimeter of the tower, Wyngalf managed to locate the key to the shackles and get his hands free. The ex-mayor, Dwalen, mustered his courage and darted forward, picking up Lord Popper's rapier where it had fallen on the stones.

"See here," Dwalen said, waving the rapier uncertainly in Wyngalf's direction. "There's no call for this sort of—"

His speech was cut short as Wyngalf lunged forward, ducking past the blade of the rapier and bringing his right hand, still holding one of the cuffs, up in an arc toward the man's face. The other cuff struck Dwalen's jaw with a loud crack, and he reeled backwards and fell limply to the stone. Without slowing, Wyngalf helped Tobalt to his feet and handed him the key.

"You have some sort of plan, I take it?" asked Tobalt, removing the cuff from his left hand.

"None whatsoever," said Wyngalf. As he spoke, he caught a glimpse of Scarlett darting between two distant spires, closely pursued by Verne. The tiny figure of Evena remained perched on Scarlett's back. "Let's go."

Twenty

Wyngalf and Tobalt ran past the dazed and frightened dignitaries. If any of the others had ideas of stopping the two prisoners, they thought better of it when Tobalt bared his fangs at them, his face still smeared with the blood of Lord Popper. The two companions scampered down the steps past more guards who yelled at them to stop but seemed too confused about what was happening to take any decisive action. They emerged from a side door from the palace into a narrow alley. With no plan in mind other than bypassing the crowd in front and somehow rescuing Evena, Wyngalf took off down the alley, Tobalt following closely behind. Behind them they heard shouts and the clanking of armor on cobblestones, but the two fugitives quickly lost their pursuers in the maze of side streets around the palace.

Eventually they came out onto a main artery that allowed them a mostly unobscured view of the sky, and after a moment Wyngalf caught sight of Verne pursuing Scarlett over the slums to the south. Scarlett seemed to be flying a bit cautiously, not wanting to lose Evena, but even so, Verne was having trouble keeping up. Wyngalf realized after a moment that Verne was being forced to crane his head at an unnatural angle to keep Scarlett in view, which was affecting his ability to fly straight. It seemed that although Tobalt had failed to blind him, he had succeeded in doing some damage to his vision. Occasionally Scarlett would make a beeline to the north, evidently attempting to return to Brobdingdon with Evena, but on the straightaways Verne would overtake her, blasting her with fire.

Each time, Scarlett was able to shield Evena from the worst of the blast, but clearly she wasn't going to keep this up forever.

For some time, Wyngalf and Tobalt ran to and fro across the city, trying to keep the two dragons in sight. Eventually they ended up running unwittingly down a side street right smack into the city square in front of the palace. Fortunately the crowd had thinned somewhat by this point, and those that remained were too distracted by the spectacle of the two dragons chasing each other overhead to pay much attention to the two fugitives. To the right, Lord Popper and the other city officials gaped at the scene from the balcony. Wyngalf and Tobalt stopped in the square, drenched with sweat and exhausted from their pursuit.

Scarlett shot overhead, Verne following seconds later. Just as Verne closed within range of Scarlett, the red dragon banked sharply to the right. Wyngalf's breath caught in his throat as he watched Evena sliding across Scarlett's back, barely keeping hold of the base of Scarlett's right wing. It took Verne only a split-second to adjust his own trajectory; he was getting better at anticipating Scarlett's moves without being able to see her. If this kept up, Evena was going to be in trouble.

"There they are!" cried a voice from across the square, and Wyngalf turned to see a trio of guards running toward them. He and Tobalt groaned and took off running again, dodging the confused spectators in their path. Scarlett shot overhead again, this time from their left, so close they could feel the breeze from her wings. Verne continued to close the gap between them.

"Give up, sister!" they heard him bellow. "I've always been faster than you!"

"Faster, maybe," called Scarlett in response, "but not smarter." She banked left and for a moment disappeared behind a row of buildings. The guards continued to gain on Wyngalf and Tobalt; the two fugitives were simply too worn out to make very good time.

"We're caught," gasped Tobalt.

"Don't stop!" cried Wyngalf, but every muscle in his body screamed at him to do just that. They made it nearly to the edge of the square before collapsing in exhaustion. Spectators backed away from them as the footsteps of the guards grew louder.

Wiping the sweat from his eyes, Wyngalf ventured a glance at the horizon. After a moment, he caught sight of Scarlett shooting above a row of buildings in the distance and arcing back toward the square, with Verne close on her heels.

"On your feet!" snapped a gruff voice behind them. Wyngalf groaned and staggered to his feet. Tobalt, still panting on the ground next to him, made no sign of having heard the command. Wyngalf seized the goblin's arm and tried to help him to his feet, but Tobalt's body remained limp.

"I said, on your feet!" the voice barked again.

"Come on, Tobalt," urged Wyngalf. "We'll get through this somehow. You and me. Don't give up yet."

Tobalt nodded wearily and allowed Wyngalf to pull him upright. Wyngalf watched as Scarlett banked again, just ahead of a blast of fire from Verne. She neared a pair of tall buildings at the edge of the square. Wyngalf was beginning to anticipate Scarlett's moves: if she were true to her pattern, she would bank left just past the buildings, flying over the square and back the way she had come. But if Wyngalf could see this, he had to assume Verne could too. If he were smart, he'd bank just short of the buildings and intercept Scarlett on her way back over the square.

"Turn around!" the voice barked, and Tobalt dutifully turned to face the guards. But Wyngalf couldn't tear his eyes from the spectacle. He could see it in his mind: Scarlett banking as she passed the two buildings and Verne banking around them the other way, surprising her with a blast of fire as they met over the square. He could only hope Verne's timing was good: if he released his torrent of fire a split second too early or too late, Evena would be badly burned but not killed. On the other hand, she'd never survive a fall from Scarlett's back, so she was dead either way.

Something hard struck Wyngalf on the back of his skull, and for a moment his vision blurred and his knees buckled. "Simply Wyngalf!" cried Tobalt, doing his best to catch Wyngalf as he slumped to the ground.

"Get up!" barked the voice behind Wyngalf again.

"If you want him ambulatory," Tobalt gasped, "might I suggest refraining from further bludgeoning?"

Wyngalf heard another whack, and he was vaguely aware of Tobalt slumping to the ground next to him. But Wyngalf's attention remained focused on Evena, clinging in terror to the back of the dragon. She was going to die, and it was all his fault. He didn't care about his own death, and he could only feel so much responsibility for Tobalt, who hadn't exactly had a promising career ahead of him when Wyngalf found him in the ruins of Sybesma. But Evena was just a girl, clever, beautiful and full of promise. And now, because Wyngalf had wanted to impress her by making himself out to be some kind of bold adventurer, she was going to die.

But as he watched, Scarlett banked more sharply than he expected, and he realized that she intended not to go around the two buildings, but *between* them. The buildings were barely far enough apart for a narrow street to run between them, and Wyngalf was almost certain that there wasn't enough room for Scarlett to make it through.

Verne, who had already begun banking sharply to intercept Scarlett, seemed puzzled as well. If she made it through the narrow gap, he'd end up in front of her, which was not where he wanted to be. Verne widened the angle of his turn, attempting to follow her through the buildings.

But while Scarlett had planned her move with precision, banking so that her wings were stretched perfectly vertical as she slipped through the gap, Verne's turn was abrupt and awkward. Scarlett, with Evena pressed flat against her back, missed the walls by mere inches on both sides. Verne did not.

Having intended to turn more sharply, Verne had to level out slightly to angle himself toward the gap between the buildings, but this meant that as he approached, his wings were less than fully vertical—and there was no margin for error between the buildings. Realizing his mistake, Verne spread his wings in an attempt to slow his approach, but this only made things worse. The underside of Verne's wings struck the stone corners, bending the wings backwards. Verne howled in pain as the joints dislocated and the wings folded behind him. Unable to halt his movement, the great green dragon continued through the gap, plummeting toward the square below.

Wyngalf realized without a moment to spare that Verne was heading directly for him, and threw himself to the ground next to Tobalt. A shadow passed over them, followed by a crash of metal on stone, and Wyngalf turned to see that the three guards had been bowled over by the crippled dragon, who was rolling to a halt near the center of the square. Scarlett, meanwhile, soared across the open space, her body still angled sharply to the side, heading directly for the palace. At first Wyngalf couldn't determine why she wasn't leveling out, but then he realized that Evena had tumbled off Scarlett's back and was now hanging off the tip of her wing, weighing the dragon down.

Scarlett was gradually righting herself, but with the added weight of Evena on her wing she was never going to clear the palace in time. Scarlett must have realized this, because at the last moment she braked in an attempt to soften the impact. With the sudden movement of Scarlett's wings, Evena lost her grip and tumbled through the air. Wyngalf held his breath as she fell—and exhaled with relief as she landed with a splash in the fountain in front of the palace.

Scarlett was not so lucky. Despite her attempts to slow herself, she continued to rocket toward the palace. Lord Popper and the other dignitaries, who had been watching the show from the balcony, suddenly realized they were in danger and began to retreat inside, but it was too late. Scarlett crashed into the palace, shattering two of the stone pillars that held up the balcony and demolishing most of the front wall. The balcony collapsed, sending its occupants crashing to the pavement below. Those that weren't buried in rubble lay unmoving on the street.

After a moment, Scarlett raised her head woozily, like a drunk who had fallen off a barstool. The sound of cracking stone echoed through the square, and before Scarlett could extricate herself from the rubble, the rest of the palace collapsed on top of her. For several seconds the only movement was the cloud of dust rising from the rubble. Then the shifting of hunks of marble at the top of the pile indicated that Scarlett was still alive.

In the meantime, Verne had gotten uneasily to his feet, his broken wings hanging uselessly at his side. He staggered forward, and for a moment Wyngalf feared that he was going after Evena, who was climbing out of the fountain. But Verne walked right past her, intent on the shifting pile of rubble on the far side of the square. "You have broken my wings, sister," he growled, dragging his wings pathetically behind him, "but I will tear your head from your body!" He climbed on top of the rubble and began tossing debris aside with his claws in an effort to get to Scarlett. Evena, dazed and dripping wet, cowered behind the fountain as chunks of brick and stone flew in every direction.

Wyngalf wrenched his attention from the scene to tend to Tobalt, who was struggling to get to his feet. As Wyngalf tried to rouse him, Tobalt murmured, "I'm okay... help Evena."

"Wait here," Wyngalf said. "I'll be right back."

Tobalt nodded, and Wyngalf took off running past the still-prone guards toward the fountain. As he approached, Verne tossed a chunk of marble in his direction, and he dived underneath its path, ending up sprawled on the pavement next to Evena. She was crouched behind the base of the fountain, shivering with cold or fear, and as Wyngalf pulled himself up next to her, he couldn't help think of the night they spent together on the island before Verne found them. He had gotten her into this mess, and now he was going to get her out.

"We need to get out of here," he urged, speaking loudly so as to be heard over the sound of crashing stone.

Evena shook her head. "Can't walk," she murmured, and as Wyngalf looked at her feet he saw what she meant. Her left ankle was badly swollen, having been sprained or maybe even broken in the fall.

"I'll carry you," he said, and she grunted something that he took as assent. He bent over to allow her to wrap her arms around his neck and scooped her into her arms. He was still a little woozy from being struck on the back of the head, but if he could run with Evena in a more-or-less straight line to the edge of the square, they could conceivably find a hiding place in an alley where Verne wouldn't be able to get to them.

As he picked her up, though, a sense of vertigo came over him, as if the ground were pitching beneath him. When he noticed water spilling out of the fountain toward what was left of the palace, he realized he wasn't imagining it: the pavement was sloping toward the rubble pile.

"What in the name of Abasmos...?" Wyngalf asked, with a puzzled glance at the water pouring over the lip of the fountain.

"The caverns!" Evena exclaimed. "The ground is collapsing!"

It was true. The collapse of the palace must have caused a cave-in in the caverns below. A deep depression had begun to form, with the pile of rubble at the epicenter. Already the walls of the buildings behind the palace were cracking as they slumped toward the deepening hole. Verne was so preoccupied with getting to Scarlett that by the time he noticed they were sinking, it was too late. He and Scarlett—whose head was now visible at the top of the pile—stared for a moment at the water pouring down the pavement toward them, trying to make sense of the situation.

"Uh-oh," said Verne, as his broken wings flailed helplessly in a vain attempt to get him airborne.

"You idiot," said Scarlett, and the two of them disappeared as the bottom fell out beneath them. Their howls of terror gradually faded as they plummeted into the cavern. The pit continued to widen as large chunks of pavement and earth crumbled from the edges, and shops and houses behind the palace began to slide into the hole.

"Run, Wyngalf!" Evena cried.

Wyngalf ran. Exhausted, his head aching, Wyngalf ran up the cracked and rapidly steepening pavement of the square, holding Evena before him. His legs burned with the effort, and at times the pavement slid out from under his feet, nearly causing him to stumble, but he kept going, urged on by Evena's terror and the sound of entire buildings collapsing into the gaping hole behind him. Beside and ahead of him, city guards and townspeople ran screaming across the square, radiating outward from the sinkhole. Only one figure stood unmoving near the edge of the square, staring awestruck at the scene.

"Tobalt!" Wyngalf cried as he approached. "Help!" His muscles giving out, Wyngalf let Evena fall from his arms. Tobalt managed to break her fall and then helped her to her feet. She winced and lifted her left foot, leaning heavily on Tobalt's shoulders. Completely spent, Wyngalf fell to his hands and knees. Venturing a glance behind him, he saw that the abyss continued to grow. The ground here was still level, but beneath his feet, the pavement buckled and cracked as the earth below it gave way.

"Simply Wyngalf!" Tobalt exclaimed. "We can't stop!"

Wyngalf struggled to his feet, and he and Tobalt helped Evena to stand. The three of them made their way to the street beyond the square, not stopping until they were certain they were on firm ground. Once they were some distance down the street, they paused to rest, turning to see the devastation behind them.

Most of the city square was now a vast chasm. The palace and several other buildings had disappeared completely into the pit. Many structures near the edge were dangerously off-kilter, looking like they might slide into the abyss at any moment. There was no telling how deep the chasm went, but it was obviously gigantic. Wyngalf left Tobalt and Evena resting against the corner of a building and walked a few steps closer to the hole, looking for any sign of the two dragons. But the bottom of the pit was lost in blackness. Somewhere, far below, were the remains of the dragons and every high-ranking official in the Skaal City government.

"There they are!" barked a voice behind him. Wyngalf turned to see the three guards, their swords drawn, coming down the street toward them.

"You have got to be kidding me," Wyngalf moaned. "A gigantic sinkhole just opened up in the middle of the city, killing both of the dragons that have been terrorizing Dis for hundreds of years, along with the mayor and his flunkies, and all you can think about is arresting us?"

The sergeant at the front of the group shrugged. "Six of my men died chasing you three through those tunnels last week," he said. "We're not arresting you. We're throwing you in that hole." The two men at his side made approving grunts, and the three moved toward Wyngalf.

Wyngalf held up his hands. "I won't resist," he said. "But you have to let my friends go."

The sergeant shrugged again. "Go ahead and resist," he said. "Doesn't make any difference to us. But in the end, you're all going in the pit."

Wyngalf groaned, trying to decide if it was even worth it to put up a fight. Surely Xandiss the Auditor wouldn't hold it against him if he just gave up and let the guards throw him over the edge. On the other hand, if he put up a fight, maybe Tobalt and Evena would have a chance to get away. But as he watched Tobalt slowly help the crippled Evena to her feet, he realized he was kidding himself. There was no way out of this. They had survived two dragons only to fall victim to the petty grudge of the city guard.

As Wyngalf backed away from the swords, stepping closer to the edge of the abyss, he heard a familiar voice from behind the men.

"Let him go, Malleck," the voice commanded sternly.

The sergeant spun on his heels to face the newcomer. "Orbrecht!" the man gasped.

Wyngalf saw that it was true. The old warrior was limping down the street toward them, flanked by two more of the city guard.

"Lord Popper and his cronies are dead, along with Verne," said Orbrecht. "Salmon Brigade has taken control of the city guard. This man and his companions are heroes. They are not to be harmed." Wyngalf saw now that Orbrecht and his companions wore matching salmon-colored armbands.

Malleck laughed. "Salmon Brigade?" he said. "Is that what you and your band of nutters are calling yourselves these days? What does the color mean?"

"It means we ran out of red dye," grumbled the man at Orbrecht's left. Orbrecht glared at him, and he bit his lip.

"How many of you are there anyway, a dozen?" Malleck asked, a wry smile on his face.

"Three score in the City Guard alone," said Orbrecht. "And the number is growing by the minute. By the time the SMASHers and SAURIANs select new leaders to replace Popper and Glindeen, Salmon Brigade will have complete control over the city."

"A few funny-colored armbands don't put you in control of nothing," said Malleck. "I don't take orders from you, old man," he said. The men at his side seemed less certain about the matter, but they nodded in agreement.

"I don't have time for this, Malleck," said Orbrecht, drawing his sword. "You can fall in line, or you can fall in that pit."

"After you, old man," Malleck said.

The two men approached each other, their respective companions standing aside by unspoken agreement. As the men's swords clashed, Wyngalf scurried away behind Malleck to rejoin Tobalt and Evena, and together they watched the melee unfold.

It didn't last long. Malleck was younger and stronger, but Orbrecht fought with the fervor of the true believer, delivering a barrage of blows so rapid and fierce that it was all Malleck could do to parry them. Orbrecht gradually pushed him backwards, and Malleck was forced to glance behind him to see how close he was to the edge of the abyss. This was all the opportunity Orbrecht needed: he swung at Malleck's neck while the man was off balance, and although Malleck succeeded in blocking the attack, he was knocked to the ground, landing on his hip and rolling toward the edge of the pit. The sword fell from his hand as he caught himself, and it disappeared into the abyss.

"Please," said Malleck, crawling forward and holding up his right hand before Orbrecht. "Don't kill me. I'll join Salmon Brigade." He began staggering to his feet.

Orbrecht caught him in the chest with his boot. "No place in Salmon Brigade for cowards," he said, and gave the man a kick. Malleck tumbled backwards into the abyss, screaming as he fell. Orbrecht turned to the other two guards, who were watching in horror from the edge of the street. "Anyone else want to question my authority?" he said. The men shook their heads.

"Good!" exclaimed Orbrecht. "What are your names?"

"I'm Javik," said the man on the left. "He's Corbel."

"Welcome to Salmon Brigade, Javik and Corbel," said Orbrecht. He turned to one of the men who had accompanied him down the street. "Anders, get armbands for Javik and Corbel, please."

Anders pulled two strips of salmon-colored cloth from a satchel and approached the two men. He tied an armband around each man's right arm, then shook their hands in turn.

"I'm establishing a perimeter of guards twenty paces from the edge of that hole, all the way around," said Orbrecht. "No one is to be permitted inside. Javik, you take Fourth Street. Corbel, I want you on Sixth."

"Yes, sir," said the men in unison, and headed to their assigned posts.

Evena and Tobalt were still staring at Orbrecht in shock, and Wyngalf decided to speak up before one of them decided to make an issue of the man's summary execution of Malleck. There would be a time for judgment of decisions made in the heat of revolution, but this wasn't it.

"Thank you, Orbrecht," said Wyngalf. "I thought we were doomed."

"Not while I'm in charge," said Orbrecht. He turned to the man on his right. "Garvin, escort these three back to the Battered Goblin. The woman is injured, so you'll need to carry her."

"Yes, sir," said the man.

Orbrecht turned to the man on his left. "Anders, go with them. Make sure no one bothers them. Tell Morten they're my personal guests."

"Yes, sir," said Anders.

"I'd come with you," said Orbrecht to Wyngalf, "but I'm afraid the revolution requires my attention." A scuffle had broken out some distance down the street involving several of the city guard, and without another word to them, Orbrecht spun on his heel and headed toward it, barking orders.

"We should get off the street," said the guard named Anders. The other, Garvin, was attempting to pick up Evena over her protests. "It isn't safe out here."

"Is the lack of safety despite Salmon Brigade's efforts," Tobalt ventured, getting to his feet next to Garvin, "or because of them?"

Anders stared at the goblin, uncomprehending.

"Don't mind him," said Wyngalf. "He babbles when he's under stress. Let's get out of here."

Tobalt frowned and muttered something, but the men paid him no heed. They made their way through the streets, with Anders in the lead and Garvin carrying Evena, who had given up struggling. Wyngalf, nearly overcome with exhaustion, trudged along behind them, and Tobalt tailed behind. Several times Anders led them down a narrow alley or sidetracked to avoid looters or some other disturbance, but eventually they made it back to the Battered

Goblin. Anders and Garvin left them in the hands of Merton the innkeeper.

Merton tended to them well, quenching their thirst with beer and their hunger with soup and bread. He provided warm water for them to bathe with and nurse their wounds, and inspected Evena's ankle, concluding that it was sprained but not broken. He and Wyngalf helped her to the room they had used previously and found her several extra pillows so that she could keep her foot elevated. She fell asleep nearly as soon as she lay down. Wyngalf and Tobalt followed suit not long after.

It was dark when Wyngalf awoke, and the sounds of revelry came from the common room below them. It seemed the people of the city were already celebrating the deaths of the two dragons and the overthrow of the old government. It was hard for Wyngalf to square the celebratory sounds he heard below with his memory of the jeering, bloodthirsty crowd from earlier in the day. Perhaps the group in the tavern was not representative of the city as a whole, but Wyngalf suspected that the façade of respect for Verne had crumbled the instant the dragon fell into the abyss. Wyngalf couldn't help wondering how the people who had demanded that Verne incinerate him and his friends would greet him now. Would they still be considered enemies of the city? Heroes, as Orbrecht had claimed? Something in between? His curiosity was not enough to get him to leave their room, though; he'd had more than enough excitement for the day. He supposed they would learn their fate soon enough.

When he awoke again, it was quiet except for the sound of someone rapping insistently on the door. "Simply Wyngalf," a voice murmured quietly from the other side of the door.

His mind still hazy with sleep, Wyngalf shuffled to the door. "Who's there?" he asked.

"It's me," said a familiar voice. "I kept it safe."

Wyngalf groaned. He opened the door to see the figure of Arbliss, his bald head shining in the moonlight coming through the window. Wyngalf could just make out the oval tattoo on the man's forehead. "What do you want, Arbliss?" The man's face was covered with dust and his hands were ragged and bloody. Some part of Wyngalf's brain was aware that Arbliss should still be in the dungeon, crushed as the caverns under the city collapsed. But the collapse hadn't been total; Arbliss must have survived and dug his way out of the rubble to the surface.

"It's time," said Arbliss, holding something out to Wyngalf with both hands. "I've kept it safe. The people are ready."

Wyngalf reflexively held out his hands, finding himself holding something wrapped in a thick wool blanket. It was about the size and weight of a large cantaloupe.

"What in the...?" Wyngalf began, but Arbliss had already turned away and was hurrying back down the hall.

"Wyngalf?" said Evena's voice from inside the room. "Is someone there?"

Wyngalf tucked the thing under his arm and closed the door. "Just a drunk," he said. "Had the wrong room."

Wyngalf made his way in the near-dark across the room, shoving the blanket-wrapped object underneath his bed. He got back in bed and soon fell asleep, his curiosity giving way to exhaustion.

Twenty-one

Wyngalf awoke the next morning uncertain whether the previous day's events had been a dream. After a week of fleeing from Verne, Scarlett, and their respective minions, it seemed impossible that they were finally safe. But it was true: both dragons were dead, crushed under tons of rock at the bottom of a pit in the middle of Skaal City. Wyngalf wondered, as the three companions broke fast in the common room of the inn, whether Orbrecht's organization, Salmon Brigade, had successfully taken over the city government.

He got his answer sooner than he expected. While they were still eating, one of the guards who had escorted them to the inn the previous day, the one named Anders, appeared.

"You're Wyngalf, right?" said Anders.

"I am," replied Wyngalf.

"Mayor Orbrecht would like to see you, as soon as is convenient."

"Regarding what?" asked Wyngalf.

"That I don't know," said Anders. "I was just told to fetch you."

"What about my friends?" asked Wyngalf.

"The mayor only requested you," Anders said.

Evena, sitting across from Wyngalf, asked, "What do you think he wants?"

Wyngalf shrugged. "I guess I'll find out. You and Tobalt wait here."

"Be careful," said Evena, and Tobalt nodded his agreement.

Wyngalf got to his feet and followed Anders out the door.

The guard escorted him down the street to a stately house not far from the palace. "Temporary offices of the new city government," Anders explained. Wyngalf nodded, and Anders led him inside to a drawing room where Orbrecht stood, still wearing his soldier's uniform. He didn't appear to have slept.

"Simply Wyngalf!" Orbrecht cried enthusiastically as they entered. "That will be all, Anders." Anders gave a salute and walked out, closing the door behind him.

"The revolution appears to be going well," Wyngalf ventured.

"So far, so good," said Orbrecht. "But the SMASHers and SAURIANs are both busily plotting against Salmon Brigade. I suspect they are going to form a coalition to oust me."

"Would that be so bad?" Wyngalf asked. "I mean, the important thing is that Verne is dead, right?"

"Ridding Dis of dragons was an important step, to be sure," said Orbrecht, "and the people have you to thank for that. But I can't allow the city to fall into the hands of the SMASHers or the SAURIANs again. Ultimately, Verne was just a scapegoat for their own destructive policies. With Salmon Brigade in charge, we have an opportunity to make some real changes. But without forming some sort of alliance, we don't have the political strength to hold the city."

"Which of the two factions are you thinking of allying with?" asked Wyngalf.

"Neither," replied Orbrecht.

"Then is there a third political faction in Skaal City?"

"Yes," said Orbrecht, with a grin. "You."

"*Me?*" asked Wyngalf. "The people of this city hate me. Yesterday they were demanding that Verne burn me alive."

"Public opinion can be fickle," said Orbrecht. "The Ovaltarians have been a marginalized sect for a long time, but they've been spreading the word that you're the Ko-Haringu. And now that you've slain not one, but *two* dragons by casting them into the Pit of Darkness, you've been pretty well anointed by public opinion."

"Pit of Darkness?" Wyngalf asked, dubiously.

Orbrecht shrugged. "That's what they're calling it."

"They can call it what they like, I suppose," said Wyngalf, "but I didn't kill any dragons."

"That's not how the story is being told," said Orbrecht. "Like it or not, most of the people in this city think you're the Ko-Haringu."

"What does that mean, though?" asked Wyngalf. "What does the Ko-Haringu do after he slays the dragons?"

"The prophecy doesn't say," said Orbrecht. "Which is to our benefit, as it gives us some wiggle room. Look, lad, you've got your objectives, and I've got mine. You want to establish a Noninitarian church here in Dis, right? And I want to institute a new regime in Skaal City. I help you, you help me."

"How so?"

"You make a public statement declaring that you are the Ko-Haringu, the prophet of the one true god, et cetera, et cetera."

"But I'm a Noninitarian," said Wyngalf. "I don't even know anything about Ovaltarianism, except for the prophecy about the Ko-Haringu."

"Doesn't matter," said Orbrecht. "You're the Ko-Haringu. You can say anything you want. Tell people that the rules of Ovaltarian have been supplanted by a new revelation or something. You're a preacher, right? You can come up with the words."

"Won't the Ovaltarians resent me for coopting their religion?"

"Some of them, sure. But they've already told the whole city you're the Ko-Haringu, so I figure it's gonna be tough for them to cast aspersions on you now. Anyway, all we need to do is ride this initial wave of enthusiasm until order is reestablished. After you make your speech, I'll declare Noninitarianism the official religion of Skaal City and establish a fund to build you a big cathedral in the middle of the city."

"Hopefully not on top of a vast abyss," said Wyngalf.

"Yes," said Orbrecht, nodding. "We're going to be a little stricter about building codes."

"And what do you expect in return for this favor?"

"Only that you encourage the people to fall in line under the new government of Skaal City. If we can get control over the religious nuts—no offense—we'll have a much easier time reestablishing order."

Wyngalf shrugged off the insult. "What about my friends, Tobalt and Evena?"

Orbrecht nodded. "I've been thinking about that," he said. "The girl, of course, will want to return home, which is easy enough. The goblin is a tougher case. People around here aren't fond of his kind, as a rule, but his own clan doesn't seem to have any use for him either. Fortunately, I've come up with a solution. The archivist at the city library is a friend of mine, and he's been complaining about his work load for months. Ordinarily this would be the last of my concerns, but your situation made me think about it."

"You're going to make Tobalt a librarian?"

"Archivist's assistant," said Orbrecht. "He'll have no contact with the public, and it will require him to spend his entire day in a cramped underground chamber sorting through musty old books and documents. Do you think you could convince your goblin to take the job?"

"I think you'd have him at 'no contact with the public,'" said Wyngalf. "It would be hard to imagine a position for which he'd be more suited."

"Excellent," said Orbrecht. "Then it's settled. I negotiate passage home for Evena, get Tobalt a job in the library, and set you up as the head of the official religion of Skaal City."

"Well," said Wyngalf, "I suppose I should talk it over with my friends." He couldn't see either of them objecting; in truth, Wyngalf mostly just wanted some more time to think over Orbrecht's offer. It seemed almost too good to be true: after a week of running for their lives, they were each being offered exactly what they wanted.

"Of course," said Orbrecht. "Go talk to your friends. But we don't have a lot of time. If I don't hear from you by noon, I will have to consider an alliance with the SMASHers or the SAURIANs."

"You would ally yourself with those fools?" Wyngalf asked.

"If you don't accept my offer, I will have no choice. It is better to have some voice in the government of Skaal City than none."

Wyngalf nodded. In politics, there were always compromises to be made. "I will talk to Evena and Tobalt," he said. "I hope to have an answer for you by noon."

"Good," said Orbrecht.

Wyngalf left the house and made his way back to the Battered Goblin. As he meandered through the mostly quiet streets, he pondered Orbrecht's offer. Clearly the Noninity was at work in these events, but was Orbrecht's offer the reward for Wyngalf's faithful service to the Noninity, or another test sent by Grimilard? If it was a test, then presumably his new position would at some point require him to somehow sacrifice his principles. But Orbrecht wasn't making any such demand on him, other than to support Orbrecht's new government. And what harm was there in that? Even if Orbrecht was a bit crude in his methods, he couldn't possibly be worse than the SMASHers and SAURIANs, who had allowed the city to be terrorized by Verne. And taking a position as a religious leader—no, *the* religious leader—in Skaal City would give him a great deal of influence with Orbrecht. After all, Orbrecht needed Wyngalf as much as Wyngalf needed him. As Orbrecht said, it was better to have some influence over the government than none. Additionally, it was not only Wyngalf's own objectives he needed to think about. If he didn't take Orbrecht's deal, there was no telling what would become of Tobalt and Evena. Evena might never make it back home, and Tobalt would be forced to go back to wandering in the wilderness, scrounging for scraps of food.

He had nearly managed to convince himself that taking Orbrecht's offer would be an act of unadulterated altruism when he walked back into their room at the inn to find Tobalt and Evena waiting for him. Resting on his bed, on top of a wool blanket, was what appeared to be a very large egg. Wyngalf had somehow managed to completely forget about his encounter with Arbliss the previous night, and at first he didn't make the connection. "What is that?" he asked.

"I thought you might tell us," said Evena. "It was under your bed."

"I didn't..." Wyngalf started. "Arbliss stopped by last night. He handed me that thing, but I didn't know what it was."

"But you know now," said Evena.

"No," replied Wyngalf, but he had a sinking feeling that he did.

"My understanding of such matters is, of course, entirely academic," said Tobalt, "but judging by the size and the markings, I would guess that this is a dragon egg."

"It explains why they call themselves 'Ovaltarians,'" said Evena. "They're some kind of dragon cult."

"You don't know that," said Wyngalf.

"That assessment would seem to be consistent with my own studies," said Tobalt. "It would seem that the Ovaltarians are not interested in ridding the land of Dis of dragons as they are in replacing the old dragons with a new one."

"That's pure conjecture," said Wyngalf. "And in any case, Arbliss entrusted me with the egg, no questions asked. Maybe the Ko-Haringu is supposed to destroy the egg before it hatches."

"Is that what you're going to do?" asked Evena.

"I don't know," said Wyngalf. "Maybe. How long do we have until that thing hatches?"

"It's impossible to say," said Tobalt. "Years, perhaps. Maybe decades."

"Then in all likelihood we have plenty of time to decide," said Wyngalf. "And in the meantime, we have more pressing matters to attend to."

"Like what?" asked Evena.

"Orbrecht made me an offer. He wants my help establishing his new government in Skaal City. In exchange, he's going to give you passage home, and he's going to give Tobalt a job as an archivist's assistant in the city library."

Tobalt's ears perked up. "Will there be any contact with the public?" he asked.

"None," said Wyngalf.

"Will I be working in a cramped underground chamber sorting through musty old books and documents?"

"All day, every day," said Wyngalf.

"Tempting," said Tobalt.

"And what do you get out of this?" Evena asked.

"Orbrecht will declare Noninitarianism the official religion of Skaal City, and set me up as its official leader."

"Leveraging the public delusion that you're the Ovaltarian messiah," said Evena.

"'Delusion' is a strong word," said Wyngalf. "I realize that you don't share my faith, but I find it perfectly reasonable that the

Noninity would pave the way for the one true faith by seeding this land with a convenient pagan prophecy."

"You actually believe you're the Ko-Haringu," said Evena, shaking her head. "You think you're the messiah, come to save the land of Dis."

"What if I am?" asked Wyngalf, growing angry. "What if I'm finally getting the opportunity to do what I was put here to do, and I turn it down?"

"I don't think it works that way," said Evena. "Destiny isn't something that's handed to you. I think people make their own destiny."

"Handed to me!" Wyngalf exclaimed. "My life has been in danger ever since I got on your father's accursed ship. It's only my own faith and resilience in the face of overwhelming odds that has kept me alive until now."

"Wow," said Evena. "That must have been really hard for you, going through that all alone."

"That's not what I'm saying," said Wyngalf.

"It kind of sounds like what you're saying," she replied.

"No, I understand that you and Tobalt have been with me the whole time. What I'm saying is that our experiences over the past few days mean something different to me than they do to you."

"Because you're the vaunted Ko-Haringu, and we're just, what, supporting characters in the Wyngalf show?"

"I don't understand why you're being like this," Wyngalf said. "We're all getting exactly what we want."

"If I might be permitted to interject," said Tobalt, "Evena and I were talking while you were out, and while we admire your dedication to your faith, it seems to us that you have a tendency to oversimplify inherently complex matters, interpreting them according to a rather arbitrary and occasionally even self-serving dogma. Further, I am beginning to have second thoughts regarding this Orbrecht character."

"Tobalt," said Wyngalf, "No offense, but matters of faith and destiny are a little outside of your bailiwick."

"I'm sorry," said Tobalt, furrowing his brow. "I'm afraid I don't understand what you mean."

"Yeah, you're pretty dense when it's convenient," said Wyngalf. "Okay, let me spell it out for you: you're a goblin, Tobalt. You don't have a soul. You can memorize all the big words and philosophical theories you want, but in the end your opinion carries about as much weight as that of a trained bear."

Somehow, seeing Tobalt rendered speechless was not nearly as satisfying as Wyngalf had expected.

"How dare you?" Evena said. "After everything Tobalt has done for you. After everything we've been through together."

"I appreciate what you've both done," said Wyngalf coldly. "But it doesn't change the basic facts of our situation. Tobalt is a goblin. You're just a young girl who needs to get home."

"And you're the Messiah of Dis."

"I'm someone who has been burdened with a great sense of purpose," Wyngalf snapped. "Someone who has been given the opportunity to be a tool of the divine will."

"You're being a tool alright," muttered Evena.

"I don't have to put up with this," said Wyngalf, bending over the bed to wrap the egg in the blanket. "I'm going to tell Orbrecht I'm taking his offer. You're welcome, both of you." He picked up the bundle and put it under his arm.

"What are you going to do with that?" asked Evena.

"Whatever I feel is best," said Wyngalf. He turned and walked out of the room, slamming the door behind him.

Twenty-two

The speech was a good one, probably the best Wyngalf had ever given—a fact that was undoubtedly related to his conscious effort to avoid getting into the details of the Noninitarian religion. He did manage to allude indirectly to three of the Fourteen Points, but these asides were met with silence and confused muttering. His calls for unity, working together peacefully, and supporting the new government were much more enthusiastically received. It rubbed him a little wrong to focus so much on temporal matters rather than those of eternal significance, but he reassured himself that there would be plenty of time to bring the people of Skaal City into the Noninitarian fold after the immediate political crisis had passed. It had only been three days since the death of the dragons and the overthrowing of the old regime.

"Well done," said Orbrecht, as Wyngalf walked inside from the balcony where he had delivered the speech to several hundred people gathered in the street below. For now, this mansion—which Wyngalf learned had been appropriated from one of Orbrecht's SAURIAN enemies—served as the headquarters for the new city government. "If we maintain a unified front, the SMASHers and SAURIANs don't have a chance against us."

Wyngalf nodded pensively.

"What's the matter, lad?" Orbrecht asked with fatherly concern. "If you're worried about your friends, I assure you they've been taken care of, as I promised. Even now, Evena is on her way north to a port where she can get passage across the Sea of Dis, and Tobalt is happily toiling away somewhere in a dark alcove."

"It's not that," said Wyngalf. The problem, he realized, was that he had not fully committed to his alliance with Orbrecht. Some part of him had continued to listen to Evena and Tobalt's warnings about Orbrecht. But that was silly. If the Noninity had paved the way for him to take his position at Orbrecht's side, then obviously it wanted him to go all in. The fate of Noninitarianism in Dis rested on Orbrecht successfully retaining control over Skaal City, and he was determined that Orbrecht would not fail. And if anybody in the city knew what to do with a dragon egg, it was Orbrecht.

"I have something to show you, Orbrecht," said Wyngalf. "I'm still not sure what to do with it, but if we're going to be partners, I think you should know about it."

Orbrecht regarded him quizzically. "All right," he said. "What is it?"

"It's in my room," said Wyngalf. He led Orbrecht down the hall to the quarters that had been assigned to him. The suite was simple but tasteful and well-appointed, as suited a man of the cloth. At the foot of his bed was a wooden chest to which he held the only key.

Wyngalf fished the key out of his pocket and opened the chest. He lifted the bundle and unwrapped it, presenting the ovoid object to Orbrecht.

Orbrecht stared at it in awe. "So it *does* exist. Arbliss had almost convinced me…." He trailed off, evidently thinking better of what he was going to say.

"You know Arbliss?"

"Everybody in Skaal City knows that crazy old preacher," said Orbrecht. "May I?"

Somewhat reluctantly, Wyngalf allowed Orbrecht to take the egg.

"But you spoke to Arbliss specifically about the egg?" asked Wyngalf.

"What?" said Orbrecht, enraptured by the mottled, marble-like pattern of the egg's shell. "No, no. I never spoke to him. But he's well-known as a member of the Ovaltarian sect, and there have long been rumors that the Ovaltarians were in possession of a dragon's egg. What I meant is that I was nearly convinced by Arbliss's mad ravings on the street that the Ovaltarians were just a bunch of wackos. But I guess there was something to the rumors after all."

"So what should we do with it?"

"Well," said Orbrecht. "There isn't much we can do but wait."

"We could destroy it," said Wyngalf.

Orbrecht frowned at him. "Destroy it? Why would we do that?"

"Because it's going to be a dragon," said Wyngalf, not sure where Orbrecht's confusion was coming from. "Dragons are evil."

Orbrecht chuckled. "Dragons are unpredictable and tend toward greed and self-aggrandizement, but I think it's a bit of an exaggeration to say they're *evil*. Besides, it takes centuries for a dragon to get as big as Verne or Scarlett. Plenty of time to train it to behave properly."

"I didn't know dragons *could* be trained," said Wyngalf.

"Sure they can," said Orbrecht. "The problem with Verne and Scarlett is that they were never properly domesticated. We have a unique opportunity with this dragon, Wyngalf. To my knowledge, this will be the first dragon that is ever hatched in captivity. Just imagine the good we could accomplish with a dragon that does our bidding!"

"I suppose so," said Wyngalf. "It's an awful lot of responsibility, though."

"Does your religion teach you to shrink from responsibility?" Orbrecht asked.

"No," admitted Wyngalf.

"Of course not," said Orbrecht. "See, this is why you're the perfect person to help me train the dragon. I'm a man of action, and I'll be the first to admit that sometimes I don't think things through as thoroughly as I should. But you take all this morality and responsibility stuff really seriously. We're going to be a great team."

"Yes," said Wyngalf, without much enthusiasm. "Every team should have a member who is concerned with morality and responsibility."

"Right?" said Orbrecht. "And don't forget, dragon broods are rarely just one egg, so there are probably more out there somewhere. We don't want Skaal City to be defenseless."

"True," said Wyngalf. It was hard to deny Orbrecht's logic.

"It's good that you came to me with this," said Orbrecht. "Don't worry, I will make sure it's in a safe place."

"I didn't intend for—" Wyngalf started.

"Obviously we can't keep it in here," said Orbrecht. "If anyone found out about it, they could break in here and steal it. We can't risk the egg falling into the wrong hands. Don't you agree, Wyngalf?"

"Of course," said Wyngalf. "But I had assumed—"

"Good!" said Orbrecht. "I'm telling you Wyngalf, this is a good omen. I'm not a religious person and I don't usually buy any of that prophecy crap, but there has to be a reason we were entrusted with this egg. Great things are going to happen in Skaal City!"

Wyngalf smiled weakly, and Orbrecht left, cradling the egg in his arms.

That night, Orbrecht's fears were proven true: Wyngalf awoke to the sound of someone rooting around in his room, obviously looking for something.

"Who is that?" Wyngalf demanded, sitting up in bed. "What are you doing?"

The figure, a small creature with large ears and overdeveloped forearms, stood still at the foot of his bed for a moment, and then began banging on the lock of the chest. "Where is it?" a familiar voice asked urgently. "It's imperative that I find it."

"Tobalt," Wyngalf groaned. "Why are you skulking around in here?"

"I've been conducting research in the library," said Tobalt. "I have to find the egg before it hatches."

"It's not here," Wyngalf said irritably. "And you shouldn't be either. If Orbrecht's guards find you, they'll cut your throat."

Tobalt hopped onto Wyngalf's bed, crouching over him and clutching the front of his pajamas. "Tell me where it is!" he hissed.

Wyngalf punched the goblin square in the face, sending him reeling backwards. He tumbled off the bed and lay on the floor moaning. "You threaten me again, and I'll call the guards myself," he said. "Now tell me what's gotten into you."

"Saurianology," moaned Tobalt. "Dragon imprinting."

"Imprinting? What's that?"

"Saurians appear to be distant relatives of avians, and share with certain waterfowl an instinctual tendency to form a bond with a maternal figure."

"Tobalt, get to the point."

"When a dragon hatches, it forms a bond with the first creature it sees. It's called imprinting. Generally the creature on which it imprints is the dragon's mother. But if it hatches in captivity...."

"It will imprint on its captor," said Wyngalf, seeing what Tobalt was getting at.

"I assumed that it was still in your possession, which would have been an undesirable but comparatively benign situation," said Tobalt. "But if *he* has it...."

"His name is Orbrecht," said Wyngalf. "And he's not the bogeyman you make him out to be. He probably doesn't even know about the imprinting."

"Oh, he knows," said Tobalt, sitting up on the floor. "Why do you think he took it from you? Now I will grant you that my knowledge of the concept friendship is largely theoretical. That is, I had thought...." Tobalt broke off, momentarily unable to speak. He continued, "Orbrecht is not your friend. You should not trust him."

"It's not a matter of trusting him," said Wyngalf. "We're partners, working together to improve Skaal City."

"You may be partners now," said Tobalt, "but how long do you think that will last once he has a dragon on his side?"

"A baby dragon," said Wyngalf. "Smaller than your head."

"The time to stop it is now," said Tobalt. "After it hatches, it will be too late. My research indicates—"

"I don't want to hear about your research!" Wyngalf snapped. "Who knows if that stuff you're reading in those old manuscripts is even accurate? Are you even doing your actual job? How do you think it's going to reflect on me if they find out you're spending all your time researching dragons?"

"How it reflects on you," echoed Tobalt, getting to his feet. Wyngalf couldn't see his face in the near-darkness, but he heard the tone of disappointment in the goblin's voice. "Simply Wyngalf, I realize that I am merely a goblin and therefore unable to appreciate the sublime beauties of human religion. Despite this defect, I have always respected your faith, and I am saddened to see that you have placed the opinions of mobs and murderers above your principles."

"Oh, like you know anything," Wyngalf said lamely.

"Goodbye, Simply Wyngalf," said Tobalt. "As much as I would like to remain here, I do not want to become so enamored of my position in this city that I someday am tempted to bow to a dragon in order to keep it." With that, Tobalt slipped out of the room, closing the door behind him.

Wyngalf sighed and lay back down in his bed, but he was unable to sleep. He realized now that he should never have taken up with a goblin in the first place. The problem was that if you spent any time with a goblin, you started thinking about them as if they were people. And once you did that, you couldn't help but start to take their stupid goblin-opinions seriously.

When the sun rose, Wyngalf got out of bed and went to Orbrecht's office. Orbrecht was already up, barking orders at underlings and signing official decrees. As far as Wyngalf could tell, he never slept.

"What can I do for you, Wyngalf?" asked Orbrecht pleasantly. "You look exhausted."

"Didn't sleep well," said Wyngalf. "I've been thinking about that dragon—"

"Hold on," said Orbrecht. "Anders, could you leave us, please?"

"Yes, sir," said Anders, who had been standing at attention next to Orbrecht's desk, apparently waiting for orders. He marched out the door, closing it behind him.

"Trying to keep the existence of our secret weapon on the down-low," said Orbrecht.

"I'm sorry," said Wyngalf. "I assumed Anders knew. You must have men guarding it...?"

"It's safe," said Orbrecht curtly. "What's on your mind, Wyngalf?"

"I was thinking that perhaps we should do some research on training dragons," said Wyngalf. "So that we're ready when it hatches."

"Good thinking," said Orbrecht. "If you want to bone up on dragon training, I can hand him over to you when he's old enough to train. I understand there are some old manuscripts on saurianology in the library. Maybe your goblin friend can help you locate them." Orbrecht's eyes met Wyngalf's. His gaze was unreadable.

"Yes," said Wyngalf uncertainly. "I will... look into that."

"Excellent. Now if there's nothing else, perhaps you could let Anders back in."

Wyngalf nodded and went to the door, passing Anders on his way out. He continued down the hall, taking the stairs down to the foyer. Passing another pair of guards at the entryway to the mansion, he walked out into the dazzling sunlight of the morning and continued down the street, with no clear goal in mind.

As much as he hated to admit it, Orbrecht's response to his mention of the dragon egg seemed to confirm Tobalt's suspicions: Orbrecht knew about the imprinting process and was guarding the egg closely to make certain he was the first person the hatchling saw. He couldn't blame Orbrecht for being cautious, but it made Wyngalf wonder what else Orbrecht wasn't telling him.

Wyngalf strolled down the streets of Skaal City, stopping occasionally to return the greeting of a peasant or shopkeeper who bade him a "Good morning, Bishop Wyngalf." Technically, being named the Noninitarian bishop of a city required a formal decree by the bishop at Svalbraakrat, but Orbrecht had convinced him that Skaal City's need for spiritual leadership outweighed any procedural concerns. Once the immediate crisis had passed and Noninitarianism had been firmly established in Skaal City, Wyngalf could send word to the Stronghold formally requesting Elevation. As there would be no competition for the bishopric in Dis, the Bishop of Svalbraakrat would have little choice but to assign Wyngalf to the position, at least on an interim basis. And by the time a more experienced replacement could be found and sent across the Sea of Dis, Wyngalf would have weeks, if not months, on the job. Yes, there was very little that could interrupt his meteoric rise in the ecclesiastical hierarchy. Perhaps he would someday be the bishop at Svalbraakrat—although the potential for the church's growth in Skaal City and the rest of Dis made him wonder if he'd even take the position if it were offered to him. What a change in circumstances he had seen since being thrown overboard from the

Erdis Evena! It was clear evidence, Wyngalf thought, of what a little faith could do.

Wyngalf was marveling at how quiet the streets were when he came across a group of five young men, their hands bound, being prodded down the street by three of the city guard. He watched as the group passed, his curiosity growing as the guards directed the men down a narrow alley. Somewhat concerned that the guards intended to execute the men, Wyngalf followed quietly. To his surprise, one of the guards pulled open a grate at the end of the alley and stepped into the hole. Wyngalf realized that the man was walking down a steep stone stairway that led somewhere below the street.

"Where are you taking those men?" Wyngalf asked, and everyone in the group, including the man who was already a few steps into the hole, turned to look at him.

"None o' your business," grunted one of the guards, who seemed to be the sergeant in charge of the group. "Get lost."

One of the other guards whispered something into the ear of the sergeant, and Wyngalf saw the man's face go pale.

"Er, sorry, Bishop," said the man. "Didn't recognize you. We're just taking some troublemakers to one of the underground prisons."

"Underground prisons?" asked Wyngalf, stunned.

"Sure," the sergeant said. "Orbrecht set up prisons all over town to deal with the likes of these. The old dungeon under the palace is mostly collapsed, but there are tunnels all over the city. Orbrecht had us block off some of the tunnels to make them into prisons."

"What happens to the people after you put them in one of the prisons?"

The guard simply stared at Wyngalf, seemingly confused by the question.

Wyngalf tried again. "What crime did these men commit?"

"Like I said," the guard replied, "They're troublemakers."

"Okay," said Wyngalf, "But what does that mean, exactly?"

"They was asking a lot of questions about the underground prisons," the guard said, meeting Wyngalf's stare.

"I see," said Wyngalf. The guards were now all regarding him suspiciously, and Wyngalf decided it was a good time to change tacks. "Very good!" he exclaimed. "I was a bit worried that Orbrecht was being a little too lenient with these sorts of agitators. Are you keeping the political prisoners separate from the ordinary thugs and ruffians?"

The sergeant frowned at him. "It's all the same to us," he said. "You cause trouble, you end up in one of the prisons."

"Hmm," said Wyngalf. "You think that's a good idea? Putting these sorts of agitators in with the petty criminals is a good way to breed an insurgency."

"Huh," said the sergeant. "Never thought of that. But we ain't had much time to sort them."

"I see," said Wyngalf. "Well, I don't think Orbrecht is going to be very pleased when he hears about it, but I suppose it's too late to do anything about it now."

"I guess we could try to sort them by their crimes," said the sergeant. "I don't know how anybody'd tell which ones are political, though."

"What do you mean?" asked Wyngalf. "You are keeping a record of what you're charging them with, right?"

"Uh," said the sergeant. "Not exactly. Like I said, we ain't had a lot of time. Mostly we just round up anybody making trouble and throw them in prison. They all start to look the same after a while. Except for that guy with the big O on his head, of course."

"Arbliss?" asked Wyngalf. "You've got Arbliss the preacher in this prison?"

"Don't know his name," said the sergeant. "But yeah, he's that crazy street preacher that used to scream at people as they passed. He's one of the first people Orbrecht had us round up. In fact, Orbrecht's even been down to see him a few times."

"Really," said Wyngalf. "You know, it occurs to me that I might be able to help you sort through your prisoners and determine which of them are political agitators. Then I could report to Orbrecht that you're keeping the prisoners properly segregated."

"Wow, that would be fantastic," said the sergeant. "Do you have time right now?"

"I could spare a few minutes," said Wyngalf, trying to sound reluctant.

"Proceed, Barderic," said the sergeant to the man who was still waiting on the steps. "We're going to be giving the good bishop a tour of the prison."

The lead guard disappeared somewhere down below, and a few moments later Wyngalf heard him calling for the others to proceed. The sergeant prodded the prisoners, sullen and grumbling, down the steps, and Wyngalf followed. The remaining guard took up the rear.

As Wyngalf's eyes adjusted to the dim light, he saw that the lead guard had procured a torch and had lit it from one already burning in a sconce on the wall. Once the group had reassembled in a cavern about the size of a small dining hall, the guard in the rear lit a torch as well. While the sergeant and the guard who had been in the rear watched the prisoners, the lead guard took a key from his belt and unlocked a rusty metal gate that was set in an opening in the far wall. He proceeded through it into a long, narrow tunnel with a ceiling so low that Wyngalf had to duck most of the way through it.

Eventually the tunnel widened into a long, winding cavern with several smaller caves branching off from it. Walls of iron bars with gates in them separated the cells from the main cavern. In several of the cells stood pale, gaunt figures in torn, soiled clothing who blinked and squinted at the approaching torches. The lead guard proceeded past the first few cells and opened one on the right with another key. "Inside!" he barked at the prisoners, who proceeded docilely into the cell. He slammed the door shut behind them.

"The first few cells are filled mostly with people who were out after curfew on the first night of the Revolution," the sergeant explained. "Past them are—"

"Simply Wyngalf!" cried a voice from one of the cells ahead on Wyngalf's left. The voice was hoarse and ragged, but Wyngalf recognized it as Arbliss's. Wyngalf grabbed the torch out of the hand of the guard ahead of him and walked toward the voice.

"Bishop," said the sergeant. "If you could remain with the group…."

"I'll just be a moment," Wyngalf called back, leaving the perplexed guards muttering to themselves.

"I knew you would come!" cried Arbliss, his knuckles white as he clutched the bars.

"What are you doing down here, Arbliss?" Wyngalf asked. In the torchlight, Wyngalf could see that Arbliss was badly bruised and his ragged clothes were stained with blood.

"Not a whole lot," said Arbliss, glancing around him.

"I meant," said Wyngalf, "why are you in here?"

"I wouldn't tell Orbrecht where the you-know-what is," said Arbliss. "His men beat me for hours, but I never told them a thing."

Wyngalf began to feel sick. "So," he said weakly, "it's very important that Orbrecht not know about the... you-know-what?"

"Oh, no," said Arbliss. "It's just important that I not tell him."

"I don't understand."

"Of course not," said Arbliss, with a grin. The corners of his mouth were crusted with blood, and at least three of his teeth were missing. "That's what makes you so useful."

"Useful?" asked Wyngalf.

Arbliss sighed. "Orbrecht has to believe that an alliance with you is necessary to retain control over the city. He has to think you're the Ko-Haringu. If he knew I had given you the egg, he would think the public perception that you're the Ko-Haringu was a result of the Ovaltarians propping you up. A self-fulfilling prophecy."

"Are you saying I'm *not* the Ko-Haringu?"

Arbliss shrugged. "Doesn't make any difference, as long as Orbrecht believes it."

"But Orbrecht doesn't believe it," said Wyngalf. "He's not religious."

"No," said Arbliss, "but he's practical. If he thinks the people think you're the Ko-Haringu, then as far as he's concerned, you're the Ko-Haringu. And as long as he thinks you're the Ko-Haringu, people will believe you're the Ko-Haringu."

"That's circular," said Wyngalf.

"Faith usually is," said Arbliss, grinning. "Look, if Orbrecht starts to doubt that you're the Ko-Haringu, then he'll dump you and make an alliance with the SAURIANs or the SMASHERs. But the SAURIANs and the SMASHERs aren't going to want to share power with a dragon. They saw how that went last time. They'll try to kill the dragon while it's still young. Orbrecht will try to protect it, of course, but the SAURIANs and the SMASHERs have agents all over the city. If Orbrecht is forced to ally himself with either of those factions, odds are that dragon is going to be dead within the year. The Ovaltarians can't allow that to happen."

"So it's true," Wyngalf said weakly. "The Ovaltarians are a dragon cult. You never cared about ridding Dis of dragons. You just wanted to ensure the reign of a new dragon."

"Oh, Simply Wyngalf," said Arbliss. "How I admire your naïveté. Of *course* we're a dragon cult." He traced the circle marking on his forehead with his index finger. "Why do you think we're called Ovaltarians?"

Wyngalf nodded dumbly. He'd been a fool not to see it: the oval was a dragon's egg.

"Verne and Scarlett had grown old and sloppy," said Arbliss. "It was only a matter of time before they were slain, and then there would be a power vacuum. Human society in Dis would fall into anarchy."

"And by 'anarchy,' you mean that people would be in charge of their own business, rather than dragons."

Arbliss shrugged. "Ovaltarians are not opposed to humans running their own societies, but there will always be dragons out there. Given that fact, a human society that doesn't have a dragon to defend it doesn't have much of a chance to avoid being subjugated by a dragon."

Wyngalf's head spun as he tried to follow Arbliss' logic. "Hang on," he said. "The Ovaltarians are dedicated to making sure that a dragon be put in control of Skaal City, because otherwise a dragon will take control of Skaal City?"

"Exactly!" cried Arbliss, as if Wyngalf had arrived at some sublime truth.

"But that's insane," said Wyngalf.

Arbliss nodded. "Faith usually is."

"That isn't faith!" Wyngalf exclaimed. "It's mindless dogma! You're pretending something is true in order to make it true!"

"I don't see the distinction," said Arbliss. "What's the point of a prophecy if you don't have to do anything to make it come true?"

"The point of a prophecy is that it comes true no matter what you do!" cried Wyngalf. "That's why it's called a prophecy!"

"Very good," said Arbliss. "Then you have accepted your role."

"What is that supposed to mean?" Wyngalf snapped.

"You're the Ko-Haringu, whether you want to be or not. You are the one who will usher in the thousand-year reign of the new dragon."

"No," said Wyngalf. "I don't accept that. There has to be another reason I was brought here."

"You said it yourself," replied Arbliss. "It doesn't matter whether you accept it or not. The fact that the Ovaltarian prophecy has suddenly become inconvenient to you does not make it false."

"And the fact that it was previously convenient for me doesn't make it true," said Wyngalf.

"Fair point," said Arbliss. "Maybe you're not the Ko-Haringu. Maybe you're just a pathetic wandering preacher who happened to stumble into town a few days before Scarlett and Verne killed each other. I guess we'll find out."

"Yes," said Wyngalf. "I suppose we will. You know, I was going to try to get you out of here, Arbliss, but now starting to think the city is better off with you down here, where you can't cause any more trouble."

Arbliss laughed. "You have an exaggerated sense of your own authority," he said. "In any case, I was never getting out of here. I'll die in this prison, and I'm okay with that. I've accepted my fate. It's time for you to accept yours."

"Bishop Wyngalf," said the sergeant, who was approaching uncertainly from behind. "Perhaps we should finish the tour?"

"Tour's over," said Wyngalf. "I've seen what I need to see." He turned away from Arbliss' cell and began to walk back the way they came.

Twenty-three

If the guards were suspicious of Wyngalf's sudden lack of interest in the prison, they didn't show it. Probably they were just happy that he no longer seemed intent on informing Orbrecht of their mismanagement. They led him back out to the street, where he mumbled his thanks for the abbreviated tour and bid them good day.

He spent the next several hours wandering the streets of Skaal City in a haze, wondering if what Arbliss had said was true. The man's logic seemed unassailable: if Wyngalf really was the Ko-Haringu, then there wasn't anything Wyngalf could do about it. His destiny had been sealed. But that meant that Wyngalf's own decisions were of no consequence. On some level, he had always believed that the Noninity had predetermined everything that had ever happened; the Doctrine of Unavoidable Destiny was, after all, one of the Fourteen Points. But it was one thing to believe this notion in the abstract and quite another to be told that one had a specific role to fulfill, and that one had no choice in the matter.

But he *did* have a choice, didn't he? He could choose to abdicate his role as Ko-Haringu. All that would prove, of course, was that he'd never been the Ko-Haringu in the first place. Maybe the similarities between his circumstances and the Ovaltarian prophecy were just meaningless coincidences. The only way to be certain he was the Ko-Haringu was to accept that he was the Ko-Haringu. There seemed to be no escaping the circularity. It was either a self-fulfilling prophecy or not a prophecy at all, and there was no way to know until after the fact.

There was one thing he did know, however: neither Arbliss nor Orbrecht could be trusted. Orbrecht had lied to him about talking to Arbliss, and Arbliss had used him to further the Ovaltarians' insane desire to put a dragon in charge of Skaal City. Wyngalf needed to determine the correct path for himself, without relying on the guidance of either mad prophets or power-hungry usurpers. But searching his own soul revealed nothing, and his prayers for wisdom remained unanswered, as far as he could tell. He found himself wanting to ask Evena what she thought, but of course she was probably hundreds of miles away now, far along the coast of Dis to the north—and even if she were still in Skaal City, she would be unlikely to help Wyngalf after the way they had parted ways.

Wyngalf eventually found himself near the harbor and decided to walk down to the docks. Any evidence of Verne's destruction of the *Numinda Fae* had been cleaned up or washed away, and workers were busily loading cargo onto another ship. The work seemed to be proceeding in a relatively ordered manner; there was no sign of the chaos that had reigned on the dock when he had last arrived here. Things were moving so smoothly, in fact, that Wyngalf became curious. As far as he knew, the old clerk, Halbert, was still at the bottom of the bay, and Lord Popper had joined Verne and Scarlett in the abyss at the center of Skaal City. So who was running the Shipping Guild office?

Wyngalf strolled down the dock to the tiny Shipping Guild shack and opened the door. He was shocked to find, sitting behind the desk, Evena herself. She looked up at him as he walked in, forcing a smile. Her eyes immediately darted for a second to Wyngalf's right, and he saw that the guard who had carried Evena back to the Battered Goblin, Garvin, was standing just inside the doorway. He regarded Wyngalf suspiciously, his hand resting on the pommel of his sword.

"Hello, Wyngalf," said Evena, without emotion. She looked very tired.

"What are you doing here, Evena?" asked Wyngalf. "I thought you were on your way home."

"I decided to stay here to help out the Shipping Guild office until they can find a new clerk," Evena said. She glanced not very subtly at Garvin.

"Do you have business here, Wyngalf?" asked Garvin. Wyngalf noticed Garvin didn't bother with the honorific.

"Just stopping in to visit my friend," said Wyngalf.

"Well, your friend has work to do," said Garvin. "Does Orbrecht know you're down here?"

"I don't have to account for my actions to Orbrecht," said Wyngalf.

This got a chuckle out of Garvin. "If you say so. In any case, you'd best socialize elsewhere."

"You should go, Wyngalf," said Evena.

Wyngalf glanced at Garvin's hand resting on his sword and nodded. "Of course," he said. "Sorry to interrupt your work." He turned and left the office, closing the door behind him.

So Orbrecht had lied to him about this as well. Evena hadn't been sent home; she was being held against her will, being forced to act as an interim clerk for the Shipping Guild. At least, that was how it appeared. As he walked up the dock, Wyngalf cursed his naïveté. Tobalt and Evena had seen it, but he had been too blinded by his own ambition and misplaced sense of destiny. Orbrecht was no better than the SAURIANs or the SMASHers. He was simply using Wyngalf to tighten the reins of power over Skaal City. And his generosity toward Wyngalf's friends had been aimed at getting them out of the way, where they couldn't talk sense into him. He was lucky Orbrecht hadn't simply decided to have their throats slit. Undoubtedly he would if they ever ceased to be of use to him—and there didn't seem to be much Wyngalf could do about it.

As he passed the ship that was being loaded, the foreman—a huge, burly red-haired man—gave him a salute. Wyngalf waved back, thinking that it was odd for someone to salute a bishop, but then it occurred to him that this was the same foreman that he and Evena had worked with to load the *Erdis Evena*. The man didn't recognize him as the bishop; he had assumed Wyngalf was still working for the Shipping Guild.

"What are you loading?" Wyngalf called to the man, partly to be polite, but an idea was brewing in the back of his head.

"Spices from Quirin, mostly," the foreman replied.

"Spices?" said Wyngalf with a frown. "What kinds of spices?"

"Uh," said the foreman. "Smells like ginger and cinnamon, mostly. Maybe some peppers."

Wyngalf gave an exaggerated groan. "Didn't they tell you? That order was canceled."

"What?" cried the foreman. "This is the first I'm hearing about it."

"Yeah, things have been kind of a mess with the paperwork lately," said Wyngalf. "Evena is still trying to figure it all out. Maybe we should go talk to her."

The foreman grumbled something and set down the crate he was holding. "Take a break until I get back," he shouted to the workers, who didn't need to be told twice. The foreman made his way down the ramp toward Wyngalf, and the two began to walk down the dock to the office. Wyngalf made sure to keep the huge foreman between him and the office, so that he couldn't be seen approaching.

As the foreman approached the door to the shack, Wyngalf stepped aside and put his hand on the man's arm. "You know," he said, "maybe I should handle this. I don't want to get you in trouble. You just get your men started unloading those spice crates, and maybe nobody has to lose their job."

The foreman shrugged and grunted, then turned to walk back to the ship. Wyngalf ducked behind the shack and listened as the man barked orders to his men. These were met with groans and mutters, and then the sound of men going back to work.

Wyngalf waited for close to half an hour in the sweltering sun behind the Shipping Guild office before he heard stirring inside the building. Evena and Garvin were arguing, and the tone was getting louder and more acrimonious. Finally, the door burst open and Evena stumbled out, as if she had been pushed. She nearly fell off the edge of the dock before regaining her balance and turning to face Garvin, who was strolling out of the office behind her. Wyngalf ducked his head back behind the wall before the man saw him.

"—ask the foreman!" Evena was saying. "I didn't tell him to unload those crates!"

"We'll see about that," Garvin growled. "If Orbrecht finds out you've been sabotaging our efforts to keep trade going, you can forget about ever going home."

Wyngalf heard the sound of footsteps receding down the dock, and he stepped out from behind the shack to see Garvin walking a few steps behind Evena. Wyngalf slipped off his boots, took a deep breath, and ran after the man.

When Wyngalf was only a few paces away, his foot hit a creaky board and Garvin suddenly spun around, his hand on his sword hilt. Garvin was too slow, though: Wyngalf launched himself at Garvin, digging his shoulder into the man's ribs. Caught off-balance, Garvin stumbled sideways and fell with a massive splash into the bay. Barely able to halt his own momentum, Wyngalf nearly followed him, skidding to a halt with his toes on the edge of the dock. Garvin's head emerged from the water, angry and sputtering, a moment later. "You're a dead man, Wyngalf!" Garvin howled, splashing his way toward the dock. "I'll kill you both!"

"Run!" yelled Wyngalf. Evena ran, favoring her injured ankle, and Wyngalf followed, the dock workers turning to stare as they passed. Wyngalf glanced behind him to see Garvin pulling himself onto the dock.

They ran up the beach and into the maze of shops near the water's edge, with Garvin following close behind. They were just far enough ahead of Garvin that they nearly lost him several times in the winding alleys and side streets near the harbor, but Wyngalf, still in his stocking feet, was having a hard time keeping up with Evena. As he rounded a corner into a dark alley, she grabbed him by the arm and pulled him into a doorway. They pressed themselves against the bricks, trying not to pant loudly as Garvin ran past.

When he was out of sight, Evena darted out of the doorway back the way they came, and Wyngalf followed, doing his best to dodge the sharper rocks in the unpaved road. She led him through another series of winding avenues, making a dozen or so seemingly random turns, until they both stopped, exhausted, in a blind alley. Standing there, bent over, panting and sweating, they could only hope they had lost Garvin.

Wyngalf listened for the sound of boots approaching, but heard nothing but a whining, nasally voice pleading with someone in the distance. He realized after a moment that the voice was familiar.

"Is that...?" Evena asked, between gasps.

"Tobalt," said Wyngalf. "Come on."

Too exhausted to run, and worried that Garvin might still be nearby, Wyngalf tiptoed down the alley toward the street, with Evena following. Seeing that the street was deserted, Wyngalf turned to the right toward the sound of voices. There seemed to be two voices other than Tobalt's, and they were alternating in an animated discussion. Wyngalf continued down the street, peering around a corner where the voices seemed to be originating. He saw two city guards standing in the middle of the street, their backs to him. Tobalt was facing toward Wyngalf, but was too preoccupied with the discussion to notice him.

"So what you're saying," the guard on the left was saying, "is that totalitarianism supplants human reason by making the glorification of the state an end in itself."

"Then it's as much a religious system as a political one," the guard on the right mused.

"That's an excellent point, Javik," said Tobalt, nodding. "In the end, a totalitarian system is held together by faith in the system itself. That's why, when the end finally comes, it tends to come quickly as the collective delusion of the all-powerful... Simply Wyngalf!" Tobalt waved as he noticed Wyngalf peering around the corner. Wyngalf and Evena sheepishly revealed themselves, walking toward the group. The two guards turned to face them, hands on their swords.

"Gentlemen," said Tobalt, "You remember Bishop Wyngalf and his friend, Evena. Wyngalf and Evena, you may recall Javik and Corbel from the Pit of Darkness the other day."

"Oh, yes," said Evena. "Condolences on your friend. What was his name?"

"Malleck," said Javik. "He was more of an acquaintance, really. Stubborn bastard."

"Well, I'm sorry he, um, fell into the abyss," said Evena.

The two men nodded in acceptance of their condolences.

Tobalt cleared his throat. "We were just discussing the advantages and disadvantages of totalitarian societies, apropos to the current shifting of the political landscape of Skaal City under Orbrecht."

"Totaliwhat?" asked Evena.

"It's a term I've coined for extremely repressive societies in which every facet of life is dictated by a powerful central authority," Tobalt explained.

"And you think that's where Skaal City is headed?" Evena said.

"Revolutions, even those initiated for noble reasons, tend to result in more oppressive political structures," Tobalt replied. "And given the rate at which Orbrecht is incarcerating political opponents, I would venture to guess that the current situation will perpetuate the pattern."

"What are you doing here, Tobalt?" asked Wyngalf. "I thought you had left town."

"I intended to," said Tobalt. "But I was apprehended at the gate by representatives of the city guard. I spent the morning in a dank cave with a delightful assortment of ruffians and agitators. It was deemed, however, that solitary confinement would better suit my temperament. Javik and Corbel were kind enough to escort me to my new quarters, which I'm assured are quite cramped and dismal."

"He was getting the other prisoners worked up with his political talk," Corbel explained.

"Yeah, he does that," said Wyngalf.

"Anyway, Orbrecht wanted him moved. Speaking of which, we should get going."

"That's alright," said Wyngalf. "We'll take him from here."

"Um," said Javik uncertainly. "I know you're the bishop, but we were given direct orders by Orbrecht to move Tobalt into solitary. We're going to have to check with him." Corbel nodded.

Tobalt began to chuckle. "It appears that someone hasn't been paying attention," he said.

Javik frowned. "What do you mean, Tobalt?"

"Just a moment ago," Tobalt said, "you were explaining that totalitarianism is essentially a religious belief system. Now it's true that in more secular societies, the religious fervor of the mob tends to have a more nationalistic flavor, but in cultures with a strong religious tradition, the object of faith tends to be a figure of reputed spiritual authority."

Corbel scratched his head thoughtfully. "You're saying that Bishop Wyngalf, not Orbrecht, is the real source of power in Skaal City."

"I'm afraid you're still missing the point," said Tobalt. "The source of power in Skaal City is the shared delusion of a powerful central authority in Skaal City."

"But it's not a delusion," said Javik. "There *is* a powerful central authority in Skaal City."

"Only because people believe there is," said Tobalt. "If people stopped having faith in Orbrecht's ability to maintain order, the city would devolve into chaos. Orbrecht simply doesn't have enough men to subjugate the entire populace unless the citizens have already accepted the inevitability of their subjugation."

"And that sense of inevitability comes from the Ovaltarian prophecy about the Ko-Haringu!" cried Corbel. Javik nodded excitedly.

"No," said Tobalt, shaking his head. "Very few people in Skaal City actually believe the Ovaltarian prophecy. But a large proportion of the populace believes that a lot of *other* people in Skaal City believe in the Ovaltarian prophecy."

"So..." said Javik, "Orbrecht's power actually arises from an exaggerated sense of the importance of the prophecy."

"No," said Tobalt again. "Orbrecht's power arises from an exaggerated sense of the exaggerated sense of the importance of the prophecy."

Javik rubbed his chin. "You mean that lots of people in Skaal City assume that lots of other people in Skaal City think that a large proportion of the population of Skaal City believes in the prophecy."

"That's it!" cried Tobalt. "The whole thing is a house of cards. One grand illusion on top of another."

"And Bishop Wyngalf is the only thing holding it all together," Corbel mused.

"Correct," said Tobalt. "He's the lynchpin of the whole totalitarian system. Nobody in this town gets repressed without Wyngalf's implicit approval."

Wyngalf frowned at this but, seeing where Tobalt was going with his sophistry, he didn't object.

"So," Javik, "we were only following Orbrecht's order because of our faith in other people's faith in other people's faith in Wyngalf."

"Technically," said Tobalt, "You were following Orbrecht's orders because of your faith in other people's faith in other people's faith in other people's faith in Wyngalf, but your basic point is sound. For all intents and purposes, you're working for Wyngalf."

"In that case," said Corbel, "I suppose there's no harm in turning you over to him."

"Of course!" cried Javik. "He's the basis of the whole repressive dynamic. I can't believe we didn't see it before."

"Don't be so hard on yourself," said Tobalt. "For jackbooted enforcers at the bottom rung of a budding totalitarian regime, you two catch on pretty quickly. Speaking of which, take off your boots."

"Our boots?" asked Javik.

"Yes," said Tobalt, with a hint of impatience. "The lynchpin of the totalitarian regime needs your boots."

The two guards dutifully sat down on the ground and pulled off their boots. Judging Corbel's to be the better fit, Wyngalf grabbed his boots and slipped them on.

"Where are you taking him?" asked Javik, as he put his own boots back on. "I mean, in case Orbrecht asks."

"This way," said Tobalt, suddenly turning and shuffling away.

"Er, yes," said Wyngalf. "That way." He started after Tobalt, with Evena close behind.

"Why, what's—?" started Corbel.

From the opposite direction, the sound of footsteps approached. "Stop them, you morons!" yelled Garvin, coming around a corner. "They're fugitives!"

The two bootless guards and the clearly exhausted Garvin did their best to pursue Wyngalf and his friends, but they were unable to keep up. After a few minutes of running down side streets, the three companions emerged from an alley into a crowded bazaar, where they did their best to blend into the throng. Wyngalf led them down another alley on the far side of the bazaar, his only goal to put as much distance between them and the guards as possible. But as he neared an intersection, he heard Tobalt call out from behind him. He and Evena turned to see that Tobalt had fallen some distance behind. At first Wyngalf thought the goblin simply hadn't been able to keep up, but he realized that Tobalt had been trying doors as he went, and had found one unlocked. He beckoned to Wyngalf and Evena to follow him inside. Wyngalf and Evena shrugged at each other and went to see what Tobalt had found.

Before they even reached the door, they were struck with the wonderful, almost-overpowering aroma of fresh-baked bread. They followed Tobalt inside to find that they were in a small bakery. A rhythmic, almost musical sound arose from somewhere toward the front of the building, and after a moment Wyngalf realized it was someone snoring. Tobalt sneaked silently toward the sound, reporting back shortly thereafter.

"It would seem the proprietor is resting up after the morning's labors," Tobalt said. "He is sound asleep in a chair."

"Well," said Evena, eyeing the shelves full of still-warm bread, "I don't think we're going to find a better place to hide out and rest for a while." She sat down on the floor and took off her boot to inspect her swollen ankle.

"Agreed," said Wyngalf. He grabbed a loaf and tore it into three pieces, handing one to each of his companions. Tobalt managed to locate a small keg of beer, and the three of them sat on the floor in the storeroom of the bakery, eating bread and drinking beer from mixing bowls.

"Your tenure as bishop seems to be going well," said Tobalt, after they had sated their hunger.

"I'm having second thoughts about the job," said Wyngalf.

"About whether you're the Ko-Haringu, you mean?" asked Evena.

"Ko-Haringu," muttered Wyngalf. "I don't even know what that word means. Funny how quick we are to conform to someone else's idea of what we should be. Somebody says, 'Hey, you look like you could be the Flibbertigibbet!' And you start thinking, 'Yeah, that's me! I'm the Flibbertigibbet!'"

"What's a Flibbertigibbet?" asked Evena.

"Exactly!" cried Wyngalf, around a mouthful of bread.

"The need to find one's place in society is common to all the humanoid races," said Tobalt. "It's what holds society together. Unfortunately, it's also what makes possible the stupidity of the SAURIANs, the SMASHers, and—sad to say—Orbrecht's new regime. People would rather find their place in a terrible system than try to change the system and risk being cast out."

Wyngalf nodded. "It's true," he said. "Fortunately, I think I've finally found my place."

"Really?" said Evena. "Where?"

"Right here," Wyngalf replied.

Evena frowned. "I'm not sure we can stay in this bakery," she said. "Eventually that guy is going to wake up."

"No," said Wyngalf, "I mean here with you two."

"Wyngalf," said Evena, "I understand that you feel bad about the way things went between us, but you've got a great opportunity here. Tobalt and I will be okay. You don't owe us anything. We know how important it is to you to start a Noninitarian church in Skaal City. And like Tobalt said, Orbrecht still needs you. So if there's any way you can patch things up with him—"

"No," said Wyngalf again. "I was a fool to trust Orbrecht. There are only two ways that relationship can go. Either I become a slave to Orbrecht, or I become another of his victims. And if I'm going to die, I'd rather die with you guys."

"That's an admirable sentiment," said Tobalt, "but perhaps not as reassuring as you had intended."

"What I'm trying to say," Wyngalf said, "is that my faith is not what it used to be. I'm not sure if it's gotten stronger or weaker, but I'm finding it hard to put much stock in ancient prophecies and obscure doctrines. I prayed for wisdom, and I ran into you two. Maybe that's just a coincidence, or maybe someone really is looking out for me. All I know is that I have more faith in the people in this bakery than anyone else in the land of Dis."

"Whazzit?" grunted a voice from the front of the building. "Somebody there?" When there was no response for a moment, the man's snoring resumed.

"Not him," Wyngalf said quietly.

"Don't be so quick to judge," said Tobalt. "We shouldn't underestimate the value of having a baker on the team," Tobalt replied.

"Why, Tobalt," said Evena, smiling at the goblin, "I believe you just made a joke."

"It has been known to happen," said Tobalt.

"You guys are kind of ruining my moment," said Wyngalf.

"We get it, Wyngalf," said Evena. "Apology accepted. Right, Tobalt?"

Tobalt nodded. "I am certain I am as much to blame for our falling out as Wyngalf," he said. "My somewhat pedantic and recondite manner can be grating at times."

"Really?" said Evena. "I hadn't noticed."

"So what are we going to do?" asked Wyngalf. "By now every guard in the city is probably looking for us. We could try to escape the city, but Orbrecht undoubtedly knows all the escape routes better than we do."

"Perhaps if we threw ourselves on Orbrecht's mercy?" Tobalt offered. "He was, after all, your ally until a few hours ago. It isn't unthinkable that we could come to some sort of mutually beneficial agreement."

Wyngalf shook his head. "In Obrecht's mind—and the minds of everyone else in the city—I'm either the Ko-Haringu or a heretical imposter. There's no middle ground. If I don't go along with Orbrecht's plan to rule Skaal City with an iron fist, I'll be strung up in the city square. Or thrown into the gaping pit that used to be the city square, I guess. And I suspect he'll throw you two in with me, after all the mischief we pulled today."

"So we can't escape, and we can't surrender," said Evena. "What options does that leave us with?"

Wyngalf glanced at Tobalt, and he could see they were thinking the same thing. "Go on the offensive," said Wyngalf.

"Uh," said Evena. "Just the three of us? Against Orbrecht and all his men? Maybe we should reconsider putting the baker on the team. We could show up at Orbrecht's headquarters with, like, 5,000 cupcakes. Not enough problems are solved with cupcakes."

"I believe Wyngalf is suggesting that we break into the mansion and destroy the dragon egg."

"Or we could do that," said Evena. "Seriously, though, I think our odds are better with the cupcake thing. How are we supposed to get out of the city once we've destroyed the egg?"

Wyngalf glanced at Tobalt again. "We don't," said Tobalt.

"It's a suicide mission," Wyngalf said. "We most likely won't get out of the mansion alive. But at least we'll stop another dragon from taking over Skaal City. It's our fault—*my* fault—that Orbrecht has the egg in the first place. I can't be responsible for another thousand years of torture and suffering. Of course, I'll understand if you and Tobalt would rather sit this one out."

"I cannot speak for Evena," said Tobalt, "but if I'm going to die, I would just as soon die attempting to dismantle an authoritarian regime as huddling in fear while waiting to be discovered by the city guard."

Evena sighed. "Yeah, me too," she said. "Also, I suspect you're going to need my help."

Wyngalf frowned. "You understand that this is essentially a breaking-and-entering job, right? We don't need to organize Orbrecht's finances."

"You know," said Evena, "for somebody who is basically a really nice guy, you sure can be a condescending jerk sometimes. I'll have you know that while you were learning about angels dancing on pins in the Noninitarian Stronghold, I was finding all sorts of ways to entertain myself in Skuldred. You'd be amazed at what a girl can learn by hanging out with the wrong crowd."

Wyngalf and Tobalt both regarded her dubiously, and she smiled mischievously. Getting to her feet, she walked to the back wall of the bakery and picked a wire whisk off a hook. "This should do nicely," she said, and turned back to face Wyngalf. "Now, tell me about this mansion."

Twenty-four

A lone guard stood sentry in the street in front of the mansion that served as Orbrecht's headquarters. It was a cloudy night, and the street was dark except for the illumination from two torches in wall sconces, one on either side of the guard. The sound of footsteps on cobblestones rose out of the darkness.

"Who goes there?" the sentry demanded.

"It's just me," said a woman's voice. "I thought you might like some company."

"Who is that?" the sentry asked, but his posture had relaxed a bit. "There's a curfew, you know. I could arrest you."

"Oh, that sounds like fun!" the woman said. "I've been very bad. I need to be punished." She let out a little yelp and fell to her knees. "Darn these streets!" she cried. "I don't know how a girl is supposed to walk on these things."

The guard stepped forward to help her to her feet. "You shouldn't be out here," the sentry chided. "It's dangerous."

"Tell me about it," said Evena. A loud thud echoed down the street and the sentry slumped to the ground. Tobalt stood behind the man, a wooden rolling pin in his hand.

Wyngalf ran out of the shadows, and he and Evena dragged the man into an alley. Meanwhile, Tobalt removed the torches from their sconces and doused them in a bucket of rainwater nearby. The street was now shrouded in near darkness, and Wyngalf had to walk carefully over the cobblestones to avoid unintentionally recreating Evena's performance.

"Over here," whispered Tobalt, and they followed the sound of his voice to the front of the mansion. Wyngalf stopped when he felt the top of the goblin's head with his outstretched fingers. He could sense Evena standing next to him. "Hold out your hands," Tobalt instructed.

Unable to see anything but meaningless gradations of shadow, Wyngalf had to trust that Tobalt was in the right place. He locked his hands together and held them in front of him at waist level. Tobalt stepped on his hands and grabbed his right arm. While Wyngalf remained as still as he could, Tobalt climbed on top of him. Wyngalf winced as Tobalt's boots dug into his shoulders, and then the weight was gone. Tobalt had pulled himself up to the second floor balcony. Looking up, Wyngalf saw the goblin's silhouette against the sky for a moment, and then he disappeared.

Wyngalf and Evena retreated around the corner where they would be less likely to be seen by passersby. The night air was cold, and Wyngalf pulled Evena toward him and embraced her as they wait for Tobalt to return. He was reminded again of the first night they spent together, huddled on the island. "Evena," Wyngalf started, "I want you to know, in case we don't live through this, which we probably won't..."

"Shh," said Evena, putting her hand on his lips. "Not every moment calls for a speech."

He smiled and gave her a squeeze. True enough, he thought, but didn't say it.

They waited for what seemed like an hour, huddled together in the darkness, fearing that a contingent of the city guard would march past at any moment. But as they waited for the sound of boots approaching, they heard instead a whisper from the front of the building.

"Hurry up!" Tobalt said. "I've got the door open."

Wyngalf walked uncertainly forward, turning the corner and running his finger along the front wall of the building until he came to the door. Inside, it was even darker, but he felt Tobalt's hand reaching out to him and clutched it tightly. In turn, Wyngalf held his other hand out to Evena. The three of them moved single-file into the quiet mansion, Evena closing the door behind them. Tobalt led them across the foyer and then paused. "Watch your step," he whispered.

Tobalt began to pull upward, and Wyngalf knew that they had reached the stairs. They climbed slowly, making as little noise as possible. Light was visible at the top of the stairs from the lanterns that hung in the upstairs hallway, and as they rounded the corner, Wyngalf took the lead. "Wait here," he whispered to his companions, and crept forward in the dim light.

The hallway split into a T here, and the two branches turned at right angles about fifty feet down. Halfway to the corner, on the inside wall of each hall, a lantern hung on a hook, casting a faint, warm glow. Wyngalf knew that the hallways turned inward again another fifty feet or so, so that the upstairs hallway formed one large, unbroken rectangle. At the far side of this rectangle was the master suite, where Orbrecht slept—and presumably where he kept the dragon egg. A guard was assigned to patrol the upstairs, but in Wyngalf's experience the man could usually be found asleep in a chair on the right branch of the hallway. Wyngalf's plan was to creep down the left branch far enough to make sure it was clear, and then signal Tobalt and Evena to follow.

But as he passed the lantern on the wall and neared the corner, he heard someone walking toward him. Realizing it was too late to retreat without being seen, he stood his ground. With any luck, the guard would be unaware that Wyngalf was now a fugitive and would allow him to pass unmolested. Luck, however, was not on Wyngalf's side.

"Hey," said the guard, halting in surprise as he rounded the corner. "Who are you?"

"I'm Bishop Wyngalf. Where's Anders?"

"Anders is out sick. Aren't you a fugitive?"

"A fugitive?" asked Wyngalf. "What makes you think I'm a fugitive?"

The man reached into his belt pouch and pulled out a crumpled sheet of paper. He uncrumpled it and held it out for Wyngalf to see. On it was a crude line drawing of Wyngalf's face. At the top of the sheet was written *BISHOP WYNGALF*. Underneath the drawing was written, in big block letters: *FUGITIVE*.

"That doesn't even look like me," Wyngalf protested, although the drawing was, despite its simplicity, an uncanny likeness. "In any case, I can't be a fugitive. I'm the, you know, lynchpin of the whole repressive system."

The guard scowled and drew his sword. "The only word I understand of that was 'lynch.'"

"Look," said Wyngalf. "It's really complicated, but basically you're being fooled into arresting me by a sort of mass delusion of an authoritarian state."

"Are you calling me stupid?" the guard growled, raising his sword to Wyngalf's throat.

"No!" said Wyngalf. "I'm sorry, my friend can explain it better than I can."

"What friend?"

"The one behind you."

The guard laughed. "I'm not falling for that," he said. "Now turn—"

There was a thud, and the guard collapsed. Wyngalf caught him as he fell, trying to keep him from making any more noise than necessary. Tobalt stood behind the guard, the rolling pin in his hand. The guard's sword clattered to the ground, and Wyngalf picked it up.

"Took you long enough," Wyngalf said.

"I wanted to listen to your explanation of the totalitarian delusion," said Tobalt.

"How did I do?" asked Wyngalf.

"I would humbly suggest you stick to theology. Which door is Orbrecht's?"

Wyngalf took the lantern from its hook and then led them down the hall to the master suite. The door was a heavy slab of wood, virtually impregnable unless one had a sledgehammer and a lot of time. It was also, Wyngalf confirmed with a twist of the knob, locked. No sound could be heard from inside, and no light escaped from the crack underneath the door. They seemed to have timed their incursion well: Orbrecht was actually asleep.

"Step aside," whispered Evena, approaching the door and taking the lantern from Wyngalf. She got on her knees, examining the lock for a moment, then handed the lantern back to Wyngalf and extracted a length of wire from her coat. It was a fragment she had broken off from the whisk she had nabbed at the bakery. She bent the wire about halfway along its length, folding it back on itself. Then she made some additional modifications to the ends, bending them with her small fingers. When she was satisfied with the pick, she inserted it into the lock and began methodically squeezing the tool as if it were a pair of scissors. With her left hand, she reached up and turned the handle. There was a click as the bolt slid aside.

"That was amazing," whispered Tobalt. "I have a rudimentary knowledge of the workings of common locks, but to be able to sense the position of the—"

"Book learning only goes so far," whispered Evena with a smile. "Sometimes the only way to learn something is by doing it. A lot. Now quiet down." She turned the knob the rest of the way and pushed the door open a few inches. The room was completely dark. Wyngalf, holding the lantern in one hand and the sword in the other, shoved the door open and stepped inside. Tobalt and Evena followed, and Evena closed the door behind them.

They were in the first room of the suite, a sort of general purpose living area that Orbrecht had turned into an office. In the far wall was another door, which led to Orbrecht's private chamber. If Orbrecht was as paranoid and power-crazy as they suspected him to be, that would be where he was keeping the egg. They were going to have to break into Orbrecht's bedroom to get it. Wyngalf wouldn't be surprised if the old warrior was sleeping with the damned thing.

Wyngalf handed the lantern back to Evena. He held up his hand to her, and then crept as quietly as he could across the room. No light came from underneath this door either. Hearing the sounds of snoring from inside, he gently tried the door handle and found it unlocked. He nodded to his companions, and Evena doused the lantern and set it down. Now completely blind, Wyngalf waited for his companions to approach. He felt Tobalt slide past him, and Wyngalf stepped aside. They didn't want to waken Orbrecht with the lantern, which meant that they would have to rely on Tobalt's ability to see in near-total darkness. But if Orbrecht woke up while Tobalt was rooting around his room—as Wyngalf had the night before—they were done for. Orbrecht was a formidable fighter, and he wouldn't be as forgiving of an intruder as Wyngalf had been. So the plan was to sneak into Orbrecht's room, subdue him, and then search for the egg. Unfortunately, the only member of their team who could see in the dark was also the least intimidating of the three. Orbrecht would be unlikely to be cowed into submission by Tobalt's squeaky, uncertain voice. So Tobalt would lead the way, guiding Wyngalf to Orbrecht's bedside. Then Tobalt would locate the egg while Evena kept a lookout. That was the idea, anyway.

Tobalt crept into the room, Wyngalf following with his hand on the goblin's shoulder. The sound of Orbrecht's snoring grew louder as they approached. Wyngalf's foot landed on a creaky board, and for a moment the snoring stopped. Tobalt halted and they stood for a moment, holding their breath in the darkness. Then the snoring started again, and they continued on their way.

When Tobalt stopped again, Wyngalf could tell from the volume of the snoring that they were very close to Orbrecht's bed. He felt Tobalt's hand on his own, and realized after a second that the goblin was guiding his sword towards Orbrecht's throat. Wyngalf relaxed his arm a bit, trying to determine where Tobalt wanted the blade. When he felt resistance, he stopped moving, holding the sword outstretched in the darkness. For all he knew, he could be threatening to skewer Orbrecht's nightstand. Tobalt gave his hand a slight pat, and he felt the goblin slip silently past him. After a moment, he heard the faint sounds of Tobalt sorting through Orbrecht's possessions to find the egg.

This was the tricky part. If Orbrecht awoke on his own, he might start hollering for the guards before Wyngalf could even threaten to cut his throat. That meant Wyngalf had to wake him in a way that kept him from crying out. To that end, he pulled a rag that he had pilfered from the bakery out of his pocket and managed to wrap it around his left hand while continuing to hold the sword in his right. He moved his left hand toward what he hoped was the general direction of Orbrecht's mouth, homing in on the man's snoring as best he could. He brushed Orbrecht's nose first, but managed to slip his rag-covered palm over his mouth before Orbrecht could do more than grunt in surprise. Wyngalf put some weight on Orbrecht's mouth and let the edge of the sword rest against Orbrecht's throat.

"Make a peep and I'll—" Wyngalf started. But before he could finish, Orbrecht jerked his head backwards, slipping his mouth out from under the cloth. Wyngalf tried to put it back, but only succeeded in sliding the edge of his palm into Orbrecht's mouth. Wyngalf yelped in pain as Orbrecht's teeth sunk into his flesh. He reflexively jerked his hand away, and pressed down with the sword. But as he pressed, something was pushing the blade back toward him. Orbrecht, he realized, had grabbed the blade with his bare hands and was pushing it away from himself.

Unable to fight Orbrecht's strength, Wyngalf pulled the sword sideways, feeling it catch in Orbrecht's flesh as it went. Orbrecht gave a grunt, and suddenly the resistance was gone. Wyngalf sliced downward, but the sword only stopped when it hit the bed. Orbrecht had somehow slipped off the bed and away from him. This was not going at all as planned.

"Guards!" howled Orbrecht's voice, now on the other side of the bed. "Guards!" Behind Wyngalf, he could hear Tobalt furiously tearing open drawers and cabinets.

Wyngalf leaped onto the bed and scrambled across it, his feet landing with a thud on the other side. He gave a broad sweep with the sword, but the blade didn't connect with anything. He could only hope that Evena was still at the door; if she were nearby, he was as likely to strike her as Orbrecht. Wyngalf took a step forward, and heard someone moving a few feet in front of him. Running on pure instinct, he dodged to his right, and a moment later felt a fire erupting on his left side. Warm blood poured down his ribs. It figured the old bastard would keep a weapon near his bed. Fortunately, Wyngalf had avoided the brunt of it, the blade had bounced off his ribs, slicing open the skin but hitting nothing vital.

Ignoring the pain, he jabbed where he thought Orbrecht was, but again found only dead air. In the distance, he heard the sounds of boots thudding up the stairs. It sounded like more than one man—perhaps as many as three. Behind him Tobalt continued his furious search for the egg; all Wyngalf could do was to stay on the offensive and hope he could keep Orbrecht on the far side of the room until Tobalt could find and destroy the egg. He sliced back and forth with the sword, but still failed to connect with anything. The boots were now coming down the hall.

"I don't want to hurt you," said Wyngalf, swinging the sword in front of him, "but I can't let you have that dragon egg. It's too dangerous."

"And who are you to decide that, Wyngalf?" Orbrecht demanded. "What gives you the right?"

Wyngalf jabbed at the sound of the voice, but again connected with nothing. Orbrecht was toying with him. He backed up and swung again, thinking that Orbrecht would lunge at him while Wyngalf was overextended. But still the blade struck only air.

"I've seen what a dragon can do, Orbrecht," said Wyngalf. "So have you."

"This time will be different!" said Orbrecht. "We can train the dragon. Control it."

Wyngalf wondered if it was true. And he wondered whether Orbrecht being in control of the dragon would be an improvement. "Even if you can," he said, "what happens when you're gone? You'll have what, maybe twenty years to run Skaal City, and then the dragon takes over. A dragon can live for a thousand years, Orbrecht. You think you're going to be able to change its basic nature in twenty?"

Someone was banging on the door. "Mayor Orbrecht, are you alright?" a muffled voice cried.

"Intruders!" yelled Orbrecht. Wyngalf heard scuffling at the door.

"Wyngalf, I can't hold it!" Evena cried from across the room. There was no lock on the bedroom door, but Evena was trying to hold it shut. She didn't last long. Wyngalf heard the door burst open, and suddenly the room was bathed in yellowish light. For a moment, Orbrecht stood blinking before him, blinded by the light, holding a dagger in his right hand. His wooden leg lay next to the bed, and he stood balanced on his left. Wyngalf seized on the chance to swing at the man. Orbrecht jumped backward, but Wyngalf's blade connected with the back of Orbrecht's hand, and the dagger clattered to the ground. Wyngalf put his foot on the dagger and slid it across the room toward the door. He took a step toward Orbrecht, who was now backed into the corner. Both the man's hands were dripping with blood.

"Wyngalf, put down the sword!" a familiar voice yelled from behind him.

Glancing over his shoulder, Wyngalf saw that three men had entered the room. Standing a few feet behind Wyngalf, his sword raised, was the guard named Javik. His partner, Corbel, was standing just inside the doorway, holding a torch. Garvin, the guard Wyngalf had pushed into the harbor, stood with his sword pointed at Evena, who lay near the foot of the bed, stunned but apparently unhurt. On the other side of the room from Wyngalf and Orbrecht, Tobalt continued to root through drawers looking for the egg.

Wyngalf turned his gaze back to Orbrecht, who was blinking in the bright torchlight, unarmed and completely helpless. Wyngalf tried to will himself to stab the man through his heart. But it was one thing to swing wildly at a man in the dark and another to attack him when he stood helplessly in front of you.

"Wyngalf!" Javik growled again. "Put down the sword!"

"Where is it?" demanded Wyngalf, taking another step toward Orbrecht. Maybe he didn't have it in him to kill Orbrecht, but he wasn't about to surrender. There was no chance they were getting out of this alive, so he might as well go down fighting. If only Tobalt could find the damned egg!

Orbrecht smiled, realizing that Wyngalf wasn't going to kill him. "Give up, Wyngalf. I'll make sure your execution is swift and painless." But as he said it, Orbrecht's smile faltered slightly, and Wyngalf saw the old warrior's eyes dart for a moment toward Tobalt. Glancing to his left, Wyngalf saw that Tobalt had torn through Orbrecht's closet and pulled out all of the drawers of a bureau. Articles of clothing littered the floor. Tobalt stood in front of the bureau, baffled. The only thing on top of the bureau was a flower pot from which a small ornamental plant arose. The plant was convincing enough, but the pot was too far from any of the windows for it to get much light. A fake.

"Put down the sword! I'm not telling you again!" Javik growled behind Wyngalf. Wyngalf could almost feel the man's breath on his neck.

"Tobalt, the flower pot!" cried Wyngalf. As he spoke, he felt a strange sensation in his lower back. Looking down, he could see the point of a blade protruding from his belly, a few inches left of his navel. Then the blade disappeared and pain tore through his side. He fell to his knees, overcome with shock and pain. Javik had stabbed him.

Tobalt had grabbed the flower pot from the bureau and was now holding it over his head, as if threatening to smash it on the floor. But Garvin, having no idea that the pot was concealing a dragon egg, misinterpreted Tobalt's action, thinking he planned on using it as a weapon. He lunged toward Tobalt, his sword swinging through the air in a broad arc. Tobalt gasped as the blade cut clean through his wrist, and his right hand and the pot fell together to the wood floor. The pot shattered, revealing a bundle of dried grass in which was nestled the dragon egg. The egg hit the floor and began to roll.

Too dazed to move, Wyngalf watched helplessly as the egg rolled under the bed and came out the other side, coming to rest against Orbrecht's bare foot. At first he thought it was a trick of the torchlight, but Wyngalf soon realized he wasn't imagining it: cracks were forming on the egg's surface.

Tobalt had fallen to the ground, moaning and clutching his wrist. Wyngalf, overcome with shock and nausea, couldn't seem to make his body move toward the egg. He was vaguely aware of Garvin and Javik, standing with their swords bloodied, waiting for an excuse to maim someone else. And Evena... was she still on the floor behind the bed? He didn't know. Maybe she had managed to slip out of the room. He hoped she had. If just one of them could escape, it should be her.

The egg was now rocking slightly back and forth, and Wyngalf watched in horror as a fragment near the top of the shell broke away and a small reptilian head poked through. It was facing Orbrecht.

Twenty-five

Orbrecht crouched down next to the hatchling, eyeing in with gleeful anticipation. "That's right, little fella," he cooed. "Look at daddy."

The shell fell away around the hatchling as it spread its wings, craning its tiny head first left then right. Its scales shone reddish-gold in the dim torchlight. Somehow it registered through Wyngalf's haze of shock and pain that the creature's eyes were still closed. It wasn't too late. The dragon hadn't yet gazed upon Orbrecht.

"Hey!" cried Corbel, somewhere behind him. "Give that back!" Wyngalf heard the sound of a door slamming, and suddenly the room was plunged into darkness. Through his mental haze, Wyngalf realized that Evena had made off with the man's torch.

"Damn it!" growled Orbrecht. "Will you get a hold of that girl? Leave it to the morons on the city guard to have one torch between them."

The door opened again, and Wyngalf heard the thudding of boots and then Evena screaming. The screaming got louder and then the light returned to the room. There was another loud thud behind him as someone hit the floor, and the screaming stopped.

The dragon seemed perturbed by all the commotion; it had covered its head with its right wing.

"Give me that torch," said Orbrecht, and Corbel stepped past Wyngalf and handed it to him. "Now get back." Corbel complied.

Wyngalf was growing light-headed; it was all he could do to support his weight with his arms. He shook his head violently, trying to keep his eyes focused on the hatchling. Maybe if he could make some noise, the dragon would instinctively look his direction. Anything would be better than it imprinting on Orbrecht. But Wyngalf couldn't muster more than a faint groan.

"Come on, little guy," Orbrecht was saying, waving the torch rhythmically just over his head. "Look up here. That's it, come on. Just one little glance."

The dragon slowly lowered its wing and lifted its head. Wyngalf couldn't see the dragon's eyes from his vantage point, but he imagined the creature focusing on Orbrecht's wizened face, indelibly imprinting the power-mad old warrior's visage into its mind. Wyngalf turned away, unable to bear it.

"Good, good!" Orbrecht cried. "Just open those little eyes and—" But his words were abruptly cut short. A strained, gurgling sound followed.

"Damn it!" Garvin yelled. "He told you to get a hold of her!"

Wyngalf managed to look up in time to see Orbrecht clutching at a dagger that protruded from his throat, blood erupting from the wound like a geyser. After trying and failing several times to get his hand to clasp on the dagger's hilt, Orbrecht swooned, his eyes rolling up in his head, and he fell face-first onto the hatchling. His outstretched left arm, still holding the torch, twitched a few times and then he was still.

Corbel darted forward and grabbed the torch from Orbrecht's hand while Javik struggled to turn Obrecht over without driving the dagger even farther into his neck. It was clearly a lost cause, though: judging from the quickly growing pool of blood underneath Orbrecht, the dagger had severed an artery. Garvin stood gaping at the foot of the bed with his sword at Evena's throat.

Wyngalf, meanwhile, was preoccupied with locating the baby dragon. Pain shot through his abdomen as he moved, but while the guards were distracted by the dagger protruding from Orbrecht's neck, Wyngalf managed to climb over Orbrecht's legs to the shell fragments that lay scattered on the floor next to him. Between his own blurry vision and the long, darting shadows cast by the torch, it was difficult to see, but a sweep of his arm across the floor caught nothing but pieces of shell and Orbrecht's blood. The dragon was gone. But where?

Javik and Corbel continued to panic over Orbrecht's condition, uncertain whether removing the dagger would improve or worsen his plight, and Wyngalf crawled toward the bed, peering underneath it. He caught the sight of something skittering away from him. He groaned. There was no way he was going to catch the dragon in his current condition, and if it escaped, there was no telling who it might imprint on. It might fly out the window and land at the feet of some drunken drifter or jaded whore. It was hard to say whether either would be an improvement over the current regime.

With a huge expenditure of effort, Wyngalf managed to pull his upper body onto the bed, trying to catch a glimpse of the hatchling. Behind him, Javik and Corbel seemed to have given up on Orbrecht; Corbel, holding the torch, was now standing still, making it easier to see. Across the room, a few paces from the far side of the bed, Tobalt still lay on the ground, moaning. His severed hand lay on the floor just in front of him. He had managed to get one of Orbrecht's shirts wrapped around his wrist as a tourniquet, staunching the bleeding, but he was clearly in a great deal of pain.

"Alright, Wyngalf," said Garvin, his sword still at Evena's throat. "Stand up. You're going to pay for your crimes."

"Let's go, Wyngalf," said Javik, getting up from Orbrecht's side.

Wyngalf struggled to get to his feet, but he was too weak. He collapsed back onto the bed as across the room, something skittered toward Tobalt. For a moment, Wyngalf's vision went black. When he could see again, Corbel had moved closer to Tobalt. The hatchling pecked curiously at the goblin's severed hand. Corbel, whose training in the city guard clearly hadn't prepared him for this situation, stood dumbly holding the torch, uncertain what to do.

"Kill that thing!" Garvin growled.

Corbel nodded and took two steps forward, lifting his boot to crush the hatchling. But as he brought his foot down, the hatchling skittered away again, coming to a halt a few inches from Tobalt's nose.

Tobalt, momentarily forgetting his pain, stared at the tiny dragon. "Hello," he said.

The dragon squeaked a response at him, then lifted its wings and fluttered onto his shoulder. It pawed at Tobalt like a kitten for a moment, then turned around to face the guard with the torch.

"Just kill it, you idiot!" Garvin yelled.

Corbel nodded and swung at the hatchling with the torch. But the hatchling spread its wings and shot into the air, dodging the torch. It hovered a few feet over Tobalt, its little red eyes affixed on the guard as if daring the man to attack.

Corbel swung at the dragon again, and the dragon again dodged the attack, fluttering closer to him. Three more times Corbel swung, but each time the hatchling evaded the blow, and each time it fluttered a little closer to him. It now hovered mere inches from Corbel's face.

"I'm certainly no expert," said Tobalt weakly from the floor, "but I would avoid antagonizing the dragon. Even at this age—"

The dragon opened its mouth and let out a tiny squawk at the guard.

"Aww," said Corbel. "Do we really have to kill it? It's adorable."

"It is pretty cute," said Javik. "And it seems harmless enough."

The dragon squawked again, slightly louder.

"Well," said Garvin. "I suppose there's no harm in letting live. Let's throw these three into one of the cells under Fourth Street and then we'll—"

The dragon opened its mouth again, letting out another squawk. This time, though, the squawk was accompanied by a blast of orange flame that engulfed Corbel's face. Corbel screamed and fell to his knees, dropping the torch and burying his face in his hands. The scent of burnt hair filled the room.

"Kill it!" Garvin cried again, evidently reconsidering the wisdom of his plan. "Kill it!"

The dragon fluttered over to Garvin, the fallen torch throwing a terrifying shadow across the wall. "Back!" Garvin cried, his sword against Evena's throat. "I'll kill her!"

The dragon landed on Garvin's sword hand, latching onto his forefinger with its tiny teeth and wrapping its tail around his wrist.

"Ow!" Garvin yelped. "What the—"

Still tightly attached to Garvin's hand, the dragon began batting wildly with it rear claws, tearing into the man's flesh and spattering blood on the wall. Garvin screamed and dropped his sword, releasing Evena. Evena spun around and punched him square in the nose. Garvin reeled and fell backwards, slumping against the wall. The dragon uncoiled itself, leaving the guard to clutch his bloody hand, moaning in pain. It fluttered toward Wyngalf.

"Easy," said Javik, backing away with his hands up. "Call off your dragon, Bishop. We surrender!"

"It's not my dragon," Wyngalf moaned, managing to roll onto his back. "It's Tobalt's."

"Well, whoever's dragon it is, call him off!"

"Come here, Shelly," said Tobalt, who had pulled himself into a sitting position against the far wall. "It's okay, girl. Come here."

The dragon squawked defiantly at Javik, and then spun around and fluttered back to Tobalt, landing on his shoulder. Garvin and Corbel continued to whimper and moan, nursing their respective injuries.

"Shelly?" asked Evena, rubbing the knuckles of her right hand with her left.

Tobalt picked a tiny fragment of shell from the dragon's head. "It was the first thing that popped into my mind," he said. "I imagine we can find a more suitable name with minimal application of effort."

"No," said Evena. "Shelly is good."

Wyngalf groaned, and Evena ran to his side. She lifted his legs onto the bed and put a pillow under his head. She pulled up his tunic and made a grimace as she glanced at his wounds. "Javik," she said, turning to the man behind her. "Get me a basin of warm water, a bottle of wine, and some clean rags. Oh, and a needle and thread."

Javik hesitated, clearly not enamored of the idea of taking orders from Evena. In the distance the sound of more boots coming up the stairs could be heard. Evena stood up and looked the man in the eye. "You saw what that dragon did to your friends," she said. "If Tobalt wants Shelly to tear your eyes out, she will. And Wyngalf is Tobalt's best friend. There's been a regime change. Do you understand?"

Javik nodded. "I'll get the stuff," he said.

"Good idea," said Evena. She turned to Garvin, who was still clutching his bloody hand. "Grab that torch and bring it over here so I can see what I'm doing."

Garvin groaned, but got to his feet. He picked up the torch, which was still smoldering on the floor, and carried it to Wyngalf's bedside.

Two more guards ran into the room, looking around in confusion. One of them carried a lantern. Their eyes came to rest on Garvin. "Captain, what's—" one of them started. "Is that the mayor?"

Garvin and Javik exchanged glances. "Not anymore," said Garvin. "Get this body out of here. And clean up that blood."

The men glanced at him uncertainly, then at the tiny dragon glaring at them from Tobalt's shoulder.

"If you value your life," Garvin growled, "you'll do as you're told."

The men each grabbed one of Orbrecht's arms and began to drag him out of the room. Javik went to help Corbel to his feet and the two of them left the room while Garvin stood silently, holding the torch over the bed. He regarded Shelly stoically.

"Are we going to have a problem, Garvin?" Evena asked.

"Not s'long as everybody knows who's in charge," said Garvin, his eyes still affixed on the dragon.

Evena nodded, apparently considering this a satisfactory answer. "Tobalt, come here," she said.

Tobalt, with the dragon still perched on his shoulder, approached the bed. The shirt wrapped around his wrist was soaked with blood.

"I can't reattach your hand," said Evena, "but I can keep the wound from getting infected. Lie down."

Tobalt climbed into the bed next to Wyngalf, sitting up against the headboard. "It would seem," Tobalt said, regarding Wyngalf, "that politics does indeed make strange bedfellows."

Wyngalf began to laugh, but stopped when pain shot through his side. "I mean no offense," he managed to gasp, "you're not the member of the team I had hoped to get into bed with." He realized as he said it that it was a highly inappropriate remark, but his wounds were clouding his judgement. Also, he was fairly certain he was about to die. Even in the dim light, Wyngalf could see that Evena was blushing.

"No offense taken," said Tobalt. "I saw the way you looked at that baker."

This time Wyngalf couldn't help it. He laughed despite the pain.

Soon after, Javik returned, carrying a tray bearing the supplies Evena had requested. He set it down on the nightstand. "I'll get some lanterns," he said, glancing nervously at the dragon. "Better light than the torch."

Evena nodded, unstopping the wine bottle. Shelly seemed content to watch the proceedings from Tobalt's shoulder.

"Seriously, though, Tobalt," Wyngalf said. "You've been a good friend. I was wrong about you not having a soul. There's no one I'd rather die next to."

"You can't die," said Tobalt. "You're the Ko-Haringu."

Wyngalf shook his head. "We misinterpreted the prophecy," he said. "I'm not the Ko-Haringu, Tobalt. You are."

Tobalt's brow furrowed, considering this possibility. "Then what does that make you?"

Wyngalf smiled. "I'm the brute who talks like a man."

Evena poured wine on Wyngalf's wound, and for a moment there was nothing but pain. Then everything went black.

Twenty-six

When Wyngalf awoke, it was daytime. He had a vague sense that several days had passed since the dragon had hatched, but other than his own condition, he had no way of knowing how many. His whole lower torso was sore and bandages were wrapped around the wound in his belly and the laceration along his ribs. The sheets of Orbrecht's bed were damp and his skin was clammy, as if he'd been feverish. Tobalt was no longer next to him, and the mess in the room had been cleaned up. Only a faint bloodstain remained on the wood floor where Orbrecht had fallen.

Seeing a glass and a pitcher of water on the nightstand, Wyngalf suddenly realized how parched he was. But as he reached for the pitcher, pain shot through his body, and he nearly blacked out. For several minutes he lay in bed, breathing deeply and trying to force his muscles to relax. When he'd recovered from this grueling ordeal, he noticed a small metal bell next to the pitcher. He gingerly reached over and tried to pick it up, but succeeded only in knocking in to the floor. The bell tinkled softly as it struck the floor and then was silent. Wyngalf groaned in frustration.

But soon he heard footsteps coming down the hall. He reflexively looked around for a weapon, and then chuckled at his stupidity. He couldn't lift a pitcher of water. How was he going to fight off an intruder?

He needn't have worried: the door opened to reveal not a member of the city guard, but rather a beautiful young woman. She was dressed so finely, in a stunning topaz gown, her hair perfectly coifed, that it took Wyngalf a moment to realize that he knew her. "Evena," he murmured.

"You were expecting an Eytrith?" [4] asked Evena. "Keep dreaming, Wyngalf." She walked to his bedside, picking up the bell and placing it on the nightstand.

"I'm no warrior," said Wyngalf. "My brilliant plan to steal the dragon egg nearly got us all killed."

"It turned out okay," said Evena. "That's what matters." She poured him a glass of water and held it to his lips.

"Did it?" Wyngalf asked. "How long was I out?" He took several swallows of water and then held up his hand.

"Five days," she said, setting the glass back down. She sat down next to Wyngalf on the bed. "I wasn't sure you were going to pull through. You're incredibly lucky Orbrecht's blade seems to have missed all your vital organs."

"And incredibly lucky to have a skilled nurse at my side," Wyngalf said. "It seems there's no end to your hidden talents. Where did you learn to throw a dagger like that?"

Evena shrugged, a bit embarrassed. "I didn't," she said. "I was aiming for the dragon."

"Oh," said Wyngalf. "Well, like you said, it turned out okay." His eyes fell to her dress. "You seem to be doing well. Did you become the new mayor of Skaal City while I was out?"

She snorted. "Hardly. I've had my hands full just trying to keep you and Tobalt alive."

Wyngalf frowned. "This is your nurse's outfit?"

"No, silly," she said. "After I cleaned and sutured your wounds and bandaged you up, there wasn't much I could do for you but wait and hope you pulled through. For the past few days I've been focused more on external threats. Fortunately for you, I'm better at diplomacy than dagger-throwing."

"Diplomacy?" Wyngalf asked. "What do you mean?"

---

[4] Eytriths are the female warriors who carry the souls of dead heroes to their glorious afterlife in the Halls of Avandoor, if you believe in that sort of thing.

"Well, for starters I had to convince the city guard that Orbrecht was a power-crazed old nut who had a personal vendetta against you, and that you killed him in self-defense. I may have also played up the idea that you're the Ko-Haringu, since it seemed easier than convincing them that their much-ballyhooed messiah was a goblin. I've sworn the men who were here that night to secrecy, but rumors are rampant among the city guard that you've got a dragon on your side. That ploy actually worked better than I imagined; the last I heard, the dragon is twice the size of Verne and five times as mean. I had to keep Tobalt and Shelly in seclusion down the hall to keep the rumors going. Anyway, the city guard is more-or-less on our side, although sentiment could shift against us at any moment. Once I'd made sure you weren't in immediate danger of being murdered in your sleep, I invited the new heads of the SMASHers and the SAURIANs to a series of negotiations about the future of the Skaal City government. By playing them against each other, I think I've managed to convince them to support you as the new leader. A nominal mayor would be selected, but the office of Noninitarian Bishop would hold most of the authority in the city. Of course, either side could double-cross us, or the two factions could decide to meet behind our backs and cut us out, so we're probably going to have to cultivate some spies within their organizations. I've identified a few possible candidates, but—"

Wyngalf groaned, and a look of concern came across Evena's face. "What's wrong?" she asked. "Did the stitches tear?"

He shook his head. "No, I'm just sick to death of all these political machinations. What was the point of all this, if we're just going to replace Orbrecht's oppressive regime with our own? The one good thing about Orbrecht was that he shut out the SMASHers and SAURIANs, and now you've invited them right back in!"

"I hardly had a choice!" Evena shot back. "I was trying to keep you and Tobalt alive!"

"It doesn't matter," Wyngalf moaned. "Don't you see? It starts out as self-preservation, but ultimately it's just the same thing, all over again. A regime built on fear."

"Well, in a sense," Evena said. "But—"

"Forget it," he said. "I'm done fighting. It was inevitable that another dragon was going to take over this city eventually. I suppose it's just as well that it's one under our control. Well, under Tobalt's control, anyway."

"Wyngalf," said Evena, "you should know—"

"I know, I wanted to kill the dragon. And I'm still not certain we shouldn't. But maybe the dragon isn't ultimately the problem. And if anyone can train a dragon to act civilly and avoid, you know, wholesale slaughter and the like, it's Tobalt."

"I agree," said Evena, "but the thing is, we don't have to—"

"Ultimately the three of us will end up as puppets, I suppose. And who knows what will happen when Tobalt dies. Hopefully he'll live long enough in this poisonous political climate to impress upon Shelly the importance of—"

"Wyngalf!" exclaimed Evena. "Shut up for a second, would you? I'm trying to tell you you're getting all worked up for nothing. Tobalt is gone."

"What?" cried Wyngalf, sitting up in bed and immediately regretting it. "Gone where?"

"I don't know," said Evena. "He and Shelly were gone when I went to check on him this morning. He left this." She pulled a scrap of paper from her pocket and handed it to Wyngalf. It was written in an awkward, barely legible script.

My dear friends, Wyngalf and Evena —

It is too dangerous to keep Shelly in the city. I have set out to find a place, far away from here, where I can train her. My hope is to keep her safe from people and to keep people safe from her. Wish me luck.

Your friend, Tobalt.

Wyngalf stared at the letter. "He just *left?*"

"So it would seem," said Evena.

"I didn't even get to say goodbye to him."

"You kind of did," said Evena. "When you thought you were dying, I mean. You got pretty emotional. Frankly, I was a little embarrassed for you."

"This isn't funny," said Wyngalf with a scowl. "Fear of that dragon was the only thing keeping us alive."

"Oh, stop," said Evena. "You just got finished preaching to me about the evils of a regime built on fear."

"That's when I thought we had a dragon on our side!" Wyngalf cried. "They're going to kill us!"

"No, they're not," said Evena. "Not anytime soon, anyway. The various political factions of the city are still feeling out the new landscape. We've got some time. But you're not really worried about that."

"I'm not?"

"No," said Evena. "You're upset because Tobalt is gone. You're going to miss him."

"That's ridiculous," said Wyngalf. "Frankly I'm glad to be rid of his pretentiousness and sophistry. He probably just ran away because he was sick of losing arguments to me."

"Yes, I'm sure that's it. Anyway, you should get some rest. You've got a big day tomorrow."

"I do? What's tomorrow?"

"I'm scheduling a public address," said Evena. "You'll nominate the new mayor and explain the new power structure to the people of the city. Well, you won't actually explain it, of course. You'll deliver a bunch of platitudes and buzzwords calculated to make each faction think it's getting what it wants while failing to make any concrete commitments."

Wyngalf groaned again. "Do I have to?"

"If you want to stay alive," Evena said. "We can either play the political game to the hilt or we can surrender to one of the factions and hope for the best. There isn't any middle option, I'm afraid. We can probably wait another day or two if you're not feeling up to it, but the longer we wait before formally taking the reins of power, the more precarious our situation is."

Wyngalf nodded glumly. "No, it's better to get it over with. I'll manage all right."

"Are you hungry?"

"Famished."

"I'll get you some food. Then you should rest up for tomorrow. I'll bring your speech in the morning."

Wyngalf sighed and closed his eyes, already exhausted from the effort he'd expended. Hopefully the political maneuvering would be easier once he was fully healed, but he suspected that he'd never have a chance to really relax again. He was doomed to a life of always looking over his shoulder. His one consolation was that Evena seemed more than willing to remain by his side.

After eating a small dinner, he fell asleep again, and didn't wake until early the next morning. He managed to bathe and get dressed before Evena came in, bearing breakfast and a script for his speech. A careful examination revealed them both to be bland and tasteless.

"Do people really swallow this sort of pabulum?" he asked. He held up the sheets of paper to indicate that he was talking about the speech, and not the bowl of porridge. "I'm used to speeches with more substance."

"I've heard your speeches," said Evena. "Trust me, this is an improvement."

"You heard only a small part of the Fourteen Points," Wyngalf protested.

"And lived to tell about it," said Evena. "Look, just deliver the speech as it's written. I'm not claiming it's great oratory, but it will buy us a few days while we solidify our alliances."

"But this speech isn't *about* anything," said Wyngalf. "There isn't a single clear policy initiative in any of this."

"Exactly," said Evena. "Nothing for anybody to get worked up about. We can't afford to anger anybody until we have a better sense of who our friends and enemies are."

"Okay, but once our position is less precarious, we'll be able to make some real changes, right? I mean, things to improve the lives of the average citizen."

"We can try," Evena replied, "but we've got to be careful. I already made a lot of people angry by having the city guard close all the prisons under the city. To be honest, I suspect it's going to take all of our wits just to stay one step ahead of the SMASHers and the SAURIANs, not to mention the Ovaltarians, most of whom are still convinced you're the Ko-Haringu. They think you're indebted to them for your sudden ascendance to power. And of course we have to deal with the Shipping Guild, and the other tradesmen's guilds, and the—"

"I get it," said Wyngalf. "Politics is complicated. Maybe I should stick to theological matters and let the nominal mayor run things. If I can't improve the citizens' lives physically, maybe I can at least address their spiritual needs."

Evena shook her head. "If we don't keep control of the mayoralty, we won't last a week. Also, you can't risk alienating the Ovaltarians at this point, so any religious pronouncements are going to have to be extremely vague. And then there are the Followers of Grovlik, the cultists of Varnoth, the—"

"I'm the *bishop*!" cried Wyngalf. "How can I not be allowed to make statements about religion?"

"You're *allowed*," said Evena. "I just wouldn't advise it."

"Why have a bishop, if he can't talk about religion?"

"People love the idea of a wise, benevolent spiritual leader watching out for them," Evena explained. "But they tend to freak out about specifics."

"Ugh," Wyngalf groaned. "Why are we even doing this?"

"No choice, remember," said Evena. "We play the game or we die."

"We could run away," said Wyngalf. "It worked for Tobalt."

"Tobalt felt a responsibility to look after Shelly," said Evena. "Your responsibility is here."

"What about your responsibility?" asked Wyngalf. "Don't you need to get back home to Skuldred?"

"The threat to my home town has passed," said Evena. "When Verne doesn't come back, my parents and the rest of the townspeople will go back to their lives."

"But they'll worry about you."

"I knew that when I ran away," said Evena. "If I go back now, they'll never let me leave again. Maybe someday I'll go back home, but not yet. Anyway, you need my help. Somebody's got to run this city, and you're the only one I'd trust with the job."

"Really?" asked Wyngalf. "Why?"

"Because you don't want it."

Wyngalf groaned again.

"Look, I'll be here with you. It will be okay. We'll figure it out together."

Wyngalf managed a faint smile, and she kissed him on the forehead.

"Study your speech. I'll come get you when it's time." She turned and left the room.

Wyngalf read through the first page of the speech again and sighed. He set it down and swallowed a spoonful of cold porridge.

Twenty-seven

Wyngalf didn't bother to memorize the speech. There was so little actual substance to it that he was in little danger of missing any key themes. The greatest risk was that in ad-libbing he might inadvertently make some sort of point, which Evena would then have to spend a week attempting to explain away in meetings with the city's various political, religious, and business groups.

Evena and Javik helped him to a balcony overlooking the street. He hesitated a moment at the doorway. Down below, he could hear a huge crowd murmuring excitedly. The people would be anticipating an inspirational address from the new bishop of Skaal City, explaining the events of late and detailing plans for the future—such as what the government planned to do about the gaping abyss in the center of the city. But Wyngalf was going to leave them disappointed. Or, worse, he was going to give them the impression that the city was in good hands, and that he and the city's other leaders had some kind of plan to deal with the problems the city faced. Other than the abyss, though, he didn't even have a good sense of what those problems *were*. Crime? Poverty? Raw sewage in the streets? The threat of Verne was gone, but would his absence embolden the goblins to the east? Would it prompt the barbarian tribes to the south to attack? What would become of the relations between Skaal City and Brobdingdon, now that both dragons were dead? Would the two cities become allies against the other monsters that threatened civilization, or would they remain enemies? He supposed Evena had spent no small amount of time over the past few days considering these issues, but they were only hinted at in the broadest terms in the speech she had written for him. Hopefully at some point he could actually work on addressing the issues, but first he needed to get the people on his side. Before he could solve their problems, he needed the people to believe he could solve their problems. Another self-fulfilling prophecy, he thought ruefully.

"Ready?" asked Evena, holding his right arm.

"As I'll ever be," he said.

Evena nodded to Javik, who released his grip on Wyngalf's other arm, saluted, and walked to the corner of the balcony.

Wyngalf took a deep breath, trying to steady his nerves. The pain wasn't too bad as long as he avoided any sudden movements. He only hoped he could stand long enough to deliver the entire speech. He could lean on the railing of the balcony if he needed to, but Evena had stressed the importance of projecting an air of strength. Only by appearing vigorous and confident could Wyngalf effect the illusion that he was actually saying something. His mind wandered to Tobalt's words: *The source of power in Skaal City is the shared delusion of a powerful central authority in Skaal City.*

That's all my power is, he thought. An illusion. I'm not standing on this balcony because some divine entity ordained it, and I'm not here because the people of Skaal City want me as their bishop. I'm here because of sheer dumb luck. I was in the right place at the right time, and now everyone in the city is looking to me for answers—answers that I don't have, and couldn't act on if I did. But if I wasn't here to perpetuate the illusion, someone else would step in to fill the void. Probably someone less scrupulous. Maybe an old kook like Orbrecht, or a feckless, preening aristocrat like Lord Otten Popper, or one of the cynical, manipulative leaders of the SAURIANs or the SMASHERs. If someone has to be in charge, he told himself, it might as well be me.

And yet this argument seemed as vapid as the speech he was about to deliver. Appearances to the contrary, he wasn't in charge of *anything*. Here he was, barely able to stand, being forced to deliver an insipid speech filled with meaningless slogans and empty assurances. And he wasn't doing this in service of any sort of grand plan or principle, but merely an attempt to try to stay alive for a few more weeks. If he accepted this role, he suddenly realized, he and

Evena would be prisoners in Skaal City forever. That was what Tobalt had missed in his analysis: power was an illusion, but the illusion went both ways. The real fools weren't the people down in the street, who would go back to their normal lives once Wyngalf's vapid speech was done; it was the people who had to continue to live the illusion forever, if they were going to live at all.

"Are you okay, Wyngalf?" asked Evena. Wyngalf had no idea how long he had been standing there. The crowd had gone silent in anticipation.

"Yeah," said Wyngalf. "I just... I don't want to do this." He imagined tearing up the speech and telling the crowd what he really wanted to say—that he was just a wandering preacher who didn't know anything about politics, and that they shouldn't trust anyone who would set himself up as some sort of messiah. Maybe the people were as sick of platitudes as he was. Maybe they were ready for some real leadership for a change. Someone who would take real risks, and stand up to the entrenched interests in Skaal City. But as the thought occurred to him, he realized he was succumbing to yet another delusion: the idea that somehow he was different from the other politicians in Skaal, that he wouldn't fall victim to the desire to use his office for self-preservation and personal gain. If he really intended to tell the truth, he'd have to start by telling the people of Skaal City that he had no more business delivering a speech to the citizens than any of them—less, in fact, since he had only been in the city for a few days. Any random blacksmith or innkeeper would have a better understanding of the issues facing Skaal City than he did. If he really believed he wasn't just another politician, then the sensible thing would be to stop acting like a politician, right now, before he even got started.

"I know you don't want to do it," Evena was saying. "But you have to. Just deliver this one speech and then you can rest for a few days."

He shook his head. "No, I mean I don't want to do this. Any of it. Ever."

Evena looked at him sternly for a moment. "Wyngalf, you need to understand what you're saying. I know a little something about running from responsibility, and let me tell you, it comes with a cost."

"I'm not running from responsibility," said Wyngalf. "I'm embracing it. Ever since I left Svalbraakrat, I've been looking for some kind of shortcut to my supposed destiny. First I thought I was being guided toward greatness by the Noninity. Then I fell for the Ovaltarian prophecy. And now I've fallen into a position of authority that I didn't earn and don't deserve. The people of Skaal City don't need me to solve their problems for them."

"But you realize that if you abdicate your authority, they're just going to fall for some other charlatan. I mean, for some charlatan."

"If they do," said Wyngalf, "that's on them. I can't force them to make the right decision. For the first time in a thousand years, the land of Dis is free of dragons. The rest is up to the people."

"What do you want to do, then? Run away?"

"I hadn't really thought it through. I guess so, yes. We need to get out of the city somehow. Far away from here and anybody who knows us. Maybe go find Tobalt. I know, the odds of us escaping the city are slim, considering my current condition, and I won't blame you if you want to leave without me...."

"Don't be ridiculous," said Evena. "I'm not leaving without you. If we do this, we're doing it together. But I need to be sure this is what you want to do."

"I'm sure," said Wyngalf. "I can't stay here."

Evena let out a relieved sigh. "Thank the Noninity," she said. "Let's go." She took Wyngalf's arm and led him past Javik, who stared at them in confusion. They went back into the mansion.

"What... where are we going?" asked Wyngalf.

"I may have put together a contingency plan," said Evena.

"You mean you *knew* I wasn't going to deliver your speech?"

"I wanted it to be your decision," she replied. "I didn't want to stand in the way of your destiny, but between you and me, the sooner we get out of this city, the better. There's a carriage waiting in the alley. I appropriated it and two horses from the city guard, along with three weeks of supplies. Oh, and a chest containing 3,000 gold pieces that I found under Orbrecht's bed while you were sleeping. I already bribed the guards at the gate, so it will be some time before anyone realizes we're missing."

As she helped him down the stairs, Wyngalf turned to stare in amazement at her.

"What?" she asked. "Is something wrong? Are you having second thoughts?"

"No," he said. "It's just... I think I might be in love with you."

"Oh, Wyngalf," she said. "For such a smart man, you certainly are a bit slow at times. You've been in love with me since the day we met."

Wyngalf nodded, realizing it was true. "But you weren't in love with me," he said.

They had reached the first floor, and Wyngalf was shaky and exhausted. He was looking forward to lying down in the carriage.

"I saw potential in you," said Evena.

"Potential to do what?"

"To overcome your limitations. Specifically, your need to let other people decide your fate."

"And?"

"To be honest, I've had my doubts at times. But recent events have taken a positive turn."

They exited the mansion through a servant's entrance. As promised, a carriage and two horses waited for them in the alley. Evena handed something to a man who stood holding the reins, and together they helped Wyngalf into the carriage. He lay down on the cushioned bench and she tucked a pillow under his head. "Try to get some rest," she said. "I doubt anyone will care enough about our disappearance to come looking for us, but we should try to get a few miles outside the city before nightfall, just in case."

Wyngalf nodded, barely able to stay awake.

"Sweet dreams, Simply Wyngalf," said Evena, with a smile. "I hope you're up for an adventure."

AFTERWORD

The rest of Wyngalf the Bold's adventures with Evena are, sadly, lost to history. It isn't known whether they ever reunited with Tobalt, although that seems unlikely. They simply disappeared from Skaal City, never to be heard from again. We can, of course, hope that they had many more exciting adventures.

Skaal City fell into chaos for several months after their disappearance, until order was finally reestablished by a coalition comprised of several prominent families and the city guard. A few learned patricians from these families assembled a convention to establish the future government of the city. A written constitution, declaring Skaal City to be an "independent republic dedicated to peace and liberty," was adopted. The republic lasted for three weeks, at which point the city was overrun by barbarian tribes from the south. Garvin, the leader of the recently disbanded city guard, assembled a contingent of armed men to repel the barbarians and then declared himself dictator. He began the practice of pressing young men from the surrounding villages into military service to defend the city. To counter the resentment from these towns, Garvin's agents began promoting the idea of a region called "Greater Skaal," which encompassed most of the southwestern part of Dis. Eventually this region became known simply as Skaal, and Gavin's grandson is generally said to be the first King of Skaal. A similar course of events took place in the north, culminating in the founding of the Thoric Dynasty at Brobdingdon, and Brobdingdon becoming the capital of the nation of Ytrisk. Eventually, both nations were incorporated into the Avaressian Empire (now known as the Old Realm), but the rivalry between them continued for a thousand years, climaxing in the War of the Itchy Coat, with which you are undoubtedly familiar.

A few sketchy accounts from explorers venturing into the Kalvan Mountains in the first few years after the First Sack of Skaal City tell of encounters with a one-handed goblin engaging in abstruse philosophical discussions with a winged lizard whose size varies from that of a housecat to that of a house, but these stories have generally been dismissed by historians as the delusions of lost travelers deranged from hunger and thirst. In any case, sightings of the eccentric goblin and his dragon grew scarcer over the years, and eventually ceased altogether; goblins—even those of a philosophical bent—don't live very long. Dragons live much longer, and the fact that Shelly was not seen again for nearly a thousand years after Tobalt's death is often given as proof that the whole story is a fiction. Dragons don't simply disappear, after all.

Another explanation, though, is that Tobalt was largely successful in his training: that he managed to overcome Shelly's natural tendencies toward avarice and violence, so that even long after Tobalt's passing, Shelly refrained from attacking human settlements.

Eventually a dragon did reappear in this region, and there can be little doubt that this dragon, which briefly terrorized several towns in northwestern Blinsk, was the very same Shelly that Tobalt had trained from a hatchling. How do we explain Shelly's sudden reemergence and change of character, after nearly a thousand years of peaceful solitude? Theories on this abound, but I suspect, based on the desultory nature of the dragon's offensives, that she was not attempting to subjugate the populace so much as trying to provoke a challenge from Clovis, the Prince of Blinsk, who was widely known as a master swordsman. And of course, anyone familiar with the history of Dis will know that she got her wish.[5]

---

[5] The story of Clovis the Dragon Slayer's encounter with Shelly, as well an account of the War of the Itchy Coat and several other exciting adventures, can

Why would Shelly deliberately provoke the encounter that was result in her own doom? Perhaps she feared that in her old age, her natural tendencies would overcome her training, or perhaps she had simply decided that she had lived long enough. Either way, far from being proof of Tobalt's failure, Shelly's reappearance can be taken as further evidence that even a dragon can change its ways. And if a goblin can help a dragon overcome its murderous nature, even for a time, then maybe there's still some hope for the rest of us.

---

be found in the saga of Boric the Implacable, available from your friendly neighborhood bookseller in a volume titled *Disenchanted.*

Review this book!
Did you enjoy *Distopia*? Please take a moment to leave a review on your favorite book reviewing website! Reviews are very important for getting the word out to other readers, and it only takes a few seconds.

More books in the Dis series:
Disenchanted
Disillusioned (coming in September 2015)

More books by Robert Kroese you might enjoy:
Mercury Falls
Mercury Rises
Mercury Rests
Mercury Revolts
"Mercury Begins" (short story)
"The Chicolini Incident" (short story)
Starship Grifters
Schrödinger's Gat
City of Sand
The Foreworld Saga: The Outcast
The Force is Middling in This One

Made in the
USA
Middletown, DE